TRACK *of* COURAGE

Books by Susan May Warren

MONTANA RESCUE

Wild Montana Skies
Rescue Me
A Matter of Trust
Troubled Waters
Storm Front
Wait for Me

GLOBAL SEARCH AND RESCUE

The Way of the Brave
The Heart of a Hero
The Price of Valor

SKY KING RANCH

Sunrise
Sunburst
Sundown

ALASKA AIR ONE RESCUE

One Last Shot
One Last Chance
One Last Promise
One Last Stand

CALL OF THE WILD • 1

TRACK *of* COURAGE

SUSAN MAY WARREN

R
Revell
a division of Baker Publishing Group
Grand Rapids, Michigan

© 2026 by Susan May Warren

Published by Revell
a division of Baker Publishing Group
Grand Rapids, Michigan
RevellBooks.com

Printed in the United States of America

Library of Congress Cataloging-in-Publication Data
Names: Warren, Susan May, 1966– author
Title: Track of courage / Susan May Warren.
Description: Grand Rapids, Michigan : Revell, a division of Baker Publishing
    Group, 2026. | Series: Call of the wild ; 1
Identifiers: LCCN 2025012573 | ISBN 9780800746056 paperback | ISBN
    9780800747985 casebound | ISBN 9781493452835 ebook
Subjects: LCGFT: Fiction | Thrillers (Fiction) | Christian fiction | Novels
Classification: LCC PS3623.A865 T73 2026 | DDC 813/.6—dc23/eng/20250528
LC record available at https://lccn.loc.gov/2025012573

Cover design by Mumtaz Mustafa

Baker Publishing Group publications use paper produced from sustainable forestry practices and postconsumer waste whenever possible.

26 27 28 29 30 31 32   7 6 5 4 3 2 1

Soli Deo Gloria

1

AT THIS RATE, he'd never walk again.

Dawson Mulligan lay back on the padded bench of the leg lift machine, sweat dripping into his ears, his body soaked, his leg burning, his breaths a little vocal as they emerged from his chest. He even sounded like a guy who'd hit the mattresses.

He shook his head and glanced at his adopted dog, Caspian, who sat with his back to him, watching the front door, like he might be on duty or something. Why the dog didn't sprawl on the gym floor like every other mutt he'd owned, he hadn't a clue. He looked over at the Doberman-Labrador.

"C'mon, Casp, do me a solid. Fetch me my towel. It's right there, on the bench press seat." He motioned toward his towel, which was hanging on the red seat.

Caspian looked over at him and sighed, the equivalent of an eye roll.

"Nice. I'm not entirely sure why I keep you around."

The dog's tail thumped once, twice.

Dawson moved his foot so that it rested on top of the pad, set his watch, then closed his eyes against the burn and let his knee sink down to a straightened position.

Three minutes of burning hellfire raking through him, the crowning finale of his daily—no, three-times daily—PT.

Country music played on the loudspeakers of the workout gym in the Tooth, aka, the headquarters for his cousin Moose's Air One Rescue team. A local radio station playing, of course, a hit by country music favorite Oaken Fox. The smell of his recently nuked pepperoni Hot Pockets lingered in the air, along with the reek of his sweat. He probably should have waited to down the bottle of Gatorade until after his workout.

It wasn't like he was running any marathons anytime soon. But now his gut ached, and frankly, he'd put on ten pounds since the shooting.

Two more minutes. He should probably add a few sit-ups, work up a real sweat.

Pain sweat didn't count.

He moaned as he sat up, his heart thumping as his knee turned to flame. Caspian glanced at him, then came over and set his head on Dawson's lap.

He ran a hand over the dog's head, not sure why the animal became needy every time he finished PT. Dawson could barely take care of his own emotional chaos, but fine. "Yeah, yeah, I'm almost done." He pushed the dog away and leaned forward into a stretch. His leg started to tremble. One minute.

"Hey, boss."

Caspian let out a bark as his former partner, Flynn Turnquist, walked through the door, her copper hair pulled back in a tidy bun, her green-eyed gaze taking Dawson in. She held up her hands, glancing at Caspian, then over to Dawson's knee—probably landing on the thick vertical scar that ran from his thigh to his shin—and then back to his face. She forced a smile. "Not sure why he barks every time I come in. He knows me."

"I don't know either." He put a hand on the dog's head, and Caspian sat, his tail swishing again.

Flynn wore a pair of black pants, boots, and a heavy wool jacket that she unbuttoned. "Looks like you're having fun." She scooted his towel over and sat on the bench press, taking off her leather gloves.

"So much. It's a party. Tell me they convicted Ravak."

She sighed. "Hung jury."

He closed his eyes, bit back a word.

His watch buzzed. Three minutes. He moved his leg off the rack and eased back on the bench. He'd have to put it on the floor, bend it at the knee, but maybe not quite yet. His watch beeped, an elevated heart rate alarm. No duh.

At his feet, Caspian whined, put a paw on his knee.

He again put his hand on the dog's head, ran his thumb around the floppy ear. "I agree. Not fair." He looked at her. "What happened?"

"They couldn't agree on the charge. First-degree murder is hard to prove—not without motive."

"His motive was revenge."

"Doesn't prove premeditation. Could have been a crime of passion."

"I saw his eyes. He wanted us to watch." Wanted *Dawson* to watch. "So he waited until I got there. Until the chief told SWAT to go in—"

"Are you saying he *made* it look like he panicked and shot the girl?" Flynn asked.

"I'm saying . . ." He put his leg down straight, then closed one eye as he moved it into a ninety-degree angle. Tightened down a groan. "I should have made us go in. I knew Ravak. What he was capable of. We only spent six months watching him."

She got up and handed Dawson his towel. He glanced at Caspian and raised an eyebrow.

Yeah, bud, that's how it's done.

Caspian set his head on his knee. No shame.

Flynn patted the dog. "He's so sweet."

"He sleeps with my shoes, carries my socks around the house when he's lonely, drinks out of the toilet, sneaks my steak off the counter when I'm not looking, and sleeps in my bed. Sometimes in the middle of the night, he sleeps *on* me. Wakes me out of . . ." Well, he didn't want to say the rest.

Because then Flynn would go all psychology on him and call him damaged on the inside too. That's what happened when he partnered up with someone who specialized in criminal profiles.

"So, you two are getting along, then." She grinned and leaned down, giving the dog a face-to-face. "Good boy."

"When Shep said he was trainable, I thought that maybe I could get him to, I don't know, fetch something. Maybe stay when asked. But no. The dog suddenly appears out of nowhere when I get up, right there to trip me. Or lean against me. I've never met such a needy animal." He rubbed the top of his knee. "So, will there be a retrial?"

"Yes. I talked with the prosecutor. But"—she reached down as if to help him up, but he didn't need help, thank you.

He pushed up from the bench. "Don't start."

"You should testify. Tell them—"

"What? That I had a gut feeling the guy was going to try and kill his own daughter?" His throat burned even as he said it.

Flynn drew in a breath, her mouth tight.

"Yeah," he said. "Not a lot of evidence for my hunches."

"Except ten years on the job."

He refused to reach for the edge of something to balance himself and instead tried to walk without a limp.

Ha.

Caspian got up and walked next to him. At least he wasn't getting in his way.

"If the chief didn't believe me, I don't think a jury will," Dawson said.

"It's hard to justify a headshot made on a hunch."

He glanced at her, his gut tightening. "Might have saved a five-year-old her life."

She sighed, nodded.

Caspian, however, nudged up against him. This dog. He petted him a moment and then hobbled out of the workout room, down the hallway, past Moose's dark office and the empty locker room, all the way to the kitchen area.

A granite-topped island held a couple paper plates of unfinished sandwiches. The uneaten lunch before the team left.

He slid onto a bench at the counter and started to reach for the plates to clean them, but Flynn beat him to it, dumped them into the garbage, and began clearing the lunch debris.

Caspian sat down beside him, his back to him.

The sun hung low, casting the last of the golden light into the day, an early twilight given it was still the first week of March. Outside, fresh snow layered the ground, although a plow had shoved most of the frosting away from the tarmac and the parking area, piling it into massive drifts around the airfield.

The icy pavement made walking with his bad knee ever so fun.

"Maybe I should take Moose's advice and head down to Florida for a while, do PT in the sunshine."

"Oh, but then you'd have to be all bright and sunny, and that would seriously jeopardize the dark funk going on." She picked up the Hot Pockets wrapper, raised an eyebrow, and then dropped it into the garbage.

"I think that belonged to Axel."

"I'm a detective, Dawson. I can spot a lie."

He managed a slight smile. "How are things down in the Special Victim Unit?"

"Lonely. Busy." She wiped the island with a sponge. "There's a BOLO out for Conan Sorros. He escaped custody on his way to Juneau a month ago."

"That's right. I can't believe he got away after waiting all this time for trial."

"The case against the family took a while to put together. It involves the murder of a DEA agent, not to mention a slew of other trafficking and drug crimes. One of the brothers had a plea deal in exchange for testifying, but he was murdered a couple months back. Rumor is that the DA is bringing in a secret key witness to get their testimony secured." She held out a piece of leftover cheese to Caspian.

The dog just looked at Dawson, as if asking permission. "Go get the cheese, pal."

Caspian stood up and moved over to Flynn, his entire body wagging. She fed it to him, petted his head. "Did Shep ever figure out who he belonged to?"

"Some guy in Minnesota, but his cell phone has been disconnected. So, he's ours, at least until we can track down his original owner."

"Did you get a breed on him?"

"Part black Lab, part Doberman. You can see the Doberman in the brown markings on his face. And his body is leaner than a Lab."

Flynn crouched in front of the dog and rubbed both her hands behind his ears. Caspian leaned to one side and let out a groan. "Sounds like Axel when I give him a shoulder rub."

"That's too much information. I don't need any details about your romantic life. I get enough TMI being his cousin, thanks."

She rolled her eyes and got up. "Listen. The DA's office will be calling you. If you want Ravak for first-degree murder, you're going to have to testify. Otherwise, they'll be downgrading to voluntary manslaughter. Five to twenty. But they're saying the appearance of the SWAT team could mitigate the sentence with aggravating circumstances."

He sighed. "I just . . . I can't . . ."

Her hand landed on his shoulder. "Okay. I get it. I just wanted to warn you, boss."

He looked up at her. "I haven't been your boss for a long time. Since you left the Investigative Support Unit and joined me at the SVU."

"You'll always be my boss," she said and winked.

"Don't."

She laughed. Pointed at him, then headed toward the door. Turned. "Oh, by the way, Axel said that Deke Starr from the Copper Mountain sheriff's office called him looking for you. Said he'd left a couple messages on your phone."

He sank his head into his hands, bracing his elbows on the island.

Caspian came up, tail wagging. Put his head on his knee.

Everybody just needed to . . . Calm down. He was *fine*.

"Wait—is he trying to recruit you?" She pulled out a stool. "Seriously?"

He sighed. "No. Maybe. I don't know." He turned to her. "I don't know if I'll be back in action down here—"

"People get knee replacements all the time—"

"My knee was completely blown out. It's a little more than a knee replacement for a fifty-year-old."

She held up her hand. "I know. I remember. It scared all of us to death. We were praying you didn't lose your leg, but . . . you're seriously going to go from tracking down kidnappers and stalkers and rape victims to giving out parking tickets in Copper Mountain?"

He raised an eyebrow.

"Sorry. It's just—"

"My mother is moving back to Copper Mountain."

She stilled, frowned. "Um . . . and . . ."

"And it's not easy. There are memories, you know."

She drew in a breath. "Right. Your sister. I forgot she was one of the early victims of the Midnight Sun killer."

"Yeah. Finally, case closed. And Mom feels like maybe it's time to come back. But . . ."

"You think the memories will haunt her."

"Don't they always?"

She swallowed. Shrugged. "Depends, I guess, if you make peace with them or not."

He put his hand on Caspian's head, the soft fur between his fingers. Tried to keep his voice from shaking. "My fifteen-year-old sister was killed by a serial killer. For years, we didn't know what happened. I came home from summer camp, and she was gone, just like that. My parents fell apart, got divorced, and . . . yeah, we're a long way from peace."

She stared at him.

Okay, so he didn't know where all that heat came from. "Sorry." He schooled his voice. "I guess . . . hopefully all that is changing, and I'm thinking I should be there for that. I dunno."

"I've learned that when people want redemption, they go home. Maybe this is your mom's way of trying to make peace."

Her hand found his, and he glanced at it, frowned. But she didn't pull away.

He gave her a look.

She smiled at him. "I'm going to miss you."

"I'm not falling off the planet." He pulled his hand away. "Your boyfriend's parents live in Copper Mountain, *coz*. I'm sure you'll do your own haunting of me."

"Oh, you betcha." She patted Caspian. "I'll let you go on one condition."

"I didn't realize we were negotiating."

"Do you want me to haunt you or not?"

He managed a slight smile.

"You take this guy with you." She nodded toward the dog. "Because he's got his eye on you. And if anyone can keep you safe, it's Caspian."

"He's got his eye on my socks. And my dinner." But he looked at the animal's brown eyes glancing at him. "But yeah. He's okay." He rubbed the dog's ears. "Aren't you, bud? Even if you can't fetch or sit—"

Caspian leaned his head against his leg, moaning at his touch. "And are completely embarrassing."

Flynn laughed. "Try and eat something other than a Hot Pocket. And I'm not talking to Caspian."

Dawson shook his head. "Go fight crime or something. I'm fine."

"See you 'round, boss." She headed out the door, into the darkness of the setting sun.

And he sat in the shadows, Caspian's head on his knee, wishing he hadn't lied to the one person who still believed in him.

HER ICE HAD long-ago melted into her Coke, watering it down. A good match to her chilly french fries and now-soggy burger.

I'm pitiful.

Keely looked at the text she'd drafted a long moment before, aw, why not? She had no one else to confess to except her manager, Goldie. Which perhaps made her even more pitiful.

She sent it.

Blew out a breath and set down her phone. Clearly the country songs twanging through the speakers of the burger joint didn't emanate from local radio because she'd heard "She Had Me at Heads Carolina" by Cole Swindell twice, along with "Thought You Should Know" by Morgan Wallen.

Probably a mixed album of all the hits from the last few years picked up at a local bin at a Walmart down in Anchorage, and wow, she'd turned cynical. Just because she'd landed here—in a backcountry, snow-covered smudge under the shadows of the icy Alaskan mountain range, in a honky-tonk with a moose head overlooking an old jukebox and dartboard, a few locals hunkered up to the long bar—didn't mean that she *belonged* here.

She was just passing through Copper Mountain. For a burger. Fries.

To get a good look at her birth mother.

Then, back to reality and all the things that came with that, like Five Seasons room service and maybe a nice, long, heated-rock massage.

A woman came up to the table, her long dark hair pulled back. She wore a long-sleeve T-shirt with Midnight Sun Saloon and Grill across the chest. "You want a refresh on that Coke?"

Her name tag said Shasta, like the soda company.

Keely nodded, smiled, tried to communicate a "Yeah. That would be great." Added a thumbs-up for boost.

"Didn't like the fries? People come from miles around for one of our baskets."

All of ten people? She shook away the snark, found another smile, then motioned the waitress closer so she could whisper. "They're good. Just . . . eyes were bigger than my stomach. It started shouting 'slow down' after the first three. But yeah, they're good."

"I'd say your stomach probably needs to shut up," Shasta whispered back. "I don't think you're in danger of overeating." She winked, then picked up the plate. "We have bottomless baskets. Would you like a refresh?"

Keely leaned back against the booth, put her hands on her stomach. "So full."

"Yeah, those three bites of burger really fill a girl up. We have some great pie. Vic hired this baker out of Anchorage, and she makes fantastic blueberry pie from our preserves. I promise, your stomach will love you."

Keely sighed. Nodded.

"Attagirl. Can't let you freeze to death." She walked away, and Keely had no idea what she meant.

Maybe she referred to her thin white puffer jacket. So she wasn't wearing bearskin and leather—she hadn't intended on putting down roots. Just a quick trip up to Copper Mountain. Maybe a . . . conversation. Then back into the little Cessna puddle jumper she'd ridden up in, and she'd get on with her life.

Whatever that looked like.

Her phone pinged and she looked at the text from her manager, although she'd lately turned into a counselor, apparently.

You're not pitiful. You have questions. And you need answers. Just pretend you're going on stage, take a deep breath, and walk up to her and say hi.

"Here you go." Shasta put a piece of pie in front of her. "I warmed it, so the ice cream is a little melty." She set down a fork. "Don't wait too long to eat it."

Keely turned over her phone and nodded. "Thanks."

Shasta's gaze flicked off the overturned phone, even as she smiled. "Uh-huh."

Keely blew out a breath and picked up her fork. Actually, her stomach had been screaming *Feed me* for the past six hours since leaving Anchorage, but well, her brain had said, *What are you doing?*

Which made her legs all jumpy, and frankly, she'd nearly run out of the joint twice in the last hour. She looked at her watch. Or, rather, ninety minutes.

Whatever.

Shasta came back with her Coke. Set it down. "You look sort of familiar."

Keely lifted a shoulder, pointed at the pie, gave a thumbs-up.

Shasta's mouth opened. "Oh my gosh—you're Bliss!"

Keely sighed, held up her hand. "Please," she whispered.

Shasta cut her voice low. "Sorry. But—what are you doing *here*?"

The *very* last thing Keely needed was for someone to tweet it out, or post her image on Insta, or grab a side photo for TikTok. "I'm visiting a friend."

Shasta's eyes widened. "You have a friend in Copper Mountain?"

Aw. She should have known she'd talked to the one person who probably knew everyone in town. "It's a surprise. Don't tell anyone." She swallowed, her voice still at a whisper. "You'll find out soon enough, probably."

True, maybe. Who knew what bio mom would do once she found out?

Except—she glanced over at Vic, the way the woman filled beers, filled orders, and occasionally hollered at locals—who knew?

In fact, part of Keely's ninety-minute dilemma had been sorting out the veracity of her father's story.

Vic Dalton. Former cop who gave away her daughter and disappeared into the Alaskan frontier. It had taken a private investigator and a couple thousand dollars to track the woman down.

"Is that why you're whispering?" Shasta asked.

Not even a little, but Keely nodded. Why not? She didn't need any other rumors to start.

Bliss is losing her voice. Yeah, that would sell tickets.

She even put a finger to her lips.

Shasta grinned. "I got you." She winked and walked away.

Keely took another bite of pie. She should have started with this. The sugar hit her veins, adding a surge of hopeful what-ifs.

What if she simply got up and walked over to the bar and introduced herself to the big, tough-looking female barkeep with the blond hair and the take-no-prisoners demeanor? *Hello. My name is Keely Williams, and I believe you're my mother.*

She took a sip of her Coke, watching as the woman now talked with one of the locals, a good-looking man, late thirties, who stood next to a smaller woman in braids. She handed them a take-out bag, and they left.

And then, just like that, Vic's gaze landed on Keely.

Not just *landed*. *Held*. And the force of it caught her up, stole her breath, pinned her into place. Vic had blue eyes, not hazel-blue like hers—but for the first time, maybe, she saw her nose on someone else's face. So *that's* where she got that little bump.

Keely looked away, her heart filling her throat, slamming against her chest.

Oh boy.

Nope. Not a chance she could do this. Because really, why again had she traveled a few thousand miles to meet a stranger?

She pushed the half-eaten pie away and reached for her phone. It buzzed in her hands, and she thumbed open the text.

I got another call from Bryce today. He needs
an answer.

Yeah, well, get in line. Life was full of questions, of people needing answers.

Today was not that day.

She put her phone into her satchel propped on the booth seat beside her, pulled out a twenty, and dropped it on the table.

She got up. Turned and ran straight into—oh no, no—*Vic*.

"Hey," the woman said.

She had a deeper voice than Keely imagined and spoke with gravel in her tone, as if she might be a smoker. Broad shouldered, thin hipped, with arms that looked like they could break a person, her blond hair pulled back into a tiny ponytail.

And still, she seemed almost concerned, a frown creasing her brows. "I came over to make sure everything was okay. Were you waiting for someone?"

Yes. *You.*

Keely swallowed. Shook her head. *Aw*—

"Okay. Well, if you need—"

A shout from near the dartboard, and a flannel-shirted man

pushed another man and suddenly tables flipped over and shouts rose—

"Topher—let him go!" Vic headed into the fray, and Keely made a beeline for the door.

Run. It wouldn't be the first time.

She pushed out into the brisk night, the stars bright in the black sky. Somewhere to the north, the glaciers and mountains rose, routing a frigid wind along the main street. She tucked up the collar of her jacket and pulled out a hat.

Last thing she needed was a bout of pneumonia.

Hiking her satchel over her shoulder, she headed down the street, past a bakery and the twinkle lights of a pizza joint, a grocery store that looked like a house, and then down a side street to the Gold Nugget Inn. The two-story home had once been owned by some great-grandfather of the owners, Hal and Nora Jensen, who had turned it into a café on the main level but kept a few rooms for rent upstairs. She took the one with the private bathroom.

It was also the only B and B open for lodging in March.

They'd seemed like a nice couple when she checked in during the daylight, and now the smell of baking bread and the quiet crackle of a fireplace in the front room met her as she entered and headed up the stairs.

It calmed her, a little. Okay, so maybe . . . maybe . . .

Aw. What was she thinking. Stupid idea, thinking her birth mother might have some insight into the biggest decision of her life. Given the looks of the woman, she had as much mothering in her baby finger as Keely did.

"Are you in for the night?"

Keely turned on the stairs and spotted Nora Jensen standing at the bottom. Mid-sixties, wearing an apron, the woman gave off a Marie Barone from *Everybody Loves Raymond* vibe. A hint of meddling, maybe some overcaring in her smile.

But it wasn't a bad look for an innkeeper.

"Yes. I—"

"I know it's dark out, but it's only six p.m. Would you care for a hot cocoa, or we have a puzzle by the fire that needs attention."

"Oh. Um." Keely sighed. "I think I'm heading to bed."

Nora nodded. "Breakfast is at eight. Have a good night."

Something about the woman stirred a warmth into Keely's bones. It reminded her of her grandma, maybe, once upon a time.

She headed upstairs and set her satchel onto the rose-flowered bedspread. Eyelet curtains hung at the windows, a hurricane lamp pooled light over one dark walnut bedside table, and of course, a Bible sat on the other. A green Queen Anne chair held a doily at the nape, and with the old Panasonic television, she felt like she might be stepping into her father's den. The place held a sense of time captured, revered.

A place to rest.

To stop *thinking*.

She sat on the bed, toed off her boots, and hung her jacket on the tall bedpost. Then she pulled out her phone and opened her photos app. Scrolled to the right one.

A four-year-old girl with blond hair wisping around her cherub face and sky-blue eyes the color of a perfect day laughed into the picture. She held a dripping ice cream cone, chocolate around her mouth, and a grin that could light up the coldest night.

Zoey. She loved that name—had suggested it, actually—and they'd used it. Zoey Anne Harper. They'd even given her the middle name of Keely's adopted mother, Anne. She ran her thumb over the chocolate mouth, stared into her eyes.

Gasped.

They looked like Vic's. Piercing and solid and seeing into her soul.

Keely closed the phone. Stared at the ceiling. Listened to the wind moan and knew in her soul that, indeed, she was a coward.

Like mother, like daughter.

21

2

SHE'D SIMPLY have to learn to live with herself.

Keely stood on the tarmac outside the terminal of the Copper Mountain Air Base, burying her chin and nose in her knitted scarf. Her hat was pulled low against the biting wind careening from the jagged, gray cast of mountainscape to the north.

Yeah, give her New York City any day. Sure, the temps dropped into the low thirties, but she could go from her heated condo to her heated garage to her driver's heated Escalade, right to her studio's heated entry, where coffee from Stumptown waited for her in her office.

Although, the breakfast today at the Gold Nugget, followed by the coffee from the Last Frontier coffee shop as she'd waited for the plane's noon departure, had found a place in her heart, especially with one of the bakery's sinfully delicious cinnamon rolls. She'd watched the sunrise from the warmth of the shop, seated in a log chair, listening to the chatter of the barista about a trial of a local thug. Something about the death of a DEA agent, some takedown of drug runners.

With all the vast wilderness, it seemed logical that they'd have a plethora of crime hidden in the bush, as Alaskans called it.

"Did you weigh this?" The question brought her back to now, on the tarmac, and came from the pilot, a man named Cade "Mack" Maverick, from Maverick Air. Mid-fifties, he had a sort of Indiana Jones feel about him, with his leather jacket, baseball cap, and cockeyed grin. He grabbed her Louis Vuitton carry-on and slung it onto a cart with two other bags. It bounced and nearly fell onto the snowy tarmac.

"It's twenty-three point two pounds," she said. She'd packed little, really. A pink velour jumpsuit, a couple pairs of wool socks, extra canvas pants and a white wool sweater, her sleeping supplies—earplugs, eye mask, face tape—and makeup, a few hair products, and of course, the picture album.

Silly.

"Good. Any more, and we'd be overweight. You'd have to wait for the next flight."

"Thanks for letting me tag along." She'd prearranged for a flight out later tonight, but frankly . . .

Well, she had a life to get back to. Enough games, what-ifs, and dodging the only answer that made sense.

"Did you get breakfast? Because we have no food service on board." He winked at her.

"I ate. Twice. Once at the Gold Nugget, then again at the Last Frontier." Her voice had started to rasp already. Shoot.

"Oh, Nora makes a whopper of a breakfast. Did you get her wild rice omelet with venison?"

"No. I . . . just eggs and sausage." No more talking. She cleared her throat.

"Oh, her reindeer sausage is award winning."

Keely managed a smile. *Reindeer? Ew.*

First thing she'd do when she got home was order a slice of pepperoni pizza from Lombardi's.

"And you can't leave town without one of the Frontier's famous cinnamon rolls, so . . . good call. We'll get this stowed, and then you and the others can board." He lifted his chin to a couple other passengers standing apart from each other.

She glanced over at them. One looked like he should probably be traveling by dogsled. He was dressed in an oversized parka fringed with wool, snow pants, and leather mukluks. A pair of leather mittens stuck out from his pocket, and he carried a rucksack over his shoulder. He looked in his early thirties, maybe, brown hair, wore a hint of a dark grizzle on his chin. Kept checking the sky to the north as if expecting something.

The other seemed a woodsman of sorts. Dark eyes, a bit of a scowl, but who wouldn't be sour against this biting weather? He, too, wore a dark beard, although longer and a bit unkempt, a wool hat, and a heavy fleece coat and snow boots. A scar parted the beard on his cheek.

She looked at her shearling Prada Ugg-style boots. She'd nearly worn her slide-on slippers, but at the last minute had opted for her mini platform, ankle-height version. After all, it was *Alaska*.

An hour, maybe a little more, and she'd be at the Anchorage Airport, booking a flight home, all this nonsense in her rearview.

Mack returned, the cart empty. "Go ahead and climb in." He glanced over at one of the men, the one in the parka. "Wilder, grab the copilot spot." He looked at the other man. "Mr. Thornwood, you can sit behind me to balance out the plane."

Thornwood grunted even as Wilder nodded.

Keely followed the troop toward the small plane. A red stripe ran the length of its compact body, with the words *Maverick Air* painted on the side.

Wilder got in first, followed by Thornwood. Keely stood on the metal stairs and glanced back at the small town of Copper Mountain.

Woodsmoke rose from the collection of pines between the air base and downtown, evidence of life in the cluster of houses tucked along the dirt roads. Already, the scent of barbecue smoke sharpened the air, so clearly the Midnight Sun Saloon had fired up their stoves for the day.

Bye . . . Mom?

No, that felt weird. She had one mom, and she'd already said goodbye to her.

Goodbye, Vic.

Keely drew in a breath of cool air, then climbed in beside Thornwood. She belted into the cozy seat and dropped her backpack at her feet.

Mack closed her door, and it latched. She tried to ignore the smell of woods from her fellow passengers.

First class, Alaska Airlines, here she came.

Her eyes burned, and she blinked hard, gazing out the window at the thick forest that surrounded the airfield. To the south, the sky opened up, a beautiful blue patched with clouds.

"You sure you want to leave so quickly? You just got here," Nora had said this morning as she set a plate in front of Keely, along with a cup of whipped-cream-topped cocoa.

"Gotta get back to work," Keely had said, not remembering to whisper.

Nora had wiped her hands on her apron, then sat in a nearby straight chair in the dining room, rich with oiled walnut furniture. Keely ate off china on a lacy tablecloth.

Quaint and weirdly comforting, really.

"What do you do?"

Keely took a sip of the cocoa and made a mental note to have her assistant give Nora a jingle and pry the recipe from her. "I . . . I'm a singer." That kept it simple. Sort of.

"Really. Oh, that's lovely. Opera? Jazz?"

"Pop. And some musical theater." She didn't want to say Broadway, because that might raise follow-up questions and maybe lead to her short stint in Hollywood, which would lead to Chase Sterling and . . . all the rest. Right?

Nope.

Nora found a smile. "Hal and I are Beatles fans."

Of course they were.

Nora leaned close. "But back in the day, we liked Dylan and Joplin." She winked.

"Classics," Keely said.

"Oh, I don't think they'd want to be known as that. But yes." She'd gotten up. "Good luck to you and your music. I hope to see you back here."

Probably not.

Mack got into the plane, then turned in his seat. "Listen up, this is your safety briefing. First—keep your seat belt buckled. It can get rough, especially with the blizzard heading our way. Our flight path veers a little east before we turn south to Anchorage to dodge it, but you never know what pockets we might hit."

Nice. Maybe she shouldn't have eaten the sausage.

"In the unlikely event we need to put down, just stay calm and listen to my instructions. There is a fire extinguisher up by the copilot seat and a first aid kit under the pilot's seat. The door is opened by pulling the handle up to unlock it and then pushing outward." He handed back a couple of headsets with microphones. "This will help with the noise, and if you can't hear me, let me know."

Keely put on her headset, and he tested it. She gave him a thumbs-up.

Her father's voice walked into her head. *"Stay alert, stay alive."*

Whatever, Detective Williams.

Then she put her head back and closed her eyes. *Sorry, Zoey.* She hadn't sent the email yet, but surely this was the right answer.

Mack taxied the plane out to the tarmac, and she listened as he called in to the tower. Moments later, they lifted off, her stomach dropping a little. But as they arched out over the town, headed southeast, she opened her eyes to watch.

A muddy and frozen river ran south from the western side of the small town, the houses and cars resembling Matchbox toys. She made out the Midnight Sun Saloon, as well as the Gold Nugget Inn, and then the plane veered east to avoid the darkening clouds to the west, and the landscape turned a mix of green pine jutting from a blanket of white. In the distance, humpback mountains rose, gray-green and ominous.

They passed tiny lakes, like dimples in the earth, some of them with cabins perched on the shore. A settlement caught her eye—a cluster of buildings carved out of the forest—with cleared land around it, situated next to a frozen lake. Smaller houses circled a larger building in the center, and a massive barn on one end rose, twice the size of the main building.

Looked almost like a small town, but no roads led to it.

They flew over it, and then Mack banked south and followed a wide river, tumbling even in the extreme cold.

"Good luck to you and your music." Yeah. Time to start therapy, probably.

Movement next to her tore her attention from the scenery, and she froze as Thornwood unbuckled his seat belt.

What—?

Then he leaned forward. Her breath stopped as he put a Glock 19 to Mack's head. The ridiculous fleeting thought that her dad might be a little proud that she knew that detail left her when Thornwood growled, "Land the plane."

What—*what*—?

She gasped, and Thornwood shot her a look that made her grab the arms of her seat.

Cold, dark eyes speared through her.

"What are you doing?" Wilder turned in his seat, and Thornwood pointed the gun at him. He recoiled. "Don't shoot!"

"Land the plane," Thornwood growled again. "There, on the riverbed."

She looked down and spotted a wide shoreline, pebbled and frozen. There?

"I'm not landing," Mack said.

"Suit yourself."

She screamed—who cared about the damage to her voice—as Thornwood grabbed a long hunting knife from his duffel.

"Stop!" She nearly lunged at him.

He shoved the knife right through the seat into Mack's back.

Mack shouted, a cry of pain, and—

No, *no*—

The plane dipped in the air.

"What are you doing!" she shouted at Thornwood. "We're going to crash!"

"Land the plane!" Thornwood pointed his gun again at Wilder. "Or your passengers die."

She bit back another scream as the plane banked, hard. Mack seemed to be fighting for control, the plane spiraling.

Wilder clawed at the yoke. "Mack, give me the controls!"

Mack moaned, a rumble deep inside. "I can . . . I'll get us . . ."

Ah, blood dribbled from his mouth as he glanced at Wilder.

They were going to die. Oh, no—no, no—

God, please, if you get me out of this—aw, she was too far gone for foxhole prayers.

Still. *Please.*

Mack aimed for the frozen riverbank, the plane wobbling as he gripped the steering wheel with both hands. His entire body shook.

"Give me control!" Wilder, shouting into the headset.

"Shut up and land!" Thornwood said.

And right then, Mack glanced back at her, his face twisted, and mouthed something.

What—wait— *Hold on?*

The ground rushed up at them, coming fast—too fast, right?

28

She gripped the arms of her seat tighter, braced her legs. Sucked in a breath—

They touched down. Bounced hard, and the plane tipped.

She couldn't stop screaming.

Metal ripped, the sound of the wings shearing off tore through her ears as they hit earth again, jerking hard, then rolling—

Her backpack hit the ceiling, slammed into her body, taking out her wind—

Shouts, more crashing, the world upending. Her screams shredded her lungs as the plane ripped apart around her and plunged her into darkness.

"WE NEED TO GET GOING so we can beat the storm."

At Moose's statement, Dawson looked up from where he poured coffee into his thermos. Moose came out of his office carrying a duffel bag, set it on the table in the middle of the room. A massive map of Alaska spanned the far wall, and The Weather Channel played on the flat-screen, muted, with captions across the bottom.

"I saw it. Coming down from the north. Looks like a doozy." Dawson capped his thermos. "Think we'll make it back tonight?"

"If not, my folks will put us up. You packed extra gear, right?"

He gestured to his own duffel bag on the floor by the door, along with another one for Caspian. The dog seemed to know that he'd put food and treats into the bag because he lay near it, occasionally sniffing at it.

"When is your mom getting in?" Moose asked.

"I'm not sure."

Moose wore a red-checkered plaid shirt and a baseball cap over his dark hair, and it seemed he hadn't shaved for a couple days.

"Late-night rescue?" Dawson asked. Not that Moose looked any different than Dawson, with his own unshaven mug. But Dawson had no excuse.

Just hadn't . . . wanted to. Even now, the idea of traveling north to see his parents . . . aw, too many questions.

Too much disappointment.

But he was all they had now, so . . .

"We got back about ten," Moose said. "But I got the paperwork from the callout done before I went home. Tillie was already asleep. And this morning, she let me sleep in while she took Hazel to school." He ran his hand along his chin. "Overslept."

"How's her pregnancy?"

Moose walked over to the coffeepot. "We heard the baby's heartbeat a couple days ago. Hazel was there too—she got pretty excited, although I'm not sure a nine-year-old understands the whole picture, despite her mother's explanation. She keeps asking how the baby *got in there*." He finger-quoted the last three words.

Dawson laughed. "That's a fun conversation."

"I'm letting Tillie handle it." He filled his coffee and turned, a hip against the counter. "Meanwhile, I'm trying to keep Fluffy from figuring out how to get out of his kennel. The pup is smart. I found him in the bathroom battling the toilet paper while Tillie was at the gym."

"Fluffy?" He grinned but glanced at Caspian, who lifted his head at the mention of the Siberian husky pup.

Moose laughed too. "Don't know why he can't be like you, Casp. Good dog."

Caspian's tail thumped.

"Please. He woke me up in the middle of the night again. I was in a sound sleep and—and suddenly, there's Caspian, licking my face, waking me up." Dawson walked over to the table, where he'd set his backpack. "I haven't gotten a decent night's sleep since I got home from the hospital."

Caspian sat up, his whip tail banging the floor.

"Ever think about asking Jericho Bowie to train him for SAR work?"

"Who, Caspian?" Dawson lifted the pack and settled it on his shoulder. "He's sweet, but he's not that smart." He patted his leg, and Casp came over, sat, looked up at him.

"I'm meeting Jericho in Copper Mountain to talk about him joining Air One with Orlando. Having a SAR dog would help our searches. Why don't you let him evaluate Casp?"

"Maybe."

"You could offer SAR services for the sheriff's department—"

Dawson held up a hand. "Let's just take a step back. I'm not even sure I want to get back into law enforcement, even for Deke."

Moose's mouth made a grim line even as he nodded. "Give yourself time."

Yeah, he doubted that time might shake him free of a fail that cost so much. But Dawson forced a smile and headed for the door, trying not to limp.

Not enough. "How's the knee?" Moose followed him outside. Caspian headed out in front of them, sniffing the area, then circled back and walked beside Dawson. At least the dog could heel.

"No cane, and I'm at 125 degrees on the bend, so, I'm practically healed. Back to normal." He didn't mention the NSAID meds he'd tucked into his jacket. Or the fact that most days, he still had to ice his leg to keep down the swelling.

Moose said nothing on their walk out to the hangar. The wind swept snow across the tarmac, crisp from the north.

He gave Dawson a glance askance.

"Okay, what?"

"Just . . . God uses circumstances to wake us up, get at things inside."

Dawson stopped. "What things?"

Moose also stopped, turned. "A five-year-old girl died in your arms. And I'm not immune to the fact that we're coming up on the anniversary of Caroline's death. Plus, with your mom coming back—I don't know. Maybe there's stuff—"

"You've been married too long. Tillie's got you thinking about *feelings*." Dawson shook his head and brushed past him. "I'm fine. Things happen. Let's go before we get iced over."

Moose said nothing and followed him to his Cessna, parked in the Quonset hut next to his Bell 429 rescue chopper and a fleet of other rescue machinery—Polaris ATVs, a couple snow machines, and a four-wheel drive command truck. It still bore the snow and ice from last night's callout.

"Help me push it out." Moose opened up the cargo hatch of the Cessna and stowed his pack and duffel, then grabbed Dawson's and stowed that too.

Dawson didn't know how much of a help he was, really. Moose was a big guy and pushed the plane out easily with the tow bar attached to the nose wheel. Maybe he was just trying to help Dawson feel useful.

He returned the tow bar while Moose did the walk-around, and by the time he'd huffed his way onto the wing and into the cockpit, Moose had already started the preflight check.

Caspian jumped in and sat on the seat behind him, head on his paws, big brown eyes watching. But as Moose fired up the prop, the dog began to whine and then slid off the seat and over to Dawson, nudging his snout into Dawson's lap.

Yeah, he wasn't super fond of flying either.

"Hey, buddy. It's all good." He patted his head, and Caspian stopped whining, but Dawson kept his hand on him.

He donned his headset, listening to Moose talk to the tower as he pulled out to the runway. With winds out of the northwest, weather clogging the air, Moose confirmed his northeasterly route to Copper Mountain.

Right over the Copper River. Memories.

"Maybe there's stuff."

Nope. He couldn't live in the past—he'd decided that long ago. Unfortunately, he didn't know how to live with the future either.

"Ready?" Moose looked over at him.

Dawson glanced at Caspian, still leaning on him. "I'm going to sit back there, hang out with Casp."

"Sounds good."

Dawson switched seats, and of course the dog climbed up, put both paws on him, putting pressure on his good leg. But as he strapped in and looked out the window, his hand on the animal, his heart stopped pounding.

See, he was fine. "I'm ready for some of your mom's cinnamon rolls, so let's go."

Moose pushed the throttle, and the bird shook as it took off.

Airborne. Once he got off the ground, he could like it. The sense of leaving the weight of gravity behind, being pulled into the sky, the beauty of seeing all things from a new perspective.

They soared over Anchorage, with its grimy snow-banked roads and the clogged and muddy Knik Arm. From here, he might be able to make out Moose's home, located on the banks of the Knik River, and for sure he spotted his townhome in a cluster of other homes. Sort of a default place, because he'd been deep into work when Caroline died. She'd been the one to pick it out, and with the purchase still pending, he just . . . let it roll.

Maybe it was prolonging the pain of losing a woman he thought he was going to marry, but really, he liked the place. A three-bedroom side-by-side with vaulted ceilings and an updated kitchen, a couple car spaces, which allowed him to store his 1999 Corvette—a silly car for Anchorage, really—and a view of Campbell Lake.

Probably, someday, he should get matching furniture, but his stuff was comfortable, and just because a guy shopped off Craigslist didn't mean it was a dump. He did have an 85" flat-screen and a dope sound system. And a Masterbuilt grill smoker on his small deck.

Caroline would have no doubt had the place looking beautiful. Then again, who knew how long she would have lasted in—

"You're quiet back there," Moose said, turning northeast.

"Yeah. Thinking of Caroline. Thanks for bringing her up."

"Sorry, coz."

Dawson glanced at him. "It's okay. Her parents usually call this time of year, just to check on me."

"That's nice."

"I think it's a way for them to remind me not to forget her." He sighed. "As if."

"It's been five years. You get to move on."

Dawson lifted a shoulder. Weirdly, Flynn's comment rounded back to him. "*. . . then you'd have to be all bright and sunny, and that would seriously jeopardize the dark funk going on.*"

Right. "Maybe. I don't have time to date, and . . . I have Caspian. We bachelors need to stick together."

"A song I used to sing before I realized how stupid I was." Moose glanced back at him and grinned.

Dawson offered a grim return smile. Not stupid. Safe. For everybody.

Especially since the accident.

"Just remember this, Daws. We can't change what happens to us, but we can decide how we want to grow from what we experience."

He rolled his eyes.

They flew over the Copper River basin with its finger tributaries and splash of lakes, now frozen dots of white amid the green. A few cabin chimneys spiraled up smoke into the blue, the land a vast white. From here, the Copper Mountain range rose, the sun glinting off the high glaciers, the peaks a white rumple along the eastern horizon. Glorious and lethal. The Copper River traced its base as it ran south.

Dawson spotted the community of Willow, with the high-end vacation properties of the Silver Salmon township.

They'd cleared the land like small kingdoms.

"This is Remington land," Moose said of the swath of forest below. "And Bowie land is just north of this."

Dawson looked down over the massive plot owned by the private mining company west of Copper Mountain. "I see a cabin down there."

"That's a Forest Service cache cabin, for bivouac when needed. They come with stoves, a makeshift kitchen, and a ham radio."

"Got it. Where's Sully's place? I can't remember."

Moose pointed out the front windshield to the east. "The Bowie Outpost? We're just a few clicks away—you'll see it below. It's on the Copper River, just south of where it curves west, on the southern border of Bowie land and about two miles west of Woodcrest, the art community."

"That's right. Such a strange group."

"They're not strange. They're just . . . private. But good people. Accepting. They live off the land and make soap and jewelry and other things they sell in Copper Mountain. I think they might even have online sales to the Lower 48, although I don't think they have internet, so I think someone in town handles the sales for them."

As they flew overhead, he searched for the Bowie Outpost, tracing where the Copper River curved and—*wait*. The sun glinted off a crumple of red and white metal—

"Moose. I think there's a downed plane on the riverbank."

Moose looked out his window.

"This side. Turn the plane around—you'll see it."

Moose banked, then retraced his flight path. "I see it."

Dawson got another look too. Seemed the plane had cart-wheeled, its wings ripped off, the fuselage still intact but upside down, with gaping holes in the sides. And from the torn snow-bank and crushed pine trees, it seemed recent.

As in *today* recent.

"Can we get down there?"

Moose checked his gauges, then glanced at the horizon. "Yes." He banked and started to descend.

The riverbank widened, and Moose overshot the crash as he aimed for the shoreline. But Dawson got an up close view.

At least one person lay on the snowbank darkened with rusty blood. Luggage spilled out into the river, a gray duffel and a brown-and-gold roller bag. The wings had sheared off, and one propped against rocks in the river. The other lay embedded in a tree.

"I don't see anyone alive."

Moose nodded, his jaw tight. "Hold on. This might get rough, even with my tundra tires."

Dawson put his hand on Caspian as the dog sat up. Probably he should have tried to belt the animal in. Instead, he pulled Caspian onto his lap and grabbed him around the body.

Moose put down, the wheels growling against the shoreline, then bumping against the rocks, jolting Dawson even as he braced himself on the back of the passenger seat.

Moose brought them to a halt. "Stay here."

"Not even a little." Dawson unbuckled his belt but turned to Caspian. "You, however, stay."

He opened the door.

Caspian leaped past him, landing on the shoreline, running after Moose, barking.

"Caspian!" Dawson eased out of the cockpit, onto the wing—

Moose had stopped near the body, which lay on its back, crumpled, blood and gore puddling the snow around it.

Dawson limped up, slower than he would have liked. "Recognize him?"

"It's Mack—Cade Maverick. Maverick Air." He crouched then. "He's gone. Looks like something impaled him. And he's been shot."

Blood saturated the man's jacket and midsection, but a gunshot to his forehead said that something terrible had gone down.

Dawson's cheeks tightened, and he stepped back, a strange sweat slicking down his back, his heart a fist as it hammered against his chest.

Caspian whined and came over to him. Sat on his feet. Looked up at him.

"Me too, bud."

Moose stood up, hands on his hips, and looked around, then stepped near the fuselage.

Dawson took a breath and followed him. A seat lay on the riverbed, the belt unbuckled, but the other back seat had survived the crash. It was still in the fuselage, now upside down. The buckles dangled down.

Dawson poked his head into the cockpit. Broken glass webbed the instrument panels, but the seats survived, the belts also hanging from the ceiling. Blood coated the pilot's seat, but he couldn't see anything sharp that might have impaled Mack.

His heart stopped pounding so hard.

Moose was rooting through the debris on the roof of the plane. "He probably has a passenger list."

Dawson spotted a few papers blowing into the river.

Caspian stood at the edge of the riverbank, almost on alert, his body taut, looking into the woods.

Weird.

"Footsteps," Dawson said, now walking around the bank. "I think that's a Sorel bootprint." He pointed to a line of footprints with raised lines in the snow. "And maybe a moccasin?" He pointed to another set.

"Over here, next to the seat—there's a third. I think. I don't know." Moose chased down a paper and stomped on it, lifted it.

"What do you have?"

"Yeah, this is the weight list. Looks like three passengers. Two men and a woman. Luggage for two, plus backpacks. Plane wasn't overweight." He looked at Mack, even as Caspian started to bark. "Not sure what happened. Maybe weather, but clearly there was foul play here. I'll call it in."

But Dawson's attention stayed on Caspian as the dog rounded. Big eyes on him, muscles tensed. And weirdly, he heard a joke in his head from an old *Lassie* show. *"Help, Timmy's stuck in the well!"*

"What's going on, bud?" He took a step toward the dog.

Caspian turned, barking. Looked back at him.

Dawson took another step toward him. "Don't go—"

The dog took off into the woods.

"Caspian! Come back!"

Aw. He glanced at Moose. "I gotta get him."

"I'll make a call and then see if I can track down any survivors. But hurry up. There's a blizzard headed this way. And keep your head on a swivel for trouble."

"No doubt. I'll be right back." Dawson picked his way up around the plane debris and over to where Caspian had taken off. "I'll be right back."

3

JUST. Keep. Running.

Keely's own breath betrayed her. Her gasps slammed against her body, as branches whipped against her face. Blood dripped from her lip where she'd tripped and careened into a tree, and she'd probably twisted her ankle too. It burned, and she bit down on a whimper.

Don't look back.

Of course, that's exactly what she did, but the forest closed in, and frankly, she could be running in circles, right back to the shoreline where—

Oh. She pressed a gloved hand to her mouth, then tripped and caught herself on a birch tree. Listened.

Her heart thundered, her breaths hard. She tried to silence them, to make them tremors rather than sweeping gasps.

No crashing behind her. No bearded thug slash woodsman threatening to slice her up with a bowie knife.

No murderer catching up to leave her dead in the woods.

Maybe.

She stumbled toward a nearby pine tree and climbed under the massive shaggy arms, pulling her knees to herself.

Breathe. Just . . .

She closed her eyes. No, bad idea. Because then she landed right back at the beach, strapped into her seat, lying on her side.

It had taken a long second, maybe a few, to unravel what had happened—the plane crash, the cartwheeling, the fact she'd lived.

She'd unbuckled and fell to the snow, and then she'd heard it—the snarls of men fighting. They punched each other—Wilder and Thornwood—and then Wilder tackled the bigger man to the ground. Roared when Thornwood drilled a fist into his head.

Don't look. She cast her gaze to the plane and spotted Mack, the kind pilot, crawling away from the fuselage, leaving a bloody trail in the snow.

She ran over to him, where he'd stopped, breathing hard as he collapsed. She rolled him over. Blood covered his abdomen, and he must have hit the instrument panel, because red ran down his face, pooled in his jacket.

"Mack—what can I do—"

"Run."

"What?"

He grabbed her hand, pulled her down to him. "Go to that community . . . we flew over. It's maybe . . . five miles . . . northeast —run, get there. They'll protect . . ."

Run. Through the woods— "I . . . no—"

"I should have recognized him—"

A shout, and Wilder stood up, red down the front of him, his lip bloody.

Thornwood kicked him, his boot sending the man back.

"Get my gun!" Mack pointed to the plane. "It's under my seat."

He had a *gun*? She scrambled for the plane, the door already open. The buckles dangled down, but she spotted a hardcase wedged under the pilot's seat and pulled it out.

Thornwood jumped Wilder, bracing his knees on the man's shoulders, and even as Wilder thrashed, he couldn't break free.

The bigger man wrapped his hands around Wilder's neck.

Oh. No—no—

She opened the case, memory of how to use the weapon clicking. *Thank you, Dad.* Then she pulled out the gun, stood up, shaking.

"Get off him!" She pointed the gun at Thornwood.

He didn't even glance at her.

She pulled the trigger. The shot barked into the air, its echo shredding the cold. "The next one goes in your back." Shoot—did she really say that? She took a breath. "I mean it!"

Wilder still thrashed, but less so. Thornwood turned back to him.

She pulled the trigger.

Instinct, but she saw herself do it, more as an out-of-body experience than full-on thought.

The shot hit Thornwood in the shoulder, and he roared back, turning, falling into the snow.

Wilder rolled, scrambled up, and ran.

Ran.

Away.

As in *left her.*

Then Thornwood found his feet and rounded. Oh, no—*no*—

He took off toward her.

Another shot, not from her, clipped him again, this time across his thigh.

"Run, girl, run!" Mack, still on the ground, but he held Thornwood's Glock. He must have found it in the debris.

She looked at Thornwood, now halted, then the forest and—

Ran.

Just left poor Mack on the beach with Thornwood.

She fled into the forest as another shot breached the air. She slowed, breathing hard. She should get back to Mack, help him—

Until she'd spotted Thornwood thundering after her.

She'd turned and ran with everything inside her.

Now, she hadn't a clue how far she'd gone, she listened for the bear of a man on her tail.

Nothing but the moan of the wind, the trees creaking.

Only then did she realize she'd dropped the gun.

And now, wait—barking. The sound slivered through her, shook her bones. *Wolves?*

She got up, looking for the sun. What had Mack said—five miles northeast? That meant the sun was behind her, right? Or did the sun behave differently here in Alaska?

Hopefully not, because she took off, the sun at her back, what little of it she could see. Memories of that movie with Liam Neeson flickered through her brain, the one where the wolves surrounded him, where he fought them off with fire.

She had no fire. No backpack. Snow crammed into her short Pradas, and her legs had turned to ice. Easy prey.

The barking followed her. *God—please.*

Funny how her mother's faith bubbled up sometimes, filled her soul, as if it might actually help.

Keely spotted a dip in the forest wall, something ahead that might be a clearing, and headed for it.

The barking grew louder, and she picked up her pace, her hands in front of her. She tried not to scream. Faster, crashing through the forest—she spotted the meadow up ahead, a clear space. Maybe even the field around the community. *Please, please—*

She looked back, still running, and spotted something black coming at her, over downed logs—no, no—

Turning back, she sped up, crashed through the heavy boughs of a pine and—

Went airborne. The earth dropped out from below her, and she launched into nothing. Her arms spun, and she screamed as the earth rushed at her.

She landed hard, slamming against boulders, the snow barely

enough to cushion her fall into the depths of the ravine. She tried to catch herself, but no, the momentum pitched her right to the bottom.

Bam.

She landed so hard, her breath clogged in her throat.

Breathe!

It took a second, then air rushed back at her and she gasped, gulped it in.

Okay. Okay. She wasn't dead. And maybe not broken, although her body burned and ached. She lay back, closed her eyes, and started to whimper.

Barking. *No—no—*

She opened her eyes and spotted the animal at the top, prowling, then dropping low to bark again. A wolf, all black, and it pawed at the snow some ten feet above her, at the top of the ravine.

She lay back down. Maybe the beast would go away.

It kept barking.

But what if it brought Thornwood?

She eased up and rolled over, nearly screamed. Yeah, whatever she'd done to her ankle before, the fall had only exacerbated the sprain. She tried to put weight on it, but sank down on her hands and knees, trembling.

"Don't cry. Crying doesn't fix anything."

Yeah, well, maybe not, but she wasn't former street cop turned detective Jimmy Williams. Didn't even have his blood in her veins.

Frankly, crying seemed the right choice.

Ahead, the ravine continued cutting through the rock. Maybe she'd fallen into a creek bed, tumbled down a frozen waterfall. As long as she stayed in the river, the wolf couldn't reach her.

He kept barking, but she forced herself up, stood on one leg, then gritted her jaw as she put weight on her ankle. Okay, maybe it wasn't broken. Still, pain shot up her leg, and she got back down on all fours.

Crawling could work.

She scooted along the creek bed, her arms breaking through the icy top layer, snow tunneling up her jacket. The wolf seemed to follow her from above, still barking. She wanted to throw something at it, maybe scare it away. Her breath had slowed, her heartbeat not a fist in her chest, but she'd gone maybe two hundred feet when she sat back and rested, breathing hard.

She was going to die here.

Die, and never meet Zoey.

Die, and never meet Vic, although honestly, she'd made peace with that.

Die, and . . . she'd heard hypothermia wasn't terrible. Like going to sleep. Except for that part where you took off all your clothing because your body played tricks on you. Seemed unfair that in the end they'd find her naked body after all the fights she'd waged with photographers who wanted her to show more skin than she felt comfortable with.

It wouldn't take long for Goldie to send out a search party. And they'd certainly find the crash—Mack had confirmed their path with the tower.

But how far had she run?

Maybe the wolf would simply tear her body to shreds.

Okay. That was enough of *that*—she rolled back over and started to crawl again.

She would survive. Find her voice again.

Maybe even make peace with her choices.

Crunching sounds on the snow ahead of her made her look up.

Snowshoes. And leather boots. Snow pants and a thick leather jacket and a furry hat and a . . . *gun?* The man who stood in front of her held his rifle loosely but aimed in her general direction and . . .

She might not be thinking clearly. Might not have all her wits about her, and maybe this guy *hadn't* shown up out of nowhere to kill her. Maybe he *wasn't* tracking her, like that character Jeremy Renner played in that scary winter movie about the Wyoming serial killer.

"Don't kill me!" She lifted her arms—why hadn't she hung on to Mack's gun!

Barking—no, *snarling*—erupted behind her. She turned and spotted the wolf—no, a *dog*? A wild dog, racing toward her, teeth bared—

Stay calm, stay calm—

Not a chance. She dropped into a ball and screamed.

HE MUST HAVE A TOUCH of PTS because the scream simply lit Dawson on fire, found his bones, and shook them.

He wanted to stop, put his hands over his ears, haul in breaths. It didn't help that his knee burned, fat and stiff and cumbersome, especially after twenty minutes of hiking-slash-running and thankfully *not* falling through the snowy forest. He'd shouted a few times, hoping that Caspian might abandon the stupid rabbit or whatever he might be chasing, but the dog refused to obey, like they were playing a game.

He'd thought, early on, that he'd been actually tracking someone, but after the first ten minutes, he'd given up that hope. Especially when Caspian stopped, looked at him.

"Caspian! Get back here!"

The dog barked, then darted off again.

Ever so briefly he'd considered leaving the animal behind, but the lineup of people who might murder him started with Flynn, with Hazel close behind, and probably even Tillie, who rolled her eyes every time Fluffy scratched at the back door.

No, Dawson was in this, despite the cold and the wind and the fact that he was probably out of cell range. Moose would be the one leaving him in the bush.

He'd let out another "Caspian!" and heard the wind take his shout. His trek had spilled him out to the edge of a forest overlooking a ravine—if the animal had gone over that, all bets were off. That's when the scream lifted. Sharp and high and ripping through him.

A female scream. Maybe. Could be an eagle or a hawk. He stumbled along the edge of an old creek bed, a thirty-foot drop, and the barking turned to snarls.

As Dawson scrambled along the side of the ravine, he spotted—

Oh *no*. It looked like Caspian had attacked a man, a trapper from the look of his attire. The dog had put himself between a woman crumpled on the snow and the trapper, growling, barking, scary.

Huh.

"Stop! *Caspian!*"

Except then he spotted the rifle in the man's grip.

"Don't shoot him!" He searched for a way down, his hands up to distract the man.

The woman knelt in front of the spectacle. Her long blond hair spilled out of a white pom-pom hat, and she backed away on her knees, her hands up.

Whoever this man was, Dawson knew in his gut that Caspian had stopped him from something terrible.

All thought, all pain stripped out of him, and in that second, he shook out of the past, the ringing inside, and found himself, or at least who he'd been, and scrambled down the side of the ravine—only a few feet here—and across the creek bed.

"Stop!"

The trapper still aimed his rifle at Caspian, and Dawson cursed his injured knee. "Don't shoot him!"

But the man had backed away, as if to get a better shot, and from five feet away, Dawson launched himself, throwing his entire body weight into the man, locking his arms around his waist.

They went down together in a terrible *whump*, cushioned only by the now-trampled snow. Caspian rounded on them, barking as Dawson pinned the guy, his good knee on the man's arm. He reached for the rifle.

The man grabbed a handful of Dawson's jacket, pulling him close, as if to hit him.

Yeah, no. He was wired now, the adrenaline hot, a part of him unhinging.

The bad guys didn't get to win today. His fist balled—

"Dawson! It's me! It's Sully!"

He jerked, stilled. Stared at the man.

Golden-brown beard, a flash of fire in his pale-blue eyes.

"Sully?"

Sully Bowie, older brother of one of his buddies in Copper Mountain.

Just like that, the realization shut him down. He scrambled off the guy, backed into the snow, breathing hard.

And Caspian all but launched himself into Dawson's arms, nearly standing over him, his hackles still bristled.

"It's okay," he said, his hand on the animal's back. Looked at Sully. "What's going on here?"

Sully looked at Caspian. "That's your dog?"

Sort of. "Yes."

"Is he going to bite me?"

Seemed like it, but then Caspian sat, his bottom right on Dawson's legs. Stopped growling. That felt like the right sign. "I don't think so."

"Nice." Sully put the rifle down and looked at the woman. "Are you okay?"

Dawson, too, looked at her.

Pretty. And scared silent, the way her hazel-blue eyes rounded, looking first at Sully, then Dawson, then Caspian.

Sully got up. "I heard the barking and came to see what was going on. Don't get a lot of dogs up here signaling like that."

Dawson glanced at Caspian. Signaling? He turned to the woman. "You okay, ma'am?"

She swallowed, then shook her head, and wouldn't you know it, her eyes filled. Then Sully took a step toward her, and she drew in a breath, flinched.

Sully halted, his gaze swinging to Dawson, back to her. "I'm not going to hurt you."

She gave Dawson a dubious look, and to be fair, Sully *did* resemble something out of the wild Alaskan bush. Dawson, however, wore a parka, a normal wool hat, and boots. Like a man who *didn't* make his living tromping around in the woods dressed in the hides of animals.

Yeah, he might have been a little freaked out too, if he didn't know the guy.

"I promise, he's harmless," Dawson said. He scooted over to her. "I'm Dawson Mulligan. I'm a cop." Or was a cop. Oh, it didn't matter. "Are you from the downed plane?"

She drew in a breath. "Are you really a cop?"

"Yes. Off duty—"

"There's a man out here trying to kill me."

He stilled. But he believed her, given the gunshot in Mack's head and the way she held her arms around herself. Blood had dried on her lip, and her stuttered breathing suggested she might be having a panic attack.

"You're safe with us. Sully is . . . well, despite the Daniel Boone appearance, he's a good guy."

"I'm wearing Carhartts and a two-thousand-dollar Overland coat," Sully said. "I'm hardly a trapper from them thar hills."

The woman nodded.

Caspian came over, whining, and she recoiled.

"Aw, he's okay. He just got a little excited." Dawson put his hand on the dog's back.

"I thought he was going to jump me," Sully said. "What, you train him to be a guard dog?"

"I can't train him to fetch my shoes. No. He just took off, as if he knew she was there."

Caspian crouched down then and started to inch toward the woman.

"He followed me?" She eyed the dog.

"Yeah, I think he . . . picked up your scent at the river. I don't know. Or maybe he heard you." Dawson put his hand on the dog's head and looked at the woman. "Can you tell me what happened at the crash?"

"I don't exactly know." Her voice dropped to a whisper, and he could barely hear her, what with the wind raking the trees. She took a breath, her voice emerging louder but gravelly. "A passenger stabbed Mack and then we crashed. And then he tried to kill another passenger and then me and . . . and . . ." Her voice broke off, and she shook her head, pressing her gloved hands to her mouth.

Oh boy. To Sully, "I need to call Moose. He's on the shore, waiting for me."

"No cell service here, Daws. But I have my shortwave. I can call Kennedy back at the outpost, and she can get ahold of the FBO via the ham radio. They'll contact Moose." He picked up the backpack he'd dropped and opened it.

"How far are we from the outpost?" Dawson stood up and stifled a groan. His knee had started to ache again. And from the heat, might be swelling.

"Six miles, maybe. But the blizzard will beat us there." Sully pointed to the northwest even as he stepped away to talk on the radio.

Dark clouds jockeyed for space as they descended into the valley, turning the world to storm and shadow, the ceiling dropping fast. "If Moose doesn't leave now, he won't get off that riverbed."

"Yep," Sully said, also scanning the sky. "We need to get to shelter too."

"Can we get to your place in time?"

"Better to go to Woodcrest," Sully said. "We're only a couple miles from Woodcrest. I'm just coming from there."

"Will you make it home before the storm?"

"They have a few snow machines. I'll borrow one."

Dawson bent over to address the woman. "What's your name?"

She had stopped crying a little, stared out past him. Caspian crawled up and set a paw on her knee. Then his snout. Nudged her hand.

"Keely," she whispered. "Keely Williams."

"Okay, Keely Williams. Listen, you're going to be okay. We're going to hike to shelter—"

"I can't walk." She lifted her gaze to him. Pretty eyes, hazel-blue. Fear in them. "I hurt my ankle." Her voice emerged raspy again. Almost a whisper.

He swallowed. Straightened. Blew out a breath.

Sully walked back to him. "I got ahold of Kennedy. She'll relay the message to Moose. In the meantime, we need to get going."

"She can't walk," Dawson said, his tone low. He glanced at Keely. She'd dug her fingers into Caspian's fur. "And I . . . I'm still moving pretty slow."

Sully nodded. "I heard about the shooting. And the total knee replacement."

He looked away. Last thing he needed was sympathy, thanks. It just made him feel . . . broken.

He was not broken.

Dawson turned to Keely. "Listen. There's a blizzard coming. We need to get to safety. There's a community not far from here."

She swallowed, and something like fire came into her eyes. Better.

He held out his hand, and she hesitated a moment, then took

it. Let him help her up. He gave her his elbow, and she tried to put weight on her ankle. A whimper eked out of her, but she drew in a breath, tightened her jaw.

Yeah, this would take a couple thousand years.

"Get on my back," he said.

"Are you kidding?" Sully rounded. "Dude—"

Dawson gave him a tight-lipped glare.

"Listen," Sully said, putting his hand on Dawson's shoulder, "we need to move. I've got her." He swung off his pack and handed Dawson his gun. "Besides, if someone is out there, you're a better shot."

"Hardly," he said. Sully was former military, and there were rumors of special ops, but he never talked about it.

Dawson shouldered the pack and swung the gun strap over his neck.

"You think this guy is still out here?" he asked Keely as Sully pulled her up to his back. She locked her arms around Sully's neck.

Nodded.

Caspian set out ahead of them, and Dawson wanted to shout at the dog to stay with them, but weirdly, the animal stayed pretty close.

Now he chose to obey.

Moose's words rounded back to him about letting Jericho train him for SAR work. But then he'd need his handler present, right?

Who had to be able to *run*, right?

Dawson blew out a breath, his steps in Sully's as he fought to keep up. They walked down the frozen riverbed.

"What are you doing out here, anyway, Sul?"

"We're on Bowie land," he said over his shoulder, as if that answered the question.

"How's Kennedy?"

Silence from his friend.

"Sul?"

"She's fine."

Not fine, by the tone.

Behind them the wind started to howl, sending icy flakes into the air, skittering down his jacket collar. He glanced back.

The clouds chased them, catching up.

They left the riverbed, trudged through a cut of forest, and then emerged in an open area, headed toward a deer trail on the other side. Keely shivered, her head on Sully's shoulders.

"How much farther?" Dawson's gut tightened the minute they walked into the open. Like they might be prey. Aw, he was probably overreacting to the wind in the trees, the darkening sky, the gripping cold.

Caspian slowed, came back, nudged up against him, as if pushing him.

"It's okay, pal."

Sully turned, walking backward for a bit. "We're nearly there—"

A crack bit the air.

Sully jerked and his leg buckled.

Then, just like that, he dropped to one knee.

Keely sprawled into the snow with a scream.

Dawson dropped, went prone, and rolled to his back, searching the forest for the shooter, his heart in his throat.

Caspian scooted next to him, nearly on top of him.

Silence. Nothing but forest ahead of them, but they lay in the open, exposed. He scanned the woods, fighting to control his breathing.

Nearby, Sully groaned, a deep, angry sound of frustration.

"Sul? You shot?"

"It's just a scratch."

Dawson began to crawl to him. Blood spit on the snow around Sully.

"Just a scratch?" His breath razed his lungs. *Calm. Down.* "We need to get to cover. Can you walk?"

Sully pressed his glove against the wound on the side of his leg. "I'm good."

"He's shot?" Keely crawled over, her breathing again panicked.

"We need to get off this field, now," Dawson said, glancing into the trees. "Give me your scarf."

Her hands shook as she handed it to him.

Another shot broke the air. Snow tufted up behind Keely, barely missing her.

Caspian slammed against him, nearly knocking him over. Yeah, well, good move. "Get down!" Dawson reached out, pushed Keely down, Caspian between them.

Sully grabbed the scarf from Dawson, tied it around his leg. "Let's move." He tried to roll over but fell.

Aw. Instinct took over, settled him as Dawson reached for Keely. "I'll come back for you!"

Then he got up, gritted his teeth, and hauled Keely up against him. "Go, Casp!"

The dog shot off, and they followed in an awkward scramble, the losers of a three-legged race. Another shot hit a tree, scrubbing off bark, as he flung them into the ring of forest. He dumped her in the snow. "Take cover!"

Then he turned for Sully.

Caspian stepped in front of him.

"Stay," he said, and the dog looked up at him.

Sat.

Really?

Sully had already started to army crawl from the clearing, some twenty feet from the end, and now gathered his feet under him.

A shot cracked again, and Sully went flat, his hand over his head.

For a second, he didn't move, and Dawson's heart nearly left his chest. Then Sully poked his head up, and Dawson took off, limping, running, ducking. He got a hand on Sully's coat and half dragged, half helped him scramble to the edge of the forest.

Another shot followed them in, shredding pine needles.

"How many was that?" Sully said, breathing hard, now rewrapping the bloody scarf around his leg.

Dawson stared out across the field, searching. "How many shots? I don't know—"

"Five. I think five," rasped Keely. "A Glock 19 holds fifteen rounds. Mack fired one, so that's nine left."

Dawson stared at her. *Really?*

Sully grunted, pulling the scarf tighter.

He'd save it for later. "You good?"

"Yeah. Bleeding is already slowing." He let out a noise, however, and Dawson recognized it as a bone-deep growl of pain, maybe frustration. So, not a scratch, but not his femoral artery either.

He blew out a breath, nodding. Then he looked at Keely. "Who is this guy? And why is he trying to kill you?"

"Us," Sully said.

"Maybe. But you were holding Keely and turned a second before the shot. It would have hit her."

A beat, then Sully nodded. "Right. Okay. Let's move." Sully used a tree to pull himself up. Dawson handed him the rifle, then turned to Keely.

"My turn."

She wiped her hand across her face. "No. I can walk."

"Right." He put out his arm, crooked it, and she sighed and tucked her arm through his. He pulled it against him, steadying her.

Sully took a step and then drew in a breath and released a grunt. "Not much farther."

This day was getting funner by the minute. "Race ya," Dawson said.

Sully's eyes narrowed. "Let's go."

They started off, Sully struggling behind him, probably scanning for the shooter. Weirdly, Moose's voice came back to him. *"Maybe there's stuff."*

Right. Like God never giving him a break? *Seriously.*

And only then did Dawson realize.

Caspian was gone.

4

KEELY OFFICIALLY hated Alaska.

And why not? Because only here did she survive a plane crash and an attempt on her life—*attempts*—only to be chased down by a blizzard?

The wind roared around them, through the forest, shaking the trees, whipping against her bare neck. Icy droplets of snow pinged against her jacket, the world around them turning fuzzy and white.

She couldn't feel her toes, her fingers, her nose. Even her ankle had ceased its throbbing.

So this was what it felt like to freeze to death. If she escaped this, she would never leave her Manhattan penthouse again, thank you. She'd do her concerts via Zoom.

"You doing okay?" This from Dawson. "You're breathing funny."

She nodded, her throat brittle and scratchy.

He glanced down at her and she offered a tight smile. Dark eyes, deep blue, and they focused on her a moment, as if trying to read her.

She looked away, blew out a breath. Probably she owed him

some kind of explanation, but her throat hurt, and she needed her energy.

Of course she had to be rescued by a cop.

A *cop*.

God clearly had a sense of humor, or maybe it was her mother up there, nudging the Almighty, refusing to let well enough alone.

Although, so far, the cop wasn't arrogant and bossy, just focused. Determined.

And strong. That part hadn't escaped her as he'd tightened his hold around her waist, helping her over downed logs, steadying her as they fought snow layers and drifts.

Behind them, his friend Sully—and wasn't *that* a small world, really?—scanned for Thornwood.

She'd landed in a bizarre *North Woods* action thriller.

Not much farther turned into an hour of trudging through snow and ice and wind and—

Please, someone, save her from Alaska.

They emerged from the woods to a lake, not large, with a rocky shoreline, a layer of snow across the icy surface. In the distance, *hallelujah*, she made out a clearing, with the lodge she'd seen earlier maybe, a spiral of welcoming smoke emitting from a chimney. It seemed they were coming in from the north side, her memory laying out fields to the south and east.

"You think the ice is strong enough?"

Oh, Dawson had addressed his friend, Sully, aka Daniel Boone. Sorry, but the guy did radiate a sort of wilderness warrior vibe. Especially with her bloody scarf knotted around his leg. Hermès cashmere, she'd picked it up in London during her last tour. It'd cost nearly as much as Sully's fancy Overland coat.

She hated Alaska.

The dog—she didn't know what to think about him. One second scary, the next pushing up against her or Dawson, like he might need a hug—now bounded out in front of them through the snow, onto the ice.

"I dunno. We had a warm spell recently, but I don't think it's enough to weaken the ice." Sully glanced back. "Let's go."

Really, if she took a step back and out of this tragedy, the view could be called breathtaking. The wind swept snow off the white, pristine surface of the lake like fairy dust. Snow coated the pine trees that edged the lake with frosting, and whitened mountains rose in the distance, majestic against the darkening sky, now streaked with the lingering colors of the day—oranges and mottled purple—fighting the advance of darkness. The colors splayed upon the glistening surface of the lake as they ventured out.

Here, the snow turned solid, with a caked layer that they crashed through with every step. Slow going. Next to her, Dawson seemed to struggle with his left leg.

Sully crunched in the snow behind them, and a glance over her shoulder confirmed a sort of military alertness as he scanned the woods around them. He still limped badly, clearly in pain.

"Will we be able to call for help from the community?" She shouldn't have spoken, maybe, because her voice rasped out.

"I don't know."

"They have a ham radio," Sully said, so maybe her question had carried. "Although I'm not sure it can get a signal out with the blizzard. You may need to sit tight for a day or so."

"We could take the snow machines out to your place," Dawson said.

Sully made a sound, more of acknowledgment than agreement.

Around them the wind howled, more open here. It wound through her jacket.

The dog had vanished, out ahead of them.

She wanted a bath—a hot bath—and cocoa and her wool socks and flannel pajamas and—

A crack sounded, and for a second, she nearly ducked. But Dawson held her tight against him and froze.

"Is that the ice?"

"Could just be groaning. Ice does that," Sully said. But he, too, stilled.

Wait—what? She drew in a breath.

"This day just keeps getting better," Dawson muttered, then looked at her. "Can you swim?"

"Is that a joke?" She cleared her throat. "We go in the water, we're dead."

He glanced at Sully. "Hang back."

"What, why? Are you serious?" Keely asked.

He didn't answer her, just eased her forward.

Oh . . . please, God, get me out of this.

He slowed them, easing into each step, and she practically held her breath.

Ten feet more, and then behind them, Sully started to move.

If Thornwood had followed them, now would be the perfect time to pick them off. *Aaand . . .* she'd clearly watched one too many action movies.

Barking on the far side made her look up. The dog paced the opposite shore, then started bounding out toward them.

"Caspian! Go back!" Dawson motioned to the animal, but he didn't respond. Just kept coming.

Another crack, somewhere in the distance, and Dawson tightened his hold on her. His hip pressed against hers, and weirdly, a sort of strength strummed through her. He picked up his pace.

Caspian had nearly reached them, and now barked, turning, as if beckoning them to follow.

He bounded back to shore, now some twenty feet away.

The next crack sounded right under their feet. Dawson didn't move. "Ice is thinner near shore. It melts first, and all this snow is an insulator."

Perfect.

And then he pointed.

Maybe thirty feet away, a small opening in the ice revealed a slate-gray puddle of open water.

"It's a warm water hole," Dawson said. "A current, or even marsh gasses, can keep the water warm enough not to freeze."

She nodded. Glanced at the shore. So close. "Now what?" Her voice emerged rough-edged in the wind and snow, barely audible.

Caspian continued to bark louder, pacing the shore. Then, suddenly, he bolted and ran toward the lodge.

No, toward a *man* dressed in an orange hunting suit, towing a flat-bottomed toboggan. Another man accompanied him, carrying a ladder.

"That's Donald Cooper," Sully said from behind them. "And the one with the ladder, I think, is Griffin Talon."

Donald lifted a hand, waving.

Dawson waved back, still not moving.

The two men came to the shore, and Griffin set the ladder onto the ice, then held it as Donald stepped out, walking on the rungs, towing the toboggan.

He set it down and pushed it out to Dawson, holding a long lead.

Dawson reached out and grabbed it, pulling it closer. He started to lower Keely toward it. "Get on."

"What?"

"It'll disperse your weight. Trust me." He kept lowering her down.

She grabbed him around the neck and held on as he maneuvered her onto the sled.

"Roll over and hold on."

She didn't want to let go, but she nodded, scooted back, and rolled over, holding onto a strap dangling from the curled front edge.

Donald pulled her to the ladder. Then he helped her up to step onto it.

"I'll crawl." She took it rung by rung to the shoreline.

She rolled out onto solid ground, watching as Dawson came in, then Sully.

Dawson stepped off the ladder, limped over to her. "You okay?"

Caspian came and lay beside her, his warmth almost calming. Still, she didn't think she'd ever be okay again. But she nodded.

Sully groaned as he stepped off the ladder. "Thanks, Griff."

"Bear attack?" Griffin pointed to his leg, then walked over to put an arm around him.

"Long story," Sully said. "Let's get inside."

Dawson pulled her up, again securing her against himself. Looked at her. "See, we're going to be fine."

She waited for a gunshot to part his words, but only the wind chased them as they headed to the lodge. So maybe he was right.

Next stop, *anywhere* but Alaska.

Okay, maybe a detour to the warm and embracing lodge.

Hello, North Woods escape. She stepped into the centerfold of *Mountain Living* magazine, the rustic version, but still sweeping and inviting. The entire building bespoke craftsmanship, from the hand-hewn logs chinked with white plaster to massive, log-framed sofas padded with overstuffed cushions that circled a towering, three-story river rock fireplace. It rose from the far end of the room, flanked by windows that overlooked the frozen lake. Inside a hearth that seemed large enough to walk into, a fire crackled, emanating heat through the massive protective screen.

Wooden pine tables with long benches ran down either side of the room, and above them hung a multitiered antler chandelier the size of a Volkswagen. At the tables in clusters sat men and women with children, a few with books open, some of the children coloring, others playing games.

A balcony ran down each side of the lodge, with rooms on the upper level, and below them, more rooms, the doors closed. They bore nameplates, like Med Clinic and Supplies. Other doors had designs carved into them, one with a cross.

The delicious aromas of baking bread and maybe a rustic stew with garlic and tomatoes reached inside and roused a hunger Keely didn't realize she possessed. Following the smells, she spotted a massive kitchen behind a serving counter.

A man, mid-twenties, sat on one of the sofas in the front of the room, playing a guitar.

Caspian came in and sat as a couple kids ran over to him. His tail brushed the floor, but he didn't move, his back to Dawson.

So clearly not the attack dog she'd thought him to be.

Sully had already eased himself down on a long bench that ran the length of the entrance wall. Jackets hung from pegs, boots neatly tucked under the bench.

A man walked up, dressed in a wool sweater and pants, felt boots. "Sully, sit tight. I'll get River, and she'll take a look at that leg."

"It's really more blood than hurt, Abe. I'm fine. Just need some duct tape." He made a wry face. "But this is a gunshot. And I don't think they mistook me for a deer."

"We'll keep watch," Abe said.

Dawson eased her down next to Sully. "Let's take a look at that ankle."

Keely stopped him as he reached for her boot. "I can do it."

He looked up, then nodded, and lowered himself onto the bench next to her.

"Where am I? Castle Black?"

Dawson frowned.

"The Night's Watch? *Game of Thrones*?"

"Welcome to Woodcrest." Griffin hung his coat on a nearby peg and stomped his boots on the massive woven mat. "But yes, we're the keepers of the wall." He winked.

She didn't want to ask about any more terrors in the woods.

"Our community isn't large—this is all of us. Seven families, some with kids, some without. The Barrows have a small army." He pointed to a family playing a board game.

Donald came in, pulling the door closed behind him. One of the two kids petting Caspian ran to him, hugged him. She seemed about five or six, with long braided hair, wearing long johns under a knitted wool dress.

A woman came out of the kitchen and hugged Griffin. Petite and pretty, she had auburn hair and wore it down, along with a pair of leggings, wool slippers, and a knitted cable sweater. Clearly, the attire of choice in Woodcrest.

She came over to Sully. "What happened to your leg?"

"I was shot," he said, meeting her gaze.

She didn't flinch, just frowned. "Okay. Let's take a look and get you patched up." A glance at Griffin had him reaching for Sully, but he shook his head.

"I need to get back to my place before the storm. Kennedy is there alone."

She deduced that Kennedy might be his girlfriend, or maybe wife, and something strained on his face with his words.

"What you need is for River to take a look, get you stitched up." He hauled him up, and Sully limped toward a room near the kitchen.

The woman turned to Keely. "I'm River. Can I take a look at your ankle?"

Keely had worked off her boot, gritting her teeth, and now got a good look. Fat, for sure, but she flexed her toes and even moved her ankle a little.

River crouched in front of her and gently felt around the swollen flesh. "Can I move it?"

Keely nodded, and River eased it to one side, then the other. "I don't think it's broken. But you probably need to stay off it. We'll get you some snow to ice it."

She left, and Keely leaned her head back, closed her eyes, listened to the chatter in the room.

It felt like family here, the smells, the laughter. Or as if she had traveled back in time and was now in an episode of *Little House on the Prairie*, Alaska style.

"Sully, really!"

She opened her eyes to see the man limping out of the room. River stood at the door. "Tape is not the answer here."

"Too late. Can I borrow a snow machine?"

A man looked up from where he sat with some kids. "Sure. All the snow machines are in the machine garage. Take one of the single seaters."

Griffin came out behind him. "I should go with you."

Sully shook his head and headed over to Dawson. From the looks of his ripped pants, he had duct-taped his wound. And his pants. "The blizzard is closing in fast. I need to go." He glanced at Keely, back at Dawson. "You'll be okay here until it passes. I'll let Moose know."

Wait—*wait!* Keely summoned her voice. "Sully!" He stopped, maybe startled at her outburst, but— "You're *leaving* us here?"

"You're in safe hands. Wait it out."

But . . . oh, Goldie was going to completely freak out.

She must have worn panic in her face because Dawson cut his voice down. "I promise. I'll keep you safe and get you back to civilization."

And again, those eyes sort of reached in, held her.

He's a cop. The thought pulsed in her brain, then vanished, replaced with *Don't cry.* She managed a nod and a tight smile.

"Maybe another day in Alaska won't kill me."

He frowned at that. "Hopefully not."

She might have appreciated a more confident response.

"YOU DID THE RIGHT thing, coming here."

Dawson turned from where he sat with a cup of coffee, leg extended, staring out into the darkness as the fire flickered in the hearth, listening to the wind howl outside the massive lodge.

Truthfully, he'd been trying to sort that out for an hour or more, as darkness descended, wondering, hoping he hadn't somehow put them in danger, bringing a shooter to their doorstep.

Caspian sat, his back to him, leaning on him just a little, and he didn't realize he had run his hand into the dog's fur until Griffin Talon came up and Caspian's body tensed, just for a second.

"Sully's idea," Dawson said. "Trying to outrun the storm."

The man pulled up a chair, then straddled it, holding a cup of hot cocoa. Dawson put him in his late twenties, but with a seasoned look in his eyes. Brown hair, cut short in the back, a bit of scruff on his face, he wore a green canvas shirt, a thermal shirt under it, and black canvas pants. And a ring on his left hand.

"You would have gone through the ice without Fido here, scratching at our door." Griffin dropped a hand onto Caspian and scratched his back. Caspian didn't move from his perch at Dawson's feet.

"He probably smelled the stew, wanted inside," Dawson said.

One side of Griffin's mouth lifted. "Maybe. Good dog."

"He's a stray. My buddy took him in, but he travels a lot, so I inherited him. A little bit needy, if you ask me. And has a mind of his own. Won't fetch, but you want someone to take up all the room on the sofa? Caspian is your buddy."

Griffin considered the dog, frowned. "Interesting. Well, good thing Donny spotted you on the lake, headed for disaster. No one knows about the ice hole unless you see it from this direction." He leaned back, took a sip of the cocoa. "Wanna talk about that gunshot?"

Dawson glanced at him. "You a cop?"

"Nope. But I've seen gunshots before." He took another sip of cocoa. "And I sort of manage security around here. Just wondering what you brought to our doorstep."

Right. "That's fair." He ran a hand across his face. "I dunno, actually. I was flying up to Copper Mountain with my cousin Moose Mulligan when we spotted the plane. When we put down, we found Cade Maverick dead."

Griffin drew in a breath, then shook his head. "Oh no. I liked Mack. He dropped off supplies for us sometimes."

Dawson took a sip of coffee. His knee had stopped aching, although it still felt fat. He left his leg extended. "He was shot in the head."

Quiet. He looked over and Griffin's mouth made a grim line. "You don't say."

"Yeah."

"Any idea by who?"

"Nope. My dog took off into the woods and after about an hour or less, I came across Sully and Keely—the woman with us. She was a passenger, but I haven't gotten much from her except that apparently someone else on the plane was trying to shoot her."

"And Sully somehow got in the middle?"

"Let's just say that, for simplicity."

"You think the shooter is someone from the plane? The manifest might shed some light."

Griffin thought like a cop.

"We tried to find it, but the wreckage was scattered everywhere."

"Mack would have filed something from where he took off."

"My guess too. Sully had Kennedy get ahold of Moose, told him to take off. The investigation will have to wait. But as for bringing the shooter here . . . I don't know. I hope not. Sorry."

"Me too." He took another sip of cocoa. "We can defend ourselves, but I like to avoid trouble."

"We'll be out of your hair as soon as the blizzard passes."

Griffin nodded. "You're welcome here. I just need to know what might be out there." He glanced toward the black window panes. Sighed. "The woman looks familiar. Who is she?"

"Keely? Just . . . a passenger."

Griffin stayed silent. Took a breath, then, "You think she knows something about it?"

"Maybe. I want to talk to her, but your wife took her away to doctor her ankle."

"Yeah, River has some doctor in her. She and I got married a few months ago. She's from here. I'm not, but I like it."

"Where'd you meet?"

"River is a Certified Direct-Entry Midwife. She was apprenticing on Kodiak Island when we got together."

"And you are—"

"Jack-of-all-trades." He smiled. "Mostly I work with Don, helping him keep this place running. We just finished stocking the barn with firewood for the winter."

"It's a big barn."

"Holds all our animals—a few milk cows, goats, a handful of beef cows we're raising. Horses. Cats, sheep for our wool—we even have a llama." He laughed. "I call her Woolly Bully. She's got issues."

"I hate drama. Even in a llama."

"Look at you, a poet." Griffin raised his mug. "You'll fit right in."

Dawson laughed. "I've heard about this place, but I've never been here."

"Yeah, apparently for a while, people thought this might be a hippie commune or something. It was started by a few artists who wanted to live off the land. We're not a cult or some weird commune. Just a bunch of people of faith, trying to raise our families in community. It's not mandatory, but we do have a service on Sunday. A couple of the men take turns preaching. We have a charter, a sort of government, but everyone is here voluntarily, owns their own home, and pays into a kind of HOA to fund the animals and main buildings."

"This lodge is huge."

"We use it for big events, and there are rooms—like a hotel—although they're assigned to each family in case of emergency."

"Like a blizzard."

"It saves resources to hunker down together during a crisis. The original founders built this lodge first, and then the homes. Not everyone is here, but most of the families show up. Like a big family reunion."

Griffin got up. "We opened a room for you. It's upstairs, near the front of the lodge, right next to your friend Keely. It has a moose on the door. By the way, I'm on night shift, so don't worry about dousing the fire."

"Night shift?"

"Makes everyone feel better if someone is up and around, watching the fire. I told you it was like the Night's Watch."

"I never saw the show."

"Let's just say we're the bastion in the cold, dark night." Griffin turned the chair back around.

Dawson watched him walk over to the kitchen area, now partially closed up. His wife came out, gave him a hug, leaning against him.

Dawson looked away, staring into the fire, and for some reason, the memory of holding Keely against him, helping her through the forest, rose, took hold.

She had pretty eyes. Hazel-blue, with flecks of gold, and maybe he'd held her gaze a little too long once, trying to figure her out. What was with the whisper? Or maybe she'd just exhausted her voice from screaming.

Tough, because once she'd pulled off her boot, he imagined the pain she'd endured. And she knew guns—her answer about the shots fired and the magazine capacity of a Glock 19 hung on to him.

But frankly she also reminded him of, well, Caroline. He blew out a breath.

This time, no one died on his watch.

He closed his eyes, fatigue running fingers through him. But shoot, as if conjured by his thoughts there she was—"*Get me home, Dawson, please get me home.*"

"Dawson?"

He jerked, spilled his coffee as he opened his eyes.

Keely had come to the room, her ankle wrapped tight, leaning on a crutch. She wore a pair of thick sweatpants and a knitted sweater, her blond hair down.

He put her at five foot four, very petite, maybe too skinny, really, without all her extra padding of outerwear. She sat in the chair Griffin had vacated. Glanced at Caspian. He'd lain down, head on his paws.

She cleared her throat but her voice came out just above a whisper. "I wanted to say thank you."

Without the roar of the wind to cut off her voice, he heard her without a problem. "You're welcome. Sorry about my dog."

Caspian got up, moved over to her, and she jerked, pulled up her legs.

"He's friendly, I promise."

"Sorry. Reflex." She nodded, reached out, patted him on the head. "He's big. And he did try to eat me." She gave a little yelp when he put his snout on her lap. "He's a little forward."

"Casp—get down."

"No, it's okay." She considered Caspian a moment. "He has pretty eyes."

"Says you and every other woman on the planet."

"What, you jealous?" She smiled, winked.

And words simply swooshed out of him. *What—?* He swallowed, then managed, "No. I mean . . . what?"

She giggled, something soft, and given the last five hours, it just reached in and loosed the tough knot inside. And then, as if she realized it, she put a hand to her mouth and stared at the fire. "I think I'm drugged."

"What?"

"I don't know. First I'm in a plane crash and then chased through the woods, and now I'm here, in some sort of Alaskan Shangri-la, eating borscht and fresh bread . . . what is happening? And . . . how is it that not one, but two heroes found me in the middle of nowhere?"

Hero?

She looked at him as if he might have answers.

He shook his head. "I don't know. Believe me, I'm still trying to figure out how I got in a plane this morning and ended up outrunning a blizzard."

"You're really a cop?"

"A detective. For SVU, out of Anchorage."

"On leave."

He frowned.

"You said that, before." She pointed to his bad knee. "Something happen?"

He drew in a breath. "Wrong place, wrong time."

She considered him a moment. "How *did* you end up on a plane this morning?"

"I was on my way to Copper Mountain with my cousin Moose, and we saw the crash. Put down . . . then I just followed Caspian here. I think he might have heard you, I'm not sure."

She looked at Caspian's snout. "So, *you're* my hero?"

The dog settled on the floor at her feet.

It seemed like the right time, the fire flickering in the hearth, the room quiet. His adrenaline had settled, his heartbeat calm. "So, ready to tell me the details of what happened on the plane?"

She drew in a breath and steeled herself, nodding.

She started by describing the two passengers—two. Called one Thornwood, the other Wilder, and he didn't know either of them. He had to lean forward at the part about the attack, and the wounds Mack suffered fell into place. Then the running, and she stopped talking then, stared away a long while. She finally turned to him and caught him up to the part where he'd jumped Sully.

He sat in her story for a bit, quiet. "Could you identify Thornwood?"

"Probably. But as soon as this storm lifts, I'm out of here. I'll give a formal statement, if you need me to, but . . ." She folded her hands and shoved them between her knees. "I need to get home."

"Which is where?"

"New York City."

"Alaska is a long way from NYC. And it's not tourist season. What are you doing here?"

She looked past him, into the darkness, before sighing. "It's a long story. Let's just say, wrong place, wrong time."

Oh.

She reached for her crutch. "How long do you think this blizzard will last?"

"I suppose until the storm blows itself out."

She glanced toward the darkness. "Seems like that might take a while. Good night, Dawson." She turned away.

"I will get you home, Keely," he said softly. "I promise."

She turned back, smiled. "I believe you."

He drew in a breath even as she walked away. And tried not to let the voices of the past call him a liar.

5

"I BELIEVE YOU"?

Sheesh, maybe Keely should write him a song, declare her undying love. And since when had she turned into such a flirt? Maybe she *was* drugged.

She hadn't behaved that stupidly since the last time she was on *Fallon* and Zac Efron sat down next to her and introduced himself.

And then she went and told the whole world that she loved *High School Musical* and had a poster of him on her wall growing up—and could she be any more embarrassing?

She sank down on the lower bunk bed of her room in the lodge and wanted to bury her face into the pillow.

Hero? She'd called him her *hero*.

Maybe she could stay right here, under the blanket for the entire storm.

She didn't hate the room, or the lodge, or the borscht, and especially not the fresh bread. And River had doctored her ankle—Keely could even walk on it—so that made her feel a little like a wimp. Hello, she could do two full sets on five-inch spikes. Not a wimp.

Truth was, she'd simply been a little overcome by his concern for her, the fact that he'd stayed with her, even helped support her, despite his clear pain. And his soft, low words had only seeded a sort of grateful affection for him. *"I will get you home, Keely."*

So yeah, a hero. But not enough to earn the soft, almost desperate *"I believe you."*

Good grief. She pulled the pillow out and put it over her face. But that only conjured up the man sitting by the fire, his broad shoulders under that flannel shirt—she didn't even *like* flannel. And his dark, nearly black hair, the brush of whiskers . . . he even smelled like smoldering flames.

What*ever*. She threw the pillow away. It landed on the braided rug. Maybe she'd just been around too many guys more interested in their personal branding than . . .

Well, than rescuing a lost woman, despite a bum knee.

There was a story there, but clearly he didn't want to tell it.

And maybe she didn't want to know it—it was probably something heroic and sacrificial and . . . aw, she needed to escape Alaska at the first glimmer of light.

Maybe book an appointment with her therapist.

A knock sounded on her door. "It's open."

River stuck her head into the room. "Hey. I wanted to check on your ankle before you went to bed. Need any more snow?"

"It's feeling better. What was it that you used?"

"Witch hazel for the swelling and ginger tea." She came into the room and picked up the pillow, set it on the bed. "Is the room okay?"

"It's perfect."

"I know it's small, but we don't have a lot of guests. Sometimes kids sleep in here." She sat on a chair made with skinned logs and a thick cushion, more of the same homemade type. "That's a patchwork quilt. My mother made it."

"It's beautiful."

"It's made from scraps, but we never throw anything away here."

"Have you lived here long?"

"I grew up here." She folded her hands on her lap, took a breath. "But I did leave for a while, while I got my midwifery training."

"You're a midwife?"

"And an herbalist. My mom is too, so . . ." She looked out the window and suddenly . . . oh, wow . . . Keely got it.

"You recognize me."

River suddenly wore a conspiratorial look, her eyes lighting up. "You're Bliss."

Keely sat up, barely missing the top bunk. "Yes. But . . . I was hoping that no one would recognize me. I . . ." She made a face. "I sort of snuck out of New York City."

"Why are you in Alaska? I mean—like I know you took time off for your voice surgery, but that was six months ago . . ."

"Well, as you can hear, I'm still working on my voice." She hated the weakness, the occasional raspy tenor when she got tired. And how she still had to strain to hit the high notes.

She'd started to wonder if it would ever come back fully.

River leaned back, held up her hand. "I'm sure it'll come back. I mean, I know it's none of my business, but . . . wow. It *has* to come back. I love your music. It's . . ."

"Fun?"

"Yes. And romantic. And hopeful." Her eyes were bright. "I got your first album—*Heartstrings and High Notes*—when I was fifteen. It was perfect. I was in love with one of the Benson brothers, and he'd just broken my heart, and you sang all the perfect words. Everything I was feeling."

She was sweet. The kind of fan who she'd sung for, once upon a time. "I loved that album. I wrote every song."

"It was perfect. Especially the one about him taking your heart—"

"'Stolen Beats.' 'You took my heart with a smile—'"

"'Oh, the game you played.'" River picked up the song. "'Left me in the shadow, cold and gray.' Oh, I played it over and over and cried and cried and cried."

Keely drew in a breath. Oh, River had no idea. She'd done exactly the same thing. "I'm sorry," she said softly.

"Oh no. It was a good cry. You put to words exactly what I was feeling. And, of course, he wasn't my true love."

"You're married to that hunk who saved us out on the ice."

River grinned, held up her hand. A small diamond, a simple gold band. "Griffin is amazing and perfect and . . . well, you wrote a song about that too."

"'Forever Found.'"

"We used the lyrics in our wedding."

"What?"

"I know. Wild. But they were perfect. 'In a world full of noise, your voice was a quiet call, through the crowd, through the chaos, you saw me through it all. Like a lighthouse in the storm, you were steadfast and tall. In your eyes, I found the place where I belong.'"

"When you say it, it sounds very romantic."

"It is . . . especially when you sing it." River met Keely's eyes, leaned forward, pitched her voice low. "Are you still dating Chase?"

A beat. Wait— *Chase Sterling?*

"Yes. I thought—I mean, weren't you together? You were in that movie, and you did that duet together—"

"Oh no. No. That was publicity. And we were promoting each other's albums, and . . . no, trust me. Chase is not . . . not my type."

River raised an eyebrow. "So who is your type?"

Keely looked away, swallowed. Closed her eyes.

"Wait. Are you with Dawson?"

She looked at River and managed a "Who?" It came out a little squeaky.

"Oh, I thought . . . you know, that guy you came in with today. You were talking to him earlier—"

"Right. The cop." Oh, she could lie so easily it seemed. "Yeah, no. I've had my share of cops in my life. No thank you." That, however, was the truth.

"Because of your dad."

She stared at River, her eyes wide.

"From *Pop Muse* magazine. You did that interview a year or so ago. Talked about your mom's death, and your dad—"

"Okay. Yes. I didn't realize they were going to print all of that. But . . . okay, yes. Having a cop for a dad can be . . . well, let's just say you never want to bring anyone home." She grinned at River and winked.

Just like she would have done for Jimmy Fallon.

River bought it. "Yeah, I see that. I'm sorry about your mom, though."

Oh. The words sideswiped her, and she looked away. Breathe. *Breathe.* Fallon, think Fallon. Showbiz.

She found herself and a smile. "She was my biggest fan. I'm sure she's still cheering for me in heaven." Then Keely leaned back on her hands. "But no cop for me. Besides, I don't have room in my life for romance."

River frowned. "What? But your songs are so romantic."

Keely lifted a shoulder. "Romance is . . . a distraction."

"Not true love. It's the reason. Everything else is second."

"Is there such a thing?"

"As true love?" River was spinning her ring. "I think so."

Outside, a light flickered on around the barn, lighting up the snow. The blizzard shone in the glow, like stars in hyperspace, the sense of it almost magical. A postcard snapshot of a winter wonderland.

What was she doing here?

"I think we make choices," Keely said, reaching for the pillow. "And we live with them. Sometimes it turns out, sometimes it doesn't." She sighed, even as River's mouth opened. "I know that doesn't sound very romantic, and don't tell anyone else, but not everyone is meant to find 'The One' and live happily ever after." She'd finger quoted The One.

Weirdly, her words sat in her chest, burned.

River sighed. "Maybe you're right. Maybe it is about choices. But . . ." She looked up. "But I believe that love, and a happy ending, is also a choice. And I think you do too."

Keely frowned.

"'We stood on the edge, where the shadows meet the light, promised each other to fight the good fight. Through storms and silence, through wrong and right, we'll hold our ground, keep our dreams in sight.'" River cocked her head, crossed her arms.

"Fine. You got me." Keely didn't have the heart to tell her that she didn't write that song.

That she hadn't wanted it on her album.

But Goldie told her it would win hearts, sell millions, and every time she got up to sing it, she put on her showbiz face. And for two minutes and thirty-seven seconds, tried to believe it.

In truth, she hadn't written her own songs in a couple years.

Four years, two months and six days, to be exact. Maybe she didn't have any more authentic heart songs in her.

River got up. "I'm glad you're here. And I promise, I'll keep our secret." She headed for the door. "But, if you're interested, that hot cop that practically carried you here is sort of a big deal. My husband recognized him from our local paper. He brought down a drug dealer and human trafficker in Anchorage a few months ago. Got shot in the process too. So I know you're leaving in a few days, but not every cop is like your dad."

The kind that would break your heart? Yeah, no. She wasn't taking any chances.

"Good night, River. And thanks again."

"Stay warm. If you need anything, Griffin is on night watch." She paused at the door. "And your cop is next door."

She rolled her eyes. "Not my cop."

"Mm-hmm." River shut the door.

Keely lay on the bed, staring at the top bunk. *"I will get you home, Keely."*

She rolled over and pulled the pillow over her ear, closed her eyes. Not. Her. Cop.

The lodge had quieted, the chatter of the families no longer humming. Earlier she'd sat at a long table and watched Donald play a game of Aggravation with a homemade board and marbles. Two cute kids—they'd introduced themselves, but she couldn't remember their names. Wren? And Oliver, she thought. She'd put Wren at around seven, Oliver a little older.

Wren reminded her of herself, maybe, with blond hair in a couple messy pigtails, always swiping her hair out of her face. She wore leggings, with a hole in one knee, and sat on her daddy's lap, her arm around his neck.

Now, the image conjured up and sank in, settled in her chest, and her throat filled.

"Not every cop is like your dad." No. Not every man was like her dad either.

She might have slept, fatigue finding her bones, pressing her into the bed, but something woke her.

Whining. She heard it, near her door. Caspian? Surely Dawson wouldn't leave him out all night . . .

She got up, eased onto her foot. Not terrible. Outside, the light still glowed from the barn, pressing into the window. Balancing on the bunk bed, she worked her way to the door.

Opened it.

Caspian rose from where he lay on the floor outside the room. "Hey there."

The dog let himself in.

Went to the window, whining.

"What's going on? Did Dawson leave you out in the hallway?"

She limped back to the window, crouched next to the dog, running her hand over his neck.

He turned to her, whined again, pressing his nose into her hand.

"Oh, you are sweet. You want to stay here, with me?"

And that's when she looked out into the night at the light flickering and glowing and—

Oh. What—

In the light outside, despite the storm, she spotted a man in a green jacket lying in the snow. He seemed unmoving.

Could be a community member, out checking the barn—

She got up, using the bunk, then gave up and limped to her door.

Darkness bathed the hall, save for the flickering fire in the hearth in the opening below. Caspian pushed past her out into the hall. He turned to Dawson's room.

The man's door hung open, and she spotted the same layout as hers—a bunk bed, and in the lower bunk, a form curled up on the bed, still dressed, his arms tucked to himself, his one leg straight, the other bent. As if he'd simply fallen there.

Caspian ran past her, whining, and nudged his hand overhanging the bed.

"Stop," he mumbled. "Casp, c'mon, man—"

"Dawson?"

He sat up so fast he slammed his head into the top bunk. Then he peered at her, blinking, as if he didn't recognize her.

Oh. Um. "There's a man outside."

He frowned at her.

"He's lying in the snow."

He got up and turned to the window, where the light from outside bled into the room. "He's going to freeze to death." He turned and swept past her, out the door. She came out to see him rush down the stairs, his gait a little stiff, then grab his jacket and head for the door.

And out into the blizzard.

HOW WAS IT that Dawson went from one tragedy to the next? The blizzard turned the blackness lethal as he kicked through the snow on the stairs, his boots crunching. When Caspian ran past him at the bottom, his feet nearly went out from under him.

Light shone from the outside floodlights on the barn, as well as from the machine shed beside it, the door to the shed open.

The man lay in the puddle of light, face down.

Blood stained the snow.

Dawson ran-slash-limped over to him, grabbed his shoulders, and turned him over.

Griffin. He lay unconscious, blood seeping from a gash in his head.

"Griffin—buddy. Wake up!" He ignored the terrible coil tightening his chest. Not *now*.

Snow swirled around him, and Griffin might have given a moan.

The guy wasn't so big that Dawson couldn't carry him, a different day, a different time. But now . . .

C'mon, God. Be on my side.

Seemed like a vain ask, but why not?

Caspian danced around him, barking.

"Calm down. I know, I know." He got up, put his hands under Griffin's shoulders, and started to wrestle him toward the house.

The blizzard fought him. His stupid knee buckled, and he fell, Griffin half on him.

He lay back, breathing hard.

Caspian came up, nosing him, then plopping his head on his chest and whining.

"I know." Useless. He struggled up, again the dog bounced away, barking.

Weird that no one had heard any commotion.

"C'mon!" He repositioned his hands on Griffin's jacket, began to drag him.

A motor sounded not far away, and Dawson looked up.

A man on a snowmobile came screaming out of the shed. Big, wearing a heavy jacket, goggles, and a wool hat, heavy leather mittens gripping the handles. He seemed encrusted with snow.

"Hey!" Dawson shouted, and Caspian turned, his barking almost frenzied.

The man didn't look back as he motored up the street.

What was he doing in the garage? But it didn't matter. He kept tugging at Griffin, who'd started to rouse.

"Griff!" The shout came from behind him, and in a moment, Donald and Abe hustled down the stairs. "What happened?" Donald lifted Griffin's legs, Dawson on one arm, Abe on the other, and they shuttled him toward the lodge.

Another man came out and took Dawson's place, clearly seeing him limp.

Shoot. But he relinquished the hold, and they carried Griffin up the steps.

River caught up to them, a coat wrapped around her. Her breath shallow. "What happened?"

Dawson shook his head and turned to see the lights from the snowmobile blinking, disappearing into the night.

He glanced at the men now carrying Griffin inside, then ducked his head against the wind and headed for the garage, Caspian leading the way. Snow swirled around the overhead light, the big sliding door open. Darkness filled the expanse as he stepped inside, but he spotted the destruction anyway.

Five snow machines, their hoods open, wires and cables in a tangle, spewing chaos from them. What the—?

Nearby, a massive tracker seemed untouched, along with farm equipment—all summer vehicles.

Dawson's heart pounded, and he stood at the mouth of the shed, hands on his hips, staring out into the night, a terrible sweat running over him.

Whoever they were, they'd just destroyed any escape.

Caspian leaned hard against him, whining. "You did good, Casp."

The animal couldn't fetch, but he did seem to have a sixth sense about when someone might be in trouble.

Dawson closed the door, ducked his head, and fought his way back inside to the warmth of the lodge.

They'd cleared a table, set Griffin on it, and River had him on his side, pressing a cloth to his wound.

Donald looked over at him, left his spot at the table. "How'd you know?" He advanced, almost angry.

Dawson held up his hands. "I didn't—Keely woke me up."

"It was the dog," Keely rasped, and only now did he see her, eyes wide, standing in the oversized sweater, a blanket around her shoulders. "He whined outside my door. I let him in, and he went right to the window. That's when I saw him in the snow—what happened?"

"Someone got into the machine shed is what happened," Dawson said. "Looks like they destroyed the other snow machines before they stole the last one."

Donald frowned, but on the table, Griffin roused. He moaned, tried to sit up, but River pushed him back down. "Stay put, tough guy."

Dawson pushed past Donald, went to the table. River still held a bandage to Griffin's head, taking it off now and again to examine it. Blood saturated his face, his shirt, his hands.

His knuckles looked torn.

"You were in a fight," Dawson said.

Griffin coughed, nodded. "The machine shed light . . . went . . . on, and I went out to check on it—spotted a man. He tried to run, but I chased him." He winced with one eye as River checked the bandage.

"Can someone get me some snow? We need some cold on this," River said.

Donald headed for the door.

Griffin reached up to touch the bandage. "He came at me with a knife. I had my shotgun, and hit it away, but he wasn't giving up easy. We went around a few times—I got a few hits in, got him down, and would have had him, but he got my shotgun and slammed it against my head, and, bam"—he made a small explosion gesture with his hand—"lights out. Stupid."

"He could have killed you," River said, her voice tight.

"But he didn't."

"He disabled all the sleds," Dawson said. "Why?"

"Dunno."

His gut told him it wasn't anything good. "Maybe so no one could follow him."

"I saw him."

Keely. She stepped closer, the blanket tight around her. "After you left, I saw him out the window."

He turned to her. "What did he look like?"

"Beard, winter clothes. I don't know—it was dark."

"The bleeding has stopped. I need to get some stitches in this." River lifted the bandage. "Think you're steady enough to follow me to the infirmary?"

Griffin sat up but put his hand on his wife's shoulder. "Is this where you say you're fresh out of Novocain and you need to dip into the whiskey?"

"Sorry, tough guy. No whiskey for you. Just a good old-fashioned shot of Novocain. Keep your hand on your head." She held his arm over her shoulder, and they headed toward the room Dawson had seen earlier.

He watched them go, and his gaze connected with Keely, still standing away, her arms around her middle.

And just like that, the memory of her body against his earlier as he'd helped her through the snow, petite yet fighting, swept through him.

She was like a little Nordic Tinkerbell. And behind that followed the terrible, sudden, wild urge to protect her.

He was just tired, probably. He couldn't protect himself, let alone someone else, thanks. Which was probably why her words about him being a hero had stuck in his craw, followed him to bed, and burned in his head.

Maybe, once upon a time. Not anymore, by a long shot. Although, yes, his dog was . . . Wait. "Where is Caspian?"

Donald came in, carrying snow in a bucket. Dawson grabbed the door, looked out into the terrible darkness, the wind snarling. Oh no, if he had to go out there again—

"He's in your room," Keely said, her voice soft. "I was afraid he'd get in the way, or hurt, so I brought him upstairs. I got him something to eat from the kitchen—they had some meat scraps from the soup, and a bone. And water. And a blanket."

He had nothing, except, wow, she was pretty. A simple, sweet beauty about her, really, and it stilled him.

"Do you think that man was . . ." She swallowed. "The man from the plane?"

"Thornwood."

She nodded.

"Maybe."

"So, we're safe, then?"

He blew out a breath. His gut said no, but he smiled. "I think so. For now."

"Maybe we'll be okay, after all." She smiled then, and yes, maybe they would.

But outside, the blizzard howled, and some terrible place in his gut—call it instinct—said this wasn't over.

6

MAYBE BEING TRAPPED in a snowy version of paradise—despite the trouble from yesterday—for a day might not be so terrible.

Keely stood at the massive picture windows overlooking the snow-covered ice, the wind still howling, snow thick and gusting off the lake. The pellet-gray sky blocked the sun, the clouds dark and broody, but inside the lodge, a fire crackled in the hearth and light shone from the hanging antler chandelier.

The place reminded her a lot of Mountain Lodge in Telluride, complete with the smell of bacon and eggs, fresh bread, and the sense of holiday.

So maybe that's what she'd call this . . . a holiday. She blew on her coffee. At least that's how she'd couch it to Goldie.

Oh, her manager would be furious. And worried. But maybe she'd appreciate the fact that Keely had slept like a bear—a first in years for her, really—warm under the patchwork quilt, despite the chill in the air, the persistent howl of the wind turning into a sort of sleep-noise machine.

Okay, it had taken a hot minute to finally fall into that hard sleep, after staring into the darkness outside, the snow swirling off the roof, thinking about the look on Dawson's face when he'd come in from the cold.

A sort of anger and a worry etched into his frown. But it was the way he looked up at her not long afterward, while talking to Griffin, almost a relief casting over him.

As if he'd been worried about her?

Like she, what, *mattered* to him?

See, this was what happened when she let her song lyrics actually stick around in her head. *Like a lighthouse in the storm, you were steadfast and tall. In your eyes, I found the place where I belong.*

Oh brother. She'd been so naive.

No, she didn't believe in true love. The guy was a cop—it stood to reason he possessed an overachieving responsibility gene. And, he had made her a promise, so calm down.

Holiday, indeed. A holiday from her common sense.

Conversation hummed in the hall, families eating at the long tables. She turned, spotted little Wren eating oatmeal, still in her pajamas, her hair a tousled mess. She sat with her father and Oliver, her father appearing tired and bedraggled.

Male voices had drifted up to her room last night, and she'd bet that a few of the men had stayed up, guarding their families.

At the serving bar between the kitchen and the great room, she helped herself to oatmeal, added maple syrup—it smelled rich and tangy, as if authentic—and headed over to sit with Donald and his family.

It occurred to her then that she hadn't seen a wife, although the man wore a wedding ring.

"Good morning." She swung her leg over the bench opposite the trio. "Can I sit with you?" Her ankle had healed so much overnight that she walked with barely a twinge today.

"Morning, Keely," Donald said.

Wren grinned at her. "We're going sledding!"

"Not yet," her father said, but gave her a grin. "After the storm is over."

"That sounds fun." Yes, real maple syrup. Best oatmeal ever. "I haven't been sledding in years. I used to go with my father, on a hill near our house."

"Where are you from?" Donald asked.

"Minnesota. Minneapolis area. Very snowy, but not like this."

"It's hard to beat an Alaskan blizzard." He picked up his coffee. "And it's just getting started. Hey, Dawson."

She looked up, and Dawson walked over, also carrying a mug of coffee. He appeared a little rough today, as if he might not have slept, his dark hair rucked up, a thicker scruff of whiskers. He wore the same clothes as yesterday but smelled as if he'd just come in from the weather, a sort of windblown freshness on him.

Stop.

"Hey," he greeted her, then Donald.

Her stupid heart kicked up a little. *Calm down, sheesh.* Her heart clearly thought she'd landed in some Alaskan Hallmark movie. Did it not remember the crash, the running, the shooting, the *terror*?

She blamed the snow, the crackling fire, and the fact that the man wore flannel.

"Did you go out to check the machine shed?" Donald asked him.

"Yeah. With Griffin and a couple of the guys. Caspian needed some outside time." He stepped over the bench, glanced at her. "Is this seat taken?"

"Saved for you." *What—? For the love!*

He raised an eyebrow, and she turned back to her oatmeal. He climbed in next to her. Smelled of pine. *Whatever!*

"So, what's the verdict?" Donald asked.

Dawson sipped his coffee. "There are five snow machines, and all of them have been tampered with. Spark plug wires pulled, fuel lines ripped out. All repairable, but it'll have to be after the storm, when we can get some supplies in."

"We were lucky. And we still have the horses." Donald sighed.

The *horses*? She *was* living an episode of *Little House on the Prairie*.

Maybe Dawson sensed her thoughts because he said, "We'll just button up here and we'll be fine."

Probably, he said it for her peace of mind, but his pinched-mouth expression screamed something else.

The man was *worried*.

Donald got up, grabbed his bowl and Oliver's, and headed to the kitchen. Wren followed him, and Oliver got up too.

Caspian sat behind Dawson, staring out into the room, as if surveying traffic. Funny. Oliver walked over to him, patted his head.

The dog didn't move, although his tail swished the floor.

"What's really going on?" she asked, her gaze back on Dawson.

He considered her, then sighed. "I can't understand why the snowmobile vandal would think we'd chase after him in the storm. Unless, of course . . . he'd taken you."

His mouth pinched.

She stared at him, her breath hitching. "Wait . . . do you think he's after me?"

"I don't know. But if he did figure out a way to grab you, we couldn't catch him. So . . . maybe just stick close."

To Dawson? To the lodge? Either way, she nodded. And all the Hallmark went out of the room. "How long are we trapped here?"

"Until the storm dies. We can call Moose, have him bring in a chopper—I don't think he can land a plane on the ice. But even then, we need to get to a radio."

"They don't have a radio here?"

He took another sip of coffee, not as alarmed as he should be in her opinion. His hand dropped onto Caspian's back, fingers in the dog's fur, an almost absent move. "I asked. They have a ham, but the antenna went down in a recent storm, and the mountains interfere with the signal. The closest radio is the Bowie Outpost a couple miles away."

She pushed away her oatmeal, her appetite gone. *A couple miles away.*

He met her eyes now, his gaze a little intense. She couldn't look away. "It'll be okay, Keely. Griffin had guys on watch, and . . . well, I made you a promise." He offered a smile.

A downright lethal combination, as it turned out, because words died in her chest.

She managed to nod. And then somehow a "Why?"

He raised a brow. "Why? Why what?"

She stared at him. "You don't know anything about me. What if I'm a murderess on the lam?"

He gave her a once-over, and his mouth hitched up on one side. "Are you?"

Too much tease in his eyes for him to be serious. "No." She swallowed. "But still. Why would you make a promise—"

"Because reasons." His smile had dimmed, and he looked away.

Oh.

They sat there in silence, conversation humming around them, and now she just stared at her coffee—

"A few years ago, I was in a plane crash too."

She looked up.

He glanced at her, his mouth tight. "I was bringing my girlfriend to Copper Mountain to meet my dad, and ice took us down. It wasn't really a *crash*, just a hard landing, but we couldn't take off again, so we had to hike out. Took us three days. My cousin Moose carried out the other passenger, a guy named Pike. Caroline was . . . not prepared for three days in the bush. None of us were. But she was . . . I guess you could call her a city girl. She was from Denver, a skier, and she loved the outdoors, but she had no idea what she was getting into up here, and she . . . she froze."

"Froze?"

"Hypothermia." He ran his fingers through Caspian's fur, almost absently. "I tried to keep her warm—and we had overnight gear. Sleeping bags, a stove. A tent. Moose carries a survival pack in his plane. But she went out one night, after we'd gone to sleep—I think she had to go to the bathroom. She never made it back, and a couple hours later, I discovered she was gone. I think maybe something scared her, and she got lost in the dark— anyway, by the time I found her, she was so far gone. I couldn't bring her back . . ." He took a breath, stared again at his coffee. "I promised her I'd keep her safe and get her home."

Ah.

She got it now. She was his do-over. Keely touched his arm. "I'm sorry."

He shrugged, sighed, and met her eyes, this time his smile sweet, almost warm. "So, let me keep this promise to you, okay?"

She nodded. Then, "I know you think I'm a city girl, but I'm tougher than I look."

His mouth quirked up.

"Really. I grew up in Minneapolis. And my dad was a cop. So, you know—life skills."

"Like shooting a gun? A Glock 19?"

Huh. "Yes. My dad taught me to shoot. And some self-defense. So, you know, watch yourself. I can take you out."

He smiled now, full on, and again, lethal, a stunner of a smile that he should probably register as a weapon. It even touched his eyes. His pretty blue eyes, the color of a Minnesota summer twilight.

Oh good grief, now she was writing songs in her head.

"Anyway." She swallowed, took a sip of her coffee. "I can also fix cars."

"No you can't."

"Can. My dad was a hobby mechanic. Let me take a look at those snowmobiles."

He laughed then. "It's not up to me, but I'll tell Griffin we have Edd China in the house."

"Joke's on you. I know who Edd is. *Wheeler Dealers*. And I have better hair."

A sort of chuckle huffed out of him, as if unused, rusty. "Yes, you do." His smile touched his eyes again. "You are interesting, Keely. I think maybe I underestimated you."

She smiled as she drained her coffee. "Get used to it."

Oh *brother*. She wanted to roll her eyes at her own lameness. But she couldn't seem to stop herself.

"You're dry. Want more?" He reached for her cup.

"Thanks."

He got up, and she watched him walk over to the coffeepot set up on the serving counter. Maybe over six foot, well built, lean, wide shoulders, strong. Sure, he walked with a small limp, but it gave him the aura of a wounded warrior. Dark hair, cut short in the back, tousled in front. The man could grace an outdoor edition of *The Rake* with his serious, focused demeanor.

Except for that smile. It reached in and loosed something inside her. Or maybe it was just his words . . . interesting.

She liked being interesting. It felt layered and authentic.

So not Bliss.

He returned, set the coffee in front of her. "I thought you might be a sugar and whole milk girl." He set a small cup of milk beside her mug. "I'll be right back."

The man limped back over to the counter and grabbed his mug and a bowl of sugar.

Maybe she didn't care why he'd made a promise to her. Just that he had.

He returned and sat down, one leg over the bench, now facing her. He handed her the sugar bowl and a spoon.

She doctored her coffee as he took a sip of his, black.

"So, what are you doing in Alaska?" he asked. "Besides fixing snowmobiles and taking care of my dog?"

Speaking of, the animal had gotten up, walked with him to the coffeepot and back, and now sat again, behind him, alert to the room. "Seems like the dog is taking care of you."

He glanced at him. "Yeah. He does that. I don't know why." He reached out and petted the animal behind the ear.

And maybe it was the gesture or the warmth of the room, the sense that here, maybe her secrets didn't have to feel so bruising, so raw and naked.

She took a breath. "I was looking for my mom."

He raised an eyebrow as she took a sip of her coffee. Perfect. She'd just ignore the inner Goldie raising an eyebrow at the sugar intake.

"Your mom?"

"My biological mom," she added. "I was adopted, and when my mom—the one who raised me—was dying, she told me about the woman who'd given me away." She hated saying it like that, but it felt that way sometimes. Even if doing so had saved her life. "My bio mom was a cop in Chicago. She worked undercover in the gangs division, with a partner—my bio dad. Apparently, they were made and my bio dad was killed. My mom was pregnant, so she went into hiding . . . anyway, when I was born, she gave me to my parents. My dad—the one who raised me—was my uncle, on my bio dad's side. He was a cop in Minneapolis. She thought that I'd be safer with him. I guess she thought the gang wouldn't stop tracking her. So, Vic gave me away and disappeared in Alaska."

"*Vic*, from the Midnight Sun Saloon? She's your mom?" His voice lowered.

She shrugged. "Yep."

"Wow. I didn't see that coming."

"You know her?"

"*Everybody* knows her. She's like . . . well, the backbone of Copper Mountain. Has been running the Midnight Sun Saloon for as long as I can remember. Rumors said she'd been a cop in the Lower 48, but no one knows much about her. Not even her last name."

"It's Dalton. I had dinner at the Midnight Sun a couple nights ago, hoping to talk to her. I bought dinner and some pie, and . . . completely chickened out."

He made a wry face. "Sorry. What happened?"

"I don't know . . . I just thought . . ." She blew out a breath. "What if . . ." And now she made a face.

He softened his voice. "She rejects you, after all this time."

She nodded.

"So, why even come here? Why try to meet her?"

And that was the question, wasn't it? Maybe it didn't matter. She let the silence sit between them. She didn't know him well enough for the rest. And frankly, she wanted him to like her. For now.

She had no illusions that their little holiday friendship would shatter when they hit civilization. Because even if she did get ahold of Goldie, it would only take a fan, a TikTok, or even a social media post for the press to wake up to the fact that superstar pop singer and actress Bliss had wandered into Alaska.

Which would bring more questions and maybe even answers, and any Hallmark magic this place possessed would vanish under the bright, hot lights of her fame. So, "I just wanted to know who she was, and if there was any of me in her." That felt vulnerable enough.

He met her eyes. "I think you should give her the chance to meet you, Keely. I don't know you well, but from what I see, there's plenty of Vic in you," Dawson said. "Tough, smart, capable . . . I think probably you shouldn't leave Alaska without another go at getting what you came for."

She looked back at him then, the kind tilt of his smile. It occurred to her that maybe, just maybe, he was the kind of guy to write a song about.

And suddenly she wondered . . . just what had she come to Alaska looking for?

TINKERBELL was Vic's daughter.

Vic Dalton, who could wrestle a polar bear away from a beer and throw him out into the snow if she had to. Yeah, he hadn't seen that coming, not from her petite frame, the aura of city that radiated off Keely. But she'd been tough enough and survived a plane crash and sure, he could see a steely thread, a strength inside her.

Huh.

"We have one set of the nickel alloy plugs." Griffin's voice. He emerged from a room inside the machine barn. "And a socket wrench."

The blizzard still howled, but in the machine shed, lit by kerosene lanterns and battery-powered lights, Donald and a couple other men, along with Dawson and Griffin, attempted to fix the broken sleds.

He hadn't yet mentioned Keely's offer to look at the snowmobiles. Honestly, he didn't know what to think.

Daughter of a Minnesota cop too. Interesting.

He'd spent the night tossing in the bunk. Maybe even disturbed Caspian, because the dog nosed him twice, waking him. No wonder he felt like he'd slept in his car after a long stakeout.

"Daws?"

"I got it all cleaned up." He set down the wire brush from where he'd scrubbed the spark plug area, then reached for the replacements and the socket wrench.

"Where'd you learn to fix snowmobiles?" Griffin asked. "That's a trick they don't teach us Florida boys." He crouched next to Dawson and wiped his hands with a shop rag. He'd spent most of the morning repairing the broken motion sensor light and the lock on the machine shed.

"My grandfather. He loved to tinker with old machines. Kept a garage full on his farm."

"Here in Alaska?"

"Mm-hmm." Dawson added a small amount of anti-seize compound to the plug. "How's the head?"

Griffin still wore a bandage over his wound but he'd put a cap down over it, so only a hint of bandage peeked out. "I'm more angry than hurt. Can't believe the guy got the drop on me. That'll teach me. Train hard, fight easy."

Dawson hand-threaded one of the plugs into the socket. Glanced at him. "Which branch?"

"Army. Rangers."

"Had a friend here who served with them." He grabbed the socket wrench. "Colt Kingston."

"I know Colt," Griffin said. "Got out about the same time he did." He looked away then. "Knew some of the guys on his team. Rough."

Dawson looked up at him. Frowned.

"It's probably classified, but let's say an op went south."

Dawson replaced the spark plug boots. "Doesn't it always. Feels like no matter how much you try, things go wrong."

Griffin looked at him, his mouth tight.

"Why'd you get out?" Dawson asked.

A beat, then, "I got shot." He pulled off his hat and turned his head, held up his hair. A thin scar ran across the back of his head.

"Metal plate. Brain bleed." He put the hat back on. "I still have seizures but not as often. Missing about two years of my life too."

Dawson reached for another plug. "Sorry."

"Yeah, well, maybe that's for the good. No PTSD memories from all the less than spectacular missions. I was medically discharged and decided to fulfill a lifelong dream of working on a longliner fishing boat. Came up to Kodiak. Met River. All good."

Dawson finished hand-screwing a spark plug. Turned to him. "Seriously?"

"Absolutely. I'm convinced that nothing can happen to me in this life that isn't used or designed by God to know him better."

Interesting. Dawson finished torquing down the spark plug. "Yeah, I dunno." His knee still burned, swollen from yesterday's exertion.

Griffin closed the box. "Consider it this way. If some jerk hadn't destroyed our snow machines, we'd never have found that leaky gas line." He pointed to one of the other machines. "Who knows. This man's evil saved us from disaster out on some below-freezing trail." He tossed Dawson his rag. "That's what I call grace."

He got up, and Dawson watched him head toward the door.

The door slid open, and as snow blew into the opening, Keely came in. She wore her puffer jacket and a borrowed pair of boots and sweatpants, her blond hair down and wispy around her hat.

She peered over his shoulder. "Did you check the gap on the plugs?"

He looked up at her. "Thanks, Edd. Yes."

"What torque setting did you use?"

"13.6 Nm."

She gave him a satisfied smile, a nod.

"You were serious. I'm impressed."

"Of course. I'd never joke about a spark plug." She winked, then sat down where Griffin had been. "Still blowing pretty good out there." Her voice emerged just above a whisper, roughened, but it seemed it might be stronger.

The blizzard became a hum behind him.

"Reminds me of working with my grandfather. He had a barn full of used vehicles he was constantly stealing parts from." He tightened down the other plug.

"He lived in Alaska?"

"Copper Mountain, all his life. Loved to work with his hands. Simple work, he said. Sweating always cleared his head. I spent a lot of time with him, especially after my sister went missing. Made me feel like my life wasn't falling apart, like maybe I'd survive. Maybe he was trying to fix me too."

Oh. He looked up at her. Aw. He hadn't meant to reveal that.

Especially since her eyes widened, her face awash with a stricken expression. "Your sister went missing?"

He sighed. He hadn't meant to go this far, tell her this much. Finally, "When she was fifteen—I was seventeen, away at Boy Scout camp when it happened. Came home . . . it was bad."

"Did they find her?"

"Yeah. She'd been . . ." He lowered his voice. "Actually, she was a victim of a serial killer in the area."

Keely's hand pinned over her mouth.

"We only just caught him recently. But it . . . it devastated my family. My parents' marriage didn't survive it. Mom moved away to Montana. Want some cocoa?"

She shook her head, but he got up and walked over to where River and another woman had left a thermos on a workbench. He filled a cup. The door hung open, so he walked over to it, looked out to the swirling wind. Took a sip of the cocoa. It found his bones.

"Of course you were a Boy Scout." Keely walked over. "I should have guessed that."

He held up a three-finger salute. "Be prepared."

She laughed. It had a sweetness to it that found a place inside him that didn't feel quite so hardened over.

"Is that why you became a cop?"

"Because I was a Boy Scout?"

"Your sister."

Oh. "Probably. I don't know. My dad was an Air Force Security Force, sort of like an Army MP. He was stationed at Joint Base Elmendorf-Richardson, but my grandparents lived in Copper Mountain, so we were in town a lot. And then, after my sister died, my dad left the military and moved home." He glanced at her. "Where's Caspian?"

"Inside, playing with Wren. She found a ball and is teaching him to fetch."

He'd sort of expected Caspian to be sitting by the door where he'd left him, whining. But he didn't want to worry about the dog running away in the storm. "Good luck with that. She'd have better luck with her socks."

She laughed again. He could stand here all day. And weirdly, Moose snuck into his head . . . *"God uses circumstances to wake us up, get at things inside."*

"What things?"

"Maybe there's stuff."

Maybe.

"My mom died of cancer when I was nineteen." She wrapped her arms around herself. "She was . . . amazing. Creative—she used to paint watercolors, but she was this fantastic cook, and for a while, when I was in middle school, went back to work as a nurse." She stared past him, into the swirling white. "Wow, I miss her."

"Sorry."

"No, it's okay. She herself didn't have a great voice, but oh she loved to sing. She'd say, 'You don't have to have a perfect voice to make a beautiful song.' She played the piano really well, though, and we'd sing all sorts of hymns—'Amazing Grace,' 'It Is Well with My Soul,' 'Blessed Assurance.' She loved Jesus, and even in the end, when the pain was great, she met it with a joy and said she'd be waiting for me in heaven."

He considered her a moment, then, "My grandfather said the same thing about my sister, Aven." He didn't know why he told her that. She might be too easy to talk to.

She glanced at him. "You believe in God?"

"I believe he exists, but sometimes I wonder if he . . ." Aw, shoot. "Just . . . wondering what he thinks about . . ."

"Our mistakes?"

He looked at her.

"Wrong place, wrong time." She gave him a tight smile. "Also, River told me about the shooting." She pointed at his knee, then met his eyes. "I'm sorry."

Oh. How had they gotten here, with him suddenly naked in a snowstorm? Still. "The worst part about it wasn't my knee."

"But you got him—the drug trafficker."

He looked at her, frowned. "At the cost of a little girl's life."

He didn't mean for the words to rush out, so hard, so blunt. Her mouth opened, closed. "Oh. River left out that part."

He looked away, his chest tight, the terrible coil inside starting to take hold. "Yeah. The news media did a poor job of reporting that detail."

Now his breathing hitched, and sweat beaded his back. He braced his hand on the doorframe.

"You okay?"

"Yeah." No. Dumping out his cocoa, he set the cup on a ledge inside the barn and took off for the house, not sure why.

He made it to the porch, climbing up when— "Dawson!"

Her voice cut through the storm, and he turned, shoving his hands in his pockets. She'd run out into the wind, the snow catching on her blond hair, her eyelashes. She came up to stand next to him, her puffer jacket tight around her.

And he couldn't escape the words pressing through him, out into the open. Or their sharp edge. "I knew he was going to kill her—I *knew* it. I'd been following this guy for months. I should have moved, but I waited for SWAT to get in place, and so I sat there, negotiating with a killer and I . . . Stupid. I . . ."

His breath was knotted, and in a moment, he was at the scene, the night sky frozen above, breath in the air, his gut tight, listening to a little girl cry.

His heart hammered inside his chest so tight it burned. He should sit down— But he gripped the porch railing, hanging on, unable to stop. "When SWAT went in, I went straight for her. And that's when he shot her. Just—*shot* her. The bullet took out my knee. But it hit her. The guys behind me took him down, but . . ." And now he almost bent over, the world spinning, his words choked. "She died."

There, it was out, into the frozen air, and he just stood, his breath forming in the air.

It occurred to him then that he hadn't let the full story out since . . .

Never, at least not since his statement that night. Because who wanted to revisit *that* nightmare?

She folded her arms, shivering. They should go inside. But somehow, standing here in the shelter of the porch, his words taken by the wind, made the telling easier.

"It wasn't your fault."

He didn't mean his tone, but, "Wasn't it? I should have said something, done something. I should have convinced the chief to move."

"Maybe," she said softly. "But you can't blame yourself for other people's evil."

Oh. He drew in a breath. "Yeah, except I can't seem to escape it either."

Somewhere, the crying continued. In his brain or—

"Do you hear that?"

She stilled. Frowned. "Yeah. Someone shouting, maybe?"

He looked around, then walked to the edge of the porch.

In the distance on the lake, he spotted an orange dot through the snow and wind. "Is that a person?"

She joined him. "Maybe. I don't know."

Barking. "Is Caspian out there?"

"Do you think Wren took him for a walk?"

Her words sliced through him. "On the *lake*?"

He took off down the stairs, slipping. "Wren!" He started through the snow, barely able to make her out. "Wren!"

His steps sank in, nearly thigh deep as he headed out. Surely a little girl couldn't get through this snow—

The orange started to move across the ice, and the barking sounded louder, sharper.

"Wren!"

He reached the shore—or what he thought might be the shore. The hole in the ice had completely snowed over. The wind cut off visibility, but there, in the distance, he made out an orange blob.

Barking sounded behind him.

Turning, he thought he spotted Caspian, a black outline against the white.

He turned back, the orange drifting farther.

What—

Not a person, maybe, because suddenly it lifted off the horizon.

A hunting vest, caught in the wind—what an idiot. All that regurgitating of the past had turned him jumpy.

Except, someone was *crying*. The sound lifted above Caspian's barks.

Trust the dog. He felt it, more than heard it.

He plowed back through the snow, toward the black blur. "Wren?"

The next step simply broke out underneath him, and he went through, and through, and suddenly, water sucked at his boot.

He'd hit the hole, and with the snow, it had kept it warm enough to stay open.

Worse, Keely had fought her way out, even with her bruised ankle, through the snow, all the way to the edge of the lake. "Stay right there! Don't move!"

She turned then, as if hearing something. And then took off toward his dog.

And that's when the ice under him decided to give way. He flung himself onto the loose snow, trying to spread his weight. The effect of it felt like jumping on a floating air mattress, unwieldy.

And slowly, but surely, sinking.

Keely ran over to Caspian, and he looked up to see her in that white jacket, reaching for something.

Someone. She fell back, a child in her arms. Clearly Wren, or whoever, had been caught in a drift, unable to pull herself out.

He tried to move, managed to work himself onto the floating perch, but water sank into his boots. Of course, he was going under.

Wrong place, wrong time.

Story of his life.

7

THE LONGER DAWSON stayed down the more Keely's gut clenched. She'd seen him fall.

And not get up.

"Go inside—get your daddy!" Keely set Wren down on the porch. "Tell him Dawson is in trouble."

Maybe she was being overdramatic, but it didn't feel that way. Worse, she'd lost sight of him in the blizzard.

Caspian came bounding out of the white, barked then turned, and she kept her eyes on the blackness of him as she followed, even in the gray of the storm.

Snow filled her boots, despite being the hearty, ugly ones that River had given her. Maybe she should have accepted the oversized parka with the matted fur around the collar. Clearly warm and ugly were better than fashionable and freezing.

Keely nearly shouted, Dawson's name welling up inside her, but it would only vanish in the blizzard, and she'd already taken a shredder to her healing vocal cords yesterday.

Instead, she followed Caspian, right out to where she thought the edge of the lake might be and there—yes—spotted Dawson.

Half in the water, half out, and he seemed to be sinking.

"Hang on!" She waved her arms. "Here! Over here!" No one

showed through the blinding snow, but she kept waving, and Caspian shot off into the swirl of white. A moment later, a couple men emerged wearing parkas and snow pants and the orange hunting vest uniform of the community.

Griffin and Donald and another man she didn't know.

She pointed out into the white. "Dawson's in the lake!"

Donald stormed past her another ten feet, then dropped to his knees. "Hang on, Dawson!"

She turned back. Only Dawson's shoulder lifted out of the water, and even from here, she could see him shaking.

Donald lay on his stomach in the snow. "C'mon, Griff!"

Griffin moved out, past him, and lay down. Donald held his ankles. The third man went past them, but even Keely could do the math.

They couldn't reach him. Unless—

She took a breath and headed out into the snow.

"Keely, go back!" Griffin said.

She shook her head. "You can't reach him. I'm light—I can!"

Yes, this could be stupid. And who knew what she might do to her voice if she got sick again, but frankly, she'd left that world so far behind—and all she could think was . . .

"You were serious. I'm impressed."

Aw, that shouldn't sit in her brain, but weirdly, his words had reached down and latched on.

So she fell to her knees and crawled out past the last man. Lay prone on the ice. Hands grabbed her legs, right above her boots.

She extended her arms. "Kick, Dawson! Kick to me!"

He balanced on his elbows, tucked under his body, holding himself just barely above water. The look he gave her didn't resemble a man stricken. Or even desperate.

He seemed angry. His jaw tight, his eyes dark. "Keely—"

"Grab my hand!" She stretched farther. He narrowed his eyes a moment, then shook his head and reached out, kicking.

He lunged for her. His hand grabbed her arm, and she grabbed on, and added the other. He latched onto her other arm, his grip burning.

"Pull!" he yelled to the team, then to her, "Don't let go!"

She met his eyes. His jaw gritted as the men pulled the chain in. The ice broke beneath them, but Dawson held on, and in a bit, he got his feet under him, then climbed onto his knees on the ice.

She crawled back as Donald reached for one of Dawson's arms, Griffin the other.

They hauled him to shore.

She stumbled behind.

"Let's get him inside!" Griffin turned to River, who had come out with a toboggan. Apparently, they had a drill. But the men dumped Dawson onto the sled and dragged him to the house.

Keely followed the path, stumbling after them, Caspian behind them.

When she came inside, someone had already wrapped Dawson in a blanket. Griff was pushing him toward the men's room, a locker room on the ground floor where they had showers. "Get in a bath and stay there."

Dawson glanced at Keely, his mouth grim, then disappeared inside the room.

Over by the fire, another woman had peeled off Wren's outerwear, wrapped her in a blanket, moved her to stand in front of it.

Caspian followed Dawson to the bathroom. Sat outside the door, whining.

Keely walked over to Wren, her heart still thundering. Sank into a chair and held her hands to the hearth.

"What were you thinking, Wren?" Donald's voice rang over the room, and Keely watched him stalk toward his daughter, his hair askew from the wool hat, his eyes bloodshot, wind shorn.

Wren's mouth tightened, and her eyes filled.

"Donald, she's okay." The woman with Wren stood up.

"But she might not have been, Nance. And she knows better!" His thunder had shut down all other conversation in the room.

Aw. "Just calm down, Donald," Keely said, more strongly than she should have.

"You stay out of this." Donald turned again to his daughter. "The old well in the front yard is dangerous—"

"It was snowed over!" Again Keely, now raising her voice. Goldie would kill her.

He turned and cut his voice low. "The last thing I need is her wandering off and getting lost. I cannot . . ." He closed his mouth, looked away, a muscle pulling in his jaw.

He shuddered. Then he turned back. "You are a guest here. Don't forget that." He crouched in front of his daughter, his voice softer, as if he'd come back to himself a little. "What happened, Wren?"

"I threw the ball for Caspian, and he chased it, but he wouldn't bring it back, so I went to get it, and I fell."

He closed his eyes, ran a hand down his face, then drew in a deep breath and looked at her. "No more playing with this dog."

"Daddy—"

"And no more going outside."

"What about sledding?"

"You can forget sledding!" He took another deep breath, schooled his voice again. "Do you know what could have happened to you if Dawson and Keely hadn't seen you?"

Her eyes widened, and she bit her lip. "I'd die. Like Mommy?"

And now, all the air seemed to leave the room too. Donald stiffened, and Keely lost her ability to breathe, and even the woman by the fire—Nance?—looked away, her arms wrapped around her body.

Donald picked up his daughter, held her tight, burying his face in her shoulder. "No, baby. Nothing is going to happen to you. Not with Daddy around."

He carried her away from the hearth, and Keely still had nothing, her throat tight as she watched them go upstairs.

She sat, staring at the fire for a long time. Finally, Nance sighed.

"Ellen died four years ago," Nance said quietly. "She was cutting wood, and the saw landed on her leg. She bled out. He was out hunting and had left them low on firewood, and . . . well, he's never forgiven himself." She touched Keely's arm. "You going to be okay?"

She nodded. But no. Not even a little. Nance walked away, and Keely, knees drawn up to herself, stared at the fire.

"I guess we're even." Male voice, a little husky. She turned to see Dawson walking toward her, his dark hair wet and curly on top, wearing a pair of jeans and a flannel shirt, probably borrowed from one of the community members. He smelled good, like cedarwood and pine, probably from the homemade soaps they made here.

He held a large mug of soup and a spoon.

"How's that?"

"You dragged me out of the lake?"

"Not even close," she said, her voice soft. "You half carried me for a mile and saved me from a blizzard. All I did was hold your hand."

"That was enough." He sat on a cushioned chair. "If you hadn't gotten help . . ." He took a sip of soup. "Can't believe I went into the ice. That orange thing—a hunting vest. Maybe it escaped from the machine shed." He took another sip. "Wrong place, wrong time."

She shook her head. "If you hadn't gone out there, I wouldn't have spotted Wren. She might have gone in the well, and we would have never found her. *Right* place, *right* time."

He considered her a moment.

They sat in silence. From the kitchen, the faintest sound of singing rose. A hymn. She leaned into it, caught the tune. *Blessed assurance, Jesus is mine! Oh, what a foretaste of glory divine!*

In a breath of time, she was standing next to her mother in church, raising her voice in worship. *"Oh, Keely, you have such a beautiful voice."*

Her eyes burned, and she swallowed back the memory.

"You okay?"

She glanced at him. Probably the cop in him—he seemed to notice everything. "Yeah. Just . . . the singing. Reminded me of my mom. She loved that hymn. Had it sung at her funeral."

He seemed to listen, then. *Heir of salvation, purchase of God, born of his Spirit, washed in his blood.* "What do you suppose that means—'what a foretaste of glory divine.'"

"I suppose that maybe with Jesus we can taste on earth the peace and joy of heaven? I don't know."

He finished off his soup, set it on the hearth. "We attended church with my grandfather until Aven was murdered. Then my parents stopped going. But my grandfather still took me sometimes. I don't think they had a hope of peace, or joy."

"My father stopped going after my mother died too," she said. "He was really lost for a while. Got remarried, though, so that helped. But I think that's what my mom would say the song is about—having peace and joy because of the assurance of salvation."

The fire crackled, the warmth casting over her, despite the fury of the wind outside. The sun hadn't yet surrendered, still fighting to pour through the snow and wind, the sky a pewter gray.

"When I was a kid, we used to go to this cabin on the north shore of Lake Superior. Little town called Deep Haven. Population about a thousand, especially in the winter. We stayed at my grandpa's vacation cabin, a little two-bedroom house right on the lake. Dad would fire up the woodstove, and we'd play games and watch the waves crash against the ice shore. I loved it. Especially at night. Sometimes we'd bundle up in blankets and go outside and watch the stars—they're so crisp and bright at night. We'd watch our breath in the air, how it vanished in the darkness, and yet the stars stayed. I felt so small, but sitting with my dad, I wasn't scared." She hated how the memory crept into her throat, bruised it.

"Sounds like you had a great dad."

"He tried . . . until my mom died." She left off the rest.

Silence fell between them, and she didn't hate it, sitting here with the warmth of the fire, safe.

Not afraid.

Huh.

The aroma of fresh bread and soup filtered from the kitchen, a few families arriving at tables.

"This reminds me of winter camp," he said quietly. "We'd earn our outside badges during the day, play games at night."

"What games?"

"The classics. Monopoly. And Risk. I loved Clue."

"Of course you did. I saw a Clue game in the bookshelf." She pointed to the long bookshelf on the opposite side of the room. "But I'm not sure it's fair."

"What's that?"

"Challenging a cop to Clue."

He raised an eyebrow. "How about Battleship? I saw that over there too."

"Oh, I'd kill you in Battleship."

He smiled, and it reached in, stirred her.

She blamed the magic of the storm and the blue of his eyes.

"Where's Caspian?"

She glanced around. "I don't know. Last I saw, he was sitting outside the bathroom door, whining."

He sighed. "That dog. I got him from a friend who decided

the dog belonged with me. Shep travels a lot, so I figured why not. But he's not trained."

"He seems pretty trained to me."

"It's weird. One minute he's like a soldier, watching my six, sometimes running out ahead of me, as if he's scouting out the territory. The next, he's leaning against me, his big brown eyes on me, almost like he's worried about me. Or scared. I can't figure him out."

Oh, he possessed such a nice smile when he wasn't so dark and grumpy and serious.

In the silence of a blizzard, where the world faded to white,
I heard your laughter through the storm, a beacon in the night.

She didn't know where the words came from, but they landed on her heart, along with a tune, and she hummed it.

He glanced at her. "You have a nice voice."

"It's better when it's not broken." She didn't know why she said that. Not that she wanted to hide Bliss, but she didn't hate being free from her, just for now.

"How'd it break?"

"Virus. And then I developed a node on my voice box."

He raised an eyebrow. "Sounds serious."

"It was. And still could be if I don't take care of it."

"Hopefully you won't have to save my life again." He winked at her.

Oh. And the crazy of his words simply swept her up. Ignited something inside her. Still, "I'm no hero." So far from it, it seemed almost laughable that she had to speak it.

He gave her a wry look, then shook his head. "Whatever. I'd better find Caspian." He reached for his mug and got up. "But I'll be back, with the game, and you'll see—your ship is sunk."

He walked away, limping just a little, shoulders wide, whistling for his dog.

And she couldn't agree more.

DAWSON NEARLY shucked off the horror of freezing to death as he sat on a bench across from Keely, analyzing his Battleship board.

Outside, the blizzard still howled, the storm reaching epic proportions, the snowfall nearly two feet on the porch.

Keely's words earlier by the fire kept nudging him. *"If you hadn't gone out there, I wouldn't have spotted Wren. Right place, right time."*

Maybe.

"4B." He smiled at her.

"Miss." She grinned back, all teeth.

He made a face of annoyance and put his white pin into the board. "I know there's a destroyer out there. I'm going to find it."

"Not before I sink your aircraft carrier." She picked up a red pin. "C8."

He narrowed his eyes. "Hit. Sunk."

"That's right, it is. You can run, but you can't hide." She drew up one knee. Her blond hair tumbled down from under her blue pom-pom hat, and it only seemed to draw out the blue of her eyes. She wore the same white cable-knit sweater but had changed into a pair of blue velour leisure pants, probably from the same bin of clothing he'd rescued his flannel shirt and jeans.

"Fine. 5B."

She wrinkled her nose. "Hit."

"Bam. Now I got *you*."

She laughed and shook her head. "I'm still three ships up to your one, there, Monk."

"Monk?"

"Favorite show ever. I watched the entire last season on tou—on a trip across America last year." She suddenly stared at her board, cleared her throat.

Weird, but . . . "Monk is my kind of guy. No games, all facts, all focus."

"You do know he's OCD. 7D."

"Yeah, but it helps him notice things others don't. And that's a miss there, Captain Sparrow."

She laughed, and oh, it poured into him like sunshine, hot and bold, and lit a long-forgotten ember inside him.

She could be dangerous. Because like Caroline, she seemed tough, despite her city-girl demeanor, and that only led to terrible assumptions that could cost lives. She wasn't an Alaskan.

So, down, boy.

"Besides, his job helps him forget his losses. 6B."

"Destroyer gone. Good hit. Like the loss of his wife?"

"Yes. And maybe pieces of himself too. His OCD only started when life went out of control. As a cop, he gets to be involved in someone else's problems instead of being stuck in his own . . . stuff." And of course, that's when Moose's words stirred in his head. *"God uses circumstances to wake us up, get at things inside."*

No, this wasn't about him, or his stuff. He was here for her. To rescue her.

But he still didn't know why she called him Monk.

"I think he's sad," she said. "He's caught in the past, and the more he looks back to what might have been, the less he can function today. D9."

Oh. "Hit." Her words, too, hit him in his chest.

He studied the board.

"You okay over there? Bleeding a little?" Her tone had turned mocking.

He glanced up at her. Sorta, yes. He swallowed and didn't know why his story rose to the surface with the terrible urge to spill out. Still, he took a breath and let it. "The guy who shot the little girl—her name was Kiana, by the way—he got off on a hung jury. The prosecution charged him with first-degree murder and refused a plea request by the defense to lower the charge to manslaughter. And the jury couldn't convict, so . . . ."

"Hung. Does that mean they can try him again?"

"Yes. But they need . . ." He looked up at her. "They want me to testify."

She lifted a shoulder. "And?"

He looked at his board, the red, sunk battleships. "I can't go back there. Relive it. I gave an initial statement, and . . ." He made a grim face. "I've never felt so . . ."

"Frustrated?"

He considered her. "Helpless. Angry. I lie in bed at night, and all I hear is Kiana crying, feel her blood on my hands—and it's not metaphorical. She died, my hand over her chest." He blew out a breath as his own chest webbed, tightened. "Fact is, I stopped trusting myself that day."

At his feet, Caspian lifted his head, sat up, and put his muzzle on his knee. Maybe the dog needed to go out.

She shut her board. "Game's over." Then she reached out and touched his hand, wrapped her hand over his.

He looked at it. Looked at her. She gave him a tight smile. "You're not the villain here, Dawson."

Soft words, but they stilled him.

He took his hand away, ran it across his mouth. "You sure you want to fold?"

"You win." She leaned back. But it seemed her eyes had filled. Wait—for *him*?

Aw. "I think I need to take Caspian out." He swung his leg over the bench. Tried not to grunt as he stood up.

"Hey, buddy. Let's get some fresh air." He'd found the dog earlier in the kitchen with Wren, who was feeding him.

The children sat around the fire, listening to Nance read a story. Camp, indeed.

Caspian thumped his tail and got up, followed him to the door.

Keely stood there, pulling on a parka.

"What are you doing?"

She looked at him. "I'm going outside to stand in the cold with you."

Oh. "You don't have to—"

"I know. Let's go."

He had nothing as he put on his boots, pulled on his coat, a hat, his gloves. He followed her outside.

A crew of shovelers emerged every hour to clean off the porch and the steps, so just a thin layer coated the surface as they went outside. The blizzard raged, ferocious in the darkness.

Caspian trotted down the stairs and into the snow, eating a mouthful, as if thrilled by the drifts.

Dawson stood at the top of the steps, hands in his pockets, shivering.

Keely sat down on the top step, her hands between her knees.

Fine. He sat with her.

She leaned into him, her shoulder warm. "There was this serial killer that haunted Minneapolis for a while. Killed a number of young women—most of them were waitresses. My dad was a young cop at the time, and he landed on one of these grisly killings. It tore him up, but . . . instead of facing it, he turned his fears to me. Taught me how to use a gun and enrolled me in self-defense classes, made me camp out in the backyard just so I could endure a night alone."

"Seriously."

"I know he was just trying to keep me safe, but he scared me. He was dark and stoic and refused to admit his emotions. He didn't even cry at my mom's funeral."

He nodded. "My father didn't cry at Aven's funeral either. Just disappeared into himself."

"I took it personally for a long time. Felt rejected." She glanced at him. "For an adopted kid, that's a double whammy."

He'd completely lost Caspian in the snow, but he couldn't take his gaze from her face. Pretty, with a softness to it, snow caught in her lashes. Winter Tinkerbell, indeed. And despite the chaos, the frenzy of the blizzard around him, his usually chaotic insides had settled, his heartbeat steady.

As if here, in this pocket, his body said he was safe.

Keely stared out into the night. "He just poured himself into his work, then. Shut me out. Until a woman walked into his life. A neighbor who'd gotten divorced. I think she saw my dad and his life and wanted stability—anyway, they got married two months after she showed up on his porch and asked him out."

"Wow."

"I made the mistake of not being overjoyed. I thought it was too fast, and I was worried about him. They called me dramatic and selfish and cut me out of their lives." She swallowed. "I grieved for a long time. And then I realized . . . maybe I was scared of losing him so I hung on too tight." She lifted a shoulder.

He cocked his head. "We don't cause things to happen just because we fear them."

"I agree. My father was broken, and my mother's death only made it worse. I think I hoped things would be different, that after her death we'd somehow get close. But he only fled into his job, and then his new wife. I wasn't . . . I wasn't what he wanted. Or needed."

He had the wild urge to find this guy, tell him what he was missing.

"I did learn that fear makes us do stupid things. It makes us run. Hide. See things the wrong way. And sometimes, it causes us to make terrible choices that cost us more than we can realize."

She looked away then, and aw, he couldn't stop the urge to put his arm around her, scooting close, their parkas crunching in the snow. Her body sank against his.

"Maybe there's stuff."

Aw, he couldn't escape it.

He sighed. "I've had three months to sit on that day. Running the shooting over and over in my head. And every time the anger just . . ." He shook his head. "If they put me on that stand, I'll either come off as a cold, calculating jerk, or I'll lose it, and yes, I see myself going over to the defense table and strangling the man. So . . ."

She nodded.

"So yeah, I'm angry. And frustrated. And . . . it's completely messed . . . I think it's messed me up."

He might have let her go, disgusted by his confession, but she turned to him, put her hand on his jacket. "You're grieving."

He met her eyes, beautiful and shiny in the puddle of porch light, and frowned.

"Yes. Grieving," she said. "And maybe it started with your sister, but you're also grieving the family you should have had. And probably your mobility. And maybe even your own heroism."

He raised an eyebrow. "What, are you a psychologist?"

She laughed. "Sometimes. But the fact is, there is a lot more churning around inside here, Dawson. And none of it adds up to you being the villain."

His throat tightened. She lifted her face, searching his, so close that all he had to do was lean down and—

Oh, wow. He let her go, looked out at the night, pulling in a cool breath.

"You okay?"

"Mm-hmm. Hey, Casp!" he called out. "Where are you?"

He waited for his dog to appear. Nothing.

He called again and started to get up.

A bark, and just like that, Caspian came bounding toward them, his entire body snowy, nipping at the snowflakes. He ran up the steps, right into his lap, and slurped his chin. "Casp!"

Keely laughed.

Caspian bounced away.

"Well, he loves you," she said.

Caspian leaped up to her too, and she squealed, pushed him away.

"Clearly he's falling for you too." He let his words hang there, his heartbeat catching his words. No, that wasn't right . . .

But then she met his eyes with a slow grin, and his pulse thundered, and no . . . no . . . that was *not* going to happen. "Yeah, well I snagged him a soup bone from the kitchen, so . . ."

"I see. Bribery."

"Absolutely. Gotta wipe the memory of my screaming from the poor guy's memory."

She got up and held out her hand to Dawson.

Oh no, it was Caroline all over again. Believing in him.

"I'll get you home."

"I know you will."

And with Keely standing there in the glow of the light, the wind taking her hair, her eyes bright, he fought the dangerous urge to pull her back down, to wrap his arms around her.

To kiss that pretty mouth.

He stared at her.

"What? Sheesh. You look like you've seen a ghost."

He took her hand, let her help him up. Found words. "No. I'm just wondering what game I'm going to best you in next."

"Rematch, anytime, if you have the guts." She winked and walked into the lodge, Caspian running in front of her.

He stayed a moment on the porch, the storm behind him, dark, furious, lethal. Then he followed her into the warmth and light of the lodge.

Not feeling safe at all.

8

THE STORM HAD STOPPED.

Or at least died. The wind had quieted, the snow no longer pinging on the window in her room. Keely lay there, under the heavy peace of her blankets, her breath cool in the room.

If she closed her eyes, she might hear her mother humming in the kitchen nearby, the pungent scent of coffee percolating on the stove, pancakes sizzling in bacon grease.

Keely hadn't sat in that memory for years. Now, she drew it in. Let it saturate her, returned to her conversation with Dawson last night.

"Fear makes us do stupid things. It makes us run. Hide . . . And sometimes, it causes us to make terrible choices that cost us more than we can realize."

She closed her eyes, listening to her heartbeat. And Dawson's voice in her head. *"I think probably you shouldn't leave Alaska without another go at getting what you came for."*

He meant Vic.

She might mean something else. Because last night, sitting on the steps with him . . .

He'd very much looked like he might kiss her. And she very much, at least for a terrible, wonderful beat, wanted him to.

Oh brother. She was in the middle of one of her sad songs about falling for the wrong guy.

Wrong place, wrong time.

She could almost hear the lyrics write themselves . . .

> Wasn't looking for a spark, just a quiet night,
> But you lit up the dark, made the wrongs seem right.
> Like a flash in the pan, it happened so fast,
> In the blink of an eye, thought it was meant to last.

She flung off the covers, let the cold air rush in, then pulled the comforter around herself, and stood at the window. Ice and frost crept in around the frames, a lacy pattern that belied the frigid temperatures.

Outside, the world had turned to a wonderland, wind still stirring up phantoms of snow on the pristine lake. Snow frosted the pine trees that surrounded the community and white blanketed the black shingles of the barn, falling in massive drifts around it. People shoveled around the barn entrance, and the *brr* of a chain saw lifted in the distance.

She'd never felt guilty for sleeping late before, but now she tied back her hair, pulled on a flannel shirt and her yoga pants, pulled on her boots, and headed downstairs.

A few kids ate breakfast at the long tables, but in the kitchen, a cadre of teenagers washed dishes while Nance directed traffic.

Keely went to the counter and poured herself a cup of coffee. "Why is everyone outside?"

"There's another storm coming in, so we have just a few hours to feed the animals and repair the heating system."

No wonder the cold nipped at her. Sure, a fire crackled in the massive hearth, but ice and frost laced her bedroom window. "What happened?"

"Tree came down on the generator hut. Which shut down

the boiler. It's wood-fed, but the pump to the lodge and all the houses is electric, and it also runs the damper. The tree took out a few of the connections, which shut down the damper, which snuffed off the furnace." She handed a stack of plates to one of the younger boys. "Your man is out there with them."

"He's not . . ."

Nance raised an eyebrow, winked. Whatever. With the storm gone, they'd be leaving anyway.

Except, she'd been gone for the better part of two days. In the Alaskan bush. With an ex-cop. As if. The papers would have a field day.

Maybe she wasn't in any hurry to leave, thank you.

For some reason, the story of Donald's wife crept into her head. Keely headed for her borrowed parka and sturdy Sorels, grabbed her hat and mittens, and stepped outside.

Funny how, three days ago, she might have stopped in the mirror and grimaced. Now, she pulled the matted fur hood up and cinched it down.

The wind swept out her breath, the cold biting her nose as she clomped down the stairs. She expected to see Caspian, but maybe he was helping Dawson.

Following the growl of the chain saw, she spotted a trail that led behind the machine shed and headed around the building.

A massive Sitka spruce sprawled across the property, its firry arms broken and covered in snow, the trunk maybe three hundred feet long.

One giant, shaggy arm had landed on a fourteen-by-twenty-foot building, the back of it half crushed, broken wood scattered like shrapnel in the snow.

Atop the tree stood Griffin in a pair of brown coveralls. He was wearing glasses and chainsaw chaps and sawing through one of the branches. Dawson hauled away cut branches from the pile—she only recognized him by his dark scruff of whiskers and set of his shoulders, because he'd also borrowed a pair of coveralls. He seemed to be moving better, although maybe it was just slow going.

On top of the building, the third man from the ice—she thought his name might be Landon—ran another saw, chewing into the arms of the branch. He threw the broken branches down to Donald.

The doors to the building hung open, and she glanced inside to see yet another man—she remembered the name Abe—crouched in front of a big white box, something she might see on the roof of a hospital or behind a building.

"Anything I can do to help?"

The saw cut off her voice, so she didn't repeat herself, just stood, watching.

Dawson looked over then and waved. Smiled.

And of course, her stupid little heart jumped up and did a dance.

Hello. *Leaving.*

In twelve hours, she could be on a plane for the Lower 48.

Except, didn't Nance say another storm might be coming in? She motioned to Dawson to come over, but he held up his hand and turned back to catch a branch that Griffin sawed.

He dragged it away to a pile and then trudged through the snow to her. His reddened cheeks betrayed the cold and his hard work, and he smelled of evergreen and sap. "Hey."

"Hey. Whatchya doing?"

"Oh, you know. Just hanging out with the guys." He winked.

Stop it! Stop it!

"Where's Caspian?"

He looked around. "Don't know. He took off this morning, went bonkers in the snow. Maybe he thinks he's on a winter holiday." He laughed.

He wasn't the only one.

"It's cold out today." She shivered, blew out her breath. It caught in the air.

"Post-storm effect. It's always warmer when it snows. It'll warm up—but that will bring another blizzard."

"Yeah. That's what I came out to ask. Should we be leaving?"

She didn't know why the question landed in her heart, twisted.

He glanced at Griffin on the tree, back to her. "Yeah. I just wanted to help them get their power restored. Without heat, they might not make it through the next storm. But pack up—we'll leave right after lunch. It'll only take a couple hours to get to the outpost, and then Moose can get us."

"What am I going to pack?" She smiled at him.

He smiled back, and for a second—a terrible, perfect second— the world stopped. Just her, standing in the snow under a blue sky, the world bright and shiny. Dawson standing in front of her like some Hallmark hero, handsome and . . .

Her man.

Oh no. She stepped away. "I'll see if we can pack a lunch."

He held up a gloved thumb and turned back to the work. Nope, he definitely wasn't limping so badly today.

She crunched back around the building toward the lodge. Barking lifted, and she turned, spotted Caspian. Someone had shoveled a path down the center of the road, and the dog stood in the middle, a speck of black.

She whistled, but the dog just stood there.

Aw. The last thing Dawson needed was to go hunting for his dog, out chasing some fox.

She headed down the shoveled path toward the dog. Whistled again, patting her legs.

Caspian barked, turned in a circle, then barked again.

He wanted to play.

Scamp was right.

Picking up her pace, she hustled out toward him. He sat, his tail swishing, then got up as she drew near and began to bark and back away.

"C'mon," she said, lunging for him.

He turned and took off.

For the love. "Caspian!" But of course, her voice didn't carry. She crunched after him, past the shoveled area, out into the deep snow. It had crusted over in parts, so her steps crashed through layers, slowing her.

Caspian skittered on the top of the crust, breaking through in spots.

Only then did she spot the boot marks. Smaller steps flattened by what looked like the trail of a sled.

Her gut tightened, and she sped up.

Caspian waited for her at the edge of a field, just past the town, at the opening of what looked like a deer trail through the woods.

She paused, glanced back at the community. The bite of the chain saws still ground through the air.

"Okay. Slow down!" She fought her way to the forest edge and then into the bunker of trees. Here, the snow drifted but hadn't layered as deep. Caspian stood at the far end of the trail where it opened to a wide, cleared area. Maybe a logging trail, although it seemed nearly twenty feet wide, not painfully steep, but . . .

The sledding hill that Wren had mentioned.

Keely stepped out into the pristine white, and there, the footsteps led out to a matting of snow and sled marks.

The sledding trail cut through the snow, not deep, evidence, maybe, of a child's weight. It tracked down the slope and then . . . oh no, veered off into the trees.

"Good boy, Caspian." Keely followed the trail, running slash falling down the slope. She landed headfirst into the powder— snow plunged down her jacket—then rolled and forced herself back up, breathing hard. Caspian ran beside her, around her, nudging her.

"Okay, okay—" She stood, shook off the snow. Her cheeks burned, the snow sharp with cold.

The sledding trail led into the forest, breaking twigs and brush, and twenty feet in ended at a shaggy tree. Splinters of wood scattered the area, the broken carcass of a wooden toboggan cast to the side. Wren.

Keely worked her way to the edge of the tree and lifted the branches.

Wren. She lay at the bottom of a circle of snow near the trunk, her eyes closed, blood emitting from her mouth.

"Wren!" Keely plopped onto her stomach, reaching into the hole. Some five feet deep, easily. If Keely went in headfirst, she'd never escape.

She turned around and slid down into the hole, feetfirst.

Wren groaned as Keely touched her. "Wren? It's Keely." Wren lay on her side, but what if she'd hit her head, broken her neck—

Wren started to cry, reached up for Keely. Before she could stop her, Wren wrapped her arms around her waist. "It was too fast!"

"Okay. Shh. I'm here."

Above her, Caspian barked.

"Get help, Casp!"

The dog barked again.

She hauled Wren up. "Where did you hit?"

"My shoulder. And my body, and my arm hurts . . ." Wren wiped her lip, saw the blood, and started to hiccup breaths.

"Calm down. Okay, let me see." She met Wren's big brown eyes, searched them. Pupils looked normal, so maybe she hadn't hit her head, but Keely wasn't a doctor.

Hadn't even played one on TV. And where that thought came from she didn't know. Most likely panic, because staying out here probably meant hypothermia, given the frigid temperatures.

"You said your arm hurt?"

Wren held it up, and Keely cradled the girl's wrist in her grip. "Can you move your fingers?"

She moved her hand, and her mitten flexed.

"Anything else hurt?"

"My tummy."

"Yeah, you probably got the wind knocked out of you. Okay, let's get you home."

Wren blinked, tears clinging, frozen to her eyelashes. "Where's my sled?"

"It's not in good shape, but I'll bet your daddy can fix it." She stood up. The bank came to her shoulders. Still, if she pushed Wren out, she could probably use the tree to leverage herself out.

"Wren, can you step into my hands?" Keely bent and made a basket with her hands. Wren tried to raise her foot, then cried out and fell back.

"What's wrong?"

"My tummy hurts!"

Keely stood over her. "Okay. Listen. I have to get you out of here. Otherwise, we'll freeze to death."

"I'm scared." Wren hunkered down in the well. "Daddy is going to be so mad."

Yeah, well. And she got that. Probably better than Wren could imagine. She crouched in front of her. "Listen. Dads get worried about their little girls. They want to protect them, but sometimes they can't. They can't always protect them from all the hurt and pain that they're afraid of. Like your dad. He's sad because of your mom, right?"

Wren nodded. "He cries sometimes, at night."

She got that too. "So, we're going to forgive your dad for being scared. And raising his voice, and no, he shouldn't, but you going sledding without his permission probably wasn't a great idea, right?"

Wren's eyes welled up.

"But he'd be even sadder if something happened to you, right?"

Wren nodded.

"So, let's not make him even sadder. Let's get you out of this hole. And home. And even if he gets mad at you, try to remember it's because he loves you, and he's just really bad at showing it." Keely bit back arguments to her own explanation and reached for Wren.

The little girl put her arms around Keely's neck. Then Keely lifted her, turned her, and pushed her up, her mittens on her boots.

Wren launched out of the tree well and landed somewhere above.

Keely put her hands on the snowbank and tried to pull up, but the snow crumbled under her mittens. Right. *Think, Keely.*

Only this time, it wasn't her father in her head but stupid Chase Sterling. *"You made this decision, not me! So you'll have to deal with it."*

The memory boiled inside her. Yeah, well, she was trying, okay?

She turned, studied the tree. Branches, maybe six feet up, but if she used the tree trunk, and made footholds for herself . . .

Kicking into the snow, she made divots, then she leaned one arm against the tree, stepped into the divots, and pivoted herself up, to the branch.

It sagged, but she grasped it with the other hand and used it to kick more divots into the snow. Another leap, and she grabbed an upper branch, pulled herself up, got one foot on the lower branch, then the other.

She was Tarzan, perched in a tree, swaying in the wind, the wind sharp against her skin.

Wren sat in the snow, her arms around Caspian, who lay next to her, watching Keely, unmoving.

It felt a little like being watched by a panther.

She worked her way out to the edge of the branch. A crack, the branch jerking—

She leaped for the bank.

Purchase, mostly, but she turned onto her back and scrabbled away from the edge, landing finally beside Wren.

Caspian got up, barked again, backing away.

"I know, I know," she whispered. "That was nearly a tragedy." Then she looked at Wren. "Let's go home."

IT FELT GOOD TO HURT. To ache from a morning of hard work, Dawson's body reacting to the hauling and climbing and effort of freeing the community generator from the fallen tree.

And they'd gotten the boiler damper working, along with the generator that pumped warm water into the lodge and the other homes.

"No burst pipes on our watch." Griffin held out a fist to him as they peeled off their work gear in a snow room off the lodge entrance. Different from the front door, this entrance held all the Carhartt coveralls, shovels, fur hats, and, of course, the weapons, locked in a case on a wall.

Dawson met the fist. "You sure it's okay for us to take your only working snow machine? I don't want to leave you without a way out."

"Yeah. Just send a plane in with the rest of the plugs and a couple fuel lines. Or Sully. He'll probably be by in a week or so with Kennedy to see River. I'll snowshoe over to his place in a couple weeks and pick up the sled."

Dawson hung up his coveralls. "Why to see River?"

"Kennedy's pregnant."

No wonder Sully had been in such a hurry to get back to her.

"I hadn't realized they'd gotten married."

"Yeah, last summer. Small ceremony, here in the community. Your cousin Axel was here with his girlfriend, Flynn. She's Kennedy's sister." Griffin held open the door to him, then held out his hand. "You're welcome back anytime, Daws. Consider yourself an honorary artist." He winked and slapped him on the back.

Dawson headed inside the main room of the lodge, the smells of bread baking and something tangy, maybe pizza, or lasagna, emanating from the kitchen. Outside, the wind had picked up, the temperatures plummeted, and snow drifted from the slate-gray sky.

They'd need to leave, and soon, if they hoped to get to Sully's before the blizzard socked them in. And even if they did make it to the outpost, Moose probably wouldn't be able to fly in, the ceiling too low.

So, they'd be bunked up with Sully for a day or two, waiting out the next surge of storm.

Maybe they should stay put. And right then, the image of Keely standing in the snow, her eyes widening after he'd made that silly joke about packing something—what an idiot. Hopefully Moose had picked up the suitcases from the crash.

Probably not. Which only drove home the memory of the plane crash. It seemed so long ago, the blizzard having separated tragedy from the relative safety of the community.

"You sure you want to leave?"

The question jerked him out of his thoughts. Griffin stood there, hands in his pockets. "I can't help but feel like you're supposed to be here. To stay."

Dawson frowned.

Griffin looked over at the kitchen, then back to Dawson. "It's just . . . I don't know. I think God has you here for a reason."

He frowned. "Have you been talking to Moose?"

"Who?" Griffin shook his head, clamped his hand on Dawson's shoulder. "When I first got here, I wasn't sure this place was right for me. I felt trapped. Even like maybe I'd run away from the world. And then I realized that sometimes we need a time-out. From the world. From expectations. Even from ourselves.

The people we've told ourselves we have to be instead of who we were made to be."

"I'm not sure I know what you mean."

"I mean that the world tells you that if you look inside, you'll find yourself, and in doing that you'll find peace. But peace doesn't come from inside. It comes from knowing that you're forgiven. Accepted. Safe. It's about standing in that place of love and letting it set you free." He lifted a hand to River reading to one of the children by the fire.

Sweet. And yes, this place felt . . . well, he'd slept last night, all the way through, without his silly dog jerking him awake, so even Caspian felt it.

But he couldn't hide from life. "I'm good, Griff. And I made a promise to Keely. So . . ." He held out his hand.

Griffin gripped it. "I'll have River pack you guys a go bag. Keep the duds."

Dawson headed upstairs to his room. He decided to leave his clothing. Why not? Then he knocked on Keely's door.

No answer.

He opened it. Her bed lay mussed, her clothing on a pile in the chair.

Huh.

He went out and looked over the room below. Spotted Nance and Donald and Oliver, Griffin, and River talking, and a few other families.

No Keely.

And no Caspian.

Maybe she'd taken him outside.

He went back downstairs, grabbed his borrowed Sorels and parka, pulled on his hat, pocketed his gloves, and headed outside.

The sun barely bled through the clouds, the sky a deep gray, bruised around the edges as if it fought slumber. The wind had picked up, snow starting to billow.

Yeah, they had two hours max before everything went dark. "Keely!"

His voice hung on the wind a moment, then scurried away down the snowy main street. He whistled.

No Caspian, no bark.

Weird.

He spotted someone coming from the barn, one of the community members hauling a hay bale out to a wheelbarrow. He headed down to Landon, one of the guys who'd helped him off the ice. He had a couple of spry teenage boys who'd worked with them today on the generator. He lifted a hand. "Have you seen Keely?"

The man, late forties, shook his head.

Really weird.

Dawson headed back inside, stomping off his boots. Walked over to River and Griffin. "Have you seen Keely?"

River shook her head.

"She was trying to catch your dog."

He turned at the voice, and Oliver stood there. "I saw her right before lunch, with Caspian."

"Where?"

He shrugged. "She was going out to the field."

Dawson looked at Griffin, who also frowned. "I'll go with you."

Griffin garbed up, and they headed out into the swirling snow, the beginnings of the second blizzard. "Where would she go?"

"I don't know. She's a city girl. She doesn't wander around in the snow." But the words stuck inside him.

And maybe even Griffin felt them, because he glanced at him. "For a city girl, she seems pretty tough."

Indeed she did. So maybe he'd misjudged her.

"I'll check the barn. Let's grab the snow machine. We'll take it out to the field and see if you spot any tracks."

Dawson trekked up to the shed, opened the door. The snow machines sat quiet, and he found the one he'd fixed, the key in the ignition, fired it up.

He motored it out into the snow, and Griffin came running up. "Nothing in the barn." He got on behind Dawson, who stood on the running board and took off up the street. A plowed area led out of town, but snow had dusted it over, and in the shadows, he couldn't make out any tracks.

They reached the end of the street, and he gunned the snowmobile to push it up over the crest and into the snow. It roared across the top of the snow some twenty feet, then sank in all the drifting.

Griffin slid off, got behind to push.

Dawson gunned the machine again. It spit up snow and ice.

And then, died. A bloom of gasoline puffed out, and Griffin stepped back. "Too much snow. It packed the engine!"

Aw. He rocked the machine back and forth, tried to start the engine again.

Nothing.

Dawson got off and dug around the engine to clear it. Then he and Griffin pulled the snow machine back along the tread path.

Dawson got back on, rocked the machine again, and this time, the engine sputtered to life, then roared, a cloud of smoke puffing up to clog the brisk air.

Dawson sat and looked out into the field. "Do you have snowshoes?"

Griffin nodded. "Let's turn this around."

Dawson got off, and together they picked up the back of the machine and turned it around. Then Dawson got on, and with Griffin's weight, he gunned it.

The machine broke free of the snowpack, spitting up snow as he motored it back to the shed.

Griffin hopped off and grabbed snowshoes from hooks on the

wall. Alloy frames, double binding, sturdy. Dawson stepped into them and took the poles Griffin offered.

The man followed him out, wearing his own snowshoes, his head down into the wind.

Keely, where are you?

Dawson had half a mind to check the lodge again—maybe he'd missed her sitting by the fire or playing with Wren.

Wren.

He hadn't seen her inside either. He looked at Griffin. "What if she's with Wren? Where would Wren be?"

Griffin met his gaze. "Right. I heard her and her dad arguing about going sledding today, right before he went out to work on the genie."

"Where would she go sledding?"

"There's a hill not far from here. It was cleared years ago."

The wind had picked up, turned angry by the time they reached their mess in the meadow, but the snowshoes held them aloft, and Dawson followed Griffin toward a dent in the forest wall.

And as he stepped into the quiet shelter of the forest, barking sounded.

"Caspian!"

Griffin must have heard it too, because he picked up his pace, working hard with his shoes and poles.

The barking closed in and then Caspian appeared on the trail, a black bundle of energy and frenzied barking.

And with him, Keely, knee-deep in snow, carrying someone on her back.

Wren.

Keely was bent over, breathing hard. She looked up at them.

Wren slid off her back and sank in the snow. Keely fell to her knees in the snowpack.

Griffin reached them first. "What happened?"

He didn't hear Keely's answer. Wren started to cry.

Griffin picked the girl up in his arms. "You get Keely." He moved past Dawson, hustling back along the trail.

Keely sat back, looked up, still breathing hard.

"What were you thinking? That you'd go sledding? Today? I mean, I know you like this girl, but—"

"Seriously." Her voice rasped out. "No. I didn't go sledding. I followed your dumb dog, who I thought was running away and in fact led me to where Wren had crashed her sled." She struggled up. "Sorry for trying to do the right thing."

Oh, shoot. And now she stumbled past him, her feet crashing through the snow.

"Keely."

She ignored him.

"I'm sorry. You're right, I shouldn't have . . . You did the right thing."

She rounded on him. Stood there in the wan light, just breathing. "You know, I've spent most of my life doing the *wrong* thing. Being the wrong thing. Being the wrong person, despite everything I've done. I just . . . I was trying to help."

Aw.

"I'm sorry that I got you into this mess and stranded you here . . . if I hadn't run away from Vic, maybe . . . maybe I wouldn't have been on that plane."

"It doesn't matter."

"It *does* matter." And now her voice was dying, her pretty hazel-blue eyes glossy. "It matters because I *always* do the wrong thing. And people get hurt."

His throat thickened at her words, and he softened his voice. "No one got hurt. You saved Wren. She would have been lost in the storm."

She wiped a mitten across her eyes, her cheeks. "And yet you're out here, with your bum knee."

"My knee's fine." In fact, he hadn't thought about it all day. He took a step toward her. "I don't think you're the wrong person." He didn't know where that came from, but . . . "And I don't think you do the wrong thing."

What was he doing? But he couldn't seem to stop, suddenly, and even took another step toward her.

"No. Stop talking, Dawson." She held up her hand. "You don't know anything about me."

His voice shook. "But I very much want to."

Really, Dawson? It had just spilled out, so he threw out an amendment. "And I know *a little*. I know about your mom, and the fact she liked to sing. And that you have X-ray Battleship vision, and that . . . that you would risk your life for a child. Which . . . yeah, I get. I really get."

She stared at him, her eyes pinned to his.

"Keely. You're amazing. And beautiful, and strong, and brave . . ."

Maybe Griffin was right. He just needed to break free of the swirl of anger, and grief and . . . thinking.

Just always thinking.

He closed the gap. "But don't do that ever again."

"Do what?" she whispered, her breath wisping out.

"Disappear."

Then he let go of the swirl inside, the ever-present hum of chaos and noise, leaned down, and kissed her.

Her lips were cold, and for a second, she didn't move. And aw, this was a—

Then she gripped his jacket, hung on, and kissed him back.

Really kissed him back. As if she might be hungry, and maybe a little desperate, or eager, and sure, it ignited the need in him to be a hero, but also simply heated him all the way through and stirred to life an unfamiliar ember inside him.

He'd call it hope. Or maybe life.

He deepened his kiss, moving his arms around her, pulling

her against him. The wind stirred the trees, snow drifting down. And sure, maybe the blizzard started to rouse, to groan . . .

But right here, in this wonderland pocket, nothing could touch him.

Nothing—

She caught her breath and leaned away. He lifted his head, met her eyes.

They were wide, a hint of shock or even regret in them. "I . . . I'm sorry. This was . . . Really, Dawson. This . . . this can't work."

He frowned at her. *What—?*

Then she whirled and headed up the path, almost stumbling to get away.

Aw. No. This *wasn't* happening.

He caught up to her, stepped out ahead of her—which said something about his knee—and stopped. "And clearly you don't know me if you think you're going anywhere without me. C'mon. You know the drill." He crooked his arm.

A moment. A breath. Then she slid her arm through his. "Please don't let me hurt you."

He had a feeling it might be too late.

9

SHE HAD LANDED IN *GROUNDHOG DAY.*

Keely lay in the bed, again, listening to the wind howl outside, the snow pinging against her window. Same wind. Same smells—cotton, coffee, the scent of fire from the hearth—sneaking under her door. The room seemed warmer today, however, and . . .

No, nothing was the same.

Dawson had kissed her. And she hadn't stopped him—not soon enough, at least. Not before the lure of his kiss made her sink into his embrace and kiss him back.

Oh my.

And worse, he tasted exactly of the amazing man who raced out into the cold to find her. A hero.

She closed her eyes and let herself sink into his arms again, remember the smell of him, all wood chips and pine, the feel of his touch—desire, and maybe a little hope . . .

It was the hope that made her step away.

Despite his words—*"Amazing. And beautiful, and strong, and brave . . ."*

No, he hadn't the first clue who she really was.

"Please don't let me hurt you."

He had no idea the pain her life might level on him. Frankly, he probably deserved the truth.

But she wanted him to at least like her, so . . .

So probably she should refrain from kissing him again. *"This can't work."*

She opened her eyes, stared at the wooden ceiling, and weirdly, a song dropped into her head. Just a piece—

> In the whirl of the storm, my dreams scream loud,
> A voice lost in the wind, just trying to be found.

What was it River said—*"You put to words exactly what I was feeling"*?

Huh.

Keely got up and slipped into her fuzzy boots, pulled her pom-pom hat over her hair. She needed a brush, but really, she needed a hot bath. Her bones were achy, her hair turning a little coarse after so many days.

Outside her room, the early morning waxed the lodge in tones of somber gray, just the hearth fire flickering to shed light. The aroma of coffee lifted, but no chatter came from the kitchen.

"You know the drill." Sure, he'd said that, but then had been painfully, brutally silent during their tromp toward the lodge. And by the time they returned, the blizzard had set in again, so no leaving for them.

She'd eaten dinner with Wren and Oliver, unable to look at Dawson, who had clumped with Griffin and some of the other men, talking about the community. He'd left with Griffin while she helped clean up in the kitchen, and she hadn't seen him when she retired to her room.

Then she slept so hard she hadn't moved in twelve hours, maybe more.

Goldie would be thrilled. Her voice felt a little stronger today too.

Keely headed downstairs into the main area and over to the hearth, flanked by the long sofas. Someone had left their guitar, still in the case, by the fire, and she pulled it out, settled herself on a sofa, and began to strum.

She set the song in the key of G major and found a D–G–B combination. Threw in an F-sharp. Started to hum, heard the words surface.

> In the whirl of the storm, my dreams scream loud,
> A voice lost in the wind, just trying to be found.
> Each snowflake a shroud, each gust a plea,
> Beneath the veil of white, I'm longing to be free.

Sounded a little desperate. But maybe . . .

She started humming again, the lyrics stirring inside her. Outside, the snow gusted, rose, and fell, like a breath.

> Hear my name, as the blizzard roars untamed,
> Find my soul in the silence the snowflakes frame.
> As the world dresses in white, away from the dark of
> night,
> Hear my name, oh hear my name, in the soft dawn's
> light.

Better. Could be a chorus, maybe. She probably needed a notebook. Or maybe the song was just for her.

Keely stared out the window, her thoughts stirring up the memory of Dawson helping her home—no, not home, but to the lodge—his arm sturdy as she hung on. Wow, he was strong, and capable, and . . .

"You don't know anything about me."

"But I very much want to."

Oh . . . Her chest tightened then, but the words swept through her, emerged soft, almost a whisper.

> Trapped in the silence, where cold truths are kept,
> In the grace of new snow, my veiled tears have wept.
> But your warmth cuts through, like a promise anew,
> In the blizzard's embrace, I reach out to you.

"I like it."

The voice was soft and female. Keely turned to see River standing behind her, holding a mug of coffee.

"It's nothing." Keely put down the guitar. "Just something . . ."

"It's beautiful." River set the coffee mug on a polished wooden coffee table. "Reminds me of 2 Samuel 22:20. 'He brought me out into a spacious place. He rescued me because he delighted in me.'"

Keely raised an eyebrow. "I don't think God is delighting in me, River. C'mon—"

"Why not?" She sat down, then indicated the coffee. "That's for you. Two sugars and cream, right?"

"When my manager isn't looking, yes." She winked, picked up the coffee. "Thanks." Hopefully River would just drop—

"I think God very much delights in you, Keely. I read the article—I know you grew up in the church. You said your mother was a woman of faith."

"Yeah, but . . . I don't—"

"But now, this is what the Lord says—'Do not fear, for I have redeemed you; I have summoned you by name; you are mine.'"

Keely took a sip of the coffee. "You don't know—"

"I know that God is greater than your fears, your weaknesses, even your sins."

Keely looked away, at the fire, the flames curling around the logs.

"People think their sins, their mistakes, their bad choices will disqualify them from God's love. But that's the point—God's love saves us from all that. Forgiveness leads to abundance." River leaned forward. "To grace and promises anew."

Keely looked at her. "It's just a song."

"It was from a voice in your heart. Maybe you should start listening." She got up. "I'm making breakfast. Want something?"

"The coffee is enough."

"I'll bring you some pancakes."

She walked away, and Keely turned back to the fire, the song still humming inside her.

> Hear my name, through the storm's wild claim,
> Feel my soul in the fresh snow's tame.
> As the world turns white, I escape the night,
> Hear my name, oh hear my name, in the morning light.

She picked up the guitar again, redid the intro, and sang through the lyrics again, her voice soft but on pitch.

Healing.

"Hey, Miss Keely." Oliver plopped down on the sofa across from her. "What are you singing?" He held a muffin in a napkin, the crumbs spilling down his sweatshirt. His dark hair stuck up in all directions, and when he smiled, he showed a front-tooth gap.

"Just . . . a song I made up."

"My mom used to make up songs. And stories." He drew up one knee, his sock floppy around his foot.

"She sounds amazing."

"She's in heaven." He lifted a shoulder, and his mouth went up one side, wry.

"Yeah. My mom is too."

He looked over at her, his eyes a little brighter. "Maybe they could say hi to each other. 'Cause we're friends."

"I'll bet they could." His words found a warmth inside her,

and with it, her mother's face, her voice, in prayer. *"I place all my fears in your hands, my trust is my worship. My God is able."*

What was it about this place that seemed to rouse inside Keely everything she tried so hard to dodge?

"How's Wren today?" she asked as he got up.

He shrugged. "Still sleeping."

The aroma of the promised pancakes rose from the kitchen. Last night, as she'd helped with the dishes, she'd listened to the workers chat—mostly about the storm, but also about community life. The livestock, and food stores, and firewood, and even an update on local news—something about a criminal being finally tried. *"I heard that Wilder is going down to testify,"* Nance had said, and the name sparked something inside Keely.

But then the group had started to sing—almost as one—a hymn maybe, although she didn't recognize it. Still, she liked it here.

Too much, maybe.

Keely stared out at the swirling snow, the day now lit with moments of sunlight fighting to burn through the gray.

> Let the snowflakes fall, let them cover all,
> In the quiet, your voice is my thaw.
> Forever here, where the cold winds call,
> Hear my name, it's yours, through the snowfall's thrall.

That's for you, Mom.

"I was told to deliver these."

Of course, Dawson looked ruggedly amazing this morning, strong shoulders under that blue flannel shirt that only brought out the blue of his eyes. He still hadn't shaved, so his stubble darkened his face, but that smile . . .

She looked away, at the plate of pancakes swimming in homemade maple syrup drowning a couple of browned deer sausages. "Thanks." She set down the guitar, then took the plate.

He walked over to the hearth, opened the screen, and added a couple of fresh logs. Then he picked up the poker and stirred the fire to life, the flames biting the logs, crackling.

Closing the screen, he set the poker back and turned to her.

"You don't know anything about me." Her words raked up, almost shouting.

"But I very much want to."

Maybe he did. Maybe he didn't. But . . . the thought unlatched something inside her. To be known . . . and still loved . . .

Except Dawson didn't *love* her . . .

Caspian, however, seemed to have a soft spot for her, because he came over, nudged her leg. She lifted her plate away from his nose and set her hand on his snout. "I don't know why I was ever so afraid of him. He's got the sweetest eyes."

"Yeah, he's a charmer."

"Are you sure he's not a tracking dog? He did a good job of finding Wren yesterday."

"Or he got bored, headed back to the lodge, saw you, and decided to play a game." But Dawson crouched, and Caspian trotted over, his tail wagging as his owner rubbed his ears.

"You did hear him, right, Casp? Maligning you? Come back to me."

Caspian seemed to hear her and turned. She held up one of her sausages.

"Hey! That's not fair."

She grinned at him. "He loves me." Caspian took the sausage, then licked her fingers of the syrup. Now for sure she'd have to bathe. Still, he sat with her, his tail brushing the floor.

"Yes, he does," Dawson said quietly.

She looked at him, frowned.

He met her eyes, held her gaze.

Wait . . . what . . . ?

Oh. "Dawson, um, we need to talk."

He nodded, swallowed. "Especially since we're going to be trapped here for at least another day. Landon is the local weatherman, and according to the reports on his shortwave, this storm won't blow through until tomorrow, maybe the next day."

Oh. But the words blew through her like a fragrance, a fresh breeze, grace maybe. "Good. I like it here. I think I never want to leave."

She meant it to change the subject. Instead, Dawson's gaze steadied on hers, and he lowered his voice. "I'm a cop. There is nothing you could tell me that would shock me, Keely. And remember, I already think you're amazing."

She stilled. But wanted, *oh* how she wanted to believe him.

She found herself nodding. "Okay, so—"

"Hey, Daws!" Griffin's voice raised from the end of the room. "I need some help with the firewood."

Dawson sighed, then glanced at him and nodded. "Be right there."

But when he stood up, he said, "We have a Battleship rematch ahead of us." He winked and walked away.

She watched him go, her heart thundering.

But, in the wake, she heard the end of her song . . .

> Could it be that you see the truths I hide?
> In the snow's pure blanket, where my deepest dreams reside?
> A look, a touch in the frosty air,
> Reveals the me I've hidden, now laid bare.

And she smiled.

"YOU'RE HUMMING."

Dawson looked up from where he stood on the stacked woodpile, tossing down logs to Griffin and Landon. Overflow firewood, the cords that didn't fit in the shed, lined the back of the barn, two stalls deep.

"It's something Keely was singing earlier." He didn't know why it stuck in his head, but he liked it.

She did have a pretty voice, and today, it seemed stronger.

She seemed stronger. Not that she'd seemed weak before, but last night, as he'd struggled through the snow to get them back to the lodge, she hung on to him tighter than he would have imagined.

The kiss sat in his mind, his chest all night, the smell of her, the taste of her, as if surprised, but eager, almost curious. All the way up to *"I'm sorry. This can't work."*

Whatever. The kiss, he could blame on her next words, the part about not wanting to hurt him, as if she had secrets that might make him walk away from her.

Hello, he'd already told her his, and she hadn't run.

He wouldn't run either.

"She has a nice voice," Griffin said as he picked up a couple chunks of firewood tossed into the snow. He added them to the two-person tote made of canvas and wooden handles. Griffin and Landon had already carried in one load.

Now, Landon worked his way down the row of livestock pens, feeding the animals.

Outside the blizzard howled, relentless. Alaska.

"Probably a good thing for her to be holed up here, really. Let her voice heal."

Dawson frowned as he tossed down a few more logs, then climbed down the ladder. His knee felt tired today, but not as achy. All this regular work seemed good for it.

Good for *him*. Moose showed up in his head, as he clapped off the wood splinters from his hands. *"God uses circumstances to wake us up, get at things inside."*

Stuff. Like grief and anger and frustration . . . but here, suddenly, all of that didn't seem quite so raw. Maybe Keely's words had found root—*"There is a lot more churning around inside here, Dawson. And none of it adds up to you being the villain."*

He'd called himself the villain for so long, he didn't know what to replace it with. But maybe . . . "Yeah," Dawson said. "Like you said, maybe we were supposed to stay."

Griffin threw the wood on the pile. "I know. Despite the storm, there's a peace here, right?"

Dawson shrugged and kept working.

"Or maybe it's not the place, but a person."

He looked at Griffin, frowned. "Are you talking about Keely?"

"Actually, I was referring to Jesus. And I know he's not just here, but sometimes it's easier to see grace and abundance and mercy and all the things when we find ourselves safe and warm inside a storm."

From the last stall, the one closest to the wood, the llama shrieked, clearly ruffled at the disturbance. What did Griffin call her—Woolly Bully? The animal had already rammed her cage once, leaning down to nip at them as they worked.

"Maybe. But . . . sometimes I feel like I'm standing in the middle of it." Dawson didn't know what it was about Griffin, but he seemed . . . well, he seemed to get it.

The man picked up the feed bucket. "Cold and suffering and alone? That's not a bad thing either."

"Suffering is a good thing?" Dawson added a few logs to the tote.

"Absolutely. Suffering helps us taste just a little of what Jesus did for us. It brings a greater understanding of his love, grace, and mercy. And, hopefully, brings us a little closer to God. So, while we don't love storms, we're not afraid of them. Right, Woolly?" Griffin poured feed into a bucket attached to her pen. Turned to Dawson.

"In the ebb and flow of the world, of the terrible and the good, maybe darkness doesn't win because God's goodness is still in the world, through his people. Through his providence. Even when it feels like the darkness is winning."

He dropped the bucket back into her feed bin. "And it doesn't hurt that you get to have Keely around just a little longer, before the world finds out."

Dawson stared at him. "What?"

"She's not at all like I expected. Quieter, for one, and resilient, although anyone who stands on a stage for three hours in five-inch stilettos has to have some kind of resilience." He laughed.

Landon finished, walked over. "My boys have been freaking out for three days. They're dying for an autograph."

Again, Dawson just looked at him. "I don't . . . *what* are you talking about?"

"Don't you recognize her?" Griffin asked. "She's Bliss."

A beat while he scrolled through any recognition. Wait— "The pop singer?"

Bliss. He'd heard her songs on the radio, of course, and, "No. That's not right. I saw her perform once. She wore an all-pink bodysuit, glitter on her face, and go-go boots. I think it was—"

"The Grammys, two years ago. I saw it while I was at Walter Reed. We all did—it was memorable. But she did have pipes. Hopefully the surgery worked, and she'll get them back."

So much to unpack there, but *Bliss*?

So that was her secret. And yes, a big one.

"She never said a word."

Griffin looked at Landon. Back to Dawson. "Sorry. I thought you knew. River recognized her right away, and Bliss—Keely—asked her to keep it quiet. That's why I thought you never mentioned it. Sorry, man."

"Why would she not tell me?"

Griffin picked up one end of the canvas tote, grunted. Dawson moved in to grab the other side, but Landon beat him to it.

"Maybe she thought you already knew." He and Landon moved off with the tote.

Dawson stood in the chill of the barn. *"You don't know anything about me."*

But he did, like he said. He knew about Vic, and her dad, and the death of her mother. He knew she could fix a car and . . .

Maybe that was the part she *wanted* him to know.

The Bliss part? So, maybe he didn't know her.

Still. Okay. So she was a city girl. And famous.

Very famous.

Except, *"I like it here. I think I never want to leave."*

Yeah, he needed answers. Dawson blew out a breath and followed Griffin into the house.

He hadn't realized how long he'd been gone. A few families sat at long tables, some of them with books open. He recognized homeschool when he saw it.

Caspian went from family to family, stopping to nose a kid, get a pat, and move on. Sheesh, the guy was in some kind of heaven here. Had stopped edging up to him, pushing against him as if needy. Still sat with his back to him, however.

Maybe he should leave Caspian behind, let him be a community dog. The thought put a slight fist in his chest. Still, he hadn't been Dawson's dog, really.

He could admit a spurt of warmth, however, when the dog spotted him and came bounding over. Sat and lifted a paw.

Dawson shook it—silly dog—and then petted him.

He glanced into the kitchen, spotted River and Nance and a few others, but no sign of Keely.

Movement at the top of the stairs caught his eye.

Keely. She wore a pair of pink velour pants, her fur short boots, an oversized sweatshirt, her hair down and wet, and just like that, he saw it.

Bliss.

Maybe a memory, maybe just his imagination, but in his mind, she walked down stairs onto a stage, a million-dollar, stage-worthy smile on her face, her hair glittering, ready to wow the crowd.

What was Bliss doing here, in the backwoods of Alaska?

Vic. Right. And her story about her mom, her rejection by her father rushed back, filled in the gaps . . .

Aw, Bliss. Under all the glamour and grins was a woman who just wanted to be known. Loved.

She saw him and smiled. Took a breath.

Wait—did she look nervous?

He walked over to her as she came down the stairs. "Hey. New duds?"

"Gotta love the discard barrel. But I did get a bath. I might live."

He couldn't stop himself. "I know."

She'd reached the bottom of the steps. "Right? Something about a warm bath—I could have used a few bubbles though. Still, they have this homemade shampoo soap—"

"No. I *know*, Keely."

She stopped on the bottom step, and it could be his imagination, but the blood seemed to drain from her. "You do?"

"What you were going to tell me before"—he cut his voice down, just in case she did mean for it to be a secret—"I know. And it's okay."

She swallowed again and looked away. But in that flash of a moment, her eyes blurred with tears.

What—? "It's not a big deal."

"It's a very big deal," she said quietly, her hazel-blue eyes on his, holding them. Almost a spark in the gold of her eyes. "And it's about to be a bigger deal. Maybe. Or maybe not. I don't . . ." She closed her eyes, a tear winked out, landed on her cheek. She brushed it away, almost angrily, and turned back to him. "I'm just such a coward."

He frowned, and something shifted inside him, because, *what*?

"Not here," she said and grabbed his hand.

Then she walked him to a small room in the back of the lodge. A quiet room with a bench overlooking the lake. "What's this?"

"A prayer room." She let him go. Backed up, her arms folded. "How'd you find out?"

Oh. "Why didn't you just tell me?"

She blinked. "Because . . . frankly, it's . . . it's still an open wound. Something I can't . . ." She shook her head. "I know I should be at peace with it by now. Four years is a long time, and really, she is fine—or *was* fine—I don't know." She sighed, turned to look out the window. "I don't know what to do."

He'd frozen on the words *open wound* and had nothing by the time she got to *she is fine*.

He slowly walked over to her. Hesitated a moment, then settled his hands on her shoulders. "Keely. I think you and I might be talking about different things. I was referring to the fact that you are actually, I think, Bliss?"

She stiffened. Put her hand to her mouth. Finally let out a long breath.

When she turned, she wore a stricken expression. "I . . . should have said something. But I guess I thought maybe you knew and just didn't want to . . ." She sighed. "River recognized me. And I know a couple of the teenagers did. I thought you were helping me keep it on the DL."

"Do you want it on the DL?"

"I don't want people knowing I came here to find Vic, so . . ." She lifted a shoulder. "I guess so."

A beat. Then, "Um. You don't have to tell me—"

"I have a four-year-old daughter."

Given the clues she'd dropped, it didn't blow him over. The way she cared for—rescued—Wren. Twice. Still, it took a second for him to nod. Swallow that information down. "I see. But . . ." He frowned. "Wait. She is fine—*was* fine. What's that about?"

"I gave her up for adoption."

Oh. His chest fisted, ached, and he managed not to pull her into an embrace. But he met her eyes. "That's tough."

"Yes. And now. I mean . . . sometimes I know in my bones it was the right thing to do. But . . ."

"It's still an open wound."

"I feel selfish."

Ah. No wonder her father's words about her selfishness cut to the soul.

"I think adoption just might be the most unselfish thing in the world—"

"I used to think that. Still do, most of the time, but . . . then I land a Grammy or go on a world tour and look out into a crowd of thousands and think . . . you'd better be happy, because you gave away your kid for this."

Oh. Wow. "That's a pretty brutal thought."

"I'm saying it nicely. The words in my head don't pull their punches." Her mouth made a grim line. "And maybe they're right. Truth is, until recently, I didn't think about her every minute of every day like a mom should. Or does. I . . . walked away. And now I don't know how I feel."

"Okay. Let's just get to the bottom of this." He led her to the bench. "Let's talk about the *was* part of the sentence. Is she not okay now?"

He sat opposite her.

She sighed. "Her name is Zoey. Her middle name is Anne, after my adopted mother. I told them and they kept it."

"They sound like good people."

"They are. From Oklahoma. My manager found them for me. He's a doctor. Her mom was a nurse. They couldn't have children of their own . . . they really loved her. They'd send me pictures sometimes. Updates."

Past tense, and his chest tightened. "And then?"

"They were in a car accident over Thanksgiving. The mom was killed, the dad, Bryce, is currently paralyzed. It's possible he could recover, but it'll take years of therapy."

He nodded, swallowed, a buzz starting deep in his brain. *Not now!*

"Bryce reached out and asked me to take guardianship. Otherwise, she goes to foster care."

"Bryce doesn't have family? Grandparents?"

"His wife's parents died years ago. He just has his mother, and she's struggling with Alzheimer's. So . . ."

Oh wow. He drew in a breath.

"See, I am selfish to even consider saying no. Or a coward because then what? I tell the world what happened?"

"You could keep it private."

She cocked her head at him. "Have you seen my life?"

He made a wry face. "Sorry. I'm a country music guy."

She laughed. "Why are you so easy to talk to?"

Something about it released the tightness, just a little. "That's a first. Usually people clam up around me."

"That's because they don't know your warm and fuzzy side."

"Please do not say that to anyone outside this room."

And right then, Caspian chose to walk in and settle beside him, leaning hard on his leg.

"Aw, please." She glanced at the dog. "Someone just needs to see you with Caspian and—"

"Keely." He took her hand. "I think giving up your daughter for adoption just might have been the most unselfish thing you've ever done. The most unselfish thing anyone could ever do. And it represents a victory, not a failure. It tells me you're strong and smart and brave."

She drew in her breath. "Really?"

He nodded. "The big question is, what do you want to do now?"

Her smile vanished, and she met his eyes. "That's why I went

151

to talk to Vic. I wanted to know if she had regrets. By the look of it, no."

"You can't know that by just looking at someone, Keely. But she also hasn't walked in your shoes, in your life. What was right for her might not be right for you. Have you talked to . . . the father?"

"When I told him I was pregnant, his words were 'You made this decision, not me. So you'll have to deal with it.'"

Dawson must have made a face because she untangled her hand from his.

"Trust me, it's better this way," she said. "He's an actor, and I was a fool. I had a short bit in a film he was in, sang a song, and . . . anyway, I made some choices I have to live with."

Her words the night they arrived drummed up in him. *"Maybe we're both paying for our mistakes."*

And maybe he wasn't the one to be pouring out truth, but it seemed Moose had words for this, sitting in Dawson's brain. "We can't change what happens to us, but we can decide how we want to grow from the experience. Sometimes when I'm working on a case, I have to step back and get a different angle on it."

Weirdly, the buzzing inside him died. "From where I sit, I see a woman who was alone and wounded, and a guy came along who didn't love you right. But you turned that around, and you did the very best you could for your daughter—"

"I was—"

"Scared. And wanted your daughter to have the same family life you did. A mom and a dad, and I'm not saying that a single mom can't do that—but I am saying that's what you chose for your daughter. And that isn't selfish."

She just stared at him.

"You have to believe me. I'm a cop."

She raised an eyebrow, then she shook her head. "Seriously. That's what you're going with?"

No, actually. Because he wanted more. Much more.

Except . . . *Bliss*. And now he got her words about it not working between them. About not wanting to hurt him.

So, he sighed and touched her hand again, testing. "And I'm your friend."

Her smile dimmed, and she wound her fingers through his. "You're more than that, Dawson. Trust me, you're more than that."

He had nothing, his gaze on her face. And oh, he wanted to lean in and kiss her but . . .

She got up. Walked to the door. "Sorry I didn't tell you about my day job."

"I'm going to need an autograph."

"In your dreams. C'mon. Imma beat you in Battleship."

He got up. And prayed that the storm might never end.

10

IT MIGHT HAVE been a perfect day.

The kind of day that she never wanted to end.

In fact, Keely could stay at Woodcrest forever. Even if she had to do the dishes.

"These are amazing, Keely."

She looked up from where Nance stood in the kitchen holding one of Keely's after-dinner sugar cookies.

"They're about a thousand calories each, but oh, so worth it. My mom used to make them every time it snowed. She called them snowballs."

"I call them addictive." This from River, who had stacked the cookies on a tray, where a few kids came up to the counter for seconds.

Keely hadn't noticed Wren in the bunch, but maybe she'd missed her. Still. "Has Wren been up and around?"

"No. Her dad made her stay in bed after her fall. Says she's banged up," Nance said.

"She hit the tree pretty hard." Keely finished scrubbing the baking tray and set it on a rack.

"I checked on her earlier," River said. "She has some tenderness in her chest—I think she might have a bruised rib. Her breathing seemed okay. How are *you* doing?"

Keely grabbed a towel. "Me? I'm fine."

"Mm-hmm," River said.

Keely frowned at her even as she dried the tray.

"I saw you and Dawson playing Battleship. It looked epic. There might have been some dancing."

"I beat him." She handed Nance the tray. Then she swung the towel over her shoulder.

"He didn't look too broken up about it." River's voice was low, almost conspiratorial. "He's very hot with that beard, wearing all that flannel."

Keely gave River a look, then matched her voice to hers. "Yes. Very. But . . . he didn't realize that . . ." She glanced at Nance, who had stepped into a closet where they kept the baking sheets and supplies. "He didn't know who I was."

"Really? How could he not recognize—?"

"Please. Not the entire world knows—"

"People in Nome were singing 'Chasing Forever' for karaoke night. I think the entire world knows," Nance said.

"I'm usually wearing glitter."

River pointed at Keely. "True."

Nance picked up the tray of cookies and walked out into the main room.

Keely sighed and stuck her hands back into the bubbly water. "There was definitely a change."

River sidled up next to her. "A change? A change from what?" She reached for the next clean tray and grabbed Keely's towel off her shoulder. Raised an eyebrow.

"A change from when he kissed me."

River looked around, then held up the pan to hide their conversation. "He *kissed* you."

"In the woods."

"Even better."

"River. Please. We have such different lives." Except right here, right now, they didn't feel so different.

Only because she was living in a Hallmark movie.

Keely stared out past River into the main room.

Dawson sat with Griffin and Landon and a few other men at a long table.

"And, I'm your friend."

No, he was her *hero*. Her Alaskan, flannel hero. He and his trusty dog.

But she couldn't bring them back to her apartment in New York City like a souvenir, right?

"I had no business kissing him." She looked at River. "It won't happen again."

"Well that completely breaks my heart," River said. "Maybe you should write that song. 'Northern Light Tears.'"

"That's a terrible title."

River started to hum . . . then, "Under the glow of the aurora, I . . . found my heart? But in the cold of Alaska, our worlds were . . . far apart?"

"Your beats are all off."

"Can you do better?"

"Please." Keely turned her voice singsongy. "I was a melody, a pop star in the spotlight, you were the snow, silent in the moon-light . . ."

"I'd call him more of a storm. You've seen those blue eyes."

"Fine." She switched to the melody again. "You were the *storm*, calling through the night."

"Not bad. It's catchy."

"No. We need something like this." Keely grabbed a wooden spoon, held it up, and cleared her throat.

And then, magic. The song started softly, almost haunting, and then grew as she gave it strength.

Caught in the blizzard, your laughter was my warmth
Your eyes like the city lights, mine were the north
Snowflakes fell like secrets in the frosty air
Alaska's winter whispered, but life's never fair . . .

River backed up to lean on the counter, and a couple of kids moved over to listen. River folded her arms. "That's not bad."

"I love improv. I did some open mic songs back in college, when I was just getting started."

"Got any more?"

Funny. She might just be getting started. "Me, the hustle of New York, with dreams as wide as day. Our worlds collided magically, in the most surprising way."

"Magically?"

"It's improv. Loosen up." She thought for a moment, and her gaze landed on Dawson, who looked up, found her gaze.

It was just a song. A Bliss pop song. But she brought the spoon to her lips.

And sang.

Not quite Bliss—her vocal range wouldn't allow for that. This was huskier, a sort of blues feel about the song. But she played with the tones, nuanced them.

Felt the music thrum inside her.

In the heart of a blizzard, where the world seemed to
    pause,
I found you, an unexpected wonder, without a cause.
You, wrapped in the mystery of Alaska's endless woods,
Me, a wanderer in your snowy neighborhood.

A couple more kids came to the window, and Nance emerged from the pantry, folded her arms, and leaned against the doorframe.

Keely used the spoon like a mic, adding drama to the song.

> We talked beneath the pines, as the snowflakes
> danzzzced around,
> In the silence of the falling snow, we found a love
> profound.
> Could this be our forever, could we make this last?
> Or is this just a beautiful moment that will soon be past?

A chorus pumped up inside her. She closed her eyes, felt the song vibrate through her.

> What if we stayed here in the wild, where winter blows
> so fierce?
> Or what if we walked together, beyond the frozen
> frontiers?
> Under the aurora's glow, can we dare to dream so far?
> Finding our forever, beneath the Alaskan stars.

When she opened her eyes, Dawson was standing at the counter. His eyes pinned on her, a sort of undone expression on his face. She gave him a smile, something sad, her voice falling, sweet, soft . . .

> Imagine us together, in a cabin by the lake,
> Or walking down a city street when we awake.
> Could the magic of this night transcend the woods so
> deep?
> Could the warmth we found in the cold be ours to keep?

Silence. Her heart thumped.

Then the room exploded, the crowd clapping, then shouting. Even Dawson, who'd raised an eyebrow, clapped.

She smiled, bowed.

When she stood up, he stepped back, away from the crowd. Then he turned, walked to the door, grabbed his jacket, and called for Caspian.

The dog bounded over, and they headed out into the darkness.

River came over to her, took the wooden spoon from her hand. "That was worth a Grammy."

She sighed. "I think I just broke his heart."

"You definitely broke mine." River followed her gaze. "You should go after him."

Keely looked at the kids dispersing. How Dawson had stared at her a long time before turning away. The smells of the kitchen rose around her, the sugar cookies, the bread in the proofers, ready for baking, the lingering scent of onions and garlic from tonight's venison stew.

"This isn't my world. No matter how much . . ." She looked at River. "It's not real."

"It is to me."

"I'd have to . . ."

"Give up everything?"

"Maybe, yes. I don't know."

"You've heard of *Notting Hill*? Or that new one, *Finding You*? Regular people fall in love with insanely famous people all the time."

"Yeah. Usually they're called stalkers."

"C'mon, you don't even want to try?"

She grabbed the spoon back and plunged it into the hot water, washing it. "It's not that. It's . . . I have a big life. Complicated. And there are a lot of moving parts. He lives in Alaska, and I'd be a complete jerk to suck him into my world without . . . well, without him knowing what it's about."

River nodded.

"I don't know what I was thinking."

"I don't think you were. You were listening to your heart."

"The heart is deceitful." She pulled out the spoon and took the towel from River. "My mother said that."

"Yes. But God can align your heart to match his will. And his will is to bring you to a place of peace and joy. To sing the song you were meant to sing. You only have to ask."

She stared at River. Swallowed. Oh no—was this what this was about? God bringing her here so she could fall in love with Alaska? With a man who . . . saw her?

She lowered the spoon. "What if I'm afraid to ask?"

"Then you'll never really know what it is that will bring you joy."

"I think I know what makes me happy."

"You only *imagine* you know. But God says that no mind has conceived the things that God has prepared for those who love him."

"He was talking about heaven."

"Was he? Because God says that our abundant life starts here. In this realm. But only if we trust God, and surrender to him. Look to Christ, and you not only get salvation, but you'll be set free to discover yourself too. The person you were made to be."

Keely glanced at the door. Then she handed River the towel and the spoon. "Hold my mic."

Because why not? It had all started with a crazy prayer four days ago, as the plane went down, a foxhole, desperate prayer that she couldn't even finish.

But if she were honest, the ending went something like *God, if you get me out of this, I'll pay attention. I'll listen. And I'll trust you.*

Or something like that.

"Go get 'im, Bliss." River pumped her fist.

Sheesh, but Keely grinned as she pulled on her parka, grabbed her pom-pom hat and mittens, and headed out into the night.

The sight before her stopped her cold, right there on the steps.

No, not cold—hot, roaring, flaming hot. She stared at the barn. Not quite an inferno, flames licked out of the windows on the sides, and black smoke tunneled out the open doors, and—

Where was Dawson?

On no, no—

She turned and opened the door. "Fire! The barn is on fire!"

THE BARN HAD GONE from spark to the furnaces of hell in the space of five minutes. Why hadn't he yelled for Griffin or Landon—

But no, he had to follow his dog's warning bark, open the barn door, and then the entire world lit up.

Because he was an idiot.

And maybe not thinking straight. Keely's song took all the space in his brain. The haunting, beautiful sound of her voice reached in and stole his breath.

He'd barely had the presence of mind to clap. And hadn't a clue why he had to leave.

Just found himself outside, following Caspian, all the way to the barn, and who knew what he'd been thinking—

The back draft lit the entire back of the barn, bursting to life from whatever ember had been sizzling. If he didn't move fast, they'd lose the livestock, if not their winter fuel supply. Never mind the firewood—the fire already gnawed at it. Flames crawled up the far wall, into the haymow, toward the roof.

Smoke gathered at the peak, some three stories up, not as thick there, but the entire building could be called tinder.

He opened the first stall, found a milking cow, grabbed her halter, and pulled her out of the pen.

Voices and shouting. He let the cow go and turned to the next pen.

Griffin ran in and opened a horse stall. As Dawson ran the cow outside, Abe and Landon led out a couple more blindfolded horses.

A few other men herded the goats.

Dawson herded out a pig, turned, and spotted Oliver shouting. And next to him, Keely, her face wrecked.

Yeah, well, him too.

"Woolly!" shouted Oliver, now crying.

The stupid llama.

A couple women stumbled out, carrying chickens, lungs racking. The birds landed, scattered into the night.

The community's entire livelihood lived in the barn.

He spotted a few men with shovels throwing snow on the outside of the barn. Too little, too late.

Get the llama.

He shoved his mouth into the front of his jacket and plowed back into the barn. The stalls hung open, with even the sheep being herded out by a few of the teenage boys. He hugged the wall, heat pouring out of the building, crackling and snapping overhead. He chanced a look—flames crawled across the rafters, the hay blazing.

Only moments before the roof crashed down.

A loud, shrill sound bit through the chaos—he'd call it llama in distress—and he headed for the animal at the end of the barn.

As he got closer, he noted the open back door—maybe why the entire barn hadn't gone inferno when he opened the front door, despite the woosh of air.

Woolly Bully circled, frantic in its stall. Dawson reached for the metal latch.

The gate opened, and the llama burst through, slamming the gate on Dawson's body, his legs.

Pain shattered through his knee. He stumbled, tripping, and slammed into the dirt.

He landed on a *body.* What—? He turned, and in the light—half in the next stall—Donald lay unconscious, blood pooled around his head. No, no—

Please, just unconscious.

"Donald!" Dawson scrambled to his feet, the flames overhead dropping in small sizzles. "Donald!"

The guy wasn't so big that Dawson couldn't carry him, a different day, a different time. But now . . .

C'mon, God. Be on my side.

He rolled Donald over, spotted a terrible gash, then hauled him up under his shoulders and wrestled him out of the stall.

"Help!"

The fire ate his words, his knee buckled, and he fell, Donald half on him.

He struggled out from under him. "C'mon!" Finding his feet, he kept pulling—a fiery drip nearly hit him, sizzled in the dirt—

Don't. Look. Up.

"Don!" The shout came from behind him, and in a moment, Griffin and another man were there, lifting Donald's legs, two more on each arm, and Dawson let go to allow them to shuttle him out of the building.

He stumbled after them, out into the frigid night, sweating, coughing, bending over to grab his knee.

His gut clenched, the world shaking around him. He breathed out, hard.

River caught up to them, following the men into the lodge.

Dawson spit on the ground—black—then wiped his face. His hand trembled. He fisted it, stood up.

Around the yard, community members herded the animals into storage garages and even houses, the biting wind turning the world brutally silent, save the fire and the wind.

Shouting erupted, and a small cadre of men—maybe women too—emerged from a storage building. A couple men held a pump between them, running hard in the blizzard toward the lake. Others carried hoses.

Clearly, they had a drill. A plan.

He stood back as the group with the hoses made quick work

of setting up the pump, plunging the hoses into the lake, right at the open source where he'd gone in, then attaching the pieces and rolling the hoses out to the barn.

Less than a minute later, water sprayed the barn.

The spectacle stopped him a moment, the splash of the water landing over him, pellets of ice, the mist glistening against the fire, caught in a swirl of blizzard winds, snow peppering the air. Sparks shifted onto the street, the crackle and snap of the flames against the roar of the wind.

The entire village could have burned.

If it weren't for Caspian . . .

Sweat layered his back, and his knees wanted to buckle again, but he managed to head over to the lodge, grip the railing, haul himself inside.

They'd cleared a table, set Donald on it, and River had him on his side as he coughed hard.

Abe looked over at Dawson, left his spot at the table. "How'd you know?" He advanced, almost angry, and Dawson held up his hands.

"I didn't—I went outside after Keely's song, and Caspian freaked out. Went to the barn and opened the door and *whoosh*! I wouldn't have seen Donald, except, I got the llama—" Oh sheesh, now he even sounded like an idiot. He put his hands down. "I didn't know— How is he?"

Dawson pushed past Abe, went to the table. Donald lay on his back, still coughing. River held a bandage to his head, taking it off now and again to examine it. Blood covered his face, his shirt, his hands.

His knuckles were torn. "You were in a fight."

Donald coughed, nodded. "I went outside to get one of Wren's kitties. I thought maybe it would help her feel better. But then the light . . . went . . . on—" His body racked, and he curled over and spit into a cloth. Black phlegm. Then he leaned back again, and River pressed her fingers to his neck, checking his pulse. He breathed in, cleared his throat. Eyed Dawson. "It's a battery-operated motion detector. I went outside—I thought maybe wolves, I don't know. I didn't see any, so I went inside to check, and of course the stupid llama was shrieking."

He closed his watering eyes, squeezed, and moisture escaped. Then he cleared his throat again. "I didn't see him. I heard a sound, and turned, and he came at me with a knife. I hit it away, but he wasn't giving up easy. We went around a few times—he finally hit me with a shovel and that's all I remember."

"You probably have a concussion," River said.

"He set the barn on fire," Dawson said. "Why?"

Donald wore a sort of horror on his face.

Griffin had something fierce, almost accusatory in his expression.

Oh no. It couldn't be . . . "What did he look like?"

Donald spit out more black phlegm. "Beard, winter clothes. I don't know—it was dark."

Why burn down their barn?

A few of the female community members had returned inside, some of them in the kitchen, a couple of them herding their children back to their rooms.

Oliver sat on the bench by the door, clutching a kitten.

Wait. Where was *Keely*?

And suddenly, the terror in the woods, the shooter, the snow machine thief rose, and oh, he was an *idiot*.

He stalked over to Oliver, sank down on the bench, tried to keep his voice easy. "Hey. Have you seen Keely?"

The kid seemed shocked, trembling. Yeah, well him too. "She told me to go inside. She was helping Aurora Benson take Woolly down to their barn."

Of course she was. "Where's the Bensons' barn?"

"Next door to our house—end of the street."

Dawson got up and headed outside, nearly fell down the front stairs, his stupid knee suddenly stiff and angry. The fire crew had moved inside the barn, hitting the flames hard with the spray. Outside, the blizzard seemed to be winning, the howl of the wind and the brutality of the ice causing the shovelers to abandon their efforts to save the outside of the structure, but maybe it had worked, because the fire seemed to be dying out.

The flames inside the barn had also died.

Darkness clouded the street.

He nearly slipped again as he reached the slick street, but found his footing, heart pounding, and crashed slash ran through the deepening layers toward the end. Lights flickered on as he passed—clearly the same motion-detecting devices. At the end, luminescence pooled out into the snowy street, the icy particles like flies in the glow. He picked up his pace, through puddles of gold, the wind moaning in the darkness beyond.

The last house seemed a little bigger than the others, although still a cabin, with a wide front porch and big windows. Behind it, a glow emerged from a small barn, and he pounded through a snow-covered path toward it.

He stomped at the threshold and pulled open the sliding door.

The llama stood, secured to an old open stall by its halter lead. Grunting sounds emanated from the space. "Keely?"

A head popped up. A woman wearing a knitted cap, with long dark hair, frowned at him. "No. She's back at the lodge. I think."

He just turned and headed back out to the snow. Because it made terrible, disastrous sense.

Start a fire. Bring out the community.

In the chaos, snatch Keely and vanish with her into the forest.

He picked up his pace, ignoring the burn in his knee. "Keely!"

The blizzard ate his voice. Just the faintest light pulsed from the barn.

He'd never find her. Not if Thornwood had grabbed her, dragged her out into the night. Standing in front of the barn, he looked past it, into the forest, then out to the lake, where the crew now hauled in the hoses, just an outline in the darkness.

"Keely!"

The wind gobbled up his voice. "*Keely—*"

"Here! I'm here!" The voice emerged faint on the wind, but enough, and he turned.

She stood on the porch, thin, bracing herself in the cold, her silly white puffer jacket pulled tight around her, shivering.

His knees nearly buckled again. But he ducked his head against the wind and fought his way up the stairs. She stepped back, like he might be a polar bear charging.

Maybe.

He stopped in front of her, looking down at her. His heart caught, roaring in his ears. It slowed, and he took a breath. Another. "You okay?"

She nodded. "Why?"

Oh, maybe she didn't need to know— He blew out his breath, shook his head, looked at the barn, back to her.

She tucked her arms close to herself and shivered again. "Can we go inside?"

And in her question, he heard *"Could the warmth we found in the cold be ours to keep?"*

Yes, maybe.

He met her eyes, his voice shaking. "What was that?"

She stared at him, caught her breath. "What—"

"That song in there. That . . . that . . . *love song.*"

"It was just a song—"

And maybe it was anger, or panic, or even . . . a painful, deep longing inside, but it all stormed out of him. "Not a chance, Bliss. That wasn't any pop song. That was . . . that was . . ."

"Real?"

The way she said it, soft and almost a question, shouldn't

167

have had the power to rock him back, but . . . a boulder lay in his throat, maybe his chest.

He nodded. "Maybe. It could be real, right?" He backed her up to the lodge wall without realizing it and braced a hand over her shoulder.

Wow, she was pretty. In the light of the porch lights, the gold in her eyes shone, sparkled, and he thought he recognized hope in them.

Probably reflecting his own.

Aw. His gaze traced her face. "If I kiss you again, are you going to run away?"

"Where am I going to run?" She reached up and tucked her bare fingers into his jacket lapels. "You have me trapped."

He smiled then, his heartbeat slowing, the terrible boulder dislodged. "Yes, actually, I do." And then he kissed her.

Really kissed her. Wrapped a hand around her neck, fitted his mouth against hers, and dove in. She tasted sweet, of those incredible sugar cookies, and maybe a hint of hot cocoa, and she smelled of the lavender soap from her shower. She stepped up to him and molded her arms around his shoulders.

And kissed him back.

He might have made a sound, because he felt the rumble deep inside, raking through him. It only lit to flame the fire he'd been trying to douse all day, especially since hearing her story.

No, he wasn't *remotely* interested in just being her friend.

He'd take hero, thank you. Protector. Definitely the guy who kept his promises.

Maybe even her happily ever after, but he pushed that thought away as he wrapped his other arm around her and deepened his kiss.

"What if we stayed here in the wild, where winter blows so fierce?"

Yes. Right now, yes.

He'd worry about what happened after the storm later.

Much later.

11

WHAT IF she stayed?

Keely let that thought run through her head too many times in the night, as she listened to the storm die, the memory of the song, the kiss, the *what-ifs* swirling through her. Woke up to it cemented in her brain.

She lay under the quilts, one thought circling her mind. *Please let this not be Chase Sterling all over again.* Handsome, charming—a liar, a betrayer.

"It could be real, right?"

Dawson's voice, soft, haunting, stuck to her heart.

She could say yes to Bryce's request, bring Zoey here with Dawson, build one of those cute cabins, and restart her life.

People restarted their lives all the time.

Zoey could grow up with Wren and Oliver, with Nance telling her stories, with Dawson as her daddy . . .

The thought filled her chest.

He'd make such an amazing dad.

Wow. She was really getting ahead of herself. For Pete's sake, she already had them married. But she'd had a front row seat on the disaster of a quick marriage, thank you, Dad.

No, this was . . . yep, Hallmark. Romance in a weekend,

something for the movies. Not real life, and probably she needed to stop believing so hard in her songs.

But oh, the man knew how to kiss. And protect. And make her laugh.

She'd never felt so safe in her life. At least not since her mother died.

Outside, the blizzard winds seemed less ferocious, and a glance out the window showed a pale sun breaking through the gray.

She got up and pulled on clothes, hearing voices lift from the main room. Apparently, she'd slept through breakfast. She walked out and headed down the stairs, and they silenced. She looked over to see a group of the community men and a few women seated and standing around one of the long tables. Griffin sat court in the middle, and Dawson stood opposite, his hands on his hips.

Caspian sat beside him, almost on his foot.

Dawson wore a look. Angry, his jaw tight, his eyes sparking. He glanced at her as she came down the stairs, and his mouth pinched.

"What's going on?" Her voice seemed even stronger today, so maybe yesterday's impromptu open mic hadn't stripped it again.

The aroma of coffee seasoned the air and even Nance had joined the group at the table, seated on the bench. She gave Keely a wan smile.

Dawson took a breath. "They want us to leave."

"Hey. That's not fair, Daws." This from Griffin.

Dawson rounded on him. "Yes, it is. And I don't blame you, Griff."

His words scraped through Keely, turned her hollow. "What?"

Dawson glanced at her. "We found tracks around the barn this morning. From more than one sled."

She walked over to the group. "What does that mean?"

"It means whoever attacked Griffin is back," Donald snapped. "And this time, he attacked me and set our barn on fire."

"The barn might have been an accident, Don," Nance said. "One of the propane lights could have ignited it."

Donald gave her a tight look.

Griffin held up his hand. "Whoever they are, yes, it looks like they came back."

Keely folded her arms against herself. Met Dawson's eyes. "Thornwood."

"Maybe," he said quietly. "I'm not sure where he would have spent the storm, but I can't figure out why he'd come back."

"Me?"

He drew in a breath, his expression grim. "Could be."

"I don't understand why he wants me."

"You saw him take down the plane. You can identify him."

"So can Wilder! And that's who he was after."

"Wilder Frost?" Landon stood with one foot on the bench, one arm perched on his knee. "You were on the plane with Wilder Frost?"

"I don't know his last name. Brown hair, in his thirties."

Landon nodded, put his foot down. "Sounds like Frost." He glanced at Dawson. "I heard the Sorros trial was beginning down in Juneau. I'll bet he was headed down to testify."

"What trial?" Griffin asked.

Dawson was nodding, and Keely could almost see the gears working in his detective brain. "Frost is a local musher." He folded his arms across his chest. "Three years ago, he was out with his dogs and just happened across a group of . . . well, let's call them a group operating outside of the law. Drugs and weapons, and we're not sure what else, but we do know the Sorros brothers were involved—Mars and Jago and Conan, all led by their father, Brand. Brand was caught about five years ago and charged with drug dealing. But the boys were still out, running the operation. Three years ago, Wilder witnessed them murder a DEA agent. Unfortunately, they knew this and came after him. They killed Wilder's wife, but he managed to escape with his daughter. He's been living in Copper Mountain ever since. The brothers scattered, but Conan and Jago were caught and arrested. Since Conan pulled the trigger, according to Wilder, they had him on first-degree murder charges. Then Jago was killed in prison a couple months ago. He had a plea agreement to testify against Conan, but when he was killed, they turned to Wilder. They were probably bringing him in to testify . . ."

Dawson glanced at Keely. "Can you describe Thornwood again?"

"Just a lumberjack. Dark beard, kind of scraggly, and he had a scar on his cheek, right here." She touched a place under her eye. "Big guy."

"Could be any of the Sorros brothers," Landon said.

"Conan Sorros escaped from prison during a transfer a month ago," Dawson said quietly.

A chill spread through Keely. "Are you saying that Thornwood is Conan Sorros and that's who was on that plane?"

"I don't know," Dawson said.

"If Wilder knew him, why didn't he recognize Sorros?" Landon asked.

"Sounds like he wore a disguise. Or—"

"Thornwood got on the plane last," Keely said. "He sat in the back seat with me. Maybe Wilder didn't get a good look at him. They were sort of standing apart from each other."

"If Thornwood really was Sorros, and he was tasked to take out Wilder, then there's no way he'd want a witness." He turned back to Griffin. "And he's not going to quit."

Silence, and she clamped her mouth shut. She refused to let tears spill out of her stinging eyes.

"You can wait for the blizzard to end," Griffin said softly. "We'll post guards, keep everyone inside—"

"They can't wait."

These words came from River, who had joined them, standing at the end of the table. She wore her hair back in a handkerchief, fatigue in her eyes. "Wren isn't doing well."

Donald stood up. Groaned and braced himself on the table.

"And Donald has a concussion."

"I'm fine."

River held up her hand. "I think Wren has some internal bleeding. Maybe a broken rib nicked something, but she has some abdominal pain and more bruising has appeared. It could be from the fall, but . . . she's pale and still confused and lethargic. She needs more medical help than we have here." Her gaze settled on Dawson. "We can't wait for the blizzard to die."

"It's already subsiding," Landon said. "According to the weather service, this is the tail end. It's clear skies west of Copper Mountain."

Griffin turned to Dawson. "Take the snow machine and a sled. With the drops in temperatures, the snow should stay powdery enough for you to get through."

"I should go," Donald said, his hands braced on the table.

"Yeah, and you'll pass out along the way, and then you'll both die." This from River, and even Keely turned brittle.

Donald gave her a wretched look, so much pain in it, Keely had to look away.

Despite his rough-edged demeanor, the man did love his daughter.

"I'll bring her to Sully's and call Moose," Dawson said. "He can bring a chopper in, and if not, the outpost should have an all-weather ATV. We'll get her to safety."

"No. You don't understand," River said. "We can't move her.

The bleeding will only increase. You need to go get help and bring it here." She looked at Donald. "You stay here with Wren. She needs her dad."

The man looked away, swallowed, his face twisted. Nodded. Poor man.

"Maybe I should go," Griffin said.

"No, you should stay. Do your job, and let me do mine," Dawson said. "I'll get to Sully's." His gaze went to Keely. "Maybe you should stay."

"Not a chance." She raised an eyebrow at his wide-eyed expression. "Thornwood is after me. If I'm not here, then . . ." A shoulder lifted, and she gave Donald a tight smile. "We'll get help. I promise."

More silence, during which Dawson gave her a dark, almost fierce look, as if biting back an argument. Then he looked at Donald and nodded.

And just like that, the movie ended.

Time to leave.

"I'll pack you a survival kit," Nance said and got up.

"You're going to need warmer clothes." River looked at Keely and exited the room.

Caspian whined.

Dawson petted his head. "Not you, buddy. You stay here. We'll get you when we come back."

The dog got up, as if in protest, but Dawson turned to Griffin. "Watch my dog?"

"I doubt he'll stay with me. He's pretty stuck to you."

Dawson glanced at the dog. "It's too dangerous for him." He headed toward the small room where they kept their outdoor gear.

River returned with a full body snowsuit and a pair of knitted wool socks. "You'll need this. And the parka. And a scarf and double mittens."

"You're scaring me."

"Alaska." She handed them to Keely, who put on the gear, took off her fuzzy Prada boots, and pulled on the wool socks. "You'll need the Sorels I loaned you," River added.

"I guess I'll trade you." Keely handed her the boots. River looked them over, raised an eyebrow.

"I thought these were Uggs. Add a couple zeros."

Keely shrugged. "The zeros don't matter when it's below freezing."

"There's the Alaska girl in you."

She laughed, fighting the burr in her throat as she zipped up the snowsuit, then she put on the wool underjacket that River gave her.

"Layers will save your life," River said.

She had no idea.

Keely zipped up the wool overcoat, then retrieved the boots by the door and laced them up.

River shoved a hat in her hands, one free of a pom-pom. "It's called a tuque. You wear it under this." She held up a fur hat. "Just like the old sourdoughs used to wear."

"A sourdough?"

"An original Alaskan gold miner." River plopped it on Keely's head, then wound a knitted scarf around her face.

"I don't think I can move."

"But you'll stay warm. Now, goggles." River grabbed a set from a peg by the door. "These are mine. Trust me on this."

Keely put on the goggles, then accepted River's help to slip into the parka, and finally worked on glove liners. River fitted on her leather mittens.

"I should be in some Alaskan photo shoot," Keely said, trying to laugh.

River smiled, although it, too, looked forced, sad. "Come back, Keely. You're always welcome here."

And now she *would* cry. She pulled River into a hug, and Nance came up behind her.

"Be safe," Nance said. And hugged her too. "We'll be praying. God has you in his hands."

Right. She didn't want to wonder where God's plans fit into this. So much for what her heart wanted.

And that thought stood Keely up, made her draw in a breath. Five long days ago, the thought of staying here, in remote Alaska, to build a life seemed . . .

Well, unthinkable.

And now at least a part of her longed for it.

More, that's exactly what her birth mother had done, wasn't it?

So maybe Dawson was right . . . maybe there was more of Vic inside her than she thought.

"We'll make it," Keely said, glancing over to Nance.

Then she went outside.

Dawson had bundled up, and she spotted him headed for the machine shed. He wore a pair of thick Carhartt coveralls, boots, a parka, the hood pulled up, and a face mask. Goggles sat on top of his head.

It felt like that moment before she went onstage, listening to the crowd cheer, knowing she was made for this.

River's words edged in as Keely headed down the steps to the shed. *"Trust God, and surrender to him . . . You not only get salvation, but you'll be set free to discover yourself too. The person you were made to be."*

She looked to the gunmetal-gray sky, to the sun peeking through. *Help me trust you, God.*

From the porch, Caspian barked, and she spotted Griffin holding the dog by the collar. *Sorry, buddy.*

Dawson started up the snowmobile and drove it out of the shed. He stopped and met her eyes. "You sure about this?"

"Not in the least." She pulled her goggles down and settled

behind him, the seat creaking in the cold. Putting her hands around him, she leaned forward. "Drive, James."

He laughed and pulled down his own goggles. "Hang on."

She had no intention of letting go as they drove into the snowy, gray day.

HE SHOULD HAVE LISTENED to his gut yesterday when it told him to leave.

Dawson maneuvered the snowmobile through the path in the forest, keeping the throttle open enough for the machine to skim the surface of the snow. Slowing would only make him sink.

Let his failures find root.

Yeah, he'd given in to the pull of staying, of comfort and, aw, who was he kidding? The sooner he got Keely out of the bush and to an airport, the sooner she was on a plane and back to her life.

Her real life.

Not the fake what-if fantasy he'd conjured up for himself last night after her stupid song.

No, not a stupid song. The kind of song that kept aflame the terrible hope inside him.

He wanted her. Her smile, the way that she teased him and yet made him feel like he might actually be a hero. And it didn't help that last night she'd kissed him as if she wanted the future she'd sung about too.

Even now, she held on to him, her legs tight against his, leaning into him as the snow chipped up around them and spotted his goggles. The wind whistled in his ears above the drone of the motor, but the sun had started to break through the cloud cover.

Landon might be right about the storm dying.

They'd spent the last twenty minutes cutting through the forest, after muscling their way through the meadow that had trapped him before. Now, they emerged out to a riverbed, frozen over.

"Hang on!" He slowed, motoring down the edge, into the gully.

"How do you know where to go?"

"There are markers in the trees." He pointed to an orange utility ribbon tacked high to a birch tree. "Orange goes to Sully's place. The red ones are ranger tags to the cache cabins."

He revved the motor again and followed the iced creek south. The same creek that he'd found her in, maybe a mile or so north. The route cut them south a quarter mile, and then he motored them out of the wash when it turned east and kept moving south. She pointed to an orange ribbon, and he headed toward an opening in the forest.

The snowmobile coughed as they entered the thicket, and he slowed. Please, let him not have screwed up the spark plug replacement.

It coughed again, and the engine nearly died. He slowed more, the machine rumbling under him. *C'mon—*

A hundred feet into the forest, it coughed again and then sputtered out.

They slowed, then sank into the powder. He closed his eyes.

"That sounded fuel-related to me." Keely got off. "Is it out of gas?"

"Griffin filled all of the machines when we fixed the spark plugs. I watched him." Although, he hadn't checked before they left. Stupid.

"It shouldn't have used that much gas," she said. "Maybe the fuel line was nicked."

He also dismounted, and wrenched open the cover. "I would have seen it when I replaced the plugs."

Around them, the wind shivered the trees.

He searched the engine compartment. "Nothing."

A rattle, and he looked over to see her opening the snowmobile seat. "My dad had one of these. An old one, but the fuel lines ran back to the—yep. The seat compartment is full of fuel. And it's dripping out the back." She pointed to a small black puddle forming in the snow. "How much farther to the outpost?"

"I don't know. Maybe a half mile? Less?"

"We'd better get moving." She headed out past him, tromping into the deep snow.

He grabbed the keys and left the machine. *Sorry, Griff.* But it wasn't going anywhere.

The snow wasn't as deep here, a little easier to move than he'd thought, the bottom layer icy and firm. And inside his Carhartts, he worked up a simmer.

Could be his own frustration.

Still, the forest began to thin, the pine trees shivering snow into the air, and ahead, it opened to a snow-crusted meadow. The wind cast dervishes across the plain of white, and Keely stopped a moment, as if contemplating their path.

Then she pointed.

There, in the distance, in a landscape of gray and black, a building huddled in the snow. "Is that it?"

"I think so." He headed out toward it, looking for any sign of life, but not even a light blazed from the front porch.

"It's bigger than a cabin."

The scarf muffled her words, but she seemed to be keeping up, and inside her goggles her gaze seemed lit, almost a triumph in it.

So maybe it hadn't been a terrible idea to bring her along.

"It's the Bowie fishing and hunting outpost. Part of their resort. They fly or ATV in guests, and Sully is the guide and host."

"It's like a postcard, out here in the middle of nowhere."

He nodded. "But it's off-grid. No electricity. It's really popular in the summer." A covered porch jutted off the front, with a tall A-frame roof with wings off each side. Timber framed, and a tall rock chimney protruded from the back.

No smoke wisping from the top, which seemed odd.

"Have you ever been here?" Keely asked, keeping up with him.

Wasn't hard, with his knee aching. "No."

Okay, that was a lie.

"My sister disappeared after falling into this river, so . . . I never . . ." He glanced at her.

Her gaze was on him, and then she reached out and took his mittened hand. Squeezed. "Well, then we'll do this together."

Then she let go and plowed forward in the snow.

Okay then. He followed her up the porch, to the double front door with antlers over the frame. She knocked and then tried the door.

It opened.

And his gut screamed, *No.*

He grabbed her jacket and pulled her back, and she nearly fell into his arms. He caught her, trapped her in his embrace. "Me first."

He set her behind him. "Wait."

Her eyes widened, and she nodded.

Then he went inside.

A gloomy darkness hovered through the room, dented only by the windows that allowed in the ghostly light of the day. The great room rose two stories tall, with a couple round tables in the middle and a leather sofa facing a cold, dead hearth.

He could nearly hear his heartbeat echo.

A chill ladened the air, although not freezing, so some heat remained, but on the counter sat a French press coffeepot, half full. A cast iron pan on the gas stove with standing grease, and . . .

Yes, something felt . . . off.

"Is anyone here?" Keely came in behind him.

He rounded on her. "I told you to wait."

She pulled down her scarf, and her mouth opened, and aw, he hadn't meant it that way, but . . . . "Something smells . . . oh no—"

Blood. He spotted it, a dark puddle on the kitchen floor. He put out his hand to keep Keely away, but she wasn't moving, her gaze on something else.

He turned and spotted a dish, broken on the floor. And then a trail of blood from the kitchen through the house.

"Please, stay here," he said quietly, his heart thundering, and followed the blood.

It pooled in the bathroom in the claw-foot tub, but a handprint on the wall in the hallway led him to a bedroom.

Ransacked, or at least the bedclothes torn off, onto the floor.

"Dawson?"

He headed toward the front door. She stood in the opening, pointing out, and as he came up, he spotted a couple drops of blood in the snowy debris of the covered porch. In the distance, a shed's doors hung open. He went down the steps, crunched in the snow, and stood at the edge of the shed.

Empty.

She'd followed him, now edged up behind him. "What were you hoping to find?"

"The ATV that Griffin mentioned. And maybe the snowmobile that Sully borrowed from the community."

His gaze fell on a pair of cross-country skis hanging on the wall, along with a hunting bow, and a number of rifles locked up behind a cage.

He turned to her. "Let's get inside. Warm up. We can call Moose on the ham radio."

She said nothing, and he hated how he'd barked at her.

They returned to the house and he closed the door behind her and then deadbolted it. Then he pulled off his goggles, mittens, and face mask and set them on the table. She did the same, and pulled off her parka hood, shaking out that beautiful blond hair.

The memory of his fingers tangled up in it last night swept through him. Oh boy.

He'd really been hoping Sully might be here.

"I'll get a fire going," he said. "You look for the radio." He pointed to a small adjacent office off the main room. "Could be in there."

Cordwood piled against the side of the tall fireplace. The damper lay open, so no wonder the freeze had found its way in.

He found birchbark tinder in a box, along with broken pieces of kindling, and built a log cabin fire, two bigger pieces of firewood at the bottom, a smaller one crossing it, kindling in the middle.

A box of long matches sat on the mantel, and he lit the birchbark. It caught, crackled, and for a moment, the sound of the snow and wind seemed to surrender to it.

"I will get you home, Keely. I promise."

Dawson suddenly never wanted to break his word more in his life.

"Daws. I found it."

He stood up, turning.

And a rock went through him at the sight of the handheld radio transceiver in one hand, an antenna in the other, the antenna bent, the transceiver in loose pieces.

"That's the ham."

"What's left of it."

He closed his eyes, listened to his heartbeat. Blew out a breath. Then looked at her again. "Okay. I know there's another radio at the cache cabin, a couple miles up the river. I can get there—"

"We can get there."

He swallowed, then walked over to her. Put his hands on her shoulders. "Your cop dad taught you how to shoot a Glock. Can you handle a rifle?"

"What?"

"There's only one set of skis in the shed, and the snow is way too deep to walk."

She blinked at him. "What . . . Daws—"

182

"We gotta get help." He looked away. Shoot. Maybe he shouldn't leave her. Because his gut started screaming all sorts of dangers.

Starting with Thornwood and ending in—well, all the things that could happen out there in Alaska, from grizzly to house fires, and now he needed to sit down, the coil in his chest so tight it cut off his breathing.

And all he could think was . . . Caspian. Usually, right about now, the dog would edge up to him, and he could feel the dog's fur in his hand.

It always felt like his dog was . . . well, comforting him.

"Dawson?"

"I'm fine." And when he met her gaze again, something had shifted inside her expression.

"I'll be fine. Yes, I can handle a rifle. Wren is running out of time. Go. I'll get the rifle and lock the door, and I might even try and figure out how to fix this radio."

Of course she would.

He stared at her, then bent down and pressed his forehead to hers. "Don't ever let anyone—especially you—accuse you of being a coward."

She smiled, then lifted her head and kissed him.

Sweetly, perfectly, the kind of kiss that he might hang on to, and it was all he could do not to grab her jacket and deepen the kiss, to stir up the hope of yesterday.

And maybe it was too late for that anyway, because as he let her go and met her eyes, she wore exactly that in her hazel-blue eyes.

Hope.

"Come back to me," she said.

"Stay put. I'll be back." Then he grabbed his hat and mittens and face mask, went to the gun safe, pulled out a rifle, and headed back out into the blizzard.

12

DAWSON COULD NO LONGER feel his knee. And maybe that wasn't a terrible thing, but the longer he skied, the more his entire body could be blown over by the wind. He'd followed the red markers, one to the next, to the next, and two miles had become a half century, turning him into an old sourdough miner fighting the elements back to his rinky-dink cabin to weather out the storm.

He'd even started humming. He might have preferred to call to mind Keely's song, but instead, one of the hymns the women had been singing in the kitchen roused to him.

"Blessed assurance, Jesus is mine! . . . Oh, what a foretaste of glory divine!"

The song turned into a hum from his grandfather working on a tractor or a truck. *"Hand me the torque wrench. It's the one with the black rubber grip and the long silver handle."*

Yeah, he missed his grandfather. And his faith. Something about Grandpa's big hands on Dawson's shoulders in church as Dawson held a hymnal, trying to sing along, still centered him.

He heard the words now, let them fall over him. He'd never really turned them inside out, taken a good look at them.

But maybe Griffin had, because his words pulsed inside, like a flame.

"But peace doesn't come from inside. It comes from knowing that you're forgiven. Accepted. Safe. It's about standing in that place of love and letting it set you free."

Maybe that's what the foretaste was about . . . love. Peace. Joy. Freedom from the terrible howl inside that said he was doomed.

Maybe God did use circumstances to get at the things inside.

A moaning and a whistling, and Dawson looked up, searching for the red marker. He should have seen it by now.

Please let it not have blown off in the storm. He remembered from the flyover Moose's words about the cache cabin being on the river, so he'd stuck to the bank since leaving Sully's place.

He turned and stared at the half-frozen river. Parts of it still ran, the current too fast to close it completely, but ice and snow patchworked the surface, the water in the middle dark and mysterious.

A vapor misted off it, caught in the swirl of the blizzard, as if it held secrets, a lethal breath. Aven hadn't died in this river, not really, but the old ghosts could still turn his bones brittle.

A shot cracked the air, and he ducked, turned.

Silence.

Probably a tree cracking under the weight of the snow. But in the distance, he spotted it—a small cabin, nearly snowed under, a stovepipe angled out of the top.

The cache cabin.

Thank you, God.

Dawson turned his skis and headed for it, the light bleeding from the day. He'd need to get in, call the Copper Mountain FBO's ham radio, and see if they could track down Moose, then get back to Keely before nightfall.

He refused to let her spend the night in Sully's cabin alone.

Who knew what had gone down there, with the bloody mess. He should also call Deke at the sheriff's station, but he'd get to that.

Footprints, the track of snowmobiles, and wide ATV tires dented the snow as he skied nearer. And the deck seemed half cleared.

Maybe Sully came here, especially after the destruction of his radio.

Dawson unclipped the skies and pulled the rifle off his back, holding it as he climbed the steps. Yep, his knee had tightened up.

"Sully?" He eased the door open.

Empty, but recently used, a fire snuffed in the stove, and empty coffee cups on the table, the smell of bodies, and a couple sleeping bags mussed on the bunks.

No blood, but whoever had used the place might be coming back. Could be rangers—Peyton Samson studied a wolf pack out this way as part of her ranger service. Or it could be locals—trappers, maybe, caught in the storm, although they were on the edge of private land and federal property, so maybe not.

He shut the door and locked it behind him. Opened the stove. Embers, almost dead. He stirred them with a nearby poker, then added some tinder and kindling, got that lit and then added a small log.

Heat filled the small room, and he went hunting for the ham radio. A couple summers ago, his former partner Flynn had saved Axel's life with the ham, and he'd heard the story so many times, he knew the radio had to be here.

He found the machine in a cupboard. Dawson brought it to the small table, pulled out a chair, and turned it on.

Hallelujah, it still had battery juice. He lifted the antenna. *Please work, please work.*

The radio buzzed and crackled. Once upon a time, his grandfather had one of these, but of course he couldn't drag up *that* useful memory.

He didn't touch the frequency—certainly they had it set for Copper Mountain.

"Um, hello? Hello? Can anyone hear me? I have an emergency. Come in."

A crackle, and in a moment. "This is AL7SKY, I read you loud and clear. Who is this?"

"It's Dawson Mulligan."

"Dawson. It's Echo Kingston. Read me the call sign on the front of your radio."

He leaned down to read the faded tag. "It's AL7RAC, Alpha Lima 7 Romeo Alpha Charlie."

"Gotcha. Please go ahead with the details of your emergency. Over."

"I need Moose. There's a little girl at Woodcrest who fell and might have internal bleeding. As soon as he can get a chopper or a plane up, she needs evac."

"Understood, AL7RAC. Moose is at the police station, working calls. Want me to call him?"

"Yes."

"Stay on the line."

He blew out a breath, then pulled his chair up to the fire and held his hand to it. *C'mon, Moose*—

"Dawson." His cousin's voice emerged through the speaker, a little grainy, and Dawson guessed Echo held the phone to her mic. "You okay? Sully said he left you at Woodcrest."

"Yeah. We're good. I found the passenger that Caspian ran after. A woman. She's safe." It occurred to him then that maybe Keely might want someone to know that. Like . . . Vic?

Or maybe not his news to tell.

"What's going on with this little girl?"

"She hit a tree sledding, and the nurse on-site thinks she might have internal bleeding."

"Where are you?"

"Sully's place—no, actually, I'm at the cache cabin about two clicks west. But I'm headed back to the Bowie Outpost. But . . . have you heard from Sully? There was blood—"

"Yeah. Sully and Kennedy are in town." A sigh on his end, then, "Kennedy lost her baby."

Dawson closed his eyes. "I'm sorry."

"Yeah. He nearly lost her too. Can you sit tight for a day? I'll get out there as soon as I can. Storm's dying, but I'm losing my ceiling. I'll barely make it to Woodcrest and back."

"Yeah. I'm good." Maybe better than that.

"Good to hear your voice, coz. Not going to say I was worried. Sully briefed us on your whereabouts. But . . ."

"Moose, have you heard anything about the Sorros brothers being around?"

A pause. "No."

"Keely—the woman from the plane—says that a guy named Thornwood took that plane down at gunpoint. Wilder Frost was on the plane."

A beat. "You think this Thornwood fellow is really a Sorros?"

"Could be. He attacked a couple of the men at the community and tried to burn their barn down."

"Seriously. You guys safe?"

He didn't know what to say. "The sooner you can get here, the better."

"I'll let Deke know. He'll look into it."

"Anyone seen Wilder?"

"I dunno. Keep your head on a swivel."

"Yeah. Did my mom make it to town?"

"She and your dad are out at his place."

Interesting.

"Stay safe. I'll get there as soon as I can."

Static, then Echo's voice came back. "I'll talk to Dodge. We're still grounded at Sky King Ranch, but if Moose can make it to Woodcrest, maybe Dodge can pick you guys up at the outpost."

"Thanks, Echo."

"AL7SKY out."

He turned off the radio, his heart thumping. His knee had started to thaw, to ache, but with the fading light, he needed to get moving.

His hands and face had at least warmed up. Retrieving snow from the porch, he doused the fire, then replaced the ham and closed up the place behind him.

The wind had died, the cold biting but not as savage as he clipped on his skis, grabbed the poles, and headed out on his trail. Easier going back with the trail already cut, and he found a rhythm for himself, moving above the riverbank, just outside the edge of the forest. His knee had gone silent again, his body working up a sweat as he raced the setting sun. It bled out fire along the river, long shadows stretching before him.

"Or what if we walked together, beyond the frozen frontiers? Could the warmth we found in the cold be ours to keep?"

His own voice came back at him. *"The sooner you can get here, the better."* Shoot. Probably for the best, but at least now he knew Sully's place wasn't a crime scene. Moose's words about Sully made him ache, but at least they hadn't been murdered, or something just as terrible, and the fact that was where his brain led him made him wonder if perhaps . . .

What if he made his leave of absence permanent?

And now the cold and the wind and Keely's sweet goodbye kiss had infected his brain. All he'd ever wanted to do, to *be*, was a cop.

He glanced at the river, listening to the soft swish of his skis. No . . .

All he ever wanted to do was protect the people he loved.

He could protect Keely. Maybe . . . what if she said yes to becoming the guardian for her child? He could . . .

What? Be a dad? He could barely care for his stray dog. In fact, it seemed Caspian took care of *him*.

Still, the thought became an ember inside Dawson as he skied. He didn't have to stay in Copper Mountain. And if his mother and father were somehow getting along . . .

Bliss wasn't Keely—he knew that. He'd *met* the real Keely. Maybe they could find something real and true and forever off the stage, out of the limelight.

And if she decided to step back in, could he stand on the sidelines, watching?

But what about the tragedy and darkness and danger that seemed to chase him?

Or perhaps *he* chased it.

Could be it didn't matter. Could be that the point wasn't the danger and tragedy but what he did with it, just like Griffin had said.

"I'm convinced that nothing can happen to me in this life that isn't used or designed by God to know him better."

He looked up at the encroaching darkness, a few early stars speckling the sky. Maybe it wasn't about escaping his mistakes, but letting God change him because of them.

The red flags on the trees wagged in the breeze, snow starting to blow over his tracks. If he remembered correctly, the outpost was just a quarter mile, maybe less—

A shot cracked the air, and he ducked, then shook it away. Branches falling, trees adjusting to the cold.

Calm down—

Another shot. This time, bark chipped off a nearby tree.

What—?

A third shot, and he reached for his rifle—

Tripped, his skies tangling. He got the rifle around, even as he fought for balance, the skis trapping him. His numb knee tore, heat spiking through him, as momentum pulled him back . . .

And over the edge of the riverbank.

Then he was tumbling, hitting rock, slamming against the boulders, and finally plunging into the lethal cold of the Copper River.

KEELY WASN'T just going to sit here and do *nothing*. Like she might be a princess or something.

For one, she'd discovered the outpost ran on a generator, like the community, only this one was located in the back of the house, in a closet. She switched it on and voilà, let there be light. The instant hot water heater also worked, so that meant the dishes got cleaned, along with the floor. She should clean up the blood, but maybe it was a crime scene . . .

And in that case, she'd made a mess of it.

Except, then she discovered, in the bedroom with the missing comforter, a small cradle in the corner, covered in a blanket. She did the math and wanted to weep for the scenario she saw in her mind.

So yes, after she took off her underjacket—thanks to the warming house—she cleaned the blood and the plates off the floor, and made the bed with new, fresh sheets, and then swept the place, which left her with nothing to do except root through the cupboards for food stores.

Potatoes, onions, and canned meat. Dried garlic and some kind of herb—smelled like dill—and she found a pot and dumped it all together, added a can of tomatoes, and after a bit, the place smelled homey and stirred up memories of the community.

Please, Dawson, come back.

He'd been gone for hours. At least three, maybe more, and night crept into the room.

"Stay put. I'll be back."

She simply refused to believe anything else.

With the soup simmering, she headed to the office. Small, tidy. A map hung on the wall with tacks marking locations. One tagged the community, another a cabin on the river. She guessed that might be where Dawson went.

"Stay put."

She'd put the handheld transceiver of the ham radio on the desk, and with the smell of soup filling the cabin, she pulled out a chair and took a look at it. The back of the device had dented in, the case breaking open, and the antenna had broken off, so maybe it took a hard fall.

Like a guy trying to call for help only to have his wife collapse in the kitchen, breaking the plate she was holding, causing him to drop the transceiver.

She should be a detective.

Please, God, bring Dawson back.

It felt like a perfect prayer, easier than she'd thought.

Screws held the back in place, so she rooted around the desk drawer, past more tacks and duct tape and pencils, and found a small screwdriver.

In a moment, she had the transceiver open.

The light waned, and a glance out the window said the sun had surrendered. *Oh, Dawson, please don't get lost.* She found a flashlight in another drawer and flicked it on. Shined it on the back of the handheld.

A circuit board and wires and fuses and—bingo. One of the fuses had turned black.

She should have taken a look at this before Dawson left. Except, a search through the drawers didn't unearth any extra fuses.

Maybe they had tinfoil somewhere. She got up and rooted around the kitchen. Nothing.

A pantry held dishes and foodstuffs, mostly canned goods—wait. There, in a basket, a few lunch-sized Cheetos bags.

She grabbed one, opened the bag, munched a Cheeto—Goldie would have a coronary at the free license she'd taken on her eating—and then took the bag into the office. She cut off a piece and wrapped the foil around the fuse, then put it back in.

It snapped and burned out.

What? Shining her light on it, she discovered the problem—the metal prong touched the fuse and grounded it out.

Taking the fuse back out, she inserted the edge of the screwdriver and bent the metal, ever so slightly, away from the fuse.

Then she ate another Cheeto, wrapped more foil around the fuse, and inserted it. Turned the radio on.

Joy to the world and hallelujah, it lit up. She almost wanted to sing.

She depressed the mic. "Hello? Hello? Anyone out there? Hello?"

Static.

She tried again. "This is the . . ." She looked around, searching for a call sign, and spotted a calendar turned to March with the name Bowie Resorts on top. It showed a man standing in gaiters in the middle of a frothy river, hauling in a fish.

Bowie. That sounded right. "Bowie Outpost. Anyone there?"

More silence. Shoot, she'd really hoped—

"Hello, Bowie Outpost. Is this a Mayday?" Male voice.

"Um. Yes. Sort of. I mean . . . no one is hurt, except at Woodcrest. There's this little girl. But . . ."

"We know about the little girl, Bowie Outpost. Are you in danger?"

She looked out the window. No Dawson, and her chest tightened. "Yes. Yes, we are. My . . . my friend is out in the storm, and he's not back yet, and . . . I'm worried."

"Understood, Bowie Outpost. And your name?"

"Keely. Keely . . ." Aw, this could go south, if the person on the other end knew anything about Bliss. Which sounded ridiculous, but something simply gripped her, and suddenly she found herself saying, "Dalton. Keely Dalton."

"Keely, can you tell me if you were in a plane accident a number of days ago?"

Oh. "Um, yes. Uh, is this—" What was the name of Dawson's friend—"Moose? Is this Moose?"

"Yes. Yes, it's Moose. Sit tight, Keely Dalton. We're coming to get you."

She set the handheld in her lap and blew out a breath. Okay. So, it was over.

Warm clothes, a bath, pizza, civilization.

Back to her life.

Then why, suddenly, did her throat tighten, her eyes burn?

Because that wasn't her life. It was a life she'd created. But here, maybe, she'd discovered a person she longed to be. Strong and capable and smart and . . . maybe she could even be a decent mother.

She could at least try.

Maybe losing her voice had been the best thing that ever happened to her. That, and a plane crash, and an overzealous dog, and a grumpy ex-cop.

And maybe it was too soon—way too soon—and the lingering memory of their Hallmark getaway, but . . .

She could love this man. Could even be on her way . . .

Oh boy. But what was she supposed to do with a man like Dawson? Sweet and considerate and self-sacrificing and . . .

So this was how it felt to want to love, the urge to give them the best of yourself, to shed all the fears and lies and simply . . . love back.

Bliss suddenly felt so far away, a costume, really, that it was time to shed.

Time to be set free.

A scratch at the door made her sit up. Set the handheld on the desk. "Dawson?"

She got up. Another scratch, and this time whining.

What—? She unbolted the door and—

Caspian?

Snow covered his dark fur, and the dog wiggled in past her, turning and barking, his entire back end wagging.

"What are you doing—wait, did you *follow* us? All the way from the community?" She crouched, and Caspian came over and nudged her, then lay down on his back.

"Tummy rubs, huh?" She scratched him. Oh, he was cold. But clearly alive, because he rolled back to his feet and shook off the snow, then started running and sniffing through the house.

She stood, watching him. He sniffed at the fire for a long time, then over to the area where blood had dropped, went into the bedroom, and came back out, then came over to her and sat. Looked up at her with those big brown eyes. She rubbed his ears with both hands. "I s'pose Dawson couldn't really live without you. Don't worry. Rescue is on the way."

The door had eased open, and she walked over to close it when Caspian stood up, headed toward it, and stood in the opening. Outside, the wind cast snow across the porch. She found a porch light and flicked it on.

Caspian took off, across the porch, down the stairs, barking. What now? "Caspian!"

She stepped out onto the porch, her arms around herself, and—

Oh no. Caspian had stopped, just outside the ring of light, pawing at a form—a body.

No, no—

She had taken off her boots, but kept them by the door, and now she shoved into them, didn't bother to lace them as she reached for her jacket, just ran down the stairs into the snowy yard, the light reaching out past her to nudge the man in the snow.

Dawson. He lay unmoving, no skis, his knees drawn up, his hat off, his dark hair tipped in white. Caspian licked his face, trying to rouse him.

She reached him and pushed him over.

He seemed dead. Except for the tiniest huff of breath.

"C'mon, Caspian, help me!" She rolled Dawson over and grabbed his jacket. She wasn't serious, but Caspian clamped onto the scruff of his coat and, with her, began to pull. The man weighed a thousand pounds. She didn't have a hope of getting him to the house or up the stairs— "C'mon, Dawson!" The shout lifted, high and loud, and tore through. "Wake up!"

Movement, and he groaned and then reached up and caught her arm. Squeezed.

She let go. "You're alive."

He grunted as he rolled over to his hands and knees, the sound deep inside him, as if he might be trying to rev something. His heart, probably.

He sat up, and she slammed herself into him, her arms around his neck. "You came back. You came back!"

He was soggy and frozen and unsteady. Even put a hand out as she nearly knocked him over. She grabbed his arms, pulled him back. "Are you okay?"

He leaned forward, put his hand down, and grunted. "Yeah, but I don't think my knee . . . I think I left it back in the river."

She hadn't a clue what he meant. But she got her arm around him, and he leaned hard on her as they struggled up, then to the porch, up the stairs, into the house.

He sank into a nearby chair. "Bolt the door."

She obeyed, and when she turned, he was trying to pull off sodden mittens. Failing.

"Why are you wet?" She yanked off his mittens. Oh, his hands were icebergs.

"I went in the river."

"What? How?" She knelt and untied his boots and eased those off. Ice clung to his wool socks, stiff, not a hint of warmth remaining. He attempted to unzip his jacket, but she got there first and dragged the wet parka off him.

His Carhartts were stiff with ice.

She unzipped them, all the way down. A flannel shirt and jeans underneath, less cold, but still, he shivered.

"I'll draw you a bath. I cleaned it out."

"They have hot water?"

"And there's soup on the stove."

He looked at her, fatigue in his eyes. "I think I love you."

She smiled and laughed, a stupid giggle, because he didn't mean it.

But it still felt good.

She stood up, put her hands on his whiskered face. "You're so cold."

He caught her hands, met her eyes. "I'll be okay."

"What happened out there?"

"I think I was shot at." He let go of her hands. "I fell in the river but managed to hang on to my gun. I fired a couple shots in return . . . and then nothing. And then I was freezing to death, so I ditched the skis and just got here as fast as I could. I tripped in the yard, and I don't know . . . I guess I just laid there, trying to find the energy for the last fifty yards."

"And then Caspian showed up like your guardian angel. I would have never seen you." She grabbed a blanket from the sofa, brought it to drape around his shoulders. "I can't believe you fell in the river."

He nodded, but leaned back, arms over himself. "But I beat it, Keely. I beat it."

She frowned even as she went over to stir the soup.

"For years, the river . . . I had nightmares of it swallowing Aven, then grabbing me. I'd wake up fighting, and angry, and all I could think was that I somehow let her down. Like I was supposed to be there. She was my little sister."

She walked over, sat in the chair next to him.

He looked up, swallowed. "She was fearless. She'd get herself in all sorts of trouble. Stuck in trees, or in a kayak—and every time I was there to help her. Because that's what I did. And she had this nickname for me—the Eagle Scout."

"I can see that."

"Yeah, well, I was always there. Always prepared . . ."

"And then you weren't there."

"Yeah." He looked away, closed his eyes. "And I blamed the river, and I blamed my parents, and I blamed God . . ."

"And you blamed yourself."

He opened his eyes.

Aw. They'd filled, and she couldn't stop herself from touching his hand. "But it wasn't your fault."

He said nothing.

"Dawson."

"I realized that, today. When I fell in. The current—I'd forgotten how strong it was. It took a minute for me to get out. And then it hit me that . . . even if I had been there, maybe I couldn't have rescued her . . ."

"And maybe you need to stop blaming yourself for stuff you have no control over."

He finally made a sound. "Stuff."

"Stuff?"

"I had stuff. Anger, and frustration, and guilt, and . . . stuff."

"We all have stuff."

"My stuff kept me trapped. I'm tired of being trapped."

Stuff. "God, if you get me out of this, I'll pay attention. I'll listen. And I'll trust you."

He frowned at her.

"I started asking God for help when the plane went down.

198

And then you showed up. I prayed again right before the barn fire that, well, if he got us out of this, then I'd pay attention." She swallowed, nodded. "I think it's time for me to listen. To trust. To believe that God has something good for me and to stop trying so hard to make it happen on my own."

He nodded. "Me too. I'm tired of always trying to stop everything from blowing up."

"Oh, no, you need to stop stuff from blowing up. But if it does, you stop blaming yourself."

He smiled. "Have I told you how beautiful you are?"

"Your brain is just frozen."

His gaze ran over her, and in his eyes she saw a desire, something deeper than simply physical, but a longing, maybe. *"Could the warmth we found in the cold be ours to keep?"*

She met his gaze. *Yes, Dawson.*

Then, "You really made soup?"

She laughed and rolled her eyes. "Yes, but you're shivering. Bath first, Iceman."

She headed to the bathroom and opened the faucet to the claw-foot tub. Water cascaded out, and she kept it lukewarm so as not to shock his body.

River's advice when they'd been drawing a bath for Wren, after the fall in the woods.

He came into the bathroom and stood in the doorframe, holding on. He'd taken off his socks.

"My mom used to do this after I went ice skating," he said. "My feet would be so cold. She'd draw a bath, and I'd soak my feet in it until the feeling came back."

"Where'd you go ice skating?"

"On a pond near our house. My cousins and I would play hockey for hours."

"Of course you did. I bet you wanted to go pro."

"On no, that was Moose. Still addicted to the sport."

"Yeah. I get that. Something that gets in your blood, you can't escape it. Oh, by the way. I fixed the ham radio and got ahold of Moose."

Silence, and she tested the water. Warm. "You can add more hot water when your body adjusts."

She got up, but he was staring at her, frowning.

"What?"

"You got ahold of Moose?"

"Yeah. He said he knew about Wren. And that he was on his way to get us."

He looked at her, then sat on the edge of the tub. "When was this?"

"Just before—hey, where's Caspian?"

He blinked and seemed to come back to himself, looking around. "Caspian?"

"I'll find him. Don't worry. Take a bath. I'll see if I can steal some clothes for you."

She went out into the bedroom, rooted through the standing closet, and found a pair of flannel-lined jeans and a thermal shirt.

Then she knocked on the door. "I'll put them on the floor in the hallway."

Barking sounded outside.

"Thanks," he said through the door. "Keely, um—are you sure you talked to Moo—"

"Just a second. I think I hear Caspian."

She headed for the door and opened it.

Her mouth gaped in a scream that didn't emerge as Thornwood reached out and grabbed her by the scruff of her jacket and pulled her into the night.

13

SOMETHING DIDN'T FEEL RIGHT. Even after Dawson shut off the bath faucet and turned on the shower. He hadn't wanted to hurt her feelings, but he wasn't a child anymore.

Still, as he stood in the spray, his feet warm in the receding bathwater, he could admit to needing the heat to rewarm his bones.

He'd been perilously close to hypothermia, probably.

As he let the water warm him, her words sat in his brain. *"He said he was on his way to get us . . ."*

Except, how could Moose be on his way to the cabin when he was supposed to be getting Wren?

Or maybe she hadn't talked to Moose, but to Dodge, Echo's husband, who ran one of the other rescue choppers in the area.

He turned off the shower and grabbed a towel, wrapped it around his waist. The heat sank into his bones, and he'd stopped shivering, although a cold nip still hung in the air, seeping through the bottom of the door.

She'd said she'd left clothes for him outside. He opened the door, found them.

The fire still flickered in the hearth, but a chill hung in the room, the blizzard a little louder. The wind must be whipping up with the night. And maybe the steam had overwarmed him.

He grabbed the clothes, put them on. She'd forgotten socks, but maybe he'd root around in Sully's gear and ask forgiveness later.

A flannel shirt, a pair of jeans, and he ran his hands through his hair to slick it back. Stared at his whiskered mug in the mirror. Such a catch. He shook his head. What was he doing?

How did you ask a megasuccessful pop singer to ditch it all and join your life in the last frontier?

"Something that gets in your blood, you can't escape it."

You didn't.

You followed her to New York City.

He braced his hands on the sink edges, considered himself. He didn't see himself as a New York cop.

But maybe that was the point. Maybe this was his chance to start over. He could become a detective—

Barking sounded, distant, as if outside. He frowned and opened the door, stepped out of the bathroom.

The front door hung open, the wind casting snow into the room. The barking came from the darkened yard.

"Keely?" He glanced into the bedroom but didn't see her, then ducked into the office.

Empty.

He walked to the front door. "Caspian! Come!"

The dog stood in the ring of light in the yard, looking out as if . . .

His gut clenched. No—wait— "Keely?"

He went to the porch. Stared out into the night.

On the front steps, footsteps matted the snow, more than one set—oh no, no— "Keely!"

His feet turned to ice, and he raced back inside, grabbed boots and shoved them on, then a jacket, and hustled back out to the yard.

Snow machine treads churned up the yard. Two sets. He ran

down one track, into the darkness, and spotted Caspian, who'd run out ahead of him, standing at the river's edge, barking into the night.

No, *no*— The world started to spin, his chest webbed, his breathing cutting out. He caught up with the dog, and in the distance—way down the riverbank—he spotted headlights, disappearing, then winking out.

"Keely!" Now his knees did buckle.

Caspian practically threw himself on top of him, licking his face, barking.

"I know—" He put a hand to his mouth and fought the urge to be sick. *How*—

Except, maybe they'd followed him from the cache cabin. It only made sense—he knew someone had been there, and certainly someone had shot at him.

He should have listened to his gut.

Caspian kept barking, all the way until he climbed to his knees. Then Caspian pushed against him and forced Dawson to put a hand on him.

The action centered him, just for a moment, brought him back to himself. Cleared his head. Okay, then . . .

"Let's get help." He stood and fought the wind and snow back to the lodge, Caspian running out ahead of him.

He barreled up the porch, then into the house, and by the time Dawson had followed, stood at the sofa, where her knit sweater lay, sniffing at it.

He rounded back to the door, barking.

"I know. I know!"

Dawson headed to the office and pulled up the radio. Turned it on and switched the frequency to the one he'd used at the cache cabin. "Echo, come in. This is . . ." He looked at the call sign on the base. "This is AL7BRP. Come in, Mayday, Mayday."

Static. He tried again.

A male voice answered. "AL7SKY, I read you loud and clear. Who is this and what is your Mayday?"

"It's Dawson Mulligan. I'm at the Bowie Outpost, and I think . . ." What? Please let him not sound crazy. "I think my girlfriend has been kidnapped."

So much in that sentence, but he let it sit.

"Come again, AL7BRP. Kidnapped?"

"Yeah. Listen, Moose was supposed to fly into Woodcrest and get a little girl, but my, um, girlfriend, Keely, called him, and he said he was coming here. But I don't think so—"

"That's a negative. Moose is enroute in my Beaver for the community."

His Beaver. "Dodge?" Moose's Air One Rescue team had a branch in Copper Mountain, run by local bush pilot Dodge Kingston. So, yes, that made sense.

"Yeah, Daws, it's me. Moose left about an hour ago, maybe more, for Woodcrest. Took my heavy plane, in hopes the weight helped. The wind had died, for the moment, but it's slated to pick back up—"

"I need . . ." What? A plane? A chopper? A SWAT team? "Listen. I think one of the Sorros brothers—maybe more than one—grabbed her. I think he was on a plane with her that went down before the blizzard and has been hunting her since." Although why would he take her instead of simply killing her?

That question sat in his gut and gnawed.

"They grabbed her, and they had snow machines."

"Which means they can't get far, not in this storm," Dodge said.

Right. "I think they were camped out at the cache cabin on the edge of Bowie land. Maybe they took her there."

"All right, listen. If they're smart, they'll hunker down while the last of this storm blows out. You do the same. I'll be in at first light to pick you up."

He closed his eyes, pressing his forehead to the mic. "Dodge—"

"Dawson. We can't land a plane on Sully's land—it's too forested, and the riverbank isn't wide enough. But, if you hang tight, I can get my chopper in. First light. I'll do everything I can to get there."

Dawson ran a hand over his forehead. "Maybe I should go after her."

"You won't be any good to her dead."

Caspian came over, set his muzzle on Dawson's knee.

He put a hand on the dog's soft fur, clenched his jaw.

His heart said go. His gut agreed with Dodge.

"Fine. First light. AL7BRP out." He set down the handheld, rubbed his hands on his jeans. Then got up.

Dodge gave his final "AL7SKY, clear," and the line cleared.

His knee ached, his gut churned, and he just barely stopped himself from punching Sully's office wall.

He headed to the kitchen, stared at the soup, still simmering.

How could you let this happen, God?

The thought punched him, and his throat burned. But really—"When is it enough? I get it—I do. I get it. Life happens. But—*c'mon.*" He shook his head, then turned off the heat.

Stared at the flickering fire in the hearth.

No. No way could he wait all night—

He headed toward Sully's room for socks.

"AL7BRP, this is AL7SKY, over." The sound came from the handheld, and he turned and hustled to the office, picked up the ham.

"AL7SKY, this is AL7BRP. I received your call. What's up?"

"Echo and I took a look at the weather. There's a higher pressure system over the area right now. It's clearing the clouds in your area. I can make it, if we hurry. I'm on my way."

Dawson sank into the chair. "Thank you."

A female voice came on the line. Echo. "Button up—it's going to get cold, Dawson. I'll call Deke and let the sheriff's office know what's going on. These Sorros brothers are bad news."

"Yeah. I'm not sure how they found us."

"If they're working with the local militia group that was shut down last summer, there were camps located all over this area. Drug manufacturing and trafficking, as well as human trafficking. Heavily armed. I've run into them a few times, accidentally, when I've been out mushing, or tracking for the forest service. And summer wildfire teams have bumped into them too. There could still be some groups operating. If she really was taken by the Sorros brothers, then you'll need more than you to find her."

Caspian had again come over, settled his muzzle on his lap. Whined, as if in solidarity. Again, he put his hand on the dog's head, more for himself, maybe.

He drew in a breath, then, "Can you call Flynn?"

"She's already in Copper Mountain. Drove up a couple days ago to be with her sister, according to my mom."

Echo's mom, the OB-GYN. "How's Kennedy?"

"She had an ectopic pregnancy. Lost a lot of blood and, of course, had emergency surgery."

That accounted for the blood.

"If Sully hadn't gotten her out in time, she would have died. She's still in critical condition, I think."

He could call himself a jerk for still wanting to call Flynn and ask for help. "What about London?" He hadn't seen the Air One Rescue chopper pilot slash former spy recently, but—

"I think she's still in Anchorage, with Shep."

Seemed right that Moose would have someone on duty at HQ while he was stranded in Copper Mountain.

Dawson needed a team. Deke, yes, but he worked with a skeleton crew of youngsters—

What about Vic? The question simply flashed into his brain, bold and scorching.

Vic had been a cop, in seedy underworld Chicago. And he didn't need to betray Keely to ask for Vic's help.

"Dawson." Echo's voice broke through the static again. "*Why was she taken by the Sorros brothers? Like you said, if they wanted to eliminate her, then why not kill her?*"

Maybe it was just the ham static, making her words brutal. But the question slid in between his ribs, turned. Stole his breath.

"They need her." His gut gave the answer, but it seeded in his bones, felt right. "For some reason, they need her."

"For what?"

He shook his head. "Ransom? She's . . ." And that had to be it. "She's pretty wealthy."

A beat. Then, "Who is this girl?"

Aw, he didn't want to give her away, but if he had any hope of getting her back, then all options needed a good scrutiny. "Have you ever heard of Bliss?"

"Bliss? The pop singer? Who hasn't? Vic plays her songs down at the Midnight Sun, sometimes. I actually walked in on her playing Bliss's televised concert on the flat-screen last fall. Wait—your girlfriend is *Bliss*?"

He keyed the mic. "Yeah, sorta. She was up here on . . . sort of a vacation, and . . . she's keeping it all on the down-low."

"For sure. If the world knew she'd been kidnapped—"

"Which we don't want anyone to find out. The media would lose it."

"You think they know who she is and want her money?"

"I can't put anything else together. Maybe Thornwood—Sorros—recognized her when he got on the plane. Except, why would he threaten Wilder Frost and take a plane down because of it? We thought it might be because of the trial, so that Wilder couldn't testify."

"Where did the plane go down?" Echo asked.

"Northwest of Woodcrest and the Bowie cabin."

"Near the cache cabin, then."

Right. He hadn't thought about that. Wait— "Do you think one of the other brothers was waiting for him at the cache cabin?"

"It's pretty remote. But it's safe and warm and usually uninhabited."

"They planned on the plane going down," he said quietly.

Static on the other end.

"Keely put a thorn in those plans by surviving," he said.

"Or by getting on the plane in the first place," Echo said. "You could be right. Plans changed when Sorros recognized her. Do you know what brother it was?"

"Not for sure. Keely said he had a scar under his eye."

"Oh, that's Conan."

"You know this guy?"

"The whole family, sort of. Jago, Conan, and Mars. Conan got in a fight in school, and his younger brother, Jago, sliced open his cheek with a knife. Mars has a forehead tattoo. And their cousin Sloan came around in the summers. He was a couple years older and taught them all his tricks. They terrified me. Don't you remember them?"

"Vaguely."

"They were a few years older than us. My dad got in a scrape with them once, years ago. Caught them poaching. Their dad was a mean guy. Went to jail for dogfighting for a couple years."

He couldn't help but glance down at Caspian, who met his gaze with his big brown eyes. "Sounds like a fantastic role model."

"I think their mom might have moved them to Anchorage after that."

"To start their life of crime there."

"Yeah, but they started haunting the Copper Mountain area maybe seven years ago. Poaching. Squatting. Then into drugs and trafficking, growing their seedy empire. They're not to be messed with."

Oh, he was going to mess with them.

Static. "I can't believe you're dating Bliss."

Dating seemed not the right word. "Maybe that was overstated."

"I just could never see you with someone so . . . dramatic. She once wore mechanical wings during a concert, had pulleys lift her into the air so she could fly over the crowd. And she's pretty famous for this crystal-encrusted bodysuit that she wore for her Grammy performance a few years ago."

"For a woman who's lived off the grid most of her life, you know a lot about Bliss."

"The *entire world* knows a lot about Bliss, Daws. Unless you live under a rock. Or your work. Maybe it's time to come into the light."

Right.

Well, the world might know a lot about Bliss, but he knew a lot about *Keely*. And maybe that's what mattered.

Her voice dropped. "Just don't get hurt, Dawson."

Probably too late.

"I'm seeing Dodge on radar. Looks like he'll be there soon. I'll call Deke. Be safe, Dawson. AL7SKY clear."

He hung up. Turned off the ham handheld and stowed it. Then he doused the fire in the hearth and closed the damper. Put the soup in a jar and stuck it in the freezer.

Bundled up himself and grabbed hold of Caspian's collar.

Then he shut off all the lights and went out onto the porch, hearing the chopper pounding the air in the darkness.

Or maybe that was just his heartbeat, pounding out his broken promises.

IF THE HOUR-LONG snowmobile ride through a blizzard and frigid winds didn't kill her, then the trip in the back of the closed pickup should have. But Keely had found an old packing blanket to roll up in and had warmed up enough to call herself alive by the time she arrived—wherever.

An old house, for sure, reeking of age and dust and beer. Wan kerosene light spilled onto the cement floor, and a large stove stood against one wall on bricks. A small kitchen area held broken cabinetry with many of the doors off, a cracked sink with a pump for a faucet. A hint of sewer smell saturated the place, probably from the back room toilet, which looked more like an outhouse, with a wooden box topped with a stained toilet seat.

The odors swilled together as Thornwood pushed her inside, followed by another man—could be his twin, really, clad in padded overalls and a grimy wool hat over his long hair. The men wore matching disgusting beards, and the scent of danger lifted off of them. The other man, however, boasted a forehead tattoo, a sort of insignia, high, nearly to his hairline.

Sort of like Charles Manson, so that was a calming comparison. But the mark matched with a name in her memory—Mars Sorros.

"Upstairs," barked Thornwood, and she fled up a creaky ladder to a crawl space. His twin followed her up, and for a second, her worst nightmare played out, but he simply grabbed the trapdoor and closed it, pulling the rope through a hole in the top and securing it below.

So, locked in.

The light from below pushed up into the room, enough for her to make out her surroundings. Not tall enough to stand in, she could still bend at the waist and move around. The space held a bare mattress, and the stench of mouse droppings could make her retch. At the far end, a frozen window rattled, the wind fighting to get in.

Which meant, maybe—

But if she escaped? Where would she go? In the darkness, and the tangle of wilderness, she was just as likely to get lost forever.

The stove shuddered, and a whoosh suggested someone had opened the damper, maybe would be starting a fire. Note to self—don't touch the metal.

She drew up her knees, working her fingers to get the blood flowing, then put her forehead down on her hands.

Why hadn't they killed her?

"You sure you're right about this?" One voice, a growl. "She's—"

"It's her." The other voice.

She crept over to the trapdoor and peered down.

Movement, the sound of a bottle opening, then one of them came into view, and she jerked away before he could look up and see her.

"So, what are you going to do with her?"

"After the handoff? Put a bullet in her head, probably. It's about time. I'm tired of her harassing us."

Harassing? She hadn't harassed anyone.

Not even Dawson. He'd been the one to make her promises.

Oh, he was going to be out of his mind with worry.

She scooted back, her heart a fist banging against her ribs, and put a hand over her mouth.

So they were going to hold her for ransom and *then* kill her. Maybe Thornwood had recognized her on the plane.

Her daughter would never know. Never know that she was loved by her birth mother. And of course, Dawson's words found her, in that steady voice of his.

"I think giving up your daughter for adoption just might have been the most unselfish thing you've ever done. It tells me you're strong and smart and brave."

Oh, she wanted to be brave, but . . .

Keely closed her eyes. What was it that she'd prayed before? *God, I trust you*?

This wasn't *quite* what she meant.

Still, River's voice found her. *"Trust God, and surrender to him . . . you'll be set free to discover yourself too. The person you were made to be."*

She hadn't a clue who that might be. Not Bliss—she'd become out of control, a character she wiggled into before she went on-stage. Sometimes, she even saw herself as if from a distance.

Maybe it was a good thing her mother hadn't lived long enough to watch. And the thought grabbed her by the throat, burned it. *"Oh, Keely, you have such a beautiful voice. Don't let it die."*

Yeah, so much for that voice. She'd shredded it, hadn't she? So much for healing . . .

The furnace had started to radiate heat from the metal pipe. She held her hand up to it, careful not to make contact.

From below, "When's he s'posed to get here?"

"Dunno. Early." A long burp rattled up from the room below, along with the clank of a beer can hitting the wall.

"Stay alert, stay alive."

She stilled, hearing her father's voice.

Right. Downstairs, the two men stopped talking, one of them asleep on a ratty sofa. She couldn't see the other from her peephole. But outside, the night had started to recede, just a little.

She crept up to the window, the wind curling around the frame. Ice had worked in too, lifting the top of the window from the casing, at an angle.

One good kick on the frame, and the whole thing might break.

And, by the grace of God, she still wore her Sorels, from dragging Dawson in from the cold. That, and her snowsuit and wool underjacket, thank you, River.

She leaned back and gave the frame a kick. Nothing too hard, but enough to test it. The window shuddered but didn't break.

Downstairs, snoring sawed through the floorboards. The wind still buffeted the house, but not as wild as during the blizzard, so maybe the storm had started to die.

Which boded well for her escape.

She leaned back, took a breath, and slammed her foot again into the edge of the casing.

The window wedged free at the top.

Another kick, and it bent, the glass cracking. She got on her hands and knees and pushed.

The window gave, wood breaking with a crack. She stilled, held her breath.

Snoring. No movement below. Okay then—

She stuck her head out. Below her jutted the roof of the entryway to the house. Perfect.

Then she lay on the floor and scooted out of the opening.

See, that's what came from not eating cake for the better part of a decade.

Outside, the sun had just started to edge the far eastern rim of the mountains, simmering like molten gold hope. It cast fingers of light over the land, and as she sat on the roof of the small home, she made out her escape.

A thirty-foot area around the house shone white and pristine, lethally clear. A tall barn stood sentry over the house, buried in snow, along with a couple outbuildings. The truck with the cover sat in the drive.

She could just slide—

Her movement sent her skidding, and before she could grab hold of the roof, she slid right off—*poof!*—onto the ground.

Snow filled her cuffs, tunneled up the back of her underjacket, but she managed not to scream, so hallelujah.

She rolled, then ducked down and ran to the battered red truck.

No keys. Of course not. Fine. And she had no tools to hotwire it. Hopefully Thornwood and his scary brother would stay drunk and asleep for a good long time.

How she wished for the fur hat, but she still wore the tuque, so she shoved her bare hands into her pockets, bent against the wind, and took off, through the tire tracks.

"Keep your head on a swivel." Her father, still in her head. *"Control what you can, adapt to what you can't."*

Okay, enough. Still, the words burrowed inside, burgeoned her. She could do this.

The wind fought to tunnel into her ears, but she kept her chin down, eyes on the tracks and the increasing brightness of the snow. She just needed to find a road. Traffic.

The trees shivered, the pine scent rich here. Turning once, she left the cabin behind, the trees growing up around her. *Don't wake up. Don't wake up.*

She kept going, still jogging, her boots crunching in the pack and then—ahead, a dent in the forest wall.

A road. Please—*please*—

She picked up her pace, running awkwardly with her hands in her pockets, her eyes on the opening . . . slowed.

A lake. It opened up ahead of her, white and pristine. A road ran around it, still just the tire tracks, and disappeared into the woods.

"Don't give up. This isn't over."

Again, her father. She shook his voice away and took off, head down, following the tracks.

It seemed someone might have plowed, maybe during the letup of the storm, which meant civilization, but she hadn't seen any houses.

From here, however, she watched the dawn break over the eastern horizon, bold and fiery, the flame of a new day. It cast upon the lake, turning the snow to molten rose-gold fire.

Breathtaking.

She slowed, breathing hard, and in the silence, a crack sounded, breaking through the forest.

No—*no*—

She whirled and froze. A giant bull moose, with its long legs, stepped easily out of the tangle of forest to stand on the frozen road.

Maybe forty feet from her, but she'd heard stories.

His breath puffed out in the cold.

Hers too.

Moose were fast. And lethal, and maybe if she didn't move—

It snorted at her, and did she imagine it or did its hair raise? Her heart thundered—

Then its ears flicked back.

She held up her hands. "Listen. I'm not going to hurt you. Let's just pretend we don't see each other."

The animal pawed the ground. Run? Or did she stop, drop, and roll—oh—

A gunshot spiked the air, and the moose jerked. For a second, she thought it might be hit, but it spooked and took off running in the opposite direction.

She pressed her hands to her throat, checking to see if her heart had escaped, then turned.

A man stood in the road in front of a newer model Dodge Ram. Expensive and clean, and when the man lowered his gun, she let out a breath.

He wore a puffer jacket, a scarf, a wool hat, and normal boots, like he'd just stepped off the plane from any of the tame Lower 48 states where moose didn't try and eat you, and you didn't get stranded in the forest during a blizzard. Okay, maybe that happened in Minnesota. Or Washington state.

But the man looked worried as he lowered his gun. "You okay?"

She nodded, shoved her hands into her pockets, and walked toward him. "I was . . ." What? Out for a morning walk? "I didn't see him. He just appeared."

"Right. They do that. Silent but deadly." He smiled. Glanced past her. "You out here alone?"

She tried not to read into that. *Please don't be a creep.* "Not really." She'd had a few voices in her head to keep her company, right? "I'm, um, from out of town though. I must have gotten turned around. You don't have a cell phone, do you?"

He gave a half laugh. "Not one that works out here, but I sup-pose I could drive you to service."

Right. "I left mine back at the . . . um . . . lodgings."

"Staying at an Airbnb? This far off the grid?" He looked around, as if trying to locate it.

"The price was low."

He offered a smile, and he wasn't a bad-looking guy. Mid-thirties, maybe.

"My name is Keely," she said. "And if you're willing to give me a ride to cell phone service . . . uh, I do need to make a call."

He considered her a moment, then sighed, as if he had some-where to be, and nodded. "Okay." Walking back to his truck, he stowed the gun in the back. Then glanced at her. "It's unlocked. And warm."

She slid into his truck. Smelled new, the seats leather, and she pressed the button on the door to heat them up.

He got in, and her pulse moved to her throat, but he just glanced at her and smiled as he got in. "I'm Sloan, by the way."

Then he put the truck in reverse, kept his gaze on the display, and started to back up. "Can't turn around here. Need to head backward, to the nearest driveway."

They pulled into a plowed driveway, and she spotted a nice-looking cabin in the sideview mirror, heat pumping out of a chim-ney. A few more yards and she would have seen it too. Her hand nearly went to the door, but maybe they didn't have cell service either.

And he did turn around, heading toward town, hopefully.

"Seat belt," he said when the car dinged.

Right. She pulled hers on, finding Goldie's number in her memory. She'd call her, and Goldie would do the rest.

Including get ahold of Dawson.

He'd be so relieved. She hated thinking about what might have happened if—

The man pulled over. "We can get service here." Opening his console box, he pulled out a phone. Looked like a burner phone, which felt weird for a man with such nice wheels, but . . .

"I need to make a call first, okay?"

She nodded. Looked away. *Hey, Goldie, sorry for the radio silence. Funny thing happened—I was in a plane crash and then spent a blizzard—*

"Hey. Yeah, I have her."

She stiffened. Looked at the man, her heart caught. *What—?*

"I know. Do better."

She reached for the door handle, but his hand clamped on her throat, tight. She hit his arm with her fist, and his grip loosened.

It didn't touch his voice.

"Listen, I'll make the call. And then we end this."

She fought her seat belt. It unsnapped.

He grabbed at her, but she slammed her unmittened hand into his jaw.

Self-defense class skills, *bam.*

His head jerked back, and she barreled out the door. His hand grabbed her jacket, but she ripped away and slammed the door on his hand.

Or, almost.

She took off. *Run for the house. Run for the—*

Feet crunched in the snow, and she made the mistake of looking back.

Sloan was closing in, too fast, and as she turned back around, he grabbed the back of her snowsuit.

Jerked hard. She slipped in her rubbery Sorels and landed on the ground. He rolled her over, jumped on her, pinning her arms. "Where do you think you're going, Bliss? You have family to meet."

Then, just like that, he hit her.

And the world went black.

14

"DO NOT TELL ME to calm down. Again." Dawson met Moose's gaze, and his cousin held up one hand. Backed away.

Dawson walked over to the map of the area, his hands folded together behind his neck, stretching, trying not to punch something.

The morning sun lit the conference room of the Copper Mountain sheriff's office, sliding over the maps and statements and photos of the crash and anything they could grab hold of.

Keely had simply disappeared off the planet.

"All right, everyone, just grab some coffee. It's been a long night, and we're tired."

Dawson shot Sheriff Deke Starr a look as the sheriff slid off the long table.

He wasn't tired.

He was furious. And no amount of pacing seemed to quell the terrible roil inside.

"We'll find her," Moose said, handing him a cup of black coffee.

Beside him, Caspian sat up, whined.

"I know, buddy. You probably need to go out." He took the coffee from Moose. "Just let me wake up a second, then we'll take a walk."

"Might do you good to air out your brain." This from Moose's brother, Axel, fellow Air One Rescue tech. He'd gone with Moose to pick up Wren, who was now at the clinic in Copper Mountain with her father.

Axel and Moose had met Dawson at the FBO when Dodge dropped him off, well after midnight.

They'd driven him to their parents'—his aunt and uncle's—home, despite his protestations.

They did stop over at the sheriff's office, and the deputy on duty said Deke had put out a BOLO to all the highway patrols but couldn't do anything until morning.

Dawson had left a message to the tune that morning might be too late. But given different shoes, a different situation, he might have told a distraught family member to do the same.

Especially without any leads.

So, Dawson had spent the night on his uncle's den sofa, staring at the ceiling, hating that evil always found a way to win.

Now, he looked at Axel, who leaned against a table in the conference room. "I should have known that it wasn't Moose on the call. I felt it in my gut—"

"C'mon, Daws. Your gut isn't infallible." Axel leaned up. "I'm going to get Flynn from the Gold Nugget Inn. She said that Kennedy is being released today, so she's on board to help with the investigation."

He'd heard the story from Moose, about how Sully had gotten Kennedy out on a snowmobile, all the way to the highway, where a state patrol had met them. How she'd nearly died in his arms. So he understood if Flynn wanted to hang around her sister—

Axel might have read his mind because he clamped a hand on Dawson's shoulder. "Trust me. She's antsy after sitting in the hospital for nearly a week. She's all in. We'll find Keely."

He stepped back then and offered a smile. "Although seriously,

Bliss? You do know her last boyfriend was Chase Sterling, the actor."

He stared at him, and Keely's story needled in. Wait. Chase Sterling wasn't the father of her baby, was he?

It didn't matter. "Go get my partner."

Axel headed out the door and brushed by Dodge, on his way in. Dodge carried a bag of donuts from the Last Frontier Bakery and set the greasy bag on a table. "Fresh cinnamon rolls from your aunt. On the house."

Dawson walked over, looked in the bag, but had no appetite.

"So, how's it going? Any leads?" Dodge stood with his hands in his leather jacket pockets. Dark hair, grim slash to his mouth, he'd taken over Sky King Ranch bush services when his father started going blind. Tragedy, although in the suffering, Dodge had also reconnected with his ex-girlfriend, Echo, and remade his life.

It also brought his other brothers home for a face-off with the past, not an easy reunion after a decade of silence. But Dawson had been there for the Great Fight that had decimated the family, so yeah, he got that.

He might walk away too, if he got betrayed like Dodge had been.

Now the man stared at the map littered with tiny pushpins. "What are these pins?"

"All the sightings of a Sorros brother over the past seven years." Dawson grabbed his mug and stepped up beside him, the coffee dark and brutal, fortifying his bones.

"These are old mining camps." Dodge pointed to a couple out west. "And this one was an abandoned Army communications building."

"Apparently, they know this area as well as we do."

"They have to know we'd look for them at their old haunts."

Moose came back in with Deke, who walked straight to the bag. "Cinnamon rolls. Your mom is a gift to the universe, Moose."

Flynn chose then to arrive with Axel. She walked right over to Dawson, her copper hair tied back in a bun, and pulled him into an embrace.

"Don't fight it. Just breathe, boss."

He managed one arm around her and a smile when she pulled away. "Axel briefed me in the truck." She unzipped her jacket. "I'm going to need coffee."

Shasta Starr, who worked reception at the sheriff's office, came in and handed her a cup. "I just poured it. I'll get another."

Flynn held it in two hands, breathed in the smell. "Had breakfast with Nora, but there's just something about police station coffee." She winked at Dawson.

And weirdly, the clench in his chest released, just a little.

"Okay. And you're sure it's the Sorros brothers after her?" She turned to study the map.

"No. But the puzzle pieces make sense. Keely said that a man named Thornwood was after Wilder. Who got on that plane to go to Anchorage enroute to testify against Conan."

"We got a report a while back about Conan," Deke said. "He was in Goose Creek until they transferred him last month. Escaped during transfer. Been at large since." Deke took a bite of his roll. Made a noise of appreciation. "The US Marshals were tracking him in Anchorage, so we didn't suspect he'd be back here, although we did have a BOLO out. Maybe that's why they asked Wilder to get on a plane—to make sure they could keep him safe."

"Do you think he knew Conan was out?"

"I don't know," Deke replied. "You'd think they would have told him that before he got on the plane, but maybe they thought he'd spook and go into hiding."

Not a terrible idea. "And Mars?" Dawson asked. "What's his last known location?"

"He went off the map last summer, after a big bust of a local militia camp. We had him on a BOLO list." He pointed to a picture of both the brothers on the wall.

Dawson walked over to it, along with Flynn.

"Mars is real pretty," she said, sipping her coffee. "A forehead tattoo. What is that, a star?"

"I think it's barbed wire." Dawson pointed to the other picture. "Echo said that scar on Conan's cheek is from a fight with Jago when he was a kid."

"Sounds like a fantastic family." She turned to him. "You know them?"

"Not really. I went to school with them as a kid."

Flynn stared at him, frowned, then turned back to the map on the wall. "They still live here?"

"I don't know," Dawson said. "I've spent most of the last decade in Anchorage."

Dodge had found himself a donut. "They moved away with their mom before high school. But I saw them in the summers with their dad, and I remember a particular fight Jericho Bowie had with one of them the summer after our senior year."

Dawson took a sip of coffee. "I remember that fight. I just didn't remember it was with the Sorros brothers." He met eyes with Deke, who also nodded.

"What about their dad, Brand?" Flynn asked. "He still around?"

"No," Deke said. "He went to prison a few years ago after a drug bust."

"He still there?"

Silence.

"Someone check on that," Flynn said.

"Where'd they live?"

Dodge studied the map, then pointed to an area north of Copper Mountain. "I think in this area."

"Their old house is not far from the Boy Scout camp I attended," Dawson said. "Just over the river."

"Anyone check the place?" Flynn took a sip of her coffee.

"It was sold," Deke said. "A number of years ago."

"To who?"

Deke finished his cinnamon roll. "Idaho."

Dawson looked at him. "The poacher who was arrested a few years ago?"

"Mmhmm."

"He's not allowed back in Alaska," Dodge said.

"So, it's been sitting vacant for a few years?" Flynn glanced at Moose. "It's worth a flyover, to see if there's been any activity."

He nodded. "I'll head out to the FBO."

"I'll go with you," Dawson said.

Caspian, however, whined again, this time from the door. Aw. "I need to take him for a walk."

"Listen," Moose said. "Even if I see something, the forest there is too dense for me to land. I'll keep in touch. You be ready to deploy."

Dawson nodded, then whistled to Caspian. He should have a leash, but he'd lost it long ago. Still, Caspian fell into stride with him. Dawson picked up his parka as he hit the door and headed outside.

The wind swirled off the river, past Starlight Pizza, now closed, and Bowie Mountain Gear, all the way down to the bakery and the Midnight Sun Saloon.

Dawson shoved his hands into his pockets, the sky clearing, finally, blue and pristine. The chill captured his breath in small puffs. Caspian sniffed and then set out in a jog down the street. Found the right place between buildings—good dog—and emerged a few minutes later. He'd have to walk him out of town a bit because he'd forgotten a cleanup bag.

He headed down the street, the smells of the early smoke from the ribs in the Midnight Sun's smoker haunting the breeze. Vic started them early, to smoke all day and emerge dripping and juicy by dinnertime.

God, please let Vic meet her daughter. Maybe Keely didn't want to see her, but . . .

It couldn't end this way. His throat tightened, even as Caspian spotted someone and barked, as if alerting.

Vic. She stood in her parka and a pair of mukluks, on the stoop of the building, staring out into the sky.

Even from here, he spotted darkness in her expression.

He caught Caspian's collar. "Hey, Vic."

She seemed to see him then, drew in a breath. "Dawson."

And he couldn't . . . well . . . even with the team inside the sheriff's office, maybe his idea from last night wasn't terrible . . .

Vic blew on her hands. A simple gesture, but they seemed to be shaking.

"Vic, are you all right?"

Her jaw tightened and she met Dawson's eyes. Swallowed.

And again, his gut—and shoot, it was time to *listen.* "Is there something . . . I mean . . . are you in trouble?"

Caspian picked that moment to wrench out of his grip, jog over to her, sit, and whine. He put a paw up, as if to greet her.

She looked at him. "Reminds me of a dog I had who was trained to help soldiers dealing with stress."

He glanced at Caspian and suddenly, oh wow. Yes. "Like PTSD?"

"Yeah. He belonged to a friend who died, so I took him. But they're trained to notice elevated heart rates and sweating and agitated behaviors. They'll nuzzle their handler to distract them, lean on them, or put a paw on them, or even sit on their feet to calm them. Alert to panic moments. Sometimes even lead them to a different place."

He looked at Caspian. "Like wake a guy up if he's having a bad dream?"

"Mm-hmm."

"Maybe sit with their back to their handler?"

"It's called watching their six. And they'll often clear a room ahead of their handler, come back, and give the all clear."

She crouched, rubbed Caspian. "Usually, the dogs are specifically trained for their handler, but their skills are embedded, so . . ."

Caspian pushed his muzzle into her shoulder.

"Vic, are you . . . stressed out?"

She said nothing. And shoot—but he knew. Just like that, he *knew.* "Did you . . ." Aw. "Do you know someone named Keely?"

She glanced up at him.

Caspian licked her face.

"Wait. Do you know what *happened* to Keely?" He couldn't move.

Vic looked at the dog. "Still got it, huh?" She sighed and stood up. "Yes, and yes."

He stared at her. Silence rose between them. He cocked his head. "And?"

"And if I tell the police, they'll kill her." She met his gaze, something steely in it.

"Okay, so, let's say I'm not the police. I'm just a guy who cares very, very much for her."

One eyebrow went up.

"We met a few days ago," Dawson said. "And she is . . . smart and beautiful and amazing and—"

"Dawson Mulligan, are you falling for my daughter?"

The breath swept out of him. He glanced at Caspian. Now might be a good time for the dog to show up with a little stress relief. But, oh well. "Maybe, yes."

Vic sighed again. "I should have told her that I knew who she was when she came into the Sun the day before the blizzard. She just sat in the booth and didn't touch her food, and I was . . . I was such a *coward.* I just stood there, behind the bar, watching her suffer. Wondering if she'd talk to me. Thinking I should talk to her. I finally screwed up the courage just as she was leaving. But it was too late, I think."

"It's not too late," he said softly. "She'd really like to meet you." Vic's eyes misted.

"But she's in trouble— The Sorros brothers have her, and—"

"I know." She held up her phone. "Sloan Sorros just called me. If I don't . . . If I don't bring them Luna Frost, then they're going to kill Keely."

A beat. "Who is Luna Frost?"

"Wilder Frost's seven-year-old daughter. Whom I'm keeping under my protection while he goes to Juneau and testifies against Conan Sorros."

His mouth opened.

"So, I get to choose between keeping a promise and losing the daughter I love all over again."

He nodded. "Do you know where they are?"

"No. But my guess is somewhere around here, because they told me that if I delivered Luna, then they'd exchange her for Keely."

"Somewhere around here."

"When people want redemption, they go home."

And there it was. "I know where they are." He knelt and put his hands into Caspian's fur. "Did you know I'm an Eagle Scout, Vic?"

She frowned. "No."

"Yeah, well, when we make promises, we keep them." He lifted his gaze to hers. "So, will you trust me?"

AND NOW SOMEONE else was going to die because of her.

Keely sat on the grimy kitchen floor, her wrists zip-tied behind her, trying to unsnarl the conversation she'd heard before being hit.

Her face burned, bruised and swollen, and it felt like her entire head had exploded—*pow*. She'd been out of it long enough for Sloan to have shoved her into the back seat of his pickup truck, bound her hands and feet, and carted her like a sack of potatoes back to the Thornwood slash Sorros lair.

Where they now waited for her, the scent of beer heavy in their rancid breaths, dark eyes peeling away any fragment of courage that remained in her body.

Sloan had carried her on his shoulder and dumped her on the floor of the kitchen, where he'd then berated them for her escape.

There might have been some shouting.

Oh God, please get me out of here. Because what other help did she have?

Sloan had told them not to screw it up—whatever that meant —and left.

So now, Thornwood sat on a green-patterned sofa, a pump-action shotgun over his knees, his gaze on her, holding a walkie. The other Sorroses had gone outside.

Her stomach growled. The sky a crisp blue outside, the sun fighting to pour into the grimy windows of the house.

"Always know your exits."

Her father's voice had been sitting in her head pretty solidly since her failed escape. *"Eyes open, ears open."*

She'd already scoured the room for exits. Front door, yes, but also a side door in the kitchen that led out the back toward the half-frozen river cresting along the rear of the property.

Between her and Thornwood stood a round table, a couple wooden chairs, and she'd spotted a poker by the stove near a stack of fresh-cut firewood.

The stove sent out enough heat now to turn the place warm, nearly hot, or maybe that came from her own adrenaline. Still, she had a plan.

Get out of the zip ties—her father had taught her that much.

Then grab the poker, head out the back, and if she needed to, run for the river.

Or better, grab the keys on the table and make for the truck.

Preferably before whomever Sloan had called showed up to die. Because of her.

Please let it not be Dawson. Because she had no doubt he'd show up, hands in the air, sacrificing his life for hers, and . . .

She couldn't watch someone else she loved die.

The thought swept her up, heat coursing through her. And maybe it felt too early for love, but—and call her crazy—she'd spent the last two hours wondering what a new life might look like. Here in Alaska, or anywhere.

Most of all, with Dawson.

She never wanted a song to be real more in her life.

Maybe that's what this trip to Alaska had really been about—finding the parts of herself that she'd silenced.

A crackle on the walkie, then a voice. "She's on her way."

She?

Thornwood got up, walked over to Keely, and looked down at her. "You're not a big deal. You try to escape, you do anything to mess this up, and I'll kill you." His gaze bored down into hers.

She looked away.

He made a noise, then headed out the front door.

"Stay calm, think fast."

Right. She wiggled her hands down under her backside, to the front, shot a look at the door, and brought her hands down hard and fast, breaking the ties.

Then she leaned back, put her hands between her knees, then jerked them apart.

Her ankle ties snapped.

She rolled to her feet, grabbed the poker, turned, and slammed open the back door. *Sort of* slammed it open because snow blocked it, but she managed to squeeze through the opening.

And then she was in the snow, up over her knees, the depth slowing her down, but she took off.

Except, a vehicle pulled up in the driveway, its tires crunching on snow and—shoot. *Who?*

She ducked down, under the windows of the kitchen, and moved toward the front of the house.

A late model Ford 150, green and dented in places, with a white racing stripe down the side. It tugged a memory inside her. But she couldn't place it.

She crouched along the edge of the building, watching as Thornwood walked away from the house, his shotgun pointed at the truck.

The door opened.

No—what—?

Vic Dalton emerged, her short blond hair pulled back in a tight knot, wearing a thick flannel jacket, jeans and boots, *exactly* how Keely imagined her. Tough. Brave.

Unyielding.

What was she doing *here?*

Vic walked around the truck, hands up. "No one needs to get hurt."

"Did you bring her?" Thornwood shouted.

Bring who?

"No. But she's close. I want to see Keely."

The words stilled her. *What did she say?*

"The Frost kid first."

Vic shook her head.

What on earth—

Crunching in the snow sounded behind Keely, and she rounded fast, the poker up.

The man caught it on her downward swing. He wore a stocking cap and outdoor gear, but she'd recognize those blue eyes anywhere— "Dawson?"

"Sorry I took so long."

She had nothing as his arm went around her neck, pulling her to himself. For a second, she clung to him. *Dawson. Oh!*

Don't cry, don't cry!

"Let's get you out of here!"

She glanced past him, spotted another person crouched in the woods, holding a rifle. "Where did you come from?"

"Boy Scout camp." He winked. "Listen. Run for Flynn. She'll get you to safety."

"What are you going to do?"

"I'm going to make sure your mother doesn't die." He moved her behind him and took her position at the corner of the house.

Vic was still arguing with Thornwood, who had raised his rifle.

"He's going to kill her!"

"He won't," Dawson whispered. "He needs Luna."

Who?

Dawson turned back. "Run!"

But her legs wouldn't work. Not when—

And that's when she spotted the other brother. He'd parked himself in the barn, in a window overlooking the compound.

"Sniper! In the barn."

Dawson stood, holding his handgun. "I said run!"

A shot fired, and snow chipped up near Vic's feet.

She didn't move. No, no—this *wasn't* happening.

Another shot, and she screamed. "No—!"

Vic's gaze landed on her a second before another shot.

Vic jerked, falling back against her truck, then crumbled onto the ground.

And then the world simply exploded.

Maybe Dawson sensed her movement, because he reached out for her, but Keely jerked away and ran around the house, screaming.

Dawson shouted from behind her, and she only got a few steps before he tackled her from behind.

She landed in the snow, face-first, as gunshots littered the air. A motor fired up, and she fought Dawson's grip on her to see the battered red truck peeling out of the driveway.

More shots from the sniper in the barn, but Dawson rolled off her. "Stay down!" He gave her a look that should pin her to the ground.

Indeed, it sent a tremor through her, but more fury than fear.

What was Vic doing here? She shot a look at the woman, un-moving in the snow, and everything curdled inside her.

Dawson told her. Nothing else made sense—the man had be-trayed her secret to Vic, which had ignited some inner cop gene, maybe, and—

Shots fired from the woods, and she spotted a man in a sher-iff's uniform emerge from the forest by the driveway, a couple more uniforms from the other side.

They had the place surrounded.

Dawson got up and grabbed Vic by the back of her jacket and pulled her away, behind the truck. Keely ran over to her.

Vic's eyes remained closed, her breathing slight. But Keely didn't see blood—

"Get down!" The woman from the woods advanced on the house. Copper hair, white parka, she held a handgun, her eye on the shooter as she crouched where Keely had been.

Then everything went quiet.

The shooter in the barn ducked away, and for a long moment, Keely didn't breathe.

Then Dawson got up, motioned to the sheriff, and they closed in on the barn.

What were they— *Oh, Dawson, don't die, don't—*

The barn exploded. An inferno of heat and flame that made Dawson hit the snow. She ducked too, the furnace blistering.

Dawson!

But when she looked up, he was running toward her, something ferocious in his gaze.

And then Vic groaned. Keely looked down even as Vic's eyes opened.

Vic put a hand to her chest, made a throat-clearing sound, and pushed up on one arm.

What—?

No blood in the snow. Vic had unzipped her jacket, pulled it apart.

Vest. The woman wore a Kevlar vest.

"Vic! You okay?" Dawson landed in the snow next to her, on his knees.

"Wow, that hurt." She winced as she breathed in. "Did you get him?"

Dawson glanced at the fire now consuming the barn. "Dunno. Maybe one of the bullets hit a propane tank."

Then he looked at Keely. "You okay?"

She just blinked at him, her breaths coming fast. And yes, maybe she should be throwing herself into his arms but— "You told Vic."

He frowned. "What—"

"How could you tell her? How could you bring her into this—oh my gosh, Dawson, you knew how . . . you knew I didn't . . ."

"Keely—stop, it's not like that." This from Vic, who reached out to her.

She rounded on the woman. "Really? What, are you saying you already knew?"

Vic's mouth opened, and then she looked away.

And Keely gasped. Wait—*what?*

And then the redhead came over and crouched in front of Vic. "Let's take a look at that bruise. There's a med kit in the cruiser."

Vic sighed and got up, followed the redhead.

Keely shook her head. Wow. So, not the reunion she'd expected.

"Calm down, Keely," Dawson said softly.

"Don't tell me to calm down!" She rounded on him, and for a second, possessed a vision of a different ending. One where she took a breath and threw herself at him, holding on.

But, no— "The last thing I am going to do is calm down. I've been kidnapped, shot at, chased, hit in the face." She indicated her still throbbing, probably reddened wound.

He winced, his jaw tightening. "Keely. Vic already knew who you were. They called *her.* I just confirmed it—"

"So you convinced her to what—act as bait? To save my life? Have you lost your mind?"

He blinked at her. Glanced at Vic.

And she knew she'd hit it on the head.

"You put her in danger to save me." She shook her head, held up her hands. "Wow. So I could watch another mother die in front of my eyes. Perfect."

"Keely. Stop being so dramatic."

His final word was a blade, landing inside. She stiffened, narrowed her eyes. "Have you not met me, Dawson? Dramatic is who I am. Have you not met Bliss?"

"No, I haven't. I've met Keely Williams." He stepped up to her. "Bliss is just the disguise for the real Keely Williams, the one who is scared to show her true self."

"Because when I do, someone betrays me."

A beat, and his mouth opened. "I was trying to *save* you."

"Yeah, well, I don't need a hero, Dawson. And you need to stop always trying to save the day. You just end up getting yourself—and people around you—hurt."

He flinched then, and yes, she should stop talking, but anger felt like her only protection. So she stepped back, her voice shaking. "Why don't you call a press conference, tell the *rest of my secrets.*"

She could have slapped him with less effect. What looked like pain flashed in his eyes, and he shook his head.

As if she might be a child throwing a temper tantrum.

She pushed the thought away. "I should have never told you."

"C'mon, Keely, let me take you home." He reached out for her.

She backed away. "Not this time."

His hand dropped, and he sighed. "Be sure to stop by the clinic to get that wound looked at before you head out of town."

He turned away.

And that was it. The true ending of her love song.

She practically fled for the local sheriff.

He bundled her up in his SUV, a deputy on watch, and she refused to look at Dawson, her heart hammering as he talked with the sheriff.

Dramatic.

She looked out the window, her eyes burning. Then she turned to the deputy. "Could you please drive me back to Copper Mountain? I need to make a call."

And only then did she realize that her voice emerged just above a whisper, destroyed. She closed her eyes and leaned back against the seat.

And let herself weep.

15

DAWSON NEEDED to get Keely and her stupid words to him out of his head before he got someone hurt. Because everything inside him had started to whir, and yes, he got it.

He had PTS. And maybe a temporary gig, but still . . .

Even his dog had figured it out. He put a hand to his chest, did a little deep breathing, trying to quell the chaos inside.

She was safe. That was all that mattered.

Really. Send her home, safe and sound, keep his promise.

"We're going to need to let the barn burn itself out," Deke said, standing back from the flames, watching as the barn caved in on itself. Black smoke darkened the air, ash and cinder falling on the snow, melting it. Deke was right.

They'd have to wait until it burned to the ground before they could root around for a body.

Unless . . . and that was just the thing—Dawson couldn't help the feeling that the barn didn't explode by accident.

A Sorros brother haunted the woods. He could nearly feel the man's gaze on him now from the snowy forest, laughing.

Winning.

A voice came over Deke's radio—Dodge, in his chopper, still

scouting the area for a fugitive. "I'm at Bingo. Returning to Copper Mountain."

Deke glanced at Dawson. "You want to hop a ride?"

He frowned.

"Dude, you spent the last twelve hours unraveling over this woman, and you're going to just let her get away? I'm not a detective, but even I can see that doesn't add up."

"We're not done here," Dawson said.

"You're limping. And we need a statement from her, if you need an excuse."

"Yeah, well, I don't need a hero, Dawson."

"She made her intentions pretty clear. And my knee is fine. I'm going to walk a perimeter around the barn, see if I can find tracks."

Deke glanced at him, then pulled out a walkie and handed it to him. "Don't get dead. I'm going to check on what my guys are finding in the house."

He took the walkie. "Any update from Vic?"

"No. But she's made of leather. She'll be fine." He headed toward the house, and Dawson didn't disagree.

Flynn had left with her over an hour ago, and shortly after, Keely peeled out of his life. Maybe he should have gone with them—his knee *did* ache. But the sting of Keely's words kept him from getting in the car and giving in to the temptation of running after her.

Mostly because she was right. He had wanted to be a hero. Had totally seen her leaping into his arms and holding on.

She had, in fact, for a moment there.

The fire turned the snow soggy and hard around the blaze, now dying as the barn walls collapsed in on each other. He headed into the snowy banks around the structure, breaking through the surface of the glistening layer, now littered with char and ash. The air stank of burned oil and wood, rubber from whatever they'd kept in here.

Reminded him of the fire at the community. Clearly an MO.

Dawson reached the back of the barn, where it sat near the forest. Here, the tall birch stood blackened, but not burning. He looked for footprints, but fallen logs and animals marred any sign.

Maybe the shooter really had died in the fire.

Still, his senses buzzed, something not quite—

Movement in his periphery. He turned, scouted the forest. Nothing—so maybe the wind had moved a branch.

Or he could be stalked by a moose.

He stood, quiet for a long moment, then kept searching. Worked his way around the barn and stood at the edge of the forest. In the distance, he made out the faint hush of the river, half frozen, running along the back of the property. Overhead, the smoke had turned the sky hazy.

Deke's voice came through the walkie. "Anything?"

Dawson keyed his mic. "Nothing. I think—"

Movement again, this time in the forest near the river and—

A shot. The bullet hit a tree, scrubbed off bark, and he turned.

There. Some sixty feet away, through the cluttered woods—a man in a grimy canvas coat, bearded, a hat—holding a pump-action shotgun.

Yeah, well he was armed too, thank you, Deke. Dawson shoved the walkie onto his belt and ducked behind a tree, then looked and managed to pull off a shot toward the shooter, now running through the woods.

Dawson got up, ignored his limp, kept his eye on him, and followed. He picked up the radio. "I got him—he's headed to the river—"

Then he pocketed it, and slapped away a branch, ducking as Sorros looked back.

Another shot—wide.

Dawson waited, looked—no shot, but he spotted the man breaking through to the river.

He took off, fighting his own grunts as he stumbled through

the snowy forest. Sorros had vanished—if he got over the river to the forest beyond, they'd lose him.

Bursting out to the shoreline, Dawson stopped, searched downstream. The river ran dark and swift in the middle, the shoreline crusted with snow, ice embedding boulders that sat in the river like stepping stones.

No Sorros.

Dawson scanned the opposite shore, his breath sharp in his lungs. He reached for his radio—

Boots crunched in the snow, and he turned just in time to get a hand up to block the clubbing blow.

Clearly the man had run out of bullets.

Dawson caught the gun, but the hit threw him off-balance, and he staggered.

The river roared, as if hungry, the waves white-capped as Dawson spun, stepped out to catch himself.

His foot caught in a rock, wedged, and he jerked around, freeing it just as Sorros tackled him. Knee in his back, hand behind his head.

"Dawson!" Deke's voice crackled through the radio. "Where are you?"

As Sorros shoved Dawson's face into the snow, Dawson plunged his hand into the icy slush at the river's edge, and he got his grip on a rock. Slammed it back.

A grunt, and bingo—Sorros's grip loosened.

Dawson rolled, backhanded the man.

Sorros barely grunted, but blood dripped from a gash on his face. Dawson grabbed his jacket and knifed the front of his neck with the side of his hand.

The man gasped, his trachea bruised. He gripped his neck, rolled off, airless, like a fish.

Dawson got up—and his knee buckled. He pitched forward, his knee on fire.

Get up. Get up—

He caught himself with his hands, but Sorros's boot exploded into his ribs. He shouted, the blow sending him onto his back.

Sorros was scrambling up, and Dawson struggled to his feet.

Not fast enough. Sorros slammed his foot into Dawson's bad leg, and it was over. Dawson shouted, the pain eclipsing him, and he crumpled, half landing in the water.

The icy water shook him, and he looked up then to see Sorros standing over him. He'd grabbed a rock—maybe the same one Dawson had used to hit him. Blood dripped from his chin, and Sorros licked his lips, then spat at Dawson.

"She's next," he said and lifted his arm.

Dawson grabbed the man's ankle and yanked. Sorros jerked, just a little off-balance, but it was enough for Dawson to dodge the blow, for Sorros to land on one knee in the river.

Dawson launched himself onto him, still woozy with pain. He scrabbled onto the man's back, put him in a sleeper hold, even as they crashed into the water.

Sorros fought him, an elbow to his face, a fist to his ribs. Still Dawson held on, the water turning him numb.

Darkness didn't win today.

Sorros managed to turn, get a fist in his nose, and Dawson tasted blood. But the momentum of the blow landed Dawson on the man's chest.

Dawson roared, dripping blood, and grabbed the man's throat.

He shoved him down into the frigid water.

"Daws!"

Nope.

"Dawson!"

Sorros slammed another fist into his head, and Dawson barely felt it, his adrenaline hot, his body shaking.

But Sorros grabbed a rock, even as he thrashed, and this time—

Everything blinked black, just for a second, and when it cleared Dawson lay in the water and Sorros was running down the shoreline.

His gun. He needed his gun—but the cool water turned his body to lead. He pushed up, growling—his head spinning, pulsing with heat.

A blur of movement out of the corner of his eye—Deke and a couple of his deputies running hard down the shoreline.

Deke's linebacker build barreled into Sorros, taking him down with a thud over the river's roar.

Sorros shouted, but the deputies descended on him.

Dawson clawed for the shore, trying to pull himself up, but his leg didn't want to work. He lay like a beached trout, gasping.

Nice. Just perfect.

"Dawson!"

The voice was female, and he spotted Flynn running out of the forest, holding her gun, breathing hard. She ran over to him, holstered her weapon, and grabbed his jacket. "What in Sam Hill are you doing?"

He stared at her. "I dunno! Taking a dip?"

She parked her retort behind a grim slash of her mouth and dragged him onto shore. Grabbed her scarf off her neck. "You're bleeding."

Really? He couldn't feel it, but when she shoved her scarf against his nose, he flinched.

Okay, so yes, Sorros might have broken something.

"When did you get back?" he asked.

"Apparently just in time. Can you walk?" She got behind him, as he held his nose, and put her hands around his shoulders and started to lift him.

Pain shafted through him, and he nearly opened his mouth like a baby and let out a shout. But he clamped it shut and managed to let only a deep moan escape. Then, "Just give me a minute."

Down shore, Deke's deputies were cuffing Sorros. Deke crunched his way back up shore to him.

"What took you so long?" Dawson managed, his voice rough, his breath still catching in his chest.

"Just having breakfast. What were you thinking, running after him without backup?"

Yeah, story of his life. "Wrong place, wrong time."

Deke smiled. "Right. Good job." He held out a hand to help Dawson up.

Shoot, but he couldn't take it. He grimaced. "I'm going to need more than that."

Deke raised an eyebrow but glanced at Flynn, and then he got on one side, and Flynn the other, and Dawson got his good leg under him.

And now he was an invalid again as they dragged him to Flynn's SUV.

"Get him to the ER in Copper Mountain," Deke said to Flynn. Then to Dawson, "We'll take care of Conan."

Conan. Which meant Mars, tattoo-face, was the one still at large.

Keely wasn't safe until Dawson found him.

He put his leg down, trying to walk on his own, and stumbled.

"Stop," Flynn said. "Sheesh."

"Mars is still out there."

"Yeah." They reached the SUV, and Flynn opened her back door, like he might be a child. "There's a BOLO out. He won't get far."

The darkness of it all settled in his chest.

Barking made him lift his head. "Is that Caspian?"

"I know you left him with Shasta, but when I stopped by the sheriff's office, he was losing his mind. I had to bring him back with me."

Someone had attached a lead to his collar, and now the dog jumped out, circling him, the lead on the ground.

Flynn picked it up as Deke helped him into the back of the car, and he slid in, his leg on the seat. Flynn opened the back, and Caspian jumped in but shoved his face over the seats.

"Hey, buddy." Dawson rubbed the dog, still holding the bloody scarf to his face. But it seemed the bleeding had slowed. Now his face just throbbed.

He closed his eyes, pain shutting him down, and he lay back, his arm over his eyes.

And of course, Caspian scrambled right over the seats and lay smack on top of him, a blanket of comfort.

He put his hand on the animal's head.

Flynn got in. "You okay?"

Not even a little.

Flynn started up the SUV. "Oh goody, the dark funk is back."

His jaw tightened, and he said nothing.

Maybe it had never really left. Because clearly there was no light left to fight it.

OUTWARDLY, she would survive.

Keely hopped off the exam table in the ER of the Copper Mountain medical clinic as the male intern handed her a cold pack.

"Just keep icing your face, twenty minutes at a time, for the next twenty-four hours. It's a deep bruise, but it should stop swelling in twenty-four hours. Then, wait a day and get some heat on it. It'll increase blood flow to the injury and break up the bruise." He paused. "I loved your last album."

Oh. She gave him a quick smile. "Thanks." Her voice emerged scratchy and broken, and she cleared her throat, but that only stuck burrs in it.

"Your voice should clear up too. You just need to rest and drink plenty of fluids."

She had a list of home remedies, but frankly, maybe her voice was never coming back. Still, she nodded and smiled, then took the ice pack and headed out to the lobby.

No press, but no Dawson either, and stupid her, she had sort of thought . . .

"Stop being so dramatic." Truth, because maybe she did live in fairy-tale land. Which might be worse than a Hallmark movie, because there were no villains in Hallmark world.

Except her.

She'd hurt him, and she knew it, and frankly, she didn't deserve a guy like Dawson Mulligan. *"Why don't you call a press conference, tell the rest of my secrets."*

She couldn't *believe* she'd said that. Sheesh—yep, dramatic.

Outside, the day arched bold and bright, the snow glistening in piles around the medical clinic parking lot. The scent of coffee wound through the lobby and roused a beast inside her. But she needed a phone first, get Goldie to wire her some money.

Arrange a nice safe car to drive her to Anchorage.

A map of the area hung on the lobby wall in a frame, and she walked over to it, staring at it, gauging the distance from here to the Gold Nugget Inn. Maybe Nora and Hal might grant her a phone call, a shower.

"Keely?"

The voice made her turn, and she startled as Donald Cooper emerged from the coffee shop at the edge of the lobby, holding a cup in his hand. He appeared better than the last time she'd seen him, distraught, wounded, desperate—

"Donald."

Oh, her voice barely sounded. She cleared it and then held up her hand in greeting.

"Still fighting that cold, huh?" He pointed to his throat, then smiled.

Yes, definitely in better spirits. She nodded, shrugged. "How's Wren?" she whispered.

He leaned close, as if to hear. "She's better. They had to do a splenectomy." He swallowed, the memory of it flickering on his face, then he sighed. "She's upstairs if you want to see her."

She nodded and stuck her hands in her parka hanging loosely over her. Probably she should return it to Donald anyway.

He walked over to the elevator and punched the button. "Moose got to us just in time. The storm came in after him, and if you'd waited any longer, she might have—" He closed his eyes, blew out a breath, then opened them. "Anyway, thank you."

She nodded, but wanted to say that it was Dawson, really.

Dawson the hero. Saving everyone's lives.

Her eyes burned.

She got onto the elevator behind Donald, took it up one flight, and got off, trailing down the hall behind him.

He went into a room with a colored picture of a unicorn taped to the door, and she followed.

Wren sat in the bed, her blond hair a disaster of knots, wearing a pony-imprinted hospital gown, an IV attached to her arm, a congregation of toys tucked around the bed—a Barbie doll, a plastic pony with purple hair, a stuffed bear. Crayons spilled into a kidney tray, and she furiously colored a picture on the bed table.

Keely's heart just turned over, a rush of relief, maybe.

"Look who's here, Wren," her father said.

She looked up. "Keely!"

Then, she winced, whimpered.

Donald sank into the chair by her bed. "Your stomach still hurt?"

Her face twisted. "And sometimes I feel like I'm going to throw up."

He picked up an empty kidney tray on her bed. "Aim for this."

Wren made a face, then picked up a crayon and offered it to Keely. "You want to color with me?"

Keely walked over, surveyed the picture. A princess with blond hair and a bright pink dress. She took the crayon, a teal, and pointed at the shoes.

Keely sat down and started adding in the blue.

"I missed you."

"Missed you too." Shoot, she hated the quiet of her voice. Still, maybe that's exactly what Wren needed. Quiet. Calm.

Maybe they both did.

Wow, she missed the community. She looked at Donald. "Everyone okay after the fire?"

He'd leaned in to hear her, then nodded. "We closed in the back half of the barn and got the livestock back inside. When I left, Griffin was posting guards."

She glanced at Wren, then back to Donald. "No need. The, um, trouble, followed us."

His eyes widened. "Are you okay?"

"Yeah." Not even a little, but that was partly her fault, wasn't it?

"Are you coming home with us?" Wren dropped her crayon into the tray and grabbed a purple one.

Keely glanced at Wren. Shook her head. "I have to . . ."

"Sing?" Wren smiled. "I like it when you sing."

She shrugged. Maybe.

"My mommy used to sing to us. And tell us stories." She looked up at her. "Are you a mommy?"

"Wren!"

Keely held up her hand to Donald, looked at Wren, and then, for some reason, nodded.

"I thought so," Wren said, dropping the purple crayon back into the tray. She picked up the picture. "This is for you."

"Thank you," she whispered, and her eyes burned again.

A nurse came into the room, a stethoscope around her neck. "How's Princess Wren this morning?" She walked over to the IV bag. "Thirsty, I see."

"My tummy still hurts," Wren said, and made a face of pain.

"Could be the stitches."

Keely got up to let the nurse in on her side. Caught the name on her badge. Alicia.

The woman clipped a pulse oximeter to Wren's pointer finger, then affixed the stethoscope to her ears to listen to her chest.

Keely should go, probably. She folded her arms over her, glanced at Donald.

The nurse moved the stethoscope lower, frowned.

Donald sat up.

"Honey, have you gone to the bathroom since you had surgery?" She wound the stethoscope over her neck and lightly touched Wren's abdomen.

The little girl howled.

Okay, yes, Keely should leave.

"What's wrong with her?" Donald clutched Wren's leg.

"Let me call the doctor." She smiled down at Wren. "Would you like something to eat?"

"I'm not hungry," Wren said, tears squeezing out of her eyes.

"Okay. I'm going to set up her blood pressure, and then I'll call the doctor."

Donald took his daughter's hand. The nurse set up the blood pressure cuff, then stepped out of the room.

Silence followed, just the sounds of the cuff tightening and Wren's hiccups. And Keely just wanted to weep.

"Are you a mommy?"

"I should go," she said quietly.

Donald met her eyes. "Thank you."

She leaned down to Wren, wiped a tear off her cheek. "Be brave, Wren." She kissed her forehead.

Wren nodded. "Don't forget your picture."

Keely found a smile from parts unknown and took the picture. Held it to her heart.

The nurse and a female doctor passed by her as she headed down the hallway, down the back stairs, and then outside.

The wind wasn't brutal, the smell of pine fresh in the air. She folded the picture, then zipped up, pulled up her hood, and headed toward the Gold Nugget Inn.

Please, God, keep Wren alive.

Funny, she'd been doing a lot more praying lately.

The town lay buried, locals still digging out. A snowplow worked Main Street, shoving snow along the edges, while another pushed the edges down the road, toward a park. Someone had shoveled a path along the building fronts, and she followed it, crossing the street so she didn't have to pass the Midnight Sun.

Because . . . yeah.

Vic *knew.*

And Keely didn't know what to make of Dawson's words, now pounding in her head. She probably needed to add ice to her face, maybe her heart.

"Vic already knew who you were!"

Already knew. Since when? When she arrived at the Midnight Sun? When she'd confronted her before Keely left and said *nothing*? Clearly intending to let Keely walk out of her life without saying a word?

So much for wanting to see if Vic had any regrets. Clearly not.

She headed down a block. Snow piled along the cleared walkway and porch to the inn. *Please let Nora have a phone—*

"Keely."

The door opened even before she finished climbing the porch. Nora stood in her apron, shaking her head. "I heard about the crash, and I've been worried sick." She reached out and pulled her into an embrace.

And Keely couldn't move. Just . . . *what?*

"Listen, I have fresh bread and jam waiting, and a lovely venison stew on the stove."

Keely wanted to weep. "Can I borrow a phone?"

"Of course." They went into the house and Nora shut the door behind her. "Oh, honey. Your poor voice. You must have worn it out in all the trauma."

Something like that.

"Hang up your parka and boots by the door. And by the way, Moose Mulligan retrieved your suitcase and belongings. Hal brought them to your room."

Her room?

"Here's your phone. I took the liberty of charging it."

She stared at the phone, the gold bling case, the cracked window, the picture of her and her mom on the lock screen.

"Maybe run yourself a bath. I'll get you that bread and jam, and bring it up. Along with cocoa, huh?" She winked.

Keely stared at her. And then, oh no . . . "You know."

Nora frowned. "Know what?"

"Know about . . ." She unlocked her phone and swiped it open. A picture of herself as Bliss, the one from the cover of *Vogue,* filled the screen. "Bliss."

Nora looked at it, frowned, cast her gaze back to her. "I don't know who that is."

Oh.

"Get yourself upstairs." She headed for the kitchen.

Keely stood a moment, then *okay.* Headed upstairs to the cozy room where she'd stayed what felt like a millennia ago.

Her carry-on, slightly dented but cleaned, sat on the bed. She ran her hand over it, then headed to the adjoining bathroom and ran water into the claw-foot tub.

She started to call Goldie, then hung up and texted instead. No need to freak her out.

> Hey. Just checking in. Big blizzard here—no cell service. But I'm ready to leave. Can you hire me a car and have it pick me up in Copper Mountain?

She set the phone down and headed back to the tub to test the water.

That's what she needed. A hot bath, something to forget the past five—or six, whatever—days and get back to her life.

A knock at the door, and she got up, her stomach already churning. She couldn't remember the last time she ate.

She opened the door.

Stilled. *What—?*

Vic stood at the door, holding her tray of bread, jam, and hot cocoa, like a surreal maid service.

"Can we talk?" she said quietly. "Because it's time you heard the entire story."

16

"**YOU SURE** you don't want me to go in with you?"

Flynn turned into the parking lot of the Copper Mountain clinic.

"Just drive me up to the entrance," Dawson said. The last thing he needed was Flynn seeing him lose it, but the pain in his knee had bled into his brain, taken over.

He might not even make it to the snowbank.

She pulled up to the ER entrance. Glanced back at him, then at Caspian, who'd ridden the entire way with his head on Dawson's chest as he lay in the back seat.

"He's so sweet," Flynn said as she put the car in park. "Shasta said that he sat at her feet the entire time, until I showed up. Then he escaped out of the building, sniffing my car. Clearly he loves you."

He glanced down to see Caspian looking at him, worry in his big brown eyes. "I thought he just liked me because I rescued him."

"Please. This dog is obsessed with you. What does he have to do to prove it?"

Funny, despite the grasp of pain, a warmth swelled inside him. Maybe it was just that easy. Show up and never give up.

"Should I keep Caspian?" Flynn asked. The plows were out cleaning the hospital parking lot, the snowbanks nearly over his head.

Dawson only debated a second. "He's a service animal. Let him out."

Probably it had nothing to do with the fact that the dog, in fact, seemed to keep his world from completely spinning off its axis.

Caspian got up, and as Flynn opened the door, bounded out.

Flynn headed inside as Dawson eased himself out of the seat, holding on to the door.

Caspian did his scouting circle, returned, and sat next to Dawson, whined as Dawson grimaced.

"What you said, buddy."

Flynn emerged from inside the ER with a wheelchair. Oh, this was fun.

But he eased himself into it. "I got it from here."

She cocked her head.

"Go to the sheriff's office and get yourself into that interrogation. Find out if Conan knows where Mars is."

"You got it, boss. But call if you need a ride. Moose is headed back to Anchorage later today."

Maybe he should be on that plane.

"Go catch bad guys," he said to Flynn, then rolled himself through the automatic doors, Caspian at his side.

A nurse met him at the entrance. A woman in her mid-forties. "No dogs, sir."

"He's a service dog. My service dog."

"He isn't wearing a vest."

"And I'm not wearing my badge. But I can promise you we're both legit."

She looked him over. "He needs a lead, at the least."

He reached for his belt, pulled it off, and wrapped it around Caspian's collar. "I'm blaming you if I lose my trousers."

The nurse rolled her eyes. "Let's get you into the ER."

He lay on the table, trying not to wince. Or call out for pain meds. And, of course, it didn't help that Keely's words kept playing through his head. He had to find her before she left town. The sense of it ground into him, his bones. Yeah, she'd given him a stiff arm, clearly angry about Vic—and maybe she had a right to be.

"Why don't you call a press conference, tell the rest of my secrets."

Ouch. But if he looked past that, he could see her fears behind the persona. Maybe he had been blind to what he might be getting into with her.

But maybe that blindness—the blizzard, the circumstances— had been the only way to really know her.

And for her to know him, past the dark funk, as Flynn called it.

An hour later, ice wrapped around his knee, plenty of prodding from the intern, he had an MRI scheduled down in Anchorage, had traded out the wheelchair for a pair of crutches, and might be a little less edgy with the flow of painkillers in his system.

Such a hero. But at least he wasn't curled into a ball.

"You have someone picking you up?" This from the intern, who'd taken off his gloves and was petting Caspian, whose tail swished on the floor.

Hopefully. "Actually, I'm looking for a woman who stopped by here. About five foot four, blond hair, really pretty."

The intern grinned. "Yeah, she was here. A couple hours ago, maybe. She wasn't admitted."

He sighed. "She left?"

"I saw her go upstairs. But didn't see her leave."

Upstairs? He frowned, then nodded and headed for the elevator.

It opened onto the second-floor lobby. A woman with copper hair, long and flowing, who wore a pair of leggings and an oversized hand-knit sweater, sat in a wheelchair, holding a couple of parkas in her lap.

Kennedy Bowie, Flynn's sister.

Sully stood behind her, leaning on the push handles, his mouth pinched. He wore a wool cap, his hair falling out of it in the back, and a good week's growth of beard.

The image of the bloody cabin flashed through Dawson's brain as he maneuvered out of the elevator. "Hey."

"Hey," Sully said. He stepped up to catch the door, but it closed on him, so he shrugged and held out his hand to Dawson. "You okay?"

"Yeah. I, uh . . ." He glanced at Kennedy. She seemed pale and wan, and his heart bled out for her. "I'm sorry about your loss."

Caspian came up to her and put his head on her lap. Kennedy jerked, then ran her hand over his head. She looked up, offered a smile that didn't touch her eyes. "Thanks."

His chest hurt. He turned to Sully. "We were at the outpost. Keely, uh, cleaned everything up."

A beat.

Then Sully nodded, followed by a frown. "Are those my jeans?"

Oh, right. "Yeah. And socks. And I really like this flannel shirt—"

"I got it at Bowie Mountain Gear. It's a Pendleton."

Another beat. "Right. I'll get it back to you."

Sully laughed, not quite clear of pain, but he put a hand on Dawson's shoulder. "Just messin' with you, bro. It looks good on you."

Kennedy took Sully's other hand. "Thank you for . . . for . . ." She cleared her throat. "Thank you for cleaning up." Her eyes filled.

"It was Keely, really. She also fixed your ham radio."

"Wow. Skills," Sully said. "She seems . . . different than when we found her."

Dawson gave a wry smile. "She is."

"Tell her thanks," Sully said. The elevator opened again, and he moved around behind Kennedy to push her in. Dawson held the door.

"You haven't seen her up here, have you? The intern said she came upstairs."

Sully turned Kennedy around inside the elevator. "Nope. Sorry, man. But Donald and Wren Cooper are here, from the community. I think they're transporting Wren down to Anchorage."

Dawson frowned but let the door go, then crutched over to the nurse's station. "I'm looking for Wren Cooper's room?"

The nurse looked familiar, but he couldn't place her. "Down the hall, third door to the right. They're waiting for the chopper to get here."

"What's going on?"

"You'll have to talk to Donald." She gave him a smile.

Right. He headed down the hall and nearly bumped into a gurney emerging from the room. Wren lay on a transport board, belted in, under a blanket, on oxygen, a nurse carrying an IV bag.

Caspian whined and pressed against Dawson's leg. "I know, buddy."

Donald came out behind them, clearly fraying, his expression drawn. He startled at Dawson, then held out his hand. "I already talked to Keely, but I should thank you too. If you hadn't been there . . ."

Dawson met it. So this was where Keely had gone. "What's going on?"

"Wren's got an obstructed bowel, from the splenectomy. Emergency flight to Anchorage." He followed the gurney down the hall. Dawson crutched next to him.

"That's rough."

"Yeah." He dropped his voice, glanced at Dawson. "We don't have insurance."

Oh.

Donald's mouth tightened, and he shook his head. "It doesn't matter. They just need to save her life." His eyes brimmed, and he looked away, blinked hard. Took a breath. Then he turned back. "You just never know when . . ." He ran his hand behind his neck. "I can't lose her."

Dawson nodded. Next to him, Caspian jerked forward. The belt slipped through his grip.

Wren wiggled free of her bonds and dropped her hand through the gurney rails. Caspian ran up, licked Wren's hand as they waited for the elevator.

"She loves that dog," Donald said. He turned to Dawson. "Pray for us."

The elevator doors opened, and he should have guessed that London Brooks and Boo Fox from Air One Rescue might be the transport team. They came out, wearing their red rescue jumpsuits. Boo glanced at him, the crutches, frowned. "You okay?"

"Twisted my stupid knee."

Boo grimaced, as if sympathetic. "You want a ride back to Anchorage?"

He almost said yes, but . . . something made him shake his head.

Regret, maybe. Or hope?

Boo nodded, then leaned down to address Wren. They wheeled her into the elevator.

Donald followed, and Dawson grabbed the belt, holding back Caspian before the dog could join them too.

Caspian sat, whining as the elevator went to the bottom.

"You just never know when . . ."

When life would find you at the wrong place, the wrong time.

And he was just so done with it. Done with darkness winning.

Not today. Not on his watch.

The feeling in his gut solidified, took form. *"Under the aurora's glow, can we dare to dream so far?"*

Yes, maybe they could. He could.

He found the stairwell, Caspian on his heels.

He hadn't forgotten how to use the stairs with crutches and got down them faster than he'd imagined possible. Down with the bad—

He reached the landing and pushed his way out of the building, dropping Caspian's lead.

The team was still wheeling Wren to the helipad out in the lot. No wonder the plows had been out. They'd cleared a space for the red Bell 429 chopper with Air One Rescue imprinted on the side.

Caspian ran ahead, barking—good dog.

"Donald!" No chopper wash yet, and Donald turned. Waited for him to catch up. Sweat ran down Dawson's back.

"Do you know where she went?"

Donald raised an eyebrow.

"Keely. Where did she go?"

"Oh." He glanced at his daughter, the team, then back to Dawson. "She mentioned wanting to call someone to get a ride back to Anchorage. I think she was going home, man. Sorry—"

Home.

The word punched him. But of course she was.

Donald turned and caught up to his daughter. Shep and Boo were loading her into the chopper as London did her preflight check. Shep waved, grinning.

"I'm not giving him back!" Dawson yelled, not sure why, as Caspian sat next to him.

He stood there as they closed the door. Then he dropped a hand on Caspian, who leaned against him, and backed away as the chopper fired up and took off. He watched it go.

Maybe he should have gone with them.

And just like that, it was over. The sky clear, the storms gone.

The chase, the fear, the danger—
Hope.

And again, he was left standing, a little in pain, just him and his dog.

"OF COURSE I knew who you were."

Vic sat at a table in the Starlight Pizza, sharing a Twilight special with Keely—pepperoni and mushroom, green peppers, and a mozzarella-filled crust.

Genes apparently included pizza topping preferences.

Thankfully, Keely hadn't hurt Nora's feelings when she turned down the venison stew. She seemed to understand Vic's need to talk someplace private.

Private clearly meant a table next to the window in the pizza joint. Still, they sat in the corner, the place not crowded, the alluring scents of baking bread and tomato sauce sneaking from a kitchen busy with take-out orders.

Their spot in the corner overlooked the town, and Keely kept glancing out the window, searching for a glimpse of Caspian, or maybe Dawson.

A fist closed around her heart at the idea of leaving town without saying goodbye.

Or . . . maybe . . . what if? Because her stupid words stuck inside her like paste. *"I don't need a hero, Dawson. And you need to stop always trying to save the day."*

Um, she *very much* needed a hero. And if he stopped trying to save the day, she might be dead in a frozen creek bed, or even shot in the head at a cabin, and she wasn't being even a little dramatic.

But Vic's words had her attention too. She set down her slice of pizza. "You did?"

"Of course I did. Your dad and mom sent me pictures of you growing up. They knew what it cost me to give you away, and they were . . . well, your mom was sympathetic. She couldn't have kids—"

"I know."

"Maybe that gave her grace. Anyway, I've been following you and your career for years." She stirred her Coke with a straw. "I might have even downloaded a few of your albums. And caught the Grammys."

"You saw the glitter suit."

Vic laughed. "You have more courage than me."

She didn't know about that. "It took plenty of courage to give me up, right?" She didn't quite mean it as a question, but . . .

"Everything I had." Vic leaned forward, pushed her plate away. "You should know that your dad and I loved each other. And, by the way, we were married. So, there was no . . . well, no affair. Although, we did have to keep it secret, so that the chief wouldn't split us up."

"He was your partner."

"In every way. I was wildly in love with him, but we were also a team. Undercover together for five years, working in the gangs department. He'd gone in before me, so when he brought me in, it was as his girlfriend." She lifted a shoulder. "After a while, we didn't have to pretend."

It almost sounded romantic.

"We were trying to get out—we'd gotten wind of a big drug shipment coming in and told the DEA agents. They came in too early, blew Max's cover, and the gang killed him."

A story flashed through her eyes, and she looked away.

Keely didn't want to know the details. "And you ran."

"I did. I went into hiding until the trial, and by then, it was clear I was pregnant. I was terrified that someone would find us, and I knew I couldn't run with a newborn, so . . ." She met Keely's eyes. "I reached out to his brother. He was a cop in Minneapolis. His wife, Anne, was . . . she was amazing. Kind and sweet and really wanted a child, and I knew that Jimmy would do everything in his power to protect you. So yes. I fled to Minnesota, gave birth, signed the adoption papers, and vanished. For years, I got my mail at a PO box in Anchorage. When I heard that the gang leader, Razor, had died, I ditched the box. Maybe I thought you'd find me one day . . ." She offered a smile.

"Dad gave me Mom's journal when she died. She'd written down the address for the old PO box, and I hired a PI to finish the trail."

Vic sat back. "Why didn't you say something in the Midnight Sun that day?"

"Why didn't you?"

A slow smile. "You would have made a good cop."

Keely smiled back. "Sorry. That's . . . my dad. He always said—never answer a question."

Vic laughed, a deep chuckle. Funny, Keely always thought she got her voice from her birth mother, but Vic possessed a gravelly, low tone. Sort of like how Keely had sounded when she sang at the community.

"I wanted to give you the space you needed," Vic said quietly. "I didn't know why you showed up, but I didn't want to spook you. I suppose I did anyway. If I had known you were getting on a plane, I probably would have chased you down."

Keely looked away, out to the street, her throat tight.

An SUV pulled up to the sheriff's office, and her breath caught when a man—cuffed and angry—was wrestled from the back seat. "They caught him. Or at least one of them."

Vic turned, craning her neck to see down the street. "Good job, Deke."

Keely kept her gaze pinned, watching.

Dawson didn't emerge from the car, nor was he in the second SUV that pulled up.

Oh.

"You looking for Dawson?"

She glanced at Vic. "Um. No."

Vic raised an eyebrow. "I know when someone is lying, Keely."

She sat back. Drew in a breath. "Maybe."

"He seemed pretty concerned about you. Did you know that he hiked in nearly a mile through the snow to get into position? I had a feeling that he wasn't going to let anything happen to you." She cocked her head. "I think he's in love with you."

And now her eyes burned too. "It's . . . it's . . . ." She met Vic's gaze. "You know my life. It's impossible."

"I know the life you had. And I hear your voice today, and . . ." She leaned forward. "I believe everything happens for a reason."

Keely didn't flinch. "Even your husband dying and you having to give me away?"

A beat. Vic didn't move. Then, "Yes. As hard as it was, yes." She leaned back. "I've had a good life here. Quiet. Friendly. Sure, it's not the life I'd planned, but I knew you were safe, so . . . yeah. I'm at peace."

"So, you'd do it again?"

"Do what?"

"Give me up." She met her gaze.

Vic drew in a long breath. "Wow."

"I just . . ." Keely shook her head. "I didn't come here just to . . . meet you, Vic." Her mouth tightened. "I need to know. If you had to do it all again, would you give me away?" She couldn't look at her, closed her eyes.

"Keely," Vic said softly, in that low voice. "Is that what you think I did—gave you away?"

She opened her eyes. Nodded.

"I never gave you away. There wasn't a day that I didn't think about you. Wasn't a day that I didn't pray God was watching over you. Wasn't a day that you weren't stuck, dead center, in my heart. I might not have been present to raise you, but I can guarantee you that I never gave you away. I held on to loving you. But I also let go to allow you to live the life I couldn't give you."

Now Vic's eyes turned glossy, and she shook her head. "Sheesh. I have a reputation to keep." She wiped her cheek, fast, hard. But then smiled at Keely. "I don't think any mother can truly erase her child out of her heart."

Keely nodded.

"But that's the brutality of it. Because it doesn't mean we don't have to make terrible, hard, painful decisions for the good of that child. So, would I do it again? If it meant you turned into the beautiful, smart, caring, successful woman I see before me? You betcha."

Keely also wiped a hand across her cheek.

Vic considered her a moment. "Why was that answer so important that you had to hop a plane and travel four thousand miles?"

Oh.

And right then, the door to Starlight Pizza opened, a bell jangling.

Vic looked up. "Flynn."

Keely turned. The redhead from the cabin. The cop who knew Dawson.

"Hey, Vic. How are you?" Flynn glanced at Keely. "And you—you okay?" She pointed to Keely's cheek. "That's a doozy."

Keely nodded. "Yeah. I'm okay."

Vic wore something of a smirk.

Fine. "Um . . . did Dawson . . . um . . . ."

Flynn drew herself up, her mouth a little tight, maybe even protective. "He was injured taking down the suspect."

Keely gasped.

"He's going to be fine. Hurt his knee." She crossed her arms. "Last I knew, he was going to hitch a ride with Moose to Anchorage."

Right.

Flynn sighed then, loosened her stance. "We do need you to stop by the station and give a statement, when you have the chance."

Keely nodded.

Flynn glanced at Vic. "Axel wants me to bring home some ribs."

"Swing by the Sun, I'll get a box made up for you. On the house."

Flynn looked back at Keely. "Your *Heartstrings and High Notes* album was my favorite." She offered a tight smile, then walked away.

Huh.

"I liked that one too." Vic.

"It was an early one. I wrote all my own music on that one."

"Mm-hmm." Vic leaned forward. "Seemed to me you lost a little heart after that."

She met Vic's gaze. "I had a baby that I gave up for adoption."

Maybe Keely should have softened it, but she had to get it out, just in case she lost her courage.

Vic breathed out, then nodded. "I see."

"It was a mistake. My dad got remarried, and I was . . . he was . . . anyway, it was a dark time, and I ended up dating—"

"Chase Sterling." Vic shook her head, leaning back. "I never liked him."

And she sounded so much like . . . like a *mom*, that it just reached in and balmed all the raw, broken edges. "Yeah."

"Shallow, sort of a jerk."

"Completely. And when he found out I didn't have an abortion, he was mad."

"I'll bet." Vic's eyes narrowed. "Did your father know?"

"No. He never knew."

Questions hung in Vic's eyes.

"It's a long story, but he is . . . not in my life."

"Oh, Keely, your mom would be heartbroken to know that." She sighed. "Poor Jimmy."

Keely frowned at her.

"To miss out on knowing the woman you've become."

The words could take out her heart. "Really?"

"Keely." Vic gave her a soft look. "Of course."

She nodded. "Funny, but . . . when I was at the cabin, I kept . . . I kept hearing his voice. The things he taught me. Like, 'Stay alert, stay alive.'"

Vic nodded, chuckling. "Yeah. Max said that too."

"And . . . I should have probably listened to this one—'Trust your instincts. If something feels off, it probably is.'"

"Yeah. Also a Maxism. Jimmy did good."

Keely nodded. "He did his best, I think." It felt weirdly freeing to say that.

"People make terrible choices when they're hurt. Or afraid." Vic looked up, her eyes wide. "But my giving you to Anne and Jimmy wasn't that. That was thought out, not rash."

Keely held up her hand. "I get it. I struggled for nine months about what to do. I ended up giving Zoey away to a husband and wife who also couldn't have biological children. It was . . ."

"Heart-wrenching." Vic made a fist on the table, her mouth a grim line.

"Yeah."

"And every day you think about her."

Keely met her eyes. "Yeah."

Vic smiled.

Yeah.

"So, why did you need an answer to your question?" Vic asked.

"Zoey's parents were in a terrible car accident a few months ago, and . . . well, her mom died. And her dad is a quadriplegic."

"Poor kid. She's what—four?"

So Vic *had* been paying attention. "Yeah. And Bryce—the dad—wants me to take her back."

Vic's brow creased.

"They don't have relatives who can take her. So while he's in therapy—and it could be years—she'd be in foster care . . ."

"I see."

"But there's . . . Bliss."

"Bliss." Vic nodded. "Oh, Bliss." She cocked her head. "Bliss can't have a child?"

Keely lifted a shoulder. "I don't think there's room for both Bliss and Zoey in my life."

"You're creative, Keely. Figure it out."

Oh.

"You came here to ask me a question, hoping the answer would give you peace about your own answer."

A nod.

Vic cut her voice low. "The problem is that my answer is not your answer. Here's what I know, daughter. God moves in mysterious ways. Unpredictable. Uncontrollable. But nothing happens in our lives that isn't designed to give us the opportunity to know his love more."

Huh. Sounded like something River had said.

"And we don't know him more without risking our heart. And doing the hard thing. For me, it was letting someone else raise my daughter. For you . . ." She gave her a grim smile.

So that didn't help at all.

The over-the-door bell rang, and she looked out onto the street to see Flynn carrying a boxed pizza, her copper hair bright in the sunshine.

The woman had been a little peeved at her. But maybe Keely was just as peeved with herself.

> Could this be our forever, could we make this last?
> Or is this just a beautiful moment that will soon be past?

She blinked away the deep sluice of regret.

"So, what are you going to do?" Vic said, cutting through her what-ifs.

Keely shrugged. "I don't know. My voice is . . . it might never recover."

"You don't have to have a perfect voice to make a beautiful song, Keely."

Keely stared at her, hearing her mother's words. How . . .

Maybe it didn't matter. The truth was . . . they were both right.

Her cell phone buzzed, a text coming in. She flipped over her phone and opened it. From Goldie.

> Keely! I wondered if you'd gotten socked in with the storm and lost service. No can do on the driver, but I sent the jet to Anchorage. Get home.

> Bryce Harper passed away.

Oh. *Oh* . . . Keely pressed her hand to her mouth.

"What's the matter?"

She set the phone down. "Zoey's dad died."

Vic frowned, just a little, something of empathy in it. Then she reached out and caught Keely's hand. "Then we'd better get you to the airport and on a flight home."

She had the terrible feeling that home was what she might be leaving.

DAWSON SHOULD have gotten on the chopper with the rest of the injured.

But, no, he had to look like an idiot, hobbling his way along the snowy road toward the sheriff's office, his crutches landing on ice, the cold wind in his ears.

He'd call Flynn, but his phone had died, so that was perfect.

So much for finding Keely, making things right. By now, she was probably in Anchorage, getting ready to hop a flight and never look back. He didn't blame her, really. But his chest ached, and not just from the strain of working his crutches.

A honk behind him made him jump, and he turned, ready to shout—*I'm walking here!*

Or hobbling. Whatever. Caspian perched in front of him, clearly with the same thought.

Except Dawson's breath blew out as the vehicle pulled to the curb. An old yellow 1988 Suburban with a roof rack and, from personal memory, a bench seat with a tweed cover. The once-bright paint had died to a faded butter, and he guessed there must be nearly five hundred thousand miles on the odometer. But his father was never good at letting go.

What was Clay Mulligan doing here?

The driver's door opened, and although Dawson hadn't seen him in a year, maybe more, the man seemed to have barely aged. Still strong, robust, tan lines from hours outdoors, and thick brown hair with lines of gray that only deepened his blue eyes. He wore a red-and-black checked heavy flannel shirt, a padded vest, a hat, and jeans over scuffed work boots.

"Dad?"

"Hey, son. I saw Moose at the house. He said you'd hurt your knee in some go-round with a local."

Aw. Of course, news traveled like wildfire in Copper Mountain. Or Deke had called Moose, maybe. But the last thing Dawson needed was his dad thinking he had problems. He was just fine, thank you.

"Said you might need a ride from the hospital. We swung by, but they said you'd left. Figured I'd see you hoofing it on your own." He smiled, winked.

But Dawson's heart had stalled on *We*, then hiccupped as the passenger door opened. And yes, he knew she was in town, but . . .

It'd been three years since he'd last seen his mother, and then . . . then she'd been broken and angry, and he couldn't bear to listen to her pain. Or watch the damage she was doing to herself to escape it.

Now, his mom looked . . . healthy. She'd lost weight, and her blue eyes seemed brighter. She wore her blond hair back in a braid and a thick, creamy white cable-knit sweater hung to her thighs over a pair of leggings and mukluks.

"Mom."

Her smile touched her eyes as she came over to him.

Caspian offered a small warning, but Dawson touched his head. "It's okay."

Maybe very okay.

She glanced at the dog, then stepped up and wrapped her arms around him. "I missed you."

He hesitated just a second, then put his arm around her, smelled cinnamon on her skin. Probably a remnant of hanging out with Moose's mom. "Hi." He let her go. "You okay?"

"I am." She touched his cheek with her mitten. "It took a while, but I realized I was tired of living my life angry. I had a choice. Stay in the darkness or look for the light." She looked at his father. "Time for all of us to start living again."

Dawson couldn't move, just stared at her.

His mother bent to pet Caspian, as if she hadn't just dropped a bomb into the middle of his soul. "Who's this?"

His comfort dog?

"Just a guy who needed a home." His voice emerged roughened.

"Always the hero," his dad said, still smiling.

And he didn't know why he couldn't just play along, but the words landed in a hard place, acrid and salty. "Yeah, well, it doesn't matter, does it—you can do everything right and—"

"And the world still explodes around you," his mother said softly. "Your sister's death was nobody's fault, Dawson. Not mine, not your dad's, and not yours."

And it all just . . . raked up and spilled out. "She was *murdered*, Mom. It was somebody's fault." He didn't know why the fury suddenly boiled inside him, raw and fresh and—

"I get it." His mom held up her mitten as if to stop his flow of words. "For years, I lived in that fury. That injustice. And the truth is, terrible things happen. But we have a choice about how we want to let it all affect us. I chose . . . I chose to let it destroy me and our family." She looked at his dad, who'd come over, put his hand on her shoulder. "But the more I live in that pain, the less I live for today, and all I still have." She leaned into his dad. "Like your father."

He kissed her forehead.

Dawson just stared at them, rocked. What was going on here?

"And you, son." She took his hand. "I hope I still have you."

Oh no, he couldn't breathe, and shoot, his throat turned scratchy. What the—

Caspian, of course, leaned against his leg.

Yep, good dog. Because he might just be having a panic attack. *"Maybe there's stuff."*

He had to look away. What was his problem? He wasn't seventeen again, losing everything. He'd grown up, learned to live with the ache.

Maybe his father read his mind because he put his hand on Dawson's shoulder. "We've been in counseling for a while now. Apart. Together. And we've learned that even in darkness, God is trustworthy. He does not abandon us to the screaming void of grief. He holds us, if we're"—he glanced at Dawson's mom—"and sometimes even if we're not—willing to hold him. Because he does love us."

The words settled, soft, like the snow dusting off the banks, and it hit him then.

His *stuff* wasn't anger. It wasn't grief. It wasn't even frustration. It was *rejection*. The sense that no matter what he did, he couldn't escape being always in the wrong place, the wrong time.

The wrong man.

Except, maybe he wasn't.

"If you hadn't been there."

His father met his eyes, holding them. "I know it's a little late now, but . . . we're sorry. Because you are the good that God gave us in that dark time. We should have seen it then. But we do see it now." He offered a smile, the kind he'd seen his grandfather wear. "We're very proud of you, son."

And weirdly, Griffin's voice returned to him.

"In the ebb and flow of the world, of the terrible and the good, maybe darkness doesn't win because God's goodness is still in the world, through his people. Through his providence. Even when it feels like the darkness is winning."

Then his dad pulled Dawson to himself.

"C'mon, son, it's time to go home."

And wouldn't you know it, he turned into a child and let himself be held, and finally, at long last, wept.

17

"I HAVEN'T BEEN this nervous since I sang at the inaugural ball of President White." Keely stood behind the sliding back door of a simple ranch house in a suburb of Tulsa, staring out into the greening, fenced backyard.

Four-year-old Zoey sat on a red tricycle in the grass.

"You'll be fine, Keely," Alicia Robbin said from behind Keely. Zoey's social worker had met her at the house.

Maybe a good thing, because Keely sort of wanted to turn around and run. But Marnie Schultz, Zoey's foster mom, gave her a warm smile. She stood beside Keely, arms folded, her smile gentle, her brown hair curly around her head. She wore a pink pullover, a pair of jeans, a pair of sneakers, a little muddy on the bottom. The picture of a mom, at least in Keely's head, including the worry in her eyes.

Yeah, well, maybe rightly so. Keely wore leggings, her white Prada Cloudbust sneakers, and a Versace gold puffer jacket, her blond hair back and covered with a black Dior baseball cap. Quintessential Bliss.

Yeah, clearly she hadn't thought this through.

Except, she had, really—spent the past three days pacing

her apartment, talking with Goldie, her lawyer, and Bryce's representative.

Bryce had written a request that his daughter go back to Keely, had it notarized and filed. So maybe he'd known her answer before Keely had.

On paper, and on the plane, and in her heart, it made sense. Right now, however . . .

"You don't have to have a perfect voice to make a beautiful song, Keely."

She didn't know why Vic—or maybe her mother—had decided to walk into her head with that, but she blamed Marnie, who leaned a shoulder against the doorframe and said, "Just love her. That's what she needs."

Right.

And wow, Zoey was cute in real life. Her blond hair longer than the last photo that she'd seen, but now French braided down the sides. She wore a pink jacket, flowered stretch pants, and cute yellow boots, now grimy with the spring mud, despite the grassy yard.

"What if I completely screw up her life?" Her voice still betrayed the damage she'd done to it in Alaska, although the pain had lessened.

Marnie gave a short laugh. "Oh, I have no doubt you'll make mistakes. We all do. But this isn't just about her. It's about you too. Being a mother is costly, and wonderful, and challenging, and amazing."

And words from Vic found her . . . *"Nothing happens . . . that isn't designed by God . . . to know his love more."*

Marnie's gaze landed on her. "You look so familiar to me. I don't know why. Have we met before?"

"Do you have teenage daughters?"

She shook her head.

Keely lifted a shoulder. "I'm a singer."

"Oh, that might be it. My husband loves country music."

"Yeah, me too."

"What do you sing?"

What did she sing? Maybe nothing, after the meeting with her laryngologist. *"Prolonged inflammation, scar tissue, permanent hoarseness . . ."*

"Oh, you know. Songs about love and life . . ."

"Are you a folk singer?"

The words stirred up the memory of her sounds from the kitchen at the community.

"Sort of. But I think I'm taking a break."

"Well, having a four-year-old can do that. But it's worth it. We're going to miss her. We've only had her for a couple months, but she's made her way into our hearts. I wish we could adopt her, but . . . well, clearly God was saving her for you."

The words caught her, filled her.

"You should know that she hasn't spoken since she came to us. I thought it might be the trauma of the accident, but . . ." She shrugged. "Sometimes it takes a while for a child to find their voice again after their life is so drastically altered."

Keely nodded. "I get that."

Outside, Zoey pushed the trike forward, only to have it fall over in the stiff grass. She landed on the grass, rolled off the bike. Started to cry.

"Oh," Marnie said and leaned up. Then she looked at Keely. "C'mon. This is where you step in."

"No, I . . ."

"If you're going to adopt her, she needs to start coming to you."

Right. But she stood frozen as Zoey started wailing, so Marnie headed out the door, took off at a fast clip, rounded the bike, and swooped Zoey up. "You're okay, sweetie." She held her a moment, then wiped her tears. "C'mon. Let's try that again."

Zoey clung to her a moment, her big blue eyes wide. Then she cast a look at Keely.

Keely's entire body seemed to convulse, and then—

Love. It simply poured through her, heat and fire and . . . peace. So much peace.

This . . . this was her song. Finally. Perfectly. And she hadn't realized her lack until the abundance poured into her bones, but . . .

This was abundance. God pouring out his love in the struggle.

"Hey, Zoey," Keely said, walking up, her voice soft. "My name is Keely. Can I help you ride your trike?"

Zoey looked back at Marnie, who nodded at her. "She's safe."

Safe.

And as Keely knelt next to Zoey, holding the trike for her as she climbed on, she heard, *"Stay safe, Keely."* Her father, standing at the door, before she left for college, watching her with something she couldn't place in his eyes.

Maybe it was love.

Zoey held the handlebars, and Keely bent low behind her. "Put your feet on the pedals. I'm going to push." The little girl looked up at her, eyes wide.

"I won't let you fall. I promise."

Zoey turned back and put her feet on the pedals.

"I promise."

Oh, Dawson. But she bit back the memory of his voice and pushed Zoey around the yard. The little girl finally put her feet on the bar and just hung on.

And laughed.

The sound trickled into the air, warm and sweet, like the smells of the springtime day. Maybe Keely could do this.

At least she could give it her very best.

They came to rest back at Marnie's feet, and Zoey got off the trike. Headed over to the slide attached to a small playset.

Keely followed her, stood at the bottom to catch her when she came down.

"I'll go pack her bag," Marnie said.

"Don't—"

Suddenly Zoey came sliding down the ramp. She flew out, faster than Keely anticipated.

Keely caught her, stumbling back with her weight.

They went down in the grass with an *umph.*

Zoey jerked in her arms, hard.

Wet grass soaked into Keely's leggings, and Zoey started to cry. Oh—oh! "Hey. Hey . . . it's all good. It's all . . ."

Zoey looked up, as if searching for Marnie.

Keely sort of wanted Marnie too.

"I won't let you fall. I promise."

She sat up. Set Zoey in her lap. "You're all right," she said softly. Zoey was still snuffling, her eyes wet.

And somehow, the song simply rose inside her, a hum, then the words, almost a whisper . . . "You're never alone, wherever you might be. Close your eyes and breathe, feel the warmth from me."

Zoey stared at her, captured, her snuffling slowing.

"That's pretty." Marnie, from behind her. Clearly she hadn't left.

"It's just a little thing I've been working on." She turned to Zoey. "Wanna try again?"

Zoey nodded. Oh, Keely liked her spunk.

She got up, climbed the ladder. Keely stood at the bottom, arms open.

Zoey kept her gaze on her, climbed on the slide, and then pushed off.

Keely caught her, grabbing her up, twirling around.

Zoey laughed.

Oh, she could live forever on that sound.

"Did you like that?"

Zoey nodded, then pushed to get down and ran back to the slide. She climbed up the ladder again, her gaze on Keely.

Grinning.

She turned to see if Marnie caught it, but the woman had left them alone in the yard.

Huh. But maybe they'd be okay.

Keely caught her daughter again, this time bracing herself, and then again, and finally Zoey ran for the house. Keely spotted Marnie standing at the open door.

"Do you two want lunch?" The worry in her eyes seemed to have vanished.

"I'll have to text the airfield and tell them we'll be late."

"We'll make it quick, then."

They came inside and Marnie had made grilled cheese sandwiches. Zoey climbed up on a stool that slid up to the Formica counter, but Marnie shooed her off to wash her hands.

Note to self. Wash hands.

Marnie poured Zoey a glass of milk. "She loves grilled cheese sandwiches and chicken nuggets, and she hates oatmeal."

"Me too."

Marnie raised an eyebrow. "Are you related to the family? Because . . . maybe Zoey is who you remind me of."

Huh. "Sort of. I'm a family friend."

"Oh, so like an aunt?"

"Maybe." Someday—maybe, hopefully—Mommy.

Zoey came running back, climbed again on the stool, and scooped up the sandwich.

Marnie walked over to a chair at the kitchen table. "She came with a backpack." She lifted the pack, a horse on the front, fringes on the side. "I bought her new clothes, and she spent Christmas with us, so she has a couple toys in this bag." She gestured to a large paper shopping bag. "Sorry, I wish she had more."

"I got this," Keely said.

She pulled up a stool next to Zoey and ate the grilled cheese sandwich Marnie had made.

"Yes, I believe you do," Marnie said, arms folded, a hip against the counter.

She glanced at Alicia, who nodded.

Keely had rented a car and purchased a car seat, and Alicia helped buckle Zoey into the back, handing her a small stuffed panda. "You're going to go with Keely. And she's going to take very good care of you." Marnie glanced over at Keely in the driver's seat.

Keely nodded. "I promise."

Then Marnie stepped in and kissed Zoey's forehead, closed the door, and backed up to stand in the driveway, hands around her waist. She didn't even bother to wipe her tears.

Keely pulled out and hadn't gotten to the end of the block before she spotted Zoey's lip quivering.

Oh no.

"Zoey. Do you . . . like music?"

Zoey clutched her panda, buried her face in it.

At the stop sign, Keely picked up her phone, connected the car to Bluetooth, and pulled up her playlist. Clicked on her *Heartstrings and High Notes* album, because why not?

She'd written many of the songs while pregnant with Zoey.

"Okay, kiddo. Let's sing."

The voice came over the speakers, so much beauty and fear and angst and hope, and as they headed to the airport, Keely sang along, her voice husky beneath the upbeat tone of the music.

> Heartstrings and high notes, let our music start,
> Play on the chords that bind unknown hearts.
> Reach out through the mystery where you and I might be,
> In this dance of life, let's find our harmony.

Zoey looked at her, still holding the animal. But she'd stopped crying.

Keely started in on the next verse as a text popped up on the screen. She waited until she stopped at a light, about to turn on 75 South, and opened it. Vic.

Just wanted to let you know that Wren took a turn. Her bowel perforated and she's septic.

So much for the singing.

Keely wanted to cry now too.

But she swiped the text away, merged into traffic . . . and kept singing.

Because that's what mothers did.

They'd cleared three songs by the time she pulled into the international airport. She headed to the private charter area, and a valet met her there. Her Dassault Falcon sat on the tarmac, fueled, its black nose painted over a white body. She waved to her pilot standing in the doorway.

She hauled Zoey out of the back seat, and the valet retrieved the car seat, carrying it up the stairs to the plane. Keely grabbed the backpack. "Zoey, have you ever been on a plane?"

Zoey shook her head.

"This will be fun, I promise."

But Zoey didn't move.

And Keely knelt, met her eyes. "Listen. I know you're scared. I am too. I don't know how to be a mommy. But I do know that I'm going to try my very best. So, let's not be scared together, okay?"

Zoey seemed to consider her for a moment, then nodded.

"Good. We're going to get on the plane and then we're going to a place called New York City."

Zoey's mouth tightened and Keely couldn't help but gather her in for a moment, the child's tiny body pressed against hers, molding there.

Another piece of Keely's heart clicking into place.

She let her go, and they climbed the stairs. The valet had clipped the car seat onto one of the creamy leather seats, and Keely helped Zoey into it.

"More music?"

Zoey nodded, and Keely sat down and opened up her phone.

The flight attendant closed the door. The pilot had already started his preflight check.

Another text. This from Goldie.

I got your new song. "Hear My Name."
Are you sure?

She glanced at Zoey, now looking out the window, and texted back.

Did you get the doctor's report I sent?

Yes. Maybe time would heal—

She considered Zoey.

Or maybe Bliss's time is done.

She hadn't really spoken it aloud, but the truth had been sitting inside her since her exam.

The cursor blinked. Three dots, then they disappeared.

Poor Goldie.

Keely pulled up her playlist and continued playing the album, listening, watching Zoey as she held her panda and stared out the window.

Poor Donald. Poor Wren.

Her phone buzzed.

Let's record it and drop it as a single.

She stared at the message, the cursor blinking. *"You're creative, Keely. Figure it out."*

She looked at Zoey, who had started to kick her seat, almost in beat with the pop music.

"We don't know him more without risking our heart. And doing the hard thing."

Okay, here went nothing.

She got up and walked to the cockpit door. Knocked on it.

The pilot opened it. "Ma'am?"

"What would it take to reroute us to Anchorage?"

AT LEAST HE COULD WALK. It wasn't pretty, but Dawson had ditched the crutches, and after an entire week, now walked into the Tooth wearing just his knee brace.

About 2400 milligrams of ibuprofen sluiced through his veins.

So, of course, Axel came in behind him, his chauffeur.

Caspian ran ahead and circled back, tail wagging. All clear. He bent and rubbed the dog behind his ears.

Flynn had gotten here first and now pulled a pizza from the oven. She set it on the stovetop. "So?" She took off her oven mitts. She still wore her badge around her neck.

Dawson shrugged out of his black puffer and hung it on a chair. "Torn ligaments but apparently they'll heal. What kind of pizza?"

"Hawaiian."

He rolled his eyes.

"Relax. I have a pepperoni in here too."

Axel walked over to her, gave her a kiss. "We stopped in to see Donald. Wren is still in a medically induced coma."

"It just goes from bad to worse," Dawson said, shaking his head.

Axel pulled out a stool and sat down.

Dawson already perched on a stool. He rubbed his thigh. "And Donald is a mess. Says the bills are crazy."

Flynn frowned.

"No insurance," Dawson said. "They'll cut him a rate, but still . . . we're probably talking hundreds of thousands of dollars."

She blew out a breath. "The important thing is that she lives."

"Yeah."

Caspian put his head on his thigh, of course, clearly sensing stress. He rubbed the dog's ear. "I'm okay, buddy. Just . . . hate talking to DAs. They always make me feel like I did something wrong."

Flynn cut the Hawaiian pizza and slid it onto a wooden board. "You're going to testify?"

"Yeah. I sat and gave a video testimony on Ravak's case, but I told them they could call me to the stand if they wanted. She said she was going to show the defense my testimony and offer another plea deal. Second-degree, with one count of kidnapping."

"That's fifteen to ninety-nine, for just the second-degree alone. He'll probably never see daylight again."

Dawson nodded, kept petting Caspian.

"Okay, what has you so wound up?" Flynn asked.

He paused.

She pointed at Caspian.

Oh.

"Caroline's parents called while he was getting the MRI," Axel said.

Dawson looked at Axel. "Thank you for that."

"I'm a detective. I would have figured it out," Flynn said. "Are you going to call them back?"

Dawson sighed and pulled out his phone. Looked at it. "Yes. But only because it's the right thing to do. I can't change the past. I can't bring her back. And I'm not to blame."

Silence. He looked up at them. "What?"

Flynn wore a smile, something kind. "Just . . . there's something different about you. What happened to the dark funk?"

He rubbed his knee. "I'm not doing any Irish jigs over here."

She threw an oven mitt at him.

He caught it. "Listen. I do need to tell you something."

Her smile fell. "Oh no. What? You're not coming back to the police department."

He stilled. "What? Do you think I shouldn't?"

"What—no. Of course I don't."

"Because you miss me."

"I . . . I mean, everybody misses you—"

"You're a little lost without me."

"I am not lost." She reached over and took back the thrown oven mitt. "I barely notice you're gone. I look around, oh, where's the guy who's supposed to bring me coffee?"

"I never brought you coffee."

"You did. Twice." She fitted on the oven mitt and retrieved the next pizza.

"You did, Daws. I was there." Axel glanced over at him, grinning.

He rolled his eyes.

She turned, still holding the pizza, set it on a cutting board, then looked at him. "Fine. Maybe I miss you a tiny bit. The kind that happens when you have the flu—you get to miss three days, but you're miserable the entire time."

"Oh, that hurt."

She grinned. "Pizza?"

"Fine. No, I'm not coming back—at least for now. Caspian and I are going to do a little service dog refresher course, and he's going to work at the hospital."

"Really. Caspian has a *job*?"

"Apparently, he's a PTSD dog. Or, at least, according to Vic, and I made some calls to Midnight Sun Service Dog Organization. They have refresher classes, and they'll train me to be a handler."

"Good. Because you need all the help you can get." She cut the pizza and dished a piece up for him. "Can he sense when you're being an idiot too?"

His mouth opened.

"It's been a week since Keely left, and you still haven't gone after her."

He blinked, and she held up a hand. "She's not my favorite after what she said to you at the cabin, but the fact is, you *do* have a hero complex, and you *do* always have to save the day, and maybe that is a little bit annoying."

He just stared at her.

"And yet still loveable," Axel said.

"Really?"

Axel shrugged, all grins.

Flynn rolled her eyes. "I'm just saying that I saw the woman in Starlight Pizza later that day, and she asked about you. Seemed a little broken up that you'd left Copper Mountain—"

"But I hadn't—"

"I know. But I thought you were getting a ride with Moose. I didn't realize you were going to have some sort of family re-union."

Neither did he.

But it did feel like something had changed in him after spending the weekend with his folks. Seeing them piecing back together their lives.

"*You are the good that God gave us in that dark time, son.*"

Sure, he felt like a kid again, but it did do a number on the dark funk.

"It doesn't matter," he said. "I talked to Vic, and she drove her to Anchorage. She's gone, back to her life." He looked at Caspian, who'd curled into sleep at his feet. "And we're back to ours."

Silence.

Too long.

He looked at Axel, who gave him a wry face.

"What?"

"Then maybe I shouldn't show you this." He reached into his jacket pocket and pulled out a folded piece of paper. "It was in the lobby of the hospital. I picked it up while I was waiting for you."

He slid it across the granite island, and Dawson opened it. His heart gave a hard hammer.

Keely—no, Bliss—in concert, for one night.

"It's a benefit?"

"For Wren. I tracked down Donald, and according to him, Keely stopped in a couple days ago to see them."

"She's in town?"

"Dunno. But the concert is tonight. In about three hours, if you're interested. It's just a local venue—I guess it's too last minute for it to be a big deal."

"The Frostbite Music Lounge is a big deal," Dawson said. "And it says here that tickets are . . . seriously. Five hundred dollars *each*?"

"She hasn't had a concert in over a year."

"She can't sing!"

Flynn's eyes widened. "What?"

"Her voice—I mean, yes, she can sing. I heard her sing. It was beautiful. But not . . . it wasn't the Grammys." Aw. *Keely, what are you doing?*

"Maybe it doesn't have to be," Axel said. "After all, she's Bliss."

"But if she sings, she'll wreck it. I mean, *really* wreck it."

"Let me see that," Flynn said, and he handed over the flyer. "It says this is a meet and greet, with a short set. It's not even a concert." She handed it back to him. "And it says there are new songs. So . . ." She lifted a shoulder. "I'm going. I probably need a date. Should I see if Caspian is free?"

"You're taken," Axel said.

"I think Caspian is too," Dawson said. He scooped up the phone. "I'm going to make that call."

"To Keely?"

"I think he means to Caroline's parents," Axel said as Dawson got up and hobbled down the hall to the workout room.

Dawson's gut fisted, but . . .

The phone rang, and he shut the door behind him, then sat on a bench press seat.

"Dawson."

Caroline's father had never really blamed him. Tall, with snow-white hair, he pastored a small church in Texas.

"Pastor Bennett."

"We talked about this. Jonathon."

"Mm-hmm." Dawson closed his eyes, his hand across his forehead. Maybe he needed more painkillers.

"I just wanted to check in on you, son. See how you were doing."

"Actually . . . I . . ."

"Listen. Lottie and I were talking. Maybe you don't know that we're grateful for what you did to try and help our daughter. It's possible that we didn't . . . well, I know that her death weighed on you, and we didn't help lift that burden. But accidents happen, and we know that, even to strong women like our daughter."

"I'm sorry I couldn't . . ." *Keep my promise.* "Bring her home."

"I know. Her sister Heather had a baby girl this year. Named her Caroline. She looks just like her."

He didn't know what to say.

"You won't be hearing from us again, Dawson. But if you ever need anything, please reach out. Caroline cared for you, and we do too."

Oh. Uh . . . "Thank you. And, Pastor Bennett—"

"Jonathon—"

"Yeah, um. Caroline was . . . I did love her. And I never got a chance to tell her, really, but . . . in the end, you should know, she wasn't alone."

"Thank you, Dawson. I know that." His voice seemed to break a little. "Live in peace."

Dawson pressed end and stared at the phone. Yes.

He got up, and barking echoed down the hall. Dawson spotted Caspian at the front door, his hackles raised.

Axel got off the stool, grabbed the dog by the collar. "Hey, bud. Friend, not food." He pulled him back as the door opened.

A man stepped inside. Brown hair, growing out under a baseball cap, a down jacket, a military build about him. He held the leash of a black-and-brown, curly-haired Bernedoodle, who came in behind him.

Dawson took over for Axel. "Sit, Caspian." The dog sat, his body tight, gaze on the other dog.

"Jericho Bowie. I heard you were back." Dawson held out his hand. "Moose says you're joining Air One Rescue."

"Thinking about it. This your K9?"

Caspian barked, a sort of greeting, but stayed next to Dawson.

"Say hi, Orlando," Jericho said, and held his leash as the two dogs sniffed each other.

"He's not really a SAR K9," Dawson said. "Apparently, he's a PTSD-trained service dog. I'm going to do some training so we can get him certified to work at the hospital."

Jericho raised an eyebrow. Looked at Caspian. "Seems to hold himself as if he knows SAR work."

Dawson looked at him. "He did find . . . well, maybe."

Jericho knelt in front of him. "Wanna come and work for Jericho? Get a real job?"

"Hey," Dawson said.

Jericho stood up. "Aw, I'm just messin' with you. PTSD service animals are highly trained and desperately needed. Is that pizza?"

He pulled the cutting board across the island.

"Help yourself," Flynn said.

Jericho had already grabbed a piece, dropping Orlando's lead. The dog came over and sat. "None for you. Not before deployment." But he did reach into a small pouch on his belt and hand him a piece of kibble.

"You guys going somewhere?" Axel came back to the counter.

"Yeah. I'm meeting up with someone from the US Marshals office. I think it's a contractor. There's been an escape, and they want Orlando to track him down."

"Who escaped?"

He picked up Orlando's lead. "Some con escaped custody yesterday when they were transporting him to Anchorage. Apparently had help—the sheriff's car was run off the road. The guy has a murder charge on his sheet. Dangerous."

Dawson froze. "What guy?" He glanced at Flynn.

"Uh." He reached into his pocket and pulled out his phone. "It's not a priority one manhunt, but . . . here it is. Oh wow." He took a breath. "It's Conan Sorros." He pocketed the phone. "Sheesh, out of everyone . . ." The past flickered briefly on his face and Dawson nodded." He dropped a hand to Orlando's head. "We'll find him. He was spotted at an ATM camera here in Anchorage."

Everything inside Dawson shut down. And maybe the dark funk wasn't back, but . . .

Yeah, a cloud had entered his soul. "Why didn't they tell us?" He looked at Flynn. "Did you know?"

"No. But I did get a missed call from Deke."

"We need to find out where Keely is staying."

"Finally." Flynn put down her pizza.

"Listen, Yenta, it's not like that. I made a promise." And this time he planned to keep it.

18

THE SONG FOR THE SOUND check rumbled out of Keely, low and husky and reverberating through the speaker like a storm, powerful yet mysterious.

Perfect. Or she hoped so.

Please let this not be a flop.

The venue felt right. Formerly a community playhouse, with a balcony, the music lounge, despite the name, possessed the exact vibe she'd hoped for—the place seated over a thousand, good acoustics, and a low stage, close enough to the audience to make it feel intimate. Industrial lighting cast an inviting glow upon the curved reclaimed wood bar that held forty or more stools. Another bar ran along the opposite wall. The worn dance floor in the middle suggested a place where people knew how to unwind and have fun.

She'd mingle. And then she'd sing. Hopefully. *Please.* They'd had to adjust the mic for her breathy tones, but the songs—all three of them—were brand new. Starting with "Hear My Name." The second, called "The Whisper," she'd written on her flight to Alaska. She'd remixed "Forever Found" for the last, turning it into a slow, sultry ballad, just her and her guitar.

In fact, the entire three-song set would simply be Bliss—or

rather, Keely, as she'd introduce herself—dressed in a pair of Farrah skinny jeans, a plain white Gucci blouse, and a pair of Dolce & Gabbana boots.

Goldie had picked out the ensemble, along with a few other choices, and had them sent to her suites at Hotel Captain Cook ahead of her arrival. Her agent had also sent clothes for Zoey, along with a new panda and some toys, but Zoey seemed . . .

"I don't know what's wrong with her," she'd said to General Goldie after she'd arrived this morning.

"She'll be fine," Goldie had said. Early fifties, the Nashville agent wore her dyed-blond hair in a bob, all one length behind her ears, a deep blue velvet blazer over her white blouse, a pair of dark denim jeans, black boots, and a chunky turquoise neck-lace. Keely hadn't realized how tightly wound she'd been until General Goldie arrived and took over the arrangements. She'd spent most of the day wielding her phone like a weapon as she barked at stage techs trying to get the sound right.

Now, she sat in a leather high-top next to one of the long bars in the Frostbite Music Lounge, listening to the sound check.

Keely wasn't under any illusions that Goldie had flown up to support her. No—pure babysitting, to make sure she only did the three songs, signed the autographs, and didn't run off again into them thar mountains.

Not a chance.

Well, maybe not.

Aw, who was Keely kidding. In her wildest, angsty-song dreams, Dawson showed up, forgave her for her words, and . . .

What? Asked her to stay?

She couldn't stay, could she? She had a life in New York City. And Zoey . . .

Zoey.

She put the mic back on the stand and came off the stage. "How does it sound?"

Goldie's eyes narrowed, then she sighed. "You sound very Janis Joplin."

"So not terrible."

"Not terrible. Just don't hold any high Cs." She slid off the bar stool. "Your voice is . . . so husky."

"It's fine. It doesn't hurt. And maybe this is the new me."

Goldie's lips pursed.

So, clearly not happy. "I'm going to check on Zoey. You sure you're okay to keep an eye on her during the show?"

"Apparently it's what I do."

"You're a gem, Goldie."

"I know, I know. You're breakin' my heart here with this sabbatical."

"Yeah, you'll be crying all the way to the bank when I release these new singles." She winked.

Goldie wrinkled her nose. "I'm going to check on the security. There's already a line at the door. Good thing your Blissfuls know how to get the word out."

Keely had released a soft version of the first two lines of "Hear My Name" recorded on her phone, sent out a video about the charity performance, and her rabid fans took it from there.

The venue, even with the high price tag, sold out in four hours, and the GoFundMe account for Donald and Wren had six figures, on the way to seven.

So, the money would help. But Wren . . . *please God, save her.*

Goldie headed for the front door, and Keely slipped behind the stage to the dressing room. Just a large room with a wall of mirrors and a dressing table, a couple sofas and overstuffed chairs around a wooden coffee table, and a flat-screen. She'd left Zoey coloring at the coffee table with Goldie's assistant, Kaya, an intern and wannabe musician.

Petite, early twenties, with her dark hair pulled back, Kaya was sitting on the sofa, curled up, watching her phone when Keely came in.

Zoey's crayons lay on the table, along with her coloring page. But no Zoey. "Um, Kaya . . . where's Zoey?"

Kaya searched the room, sat up, looked at Keely again. "She was right here."

"Oh my—she's four. Four. Kids who are four wander off—*for the love!*" Keely turned and went back out into the darkened backstage area. "Zoey?" Shoot. "I need lights!"

Don't shout. But still . . . she rounded back to the room and nearly mowed over Kaya. "Get lights on in the backstage area—"

Kaya took off, her expression stricken. Yeah, well—

Keely headed past the stage into the hallway behind the stage that led out to the back entrance, a loading dock, and . . .

The night.

Danger.

Aw— She hit the door to the back entrance and stopped.

Zoey stood, a black dog barring her exit, just still as the little girl's arms clutched his neck.

And standing with Caspian, of course—Dawson.

He looked good. The kind of good that made her stop short, catch her breath. He wore a leather jacket, jeans, a brace on his knee, but he'd shaved, his dark hair short, almost windblown, but this was Alaska, so . . .

"Hey," he said quietly.

"Hey." Her voice emerged barely a whisper.

He looked at the little girl. Back to her. "Is this—"

"Yes."

He crouched then and held out his hand. "Hi. My name is Dawson."

Zoey gripped her panda around the neck, shied back. He just smiled at her.

After a moment, she met his grip.

"I'm a friend of your—"

"*Friend*," Keely said, making sure. They hadn't crossed over into the Mom terminology yet.

He looked at her, nodded. "Your friend Keely."

He got up. "We were just coming in . . . I mean, I saw you were in concert, so . . . and . . ." He blew out a breath. "How's the voice?"

"How's the knee?"

He looked at his brace. "Getting better."

"Me too."

She looked at him, and he met her eyes. Then, he swallowed and—

"I'm—"

"Sorry—"

He smiled then, so much warmth in his eyes, it blew through her like a storm. Wow, she missed him. He was the calm to her torrid world and the voice that said she'd be safe. He was protection and so much more than a friend.

"I missed you," she said, wrapping her arms around herself. "And I shouldn't have said what I said. I . . . I didn't mean it."

"I know." He stepped closer. Oh, he smelled good. Aftershave, cedarwood with hints of birch and musk.

And now her eyes blurred. Oh no— She looked away, blinking. Not before a performance!

"Keely."

She turned back to him.

He'd taken another step toward her. And he wore such longing in his eyes—or maybe she just thought he did, but it was . . . intoxicating. Hypnotizing and—

She kissed him. Just stepped up, her hands cupping his face, and planted a kiss right on his lips, the kind that she should have given him back at the cabin after he'd rescued her, *again*. The kind of kiss that said *hello* and *thank you* and *never leave* and *I'm yours* . . . especially *I'm yours*.

And he made the most glorious hum in the back of his throat, wrapped one arm around her, and kissed her back. Sweetly, maybe because her daughter was watching, but lingering, as if saying the same thing.

Hello. Thank you. Never leave. I'm yours.

He tasted salty, as if he'd had pizza, and maybe even a little like desperation, but she was right there with him. Desperate that this couldn't be the end.

Please let this not be the end.

A nudge at her leg, and Dawson nearly tripped away from her. Caspian, leaning against his leg.

"No, buddy. I'm not in trouble." He looked at her. "Although . . . um . . ." He sighed.

Oh no.

"I'm actually here because . . . you are. I think."

She stepped back from him. Oh . . .

"No, no—don't get the wrong idea. I'd be here even if you weren't in trouble." He put his arm around her again, but not without glancing down to find Zoey.

She'd already located her and grabbed her hand. Zoey clutched her panda but kept trying to reach out to Caspian.

"I'm here because I missed you. I missed your ridiculous ability to drive me nuts, and to beat me at Battleship, and—I'm sorry I didn't stop you from leaving Alaska."

She cut her voice low. "I had to go. Zoey's dad, Bryce . . . he um . . . passed."

"Oh. So . . ."

"I'm adopting her back." She looked down at her daughter. *Daughter.* "For now, I have full legal and physical custody."

"So what's this? Tonight?"

"It's a fundraiser. One last concert."

"But your voice—"

"I can still sing. It's just . . . different."

He smiled, and it just lit up his blue eyes. Not a storm in sight. "I can get on board with different."

She met his gaze. Debated. "Can you get on board with Bliss?"

He blew out a breath but looked down at Zoey, back at her. "Yeah. I can get on board with Bliss."

She smiled then, waggled her eyebrows.

"What?"

"Bliss is going bye-bye. At least for a while. I think maybe Zoey and I . . . and . . . Caspian need some time to get to know each other."

"I could do that."

"Mm-hmm." She put her hands on his chest. "Maybe even . . . at the community?"

"Really?"

"Yeah. I talked to Donald. They'll let me buy land and build a house and . . . I probably need personal security." She leaned in—

He jerked back. Held up his hand. "Okay, see. This is what happens. I completely lose my train of thought." He put her away from him. "Conan Sorros broke out of custody."

She had nothing.

"Thornwood. The brothers are still out there."

She went cold, right to her bones. "What?"

"Yeah. So. I'm here to protect you."

A beat. And she couldn't help but step up to him, curl her arm around his neck. "Then you'd better protect me." She lifted herself up, kissed him again.

He let her, then drew her arms down. "Hard to do that when you're kissing me."

"Maybe I should fire you."

"I don't work for you."

She wrinkled her nose.

"Listen. Do everything I say, okay?"

"Bossy."

He rolled his eyes. "The last thing I want is the woman I care about—or her pretty . . . friend—getting hurt on my watch. So, yeah, meet the bossy grump. If I have to, I'll be onstage with you."

"Fine. But I hope you can sing."

"Not even a little. But neither can you, so . . ." He winked.

And she just laughed. "Watch me, baby."

MAYBE he'd been wrong.

Dawson stood at the edge of the stage, staring out into the darkness, past where Keely sat on a high stool, her guitar over her knee, leaning into the mic, singing her first original song of the night.

He liked it. And her voice, of course. A sort of sultry, deep tone, with vibrato and a smoky whisper in some places. Not even a little like the pop and glitz of Bliss, although she possessed a showmanship, a smile, a way of wooing the crowd, that evidenced years of practice.

He'd stood beside her during the meet and greet, as they let the crowd in one by one to her signing autographs, taking pictures, each person a bestie.

Flynn and Axel came in, and he'd commandeered them for duty to watch Zoey in the wings. He spotted them now, seated on director's chairs, Flynn holding Zoey in her lap.

Caspian lay at their feet, head up, ears alert. Axel held his lead, and Dawson could imagine the poor guy felt imprisoned.

I'm fine, Casp. And strangely, he was. Sure, a live wire lit inside him, the ever-present buzz of danger, but it didn't put a noose around him, close in on him.

For now.

Maybe it was the focus, the sense of responsibility.

Getting back into the game.

Even Griffin and River had shown up for the event, escaping the community on their repaired snow machines, thanks to a delivery of parts.

Still, because Keely now sat alone in the spotlight, darkness pressing out into the crowd, and occasionally glanced his direction, he couldn't escape the sense that they might be the only two in the room.

Her song for him.

> Snowbound secrets, buried deep and wide,
> Your eyes pierce the blizzard where my fears reside.
> Through the whiteout, through the chill, I yearn for the thrill,
> To be known, to be found, against nature's will.

Maybe it was. *"You'd better protect me."* She'd been half kidding maybe, but challenge accepted. Forever and ever, amen.

So yeah, he tore his gaze and his attention off her song and onto the shadowy crowd.

Sorros, where are you?

He'd already alerted the security team to the threat, but they had a crowd to control too.

Please let him be wrong.

Still, he couldn't see anything from here, and his gut kept pinging, so he moved into the backstage darkness and spotted the security guard standing by the exit sign. He limped over, read the man's name badge. "Gil, I'm going to go around to the front, assess the crowd from the floor. Don't let anyone come through this door, except me."

The security guard, a man in his mid-forties, with a little cheese-and-chips paunch on him, nodded and held open the door for Dawson.

He headed outside into the chilly night and toward the front of the building. Stars shone from the crisp night, winking down at him, the air redolent with the scents of the city. For many years, he worked night shift. Learned to see in the dark, sense danger in the shadows.

His gut said they were here.

He greeted the security at the door, then slipped inside and worked his way into the crowd. Standing room only, every ticket had sold out, and the audience stood shoulder to shoulder, men with women leaning against each other, some holding drinks. He sidled up to the bar and glanced at the balcony, but darkness shrouded the crowd.

> Hear my name, through the storm's wild claim,
> Feel my soul in the fresh snow's tame.
> As the world turns white, I escape the night,
> Hear my voice, oh hear my voice, in the morning light.

He turned, his gaze on Keely. She sparkled under the spotlight, her boot hooked onto one rung of her stool, her blond hair down and curly as she bent over her guitar, singing with her eyes closed. She'd open them and catch on a fan and flash a smile that could grab a heart.

Focus, Daws.

Sitting in the darkness, he could make out more of the crowd, and now he simply began to move through it, watching faces, looking for anyone not mesmerized. He spotted River sitting on a stool, Griffin behind her, his hands clasped around her waist, legs braced.

Griffin glanced over at him, lifted a chin.

"You're welcome back anytime, Daws. Consider yourself an honorary artist."

He didn't hate the idea of building a life in the quiet of the Alaskan forest.

Focus.

Dawson worked his way to the front, near the side, stood at the edge of the crowd, looking back. Maybe he'd overreacted.

Her voice changed beat, took on a breathlessness as she reached the bridge.

> Could it be that you see the truths I hide?
> In the snow's pure blanket, where my deepest dreams
>   reside?
> A look, a touch in the frosty air,
> Reveals the me I've hidden, now laid bare.

He turned and looked at her. That was it, wasn't it? She saw him, despite the darkness that surrounded him, she saw through him to the person he wanted to be.

And he saw her.

Movement from the wings, and he stilled. Not Axel and Flynn —they sat on the opposite side.

Could be Gil, the security guard. He kept his eyes on the wings, even as she finished her song.

> Let the snowflakes fall, let them cover all,
> In the quiet, your voice is my thaw.
> Forever here, where the cold winds call,
> Hear my name, it's yours, through the stormy snowfall.

She let the last of her song thrum out in the chords of her guitar, then smiled at her listeners.

The crowd erupted.

The man in the wings showed himself.

Dressed in jeans and a flannel shirt, hair cut short, a beard, and the form and outline of the man Dawson had chased down by the river.

Maybe.

Or Dawson's brain could be playing games with him. Lying to him.

The man didn't move as Keely leaned into the mic. "I want

to thank you again for coming out tonight. Your support of my friend Wren and her family is huge, and for every dollar we raised tonight, I'll be matching it with my own donation."

More cheering.

"I'm going to be taking a hiatus after this. I know, I know," she said against the noise of the crowd's raucous response. "But I wanted to give you a couple new songs first. These were inspired by the wild blizzard we just survived—and yes, *we*, because I was here too."

More clapping, some cheers.

"I think you'll like this next one. It's more of a ballad. It's called 'The Whisper.'"

She leaned over the guitar and started to pick out an intro.

Dawson couldn't just stand here, not with everything inside him pinging.

But he couldn't exactly run up onstage, right?

He glanced at the wing. The man had vanished. And that was just it—

Dawson pushed through the crowd, to the edge of the stage. Security stood at the stairs. "Let me up."

He recognized the man from their briefing, and he now frowned but moved aside.

Keely glanced over as she started into her song, but he flashed her a smile—nothing to worry about—and ducked into the wing, toward the shadowy backstage.

Flynn still sat with Zoey on her lap, the little girl now playing with Flynn's phone. Axel stood behind her, Keely's manager seated on the other chair, now glaring at him.

"What are you doing?"

"Something's not right. You need to take Zoey and lock yourselves in the greenroom."

Flynn got up, handed Zoey over to Axel. "I'm going with you."

Axel leaned down and kissed her. "Stay safe."

Goldie got up, clearly torn.

"I got this," Axel said and headed toward the greenroom, holding Zoey. Caspian, good boy, followed him.

Dawson turned to Flynn. "You stay and watch Keely—"

"We have a room of people watching Keely. What did you see?" He motioned toward the opposite wing. "Movement. A man."

Flynn pushed past him, and he limped-hopped behind her.

The back door hung open, just a crack.

Where was Gil?

"Outside," he hissed over Keely's song and headed toward the door.

Gil sat on the snowy ground, bleeding from the head but still conscious. "He's getting away!" Gil pointed, and Dawson spotted a man moving through the parking lot, under the splotch of lights.

He took off, limping hard, but Flynn shot out past him.

"Go around—block his exit!" He pointed toward the other row of cars.

She ran to cut him off, her gun already unholstered.

The man stopped at an old model truck with a topper just like the one Mars Sorros had used in his escape. Dawson cut through cars. "Stop!"

His voice jerked the man. He rounded on him, and it was just long enough for Flynn to surprise him. She stopped, her gun on him. "Get down! Get down!"

He sank to his knees, arms up.

The surrender hiccupped through Dawson. Something—

"On the ground!"

Dawson caught up to Flynn. She took the man's hand, put him in a submission hold, her knee on his back. "Get backup."

He turned and spotted Gil heading their way, holding a handkerchief to his head. "Gil! Get on the radio. We need police backup."

Conan wasn't moving, and Dawson's instincts gave a jolt. After everything Conan had done to escape, this felt too easy. He turned, saw Gil on the radio, still heading their way.

"What?" Flynn said, clearly reading him.

"Something doesn't feel right," he said, glancing at Conan.

"I got this," Flynn said.

Gil huffed over. He held zip ties and now stepped over to Flynn to secure the man.

"Don't let him get away," Dawson said to Flynn, and took off, limping hard toward the theater.

Too easy. Way too easy, and that thought took him by the throat and moved him into a painful run.

He wrenched open the door, struggled up the stairs, and heard the last of Keely's song as the crowd applauded.

He stood in the dark, listening to his heartbeat.

Above the song, a whine sounded, as if from Caspian, high, worried—

His gut tightened. *Diversion!* Dawson headed toward the closed door of the greenroom, grabbed it.

Caspian jumped to his feet, barking.

Dawson froze.

Mars Sorros pointed a gun at Axel, who held both Caspian and Zoey in his grip.

He'd clearly been expecting Keely, because his jaw tightened, his eyes narrowing. "You."

"Me." Dawson pointed his gun at Sorros. "Put down the gun."

"No." And then Mars grabbed Zoey, yanked her away from Axel, and shoved the gun against her head.

It happened so fast, Dawson didn't have time to react. Caspian lunged toward the man, his teeth on his arm, ripping his grip away from the little girl.

Zoey screamed, and Axel grabbed her back, caught her, and rolled away from the man.

Dawson pulled the trigger, but Mars struggled with Caspian, shouting, and the shot only scuffed him.

Caspian was a bulldog, tearing at Mars's arm, and Dawson couldn't get another shot. The man fell back against the wall and punched Caspian. The dog yelped and must have loosened his hold, because Mars hit him again.

The dog cried, and the sound of it set Dawson on fire. He leaped at Mars, grabbing him around the waist as the man threw Caspian away. His arm bled, and Dawson slammed him against the wall.

"Don't move!"

Mars elbowed him in the ribs, but he ignored it, grabbed his wrist, fighting for a submission hold.

Behind him, Caspian was crying.

Mars turned, slammed his fist into Dawson's chest, and Dawson stumbled back.

Then Mars pointed his gun at Dawson, and—

Caspian lunged at him, maybe to again grab his arm—

The shot exploded through the room, and Caspian dropped.

Zoey screamed.

Dawson staggered to the dog. Caspian lay on the ground, blood spattering his fur, pooling on the ground, crying.

Mars pushed past him, heading for the door.

No—no—

Dawson whirled around, tried to get up, but his knee wouldn't work.

Caspian's cries shredded the air.

Mars jerked open the door—

Dawson turned back to Caspian, the animal writhing. He might not be a four-year-old girl, but his dog trusted him.

And darkness didn't win today.

Mars disappeared out the exit—hello, where was security? But Dawson focused on his dog, pressing his hand on Caspian's wound, just above his right leg, in his chest. "I know, buddy, I know—" He glanced at Axel, still holding Zoey, his hands over her ears, her back to the trauma.

"I need a cloth."

Axel tossed him a nearby T-shirt, and Dawson shoved it against the wound. "We need to get him to a vet." He scooped up the dog but struggled to stand.

Axel let Zoey go and appeared right there, a towel in his arms. "I got him."

Dawson relinquished the dog, then glanced at Zoey. She hugged her panda, her eyes wide, her lower lip caught in her teeth.

He couldn't leave her. "Where's Goldie?"

"She stayed in the wings," Axel answered. "Said someone had to watch Keely."

He got that. But he wasn't letting Zoey out of his sight.

But he couldn't leave Keely, could he? Or Caspian.

He leaned down to her. "Kiddo, let's take the doggy to the hospital, okay?"

Zoey had barely nodded when he picked her up. Turned to Axel. "Let's go."

Axel had already headed toward the door.

Griffin stood on the other side of the door. "Everything—oh wow, is that—*what happened?*" He stood back as Axel pushed past him, into the backstage area.

"Mars Sorros was here—he probably went out the back. Get security, and . . . stay with Keely."

Griffin nodded, stepped back for Dawson to follow Axel.

"He's armed."

"So am I," Griffin said.

Griffin headed for the wings, and Dawson pushed out after Axel. Zoey buried her head into his shoulder.

Axel had parked near the back entrance and now opened up the back end, set Caspian inside.

Shoot—Dawson didn't have a car seat—

"Dawson!"

Goldie appeared from the back door. She stalked toward him, picked up her pace. "Where are you going—"

"My dog's been shot."

She glanced at Zoey, then past her to Axel. "Right. Zoey can stay with me."

He considered for a moment, then shook his head. "I think—"

"Fine. Take Keely's rental." She turned and ran back inside.

He set Zoey down, his hand in hers, and turned to Axel. "Where are you going?"

"Arctic Paws Vet Center. It's right near the Tooth, about a block away, across from the hospital."

Goldie came back out, holding keys. She pressed the fob, and a nearby SUV barked.

"I'll meet you there." Dawson took the keys and tried to breathe as Axel pulled out with Caspian.

He set Zoey into her car seat. Strapped her in. Her big eyes landed on him, and he crouched by the door. "Zoey, everything is going to be okay. I promise."

She just met his gaze.

God, please let him not be a liar.

He got in, pulled out and followed Axel's rearview lights onto the highway, off on 15th, east to the airfield—

God. He's a good dog. His throat tightened. *Please.*

They pulled up to the clinic under a lighted sign that said 24-Hour Clinic.

Axel already had Caspian in his arms when Dawson met him at the door with Zoey. He held it open, and a receptionist met them in the lobby.

"He's been shot," Dawson said as a doctor came from the back.

"I'm Dr. White," she said as she lifted the towel. "Okay, get him in the back."

Axel followed her, and Dawson couldn't stop himself from following.

Caspian groaned when Axel set him on the metal table.

"I'll need you out of here," Dr. White said.

"I'm staying. He's my dog."

Axel took Zoey's hand. "C'mon, sweetie." He took her out of the room.

Dr. White turned to him. "Then stay back and say nothing."

He looked at Caspian. "Don't die on me, buddy."

19

KEELY DIDN'T HATE the sound of her voice. And not only had it held up, but it had created a sort of grounded, deeper effect from the stage, even as she finished the last of "Forever Found."

> And when the years have passed, and we look back to see,
> Every step, every dream, you were right there with me.
> In your eyes, I still find the place where I belong,
> In our world full of love, your voice is my song.

She already saw the new album—maybe she'd called it *Hearthstone*, and it would be a departure, something that spoke to the deeper themes of home and true love and . . .

The crowd erupted as the final tones ended, and she smiled into the shadowy crowd. "Thank you." Sitting back, she raised her hand, then glanced to the wings.

Dawson's friends Flynn and Axel had left—she'd seen them go when he ran onstage. She'd nearly stopped singing, but Goldie had stayed and shot her a thumbs-up, and she'd settled into finishing her set.

Now, Goldie stood, her arms akimbo, her mouth a tight line, and the entire posture strummed a thread inside her. Something wasn't right.

Keely leaned into the mic. "You've been a fantastic audience tonight. Thank you for coming out and supporting Wren and her family. Have a great night!" Lifting the guitar, she headed offstage toward Goldie.

The shouts of "Encore" lifted, the crowd clapping, chanting, and Goldie stepped back, into her path.

"What's going on?"

"Everything's fine," she said. "Your fans want an encore."

Keely looked past her and spotted Griffin standing with a couple security guards. "Is . . . is Zoey okay?"

More shouts, and the chanting continued.

"She's fine," Griffin said.

Keely headed for the greenroom, but Goldie caught her arm. "Your fans are calling!"

She yanked her arm from Goldie's grasp. "Where. Is. Zoey?"

Griffin stepped up to her. "She's fine—she's with Dawson."

The words loosened the knot in her gut. Except—"Where is *Dawson*?" She expected him to emerge from the greenroom, but a glance in that direction suggested it might be empty.

Goldie wasn't giving up. "Bliss, just one more song—"

"I'm not Bliss!" She didn't mean for her voice to emerge in a shout, but—"I'm Zoey's mom. What. Happened?"

Goldie's mouth closed, pinched. "There was an incident. The dog got shot."

The dog. "Caspian? Oh my—and Zoey?"

"She's fine," Griffin repeated. "I mean—probably a little shaken, but—"

"Probably a little shaken? What the—"

"One of the Sorros brothers got into the greenroom."

And her knees nearly buckled. She shoved the guitar at Goldie. "Tell them that everyone will get an advance copy of my newest single. That's my encore."

Then she looked at Griffin. "Take me to my daughter."

He turned and, "Out of the way!"

The security guards stepped aside, and she followed him out of the theater, into the parking lot, now lit up with the cycling red and white lights of police support.

Griffin walked her across the lot, maybe toward his car, but Flynn came running up.

"We got him, Keely. Conan, at least."

All she cared about was—"Where's Dawson?"

"He's at the vet," Flynn said.

"Please tell me that Zoey is with him."

"Axel has her. She's fine."

Sure she was. Because a four-year-old who'd just lost her parents and saw a dog get shot certainly didn't have any trauma.

"And Caspian?"

"Dunno. Axel texted that they'd gotten him to the vet okay. We can take my car—Dawson took your SUV."

She had no room to process that. Whatever. Keely slid into the passenger seat of Flynn's SUV, and Flynn pulled out, past the police presence, onto the darkened street.

Silence, then, "You were amazing tonight."

"Thanks."

"I think probably you're the best thing that has happened to Dawson." Keely's glance fell on Flynn. The woman met it. "I just have one request."

Keely raised an eyebrow.

"Just don't let him be a brokenhearted love song."

Keely's mouth tightened, but she nodded. "That's fair. But to be truthful, I think he's the *only* love song."

Flynn matched her tight smile, but it hit her eyes.

"That song 'Hear My Name' sounds more like your original stuff."

"I wrote it during the blizzard, while I was waiting for Dawson to come home." No, not home. "Back. Anyway, yeah, I guess it is more like me."

"Honest. Real. And the way you sang it—a little rough-edged but soul-true."

Soul-true. She smiled. "Thanks."

"It's going to be okay, you know. Life doesn't have to be perfect to be happy. You just have to look for the happy in the middle of all the darkness and keep your eyes on hope." She pulled off the highway. "Something I learned while I searched for my missing sister a few years ago."

"Missing sister?"

"Kennedy. Sully's wife. Long story. But I eventually found her."

Funny, it seemed that maybe she'd been on a search too. And had eventually found herself.

They pulled into the lot, and lights pushed out into the darkness from a vet clinic. She spotted Zoey sitting inside on Axel's lap, him reading to her.

Flynn turned off the car. "I really need to marry that man."

Zoey looked up when Keely walked into the vet clinic, and for a moment, the past hour, maybe more, played on her face.

Then, as Keely froze, the little girl squirmed off Axel's lap, landed on the floor, and ran for her.

Oh—*oh!* Keely crouched and caught Zoey, whose small arms clamped around her, her body shaking.

And Keely couldn't stop herself. "It's okay, baby. Mommy's here. I'm here." She picked her up, held her against herself, rocking her. Oh well, the name was bound to spill out from her heart at some point.

Flynn came in and took Axel's hand. He rose, blew out a breath.

Zoey wrapped her legs around Keely, clinging to her.

"How's Caspian?"

Axel shook his head, drew in a breath.

No.

Just then, the door to the back opened. Dawson came out, his eyes reddened.

"Dawson—"

"He's okay." Then he walked right up to Keely and wrapped her in his arms. Her and Zoey, and they stood, a clump, together.

A family, maybe. Or the beginnings of one.

She closed her eyes and sank into the abundance.

Finally, he stepped back.

"Griffin said he was shot."

"He was. But it was a glancing shot—more blood than damage. Scary though."

"To be clear, it sounded a lot worse," Axel said. "Mr. Drama howled the entire time to the vet."

"You try getting shot in the chest and see how you feel," Flynn said, whacking him on the shoulder.

"Is he going to be okay?" Keely asked.

"Yes. The doc shaved the area and just finished stitching him up. She's bandaging him so we can take him home." He settled his hand on Zoey's back. "Hey, sweetheart. You okay?"

She lifted her head, still tucked against Keely's chest, still holding on. Keely put her head down atop hers. "She doesn't sp—"

"Puppy?"

Keely stared at Zoey. "Puppy?"

Zoey reached out, looking past them.

Caspian stood at the door, a bandage across his chest, wearing a cone of shame. He barked and came over, his tail thumping as he crouched and crawled toward Zoey.

She wiggled out of Keely's arms, and Keely put her daughter down. "Puppy!"

Dawson caught her just as she advanced on Caspian. "Let's give puppy some room."

But Caspian lay down, then rolled over, his tongue hanging out, and Keely laughed. "I don't think he needs any room."

"I've never seen him do that before."

But even Keely could see the way he swallowed hard, the sudden shudder of his breath.

"He heard voices and wouldn't stay put." This from a vet who came out of the room, taking off her gloves. "Sorry. He's determined. Knows what he wants."

Dawson was half crouched next to Caspian, helping direct Zoey's hands away from his wound. But Keely's entire body lit up with her giggles.

And right then, Keely knew exactly what she wanted.

What she'd *really* come to Alaska to find.

Dawson stood up as Caspian rolled to his feet and shoved his muzzle into Zoey's hands. "How'd the concert go?"

"I think it was a hit."

"Of course it was." He picked up Caspian's lead. "Did you give them an encore?"

She stepped up to him. "I saved it for you."

Then she took his face between her hands and kissed him. Something sweet, but exactly the song she wanted to sing.

She felt Caspian lean against Dawson's leg, and she let him go, looking down.

Dawson scratched his ears. "Buddy, I promise you, I'm okay." He met Keely's eyes. "I'm very, very much okay."

She took Zoey's hand. Yes, yes they were.

"I think it's time that I finally get you home." He slid his hand into hers.

"Promises, promises," she said.

He looked at her and laughed.

And as they walked outside, in the dark of the Alaskan night, the northern lights ribboned above them. *We found our forever, beneath the Alaskan stars.*

Yes, yes they had.

EPILOGUE

THE STEADY BEEP of the heart monitor filled the dimly lit hospital room as Keely entered, Zoey's hand in hers.

Donald sat hunched in the chair next to Wren's bed, clutching her small hand like a lifeline. Stuffed animals, shiny Mylar balloons, and colorful flower arrangements covered nearly every surface. A bombardment of love from the Woodcrest community, no doubt.

A ball of heat landed in Keely's chest. Only a month had passed since she'd left the community, but already she deeply missed them.

But she was cooking up a remedy to fix that.

Donald barely glanced up when Keely came to the bed. Red rimmed his eyes, and shadows hung under them. Clearly the man wasn't sleeping.

Yeah, well, what parent would? Keely checked on Zoey so many times a night, she should probably make up a bed in her room.

"How's our girl?" Keely asked softly as she leaned down to wrap Donald in a one-armed hug.

He sighed, scrubbing a hand down his face. "Better. Breathing on her own now, and the doctors think she'll wake up any time. They're 'cautiously optimistic' she'll make a full recovery." He shook his head, his voice roughed. "I just keep hoping . . ."

Keely squeezed his shoulder. "She's a fighter, like her dad. And she's got the best care."

"I can never repay you," Donald choked out. "What you did, that concert—it covered all her bills. I don't know what I would have—" His voice broke, and he ducked his head.

"That's what family does," Keely said firmly. "We take care of each other."

The words just tumbled out, and she caught her breath. But . . . everyone at Woodcrest had felt like family, really.

But the true family was the new and precious thing between her and Dawson and Zoey. This weird sense that, yes, she'd been waiting for this her entire life. Lost . . . and found in Alaska.

More than found, really. The future seemed bright and whole and . . . healing.

The door swung open and Dawson entered, a healing but still bandaged Caspian at his heels. The dog wore an Elizabethan collar that made him resemble a furry lamp.

Zoey instantly lit up. "Puppy!" She scampered over and threw her arms around Caspian's neck, dodging the collar. The dog's tail thumped against the linoleum.

Sweet.

"Gentle, Zoey." Dawson steered her hands away from Caspian's wrapped chest. "Remember, he's still got owies."

Oh, the man was too cute when he talked like a four-year-old.

Zoey nodded, then placed the gentlest of pats on the dog's head instead. Dawson shared a grin with Keely, shaking his head. But his eyes lit with a sort of joy.

Yes, yes, this was the right decision.

"Not sure who's gonna heal faster, him or me." He limped slightly as he leaned across the bed to shake Donald's hand and then pulled Keely to his side.

Oh, she loved this man.

This life. And it was just getting started.

"Any updates?" Dawson asked, nodding toward Wren.

"Doing better," Keely said. "Doctors are optimistic."

"That's the best news I've heard all day," Dawson said. He gave Donald a grim nod.

Donald blinked hard, maybe to clear the shimmer of tears from his eyes. "I can't thank you both enough. That concert . . ."

"It was . . . well, people were really generous. And the real star was a certain hero who saved the day." Keely shot a glance at Caspian.

"Hey," Dawson said. "I wasn't just eye candy."

"No, no, that's exactly what you were." Keely winked.

He laughed and dropped a kiss on the tip of her nose.

A soft moan drew their attention to the bed where Wren had begun to stir, her brows furrowing as she surfaced from the deep pool of sleep.

Donald shot to his feet, one hand cupping Wren's cheek. "Wren? Honey, can you hear me?"

Her eyelids fluttered once, twice, then opened fully. She blinked. "Daddy?" The little girl's voice rasped through her oxygen mask.

"I'm right here." He pushed her hair from her face, pressed a kiss to her forehead.

Her gaze swept the room, taking in the balloons and flowers before landing on Keely and Dawson. A shy smile peeked out. "Keely."

"Hey there, troublemaker." Keely perched on the edge of the bed, taking one of Wren's small hands between her own.

Zoey had gotten up. "I brought you a present." She held out a slightly crumpled piece of paper covered in crayon scribbles.

"Who are you?" Wren asked, taking the paper.

"I'm"—she looked at Keely—"That's my mom."

Wren sighed. Smiled. Her eyes closed.

Caspian settled on the floor, also with a loud sigh.

"I think that's probably enough for right now," Dawson said.

He leaned down to pick up Zoey. "How about you color Wren another picture, huh?" He brought Zoey over to a chair and pulled up the bed table.

Like a seasoned father already, Dawson pulled out a pack of crayons, just three colors, then crouched in front of Zoey and handed them to her. "How about a picture of Caspian."

He'd evidently grabbed the paper place mat from the burger place where they had lunch and now unfolded it onto the tray.

The man thought of everything.

Zoey leaned over the paper, began to draw.

"Who are you?" Keely said as he walked back to her. He grinned at her, winked.

Already, Wren had fallen back to sleep.

Donald wiped his eyes again and stood up. Walked away from her.

Dawson and Keely followed.

"Any updates on the Sorros front?" Donald's jaw clenched, a muscle ticking in his cheek.

"Conan is locked down tight, awaiting trial. We all gave our testimonies, and with Keely's account of the crash, he's not going anywhere." Dawson's hand landed on the small of Keely's back, warm and reassuring. "But Mars is in the wind. Sheriff Starr thinks they spotted him in Copper Mountain. My SAR buddy Jericho has a scent dog, and apparently they were here to track Conan, but Starr has asked him to help find Mars, so the hunt isn't over."

Donald shook his head, his expression grim.

Yeah, she got that. She'd like to see all the brothers—and their evil cousin Sloan—behind bars. Frankly, she didn't feel safe with any of them on the loose.

She wound her fingers between Dawson's and held on. He tightened his around hers in response.

Dawson's voice turned low, lethal. "They'll get them, it's only a matter of time."

A knock sounded at the door and a nurse in festive Snoopy scrubs came in. She held up a digital thermometer with an apologetic smile. "Sorry, folks, but I need to check the patient's vitals."

Keely walked over to Zoey, still drawing with great fervor, and crouched in front of her. "We need to go, sweetie."

Zoey held up a picture of a pink dog.

"I think that's perfect," Keely said. She glanced at Dawson.

"Don't show Casp," he said with a shake of his head. Then he grinned at Zoey. "Great job."

Donald walked them to the door, enveloping first Keely and then Dawson in a rib-cracking hug. "Thank you. For everything," he said gruffly. "You just say the word, anything you need, anytime."

Dawson clasped the other man's shoulder, his voice thick with emotion. "Everything is going to be okay."

His words followed Keely out into the bustling hospital corridor, and she let them wash over her as they waited for the elevator. Zoey held her hand, Caspian walked with them in his cone of shame.

"Everything's going to be okay."

The elevator arrived with a muted ding, but Keely paused, turning to Dawson. "It is, right? Going to be okay?"

"Yes," Dawson said. "I'm not going anywhere."

She believed him. Really, perfectly, completely.

Dawson had taken Zoey's other hand, his gaze gentle but serious as it met Keely's. "And you . . . just try and escape me. I have resources."

She laughed. Looked at Caspian. "He's not a tracking dog."

"Tell him that." The dog had walked into the elevator and sat next to Zoey. "My guess is that he's never leaving her side."

Yeah, well . . . she so got that.

Dawson pressed a kiss to her temple as the elevator descended, carrying them down, out of the dark shadow of the hospital and into the bright promise of a future together.

Otherwise known as . . . home.

DEAR READER,

Thank you for reading *Track of Courage*! I so enjoyed writing this story of Dawson, the brave man who doesn't realize how affected he was by his traumatic event, and the sweet dog Caspian who understands him better than he thinks. I related with Dawson more than I realized as I dove into the story—we had a home invasion many years ago, and I didn't realize I suffered from PTS until much later. I could have used a Caspian in my life. Thankfully, the effects of that attack have subsided, but it made me realize how important it is to confront the wounds in our lives, and yet, find the courage to push through. This is hope on the other side.

As for Keely, I also brought a bit of my own journey as an adopted child to her story. I loved how she found traces of herself in Vic and how she also was deeply influenced by her adoptive mother. And now, she gets a second chance to experience the joy of being a mother.

God is with us during our trials, our storms, our wounds, and he does not leave us without resources. I hoped to show his provision by giving Caspian to Dawson before he even knew he needed him. And, for Keely, to provide a way for her to learn to trust again.

My hope as an author is to offer truths through the experiences of my characters, to reveal moments that might normally be unseen in our own lives, and stir the thought that God is with us, if we will just open our eyes to see him at work.

I hope you'll continue the journey with me into book 2! I can't wait for you to experience Jericho's story.

My deepest gratitude goes out to the team of people who work so hard to bring these stories to life. My sweet husband, who listens to all my wild ideas and answers things like, If you were going to sabotage a snowmobile, how would you do it? (It helps that he's a mechanic!) My writing partner, Rachel Hauck, who helps me sort through the spiritual threads and encourages me with truth. I love our Saturday breakfasts! My amazing VA, Rel Mollet, who reads everything I write and gives me honest and much-needed feedback. My amazing editorial assistant, Sarah Erredge, who keeps everything running behind the scenes so I can focus on writing. And my brilliant social media assistant, Essie Shull, who makes me look better than I am online! The fantastic team at Revell—the amazing Andrea Doering who said, "Why don't you write a book about dogs?" Brilliant as usual, and of course the editorial and marketing teams (a special shout-out to Karen Steele!) who work tirelessly to get the word out. I love working with you all!

Finally, to my readers. Thank you for cheering on the stories and going on the journey with me!

Onward!

Susie May

Susan May Warren is the *USA Today* bestselling author of nearly 100 novels with more than 1.5 million books sold, including the Global Search and Rescue and Montana Rescue series. Winner of a RITA Award and multiple Christy and Carol Awards, as well as the HOLT Medallion and numerous Readers' Choice Awards, Susan makes her home in Minnesota. Visit her at SusanMayWarren.com.

Dear Reader,

Thank you for selecting a Revell novel! We're so happy to be part of your reading life through this work. Our mission here at Revell is to publish stories that reach the heart. Through friendship, romance, suspense, or a travel back in time, we bring stories that will entertain, inspire, and encourage you. We believe in the power of stories to change our lives and are grateful for the privilege of sharing these stories with you.

We believe in building lasting relationships with readers, and we'd love to get to know you better. If you have any feedback, questions, or just want to chat about your experience reading this book, please email us directly at publisher@revellbooks.com. Your insights are incredibly important to us, and it would be our pleasure to hear how we can better serve you.

We look forward to hearing from you and having the chance to enhance your experience with Revell Books.

The Publishing Team at Revell Books
A Division of Baker Publishing Group
publisher@revellbooks.com